For my amazing daughters,
my very own elixirs.
No father could possibly be any prouder.

SANCTUARY

RAYMOND KHOURY

First published in Great Britain in 2007 by Orion books,
an imprint of The Orion Publishing Group Ltd
Orion House, 5 Upper Saint Martin's Lane
London WC2H 9EA
An Hachette Livre UK Company

3 5 7 9 10 8 6 4 2

A CIP catalogue record for this book is
available from the British Library

ISBN (Hardback) 978 0 7528 7588 0
ISBN (Trade Paperback) 978 0 7528 7589 7

Printed in Great Britain by Mackays of Chatham plc, Chatham, Kent

The Orion Publishing Group's policy is to use papers that are natural,
renewable and recyclable products and made from wood grown in sustainable
forests. The logging and manufacturing processes are expected to conform to
the environmental regulations of the country of origin.

SANCTUARY

When a distinguished . . . scientist states that something is possible, he is almost certainly right. When he states that something is impossible, he is very probably wrong.
—Arthur C. Clarke

Tempus edax, homo edacior.
(Time devours; man devours even more.)
—Ancient Roman saying

Prologue

∽∾ ∽∾

I

Naples—November 1749

The scrape was hardly there, but it still woke him up. It wasn't really loud enough to rouse anyone from a deep sleep, but then, he hadn't slept well for years.

It sounded like metal, brushing against stone.

Could be nothing. An anodyne, household noise. One of the servants getting a head start on the day.

Maybe.

On the other hand, it could be something less auspicious. Like a sword. Accidentally scraping along a wall.

Someone's here.

He sat up, listening intently. Everything was deathly quiet for a moment. Then he heard something else.

Footsteps.

Stealing up cold limestone stairs.

At the edge of his consciousness, but definitely there.

And getting closer.

He bolted out of bed and over to the French windows that led to a small balcony across from the fireplace. He pulled the curtain to one side, swung the door open quietly and slipped out into the biting night air. Winter was closing in quickly now, and his bare feet froze on the icy stone floor. He leaned over the balustrade and peered down. The courtyard of his palazzo was enshrouded in a stygian darkness. He concentrated his gaze, looking for a reflection, a glint of movement, but he couldn't see any sign of life below. No horses, no carts, no valets or servants. Across the street and beyond, the outlines of the other houses were barely discernible, backlit by the first glimmer of dawn that hinted from behind Vesuvius. He'd witnessed the sun rising up behind the mountain and its ominous trail of gray smoke several times. It was a majestic, inspiring sight, one that usually brought him some solace when not much else did.

Tonight was different. He could feel a prickling malignancy in the air.

He hurried back inside and slipped on his breeches and a shirt, not bothering with the buttons. There were more pressing needs. He rushed to his dressing table and pulled open its top drawer. His fingers had just managed to reach the dagger's grip when the door to his bedchamber burst open and three men charged in. Their swords were already drawn. In the dim light of the dying embers in the hearth, he could also make out a pistol carried by the middle man.

The light was enough for him to recognize the man. And instantly, he knew what this was about.

"Don't do anything foolish, Montferrat," the lead attacker rasped.

The man who went by the name of the Marquis de Montferrat raised his arms calmingly and carefully sidestepped away from the dressing table. The intruders fanned out to either side of him, their blades hovering menacingly in his face.

"What are you doing here?" he asked cautiously.

Raimondo di Sangro sheathed his sword and laid his pistol on the table. He grabbed a side chair and kicked it over to the marquis. It hit a groove in the flooring and tumbled noisily onto its side. "Sit down," he barked. "I suspect this is going to take a while."

His eyes fixed on di Sangro, Montferrat righted the chair and hesitantly sat down. "What do you want?"

Di Sangro reached into the hearth and ignited a taper, which he used to light an oil lantern. He set it on the table and retrieved his gun, then waved his men out dismissively with it. They nodded and left the room, closing the door behind them. Di Sangro pulled over another chair and sat astride it, face-to-face with his prey. "You know very well what I want, Montferrat," he replied, aiming the double-barrel flintlock pistol at him menacingly as he studied him, before adding acidly, "And you can start with your real name."

"My real name?"

"Let's not play games, *Marquese*." He slurred the last word mockingly, his face brimming with condescension. "I had your letters checked. They're forged. In fact, nothing in the vague snippets you've let slip about your past, since the moment you got here, seems to have any truth."

Montferrat knew that his accuser had all the resources necessary to make such inquiries. Raimondo di Sangro had inherited the title of *principe di San Severo*—prince of San Severo—at the tender age of sixteen, after the deaths of his two brothers. He counted the young Spanish king of Naples and Sicily, Charles VII, among his friends and admirers.

How could I have so misread this man? Montferrat thought with burgeoning horror. *How could I have so misread this place?*

After years of torment and self-doubt, he had finally abandoned his quest in the Orient and returned to Europe less than a year earlier, making his way to Naples by way of Constantinople and Venice. He hadn't intended to stay in the city. His plan had been to continue onward to Messina, and from there to sail on to Spain and, possibly, back home to Portugal.

He paused at the thought.

Home.

A word meant for others, not for him. An empty, hollow word, bone-picked clean of any resonance by the passage of time.

Naples had given pause to his thoughts of surrender. Under the Spanish viceroys, it had grown to become the second city of Europe, after Paris. It was also part of a new Europe he was discovering, a different Europe than the one he had left behind. It was a land where the ideas of the Enlightenment were steering people to a new future, ideas embraced and nurtured in Naples by Charles VII, who had championed discourse, learning, and cultural debate. The king had set up a National Library, as well as an Archaeological Museum to house the relics unearthed from the recently discovered buried towns of Herculaneum and Pompeii. Of further allure was that the king was hostile to the Inquisition, the bane of Montferrat's previous life. Wary of the Jesuits' influence, the king had trod carefully in suppressing them, which he had managed to do without raising the ire of the pope.

And so he had reverted to the name he'd used in Venice many years earlier, the Marquis of Montferrat. He'd found it easy to lose himself in the bustling city and its visitors. Several countries had founded academies in Naples to house the steady stream of travelers who came to study the newly excavated Roman towns. Soon, he was meeting scholars, both locals and visitors from across Europe, like-minded men with inquisitive minds.

Men like Raimondo di Sangro.

Inquisitive mind, indeed.

"All these lies," di Sangro continued, gauging his pistol, eyeing Montferrat with a glint of unbridled greed in his eye. "And yet, intriguing and rather odd, since that dear old lady, the Contessa di Czergy, claims she knew you by the very same name in Venice, Montferrat . . . how many years ago was it now? Thirty? More?"

The name spiked through the false marquis like a blade. *He knows. No, he cannot know. But he suspects.*

"Obviously, the old parsnip's mind isn't what it used to be. The ravages of time will get us all in the end, won't they?" di Sangro pressed on. "But about you, she was so insistent, so clear, so resolute and adamant that she wasn't mistaken . . . it was hard to dismiss her words as the delusional ramblings of an old crone. And then I discover that you speak Arabic with the tongue of a native. That you know Constantinople like the back of your hand and that you've traveled extensively in the Orient, posing—impeccably, or so I'm told—as an Arab sheikh. So many mysteries for one man, *Marquese*. It defies logic—or belief."

Montferrat frowned inwardly, berating himself for even considering the man a kindred spirit, a potential ally. For testing him, probing him, however cryptically.

Yes, he had totally misjudged the man. But, he thought, perhaps this was fate. Perhaps it was time to unburden himself. Perhaps it was time to let the world in on his secret. Perhaps man could find a way to deal with it in a noble and magnanimous way.

Di Sangro's eyes were locked on him, studying every twitch in his face. "Come now. I had to drag myself out of bed at this ungodly hour just to hear your story, *Marquese*," he said haughtily. "And to be frank with you, I don't particularly care who you really are or where you're really from. All I want to know is your secret."

Montferrat met his inquisitor's gaze straight on. "You don't want to know, *Principe*. Trust me. It is not a gift, not for any man. It is a curse, pure and simple. A curse from which there is no respite."

Di Sangro wasn't moved. "Why don't you let me be the judge of that?"

Montferrat leaned in. "You have a family," he said, his voice now hollow and distant. "A wife. Children. The king is your friend. What more could a man ask for?"

The answer came back with unsettling ease. "More. Of the same."

Montferrat shook his head. "You should leave things be."

Di Sangro edged closer to his prisoner. His eyes were blazing with an almost messianic fervor. "Listen to me, *Marquese*. This city, this paltry boy-king . . . that is nothing. If what I suspect you know is true, we can be emperors. Don't you understand? People will sell their very souls for this."

The false marquis didn't doubt it for a second. "That's what I'm afraid of."

Di Sangro's breathing got heavier with frustration as he tried to size up the man's resolve. His eyes flickered downwards as he seemed to catch sight of something on Montferrat's chest that piqued his curiosity. He leaned menacingly closer and reached across the table, pulling out a chain-hung medallion from underneath the false marquis's opened shirt. Montferrat's hand flew up and grabbed di Sangro's wrist, stilling it, but the prince quickly raised his gun and cocked it. Montferrat slowly released his grip. The prince held the medallion in his fingers a moment longer, then suddenly yanked it off Montferrat's neck, splitting its chain. He held the medallion closer, examining it.

It was a simple, round piece, cast out of bronze, like a large coin, a little over two digits in diameter. Its sole feature was a snake, which lay coiled around the medallion's face, ringlike, its head at the top of the circle formed by its own body.

The snake was devouring its own tail.

The prince looked a question at Montferrat. The false marquis's hardened eyes gave nothing away. "I'm tired of waiting, *Marquese*," di Sangro hissed menacingly. "I'm tired of trying to make sense of this"—he rasped as his fingers tightened against the medallion and shook it angrily at Montferrat—"tired of your cryptic remarks, of trying to read through all your esoteric references. I'm tired of hearing reports about your passing questions to certain scholars and travelers and piecing together what I now believe is true about you. I want to know. I *demand* to know. So it's really your choice. You can tell me, here, now. Or you can take it with you to your grave." He pushed his gun even closer. Its over-and-under twin barrels were now hovering inches from his prisoner's face. He let the threat hang there for a moment. "But if that were to be your decision," he added, "to die here tonight and take your knowledge with you, I would ask you to ponder one thing: What gives you the right to deprive us, to hold the world in contempt and in ignorance? What did you do to deserve the right to make that choice for the rest of us?"

It was a question the man had asked himself many times, a question that had haunted his very existence.

In a distant past, another man, an old man whom he had watched die, a friend whose death he had even—in his own eyes—helped bring about, had made that choice for him. With his dying breath, his friend had stunned him by telling him that despite Montferrat's deplorable and heinous actions, he could see the reticence and the doubt in his eyes. Somehow, the old man felt sure that the valor, the nobility, and the honesty of his young ward were still there, buried deep within, smothered by a misguided sense of duty. In his darkest hour, that friend had managed to find promise and purpose in his young ward's life, something the false marquis had himself long given up on. And with that came an admission, a revelation, and a mission that would consume the rest of Montferrat's life.

The choice had been made for him. The right to decide had been bequeathed to him by someone far more deserving than he had ever imagined himself to be.

But he had surprised himself.

He had done his best, tried his hardest, to discover what the missing pages of the codex had contained and wrest the ancient book's lost secrets.

He'd managed to evade his accusers in Portugal. He'd searched in Spain, and in Rome. He'd traveled to Constantinople and beyond, to the Orient. But he hadn't found anything to advance his quest.

He had failed.

He'd thought a return to the land of his birth would help him decide on what his next step would be. Di Sangro's interruption had put pause to all that. And in the fog that clouded his mind, one thing glowed with certainty: that holding the man who was sitting before him in contempt and keeping him in ignorance was a choice he was happy to make.

The rest of the world, well . . . that was another matter.

"Well?" di Sangro snapped, his hand wavering slightly under the weight of the pistol.

The man who called himself Montferrat leapt out of his chair and hurled himself at his adversary, reaching out and pushing his pistol away just as di Sangro pulled the trigger. The charge exploded in a deafening roar as both men grappled over the gun, its lead ball bursting out of the upper muzzle and whistling past Montferrat's ear before biting into the paneling on the wall behind him. The two men slammed into the table by the fireplace, still fighting for the gun, as the door to the bedchamber swung open. Di Sangro's henchmen rushed in, swords raised. Montferrat caught the momentary distraction in his adversary's eyes and exploited it, hammering the *principe* with a fierce back-elbow that caught him in the throat. The prince recoiled backwards under the blow, loosening his grip on the pistol just enough for Montferrat to wrest it from him. Montferrat pushed the prince away and raised the pistol, rotating its barrel and cocking its firing arm as he moved away from the first of the henchmen, who was already charging at him, and fired. The round struck his attacker in the chest, causing him to twist sideways and drop to the ground at Montferrat's feet.

Montferrat hurled the empty pistol at the second attacker and swiftly picked up the fallen man's sword. The prince had recovered somewhat, and despite being unsteady on his feet, he drew his own sword. "Don't kill him," he hissed, inching forward to join his henchman. "I need him alive . . . for now."

Montferrat gripped the sword with both hands, holding it up defensively, flicking it left and right to keep his attackers at bay. The two men
facing him were impatient, and in his experience, poise was as effective
a weapon as a sword. He would wait for them to make a mistake. The
henchman was eager to prove his worth and lunged forward recklessly.
Montferrat blocked the strike with his sword and kicked the man with all
his might, his bare foot catching the man in his thigh. The man howled
with pain, and from the corner of his eye, Montferrat noted that the
prince had held back mindfully. He decided to stay on his attacker and
swung his sword, catching the faltering man's blade with the full brunt
of his own and knocking it out from his hand. The prince screamed in
anger and rushed forward, interrupting Montferrat, whose sword was
now needed elsewhere. Montferrat managed to kick his first attacker
back before quickly spinning to face di Sangro. The henchman reeled
backwards, crashing into the table and slipping off it into the large fireplace. Sparks and embers flew out from the hearth as he yelped from the
pain in his seared hand, with which he had tried to catch his fall. Montferrat saw the man's sleeve catch fire just as the lantern, which had fallen
off the table, ignited the carpet in a swath of fire.

The false marquis struggled to parry the resurgent di Sangro's thrusts
as the flames from the carpet grew furiously and licked at the thick
velvet curtain before taking hold of it. The heat and the smoke in the
bedchamber were infernal as the prince fought on relentlessly and surprised Montferrat with a ferocious strike that knocked the sword from
his hands. Montferrat stepped backwards, trying to avoid the edge of
di Sangro's blade, which now loomed too close to his throat. Through
the rising smoke in the chamber, he noticed that the thug with the
burnt hand had managed to extinguish the flames on his coat and was
now rising to rejoin the fray. The man moved sideways, positioning
himself by the bedchamber door to block any attempt at escape by
Montferrat.

Montferrat was outnumbered and outgunned, and he knew it.

Darting nervous glances left and right, he saw a possible way out and
decided to chance it. He raised his hands and sidestepped towards the
burning curtain, his eyes locked on di Sangro.

"We need to put this fire out before it spreads to the other floors,"
Montferrat shouted, his feet circling cautiously towards the curtain.

"To hell with the other floors," di Sangro fired back, "just as long as what you know doesn't go up in flames."

Montferrat had managed to edge his way over to the burning curtain. The henchman's discarded, half-burnt coat was lying there, smoldering. Montferrat made his move. He grabbed the coat and used it to shield his hands as he reached into the flames and yanked the curtain off its rail before flinging it at di Sangro and his lackey. The flaming cloak landed heavily on the prince's man, who yelled out in horror as he furiously tried to bat it off him. It enshrouded him in its flaming embrace until he managed to flick it to the floor, where it created a barrier of fire between them and their quarry. Montferrat didn't wait. He yanked open the door to the balcony and rushed out into the night.

After the intense heat in the bedchamber, the chilly air coming in from the bay hit him like a slap. Casting a quick look back inside, he saw di Sangro and his half-burnt henchman trampling feverishly on the flames and edging around them to follow him. Di Sangro raised his gaze and locked eyes with Montferrat. Montferrat nodded, and with his heart in his mouth, he climbed onto the railing and flung himself off it.

He landed with a thud on the balcony of an adjacent chamber on the floor below. The landing sent a jolt of pain searing through his jaw and teeth and rattling in his head. He shook it off and sprang to his feet, climbing over the wrought-iron railing before hurling himself onto the roof that jutted out two floors below just as di Sangro made it onto the balcony.

"Get him," di Sangro yelled into the darkness as he stood there, backlit by the flames like a demon from hell. Montferrat glanced over at the palazzo's entrance and spotted two men rushing out into the darkness, silhouetted against the light coming from a lantern one of them carried. He clambered across one roof and jumped onto the roof of an abutting structure, sending tiles clattering to the ground below. He looked at the rooftops and chimneys ahead, mapping out his escape route. In the darkness of the densely built city, he knew he could lose his pursuers and disappear.

What concerned him more was what he knew had to come.

Once he had retrieved the precious trove he kept tucked away in a safe spot, far from his palazzo—a precaution he always took—he would have to move on.

He would have to find himself a new name and a new home.

Reinvent himself. Yet again.

He had done it before.

He would do it again.

He heard di Sangro bellowing "Montferrat" into the night like a man possessed. He knew he hadn't seen the last of him. A man like di Sangro wouldn't give up that easily. He'd been infected by a feverish greed that, once it took hold of a man, would never let go.

The thought chilled Montferrat to the bone as he slipped into the night.

II

Baghdad—April 2003

"Sir, we've just gone over the ten-minute mark."

Captain Eric Rucker of the First Battalion, Seventh Cavalry Regiment, checked his watch and nodded. He looked at the faces around him, grimy and tense, dripping with sweat. It wasn't even ten in the morning and the sun was already beating down on them with murderous heat. The heavy protective gear didn't help either, not when it was 110 degrees in the shade. But they couldn't do without it.

The deadline had passed.

It was time to go in.

With eerie synchronicity, a call to prayer from a nearby minaret cut through the dusty, stifling air. Rucker heard a creak behind him and looked up to see an old woman with half-graying, half-hennaed hair lean out from a window in a house across the street from the target. She studied him with grim, lifeless eyes before swinging the window's shutters closed.

He gave her a few moments to find shelter deeper in the house, then, with a curt nod to the XO, he initiated the assault.

A Mark 19 grenade launched from the lead Humvee whistled across the wide street and obliterated the main gate to the compound. Squad leaders rushed in with twenty or so soldiers close behind and immediately came under small-arms fire. Bullets snapped around them as they fanned out through the courtyard and ducked for cover behind anything they could find. Two men fell before the rest had managed to secure safe positions on either side of the house's entrance. They soon unleashed a torrent of gunfire onto the house as cover while the wounded were swiftly pulled back out to the relative safety of the street by men with big biceps and bigger hearts.

The house's front door was barricaded, its windows blocked out. Over the next twenty-two minutes, thousands of rounds were exchanged, but little progress was made. Another soldier was hit as the car he was crouching behind was peppered with bullets from the house.

Rucker gave the order to withdraw. The house was surrounded. The men inside weren't going anywhere.

Time was on his side.

∾∾∾

LIKE SO MANY OF THE OTHERS that followed, it had all started with a walk-in.

On that sweltering spring evening, a middle-aged man in a tattered suit and a swath of soiled cloth around his head had walked up to the soldiers manning the gate at FOB Camp Headhunter. Wary of being spotted cozying up to the enemy, he spoke low and fast. The soldiers kept him at bay while they called over a local they used as an interpreter. The interpreter listened to the man's claims and told them the man should be allowed in as soon as he could be checked for explosives. The interpreter then rushed in to alert the camp's commander.

The man had information regarding the whereabouts of a "person of interest."

The hunt was on.

Tracking down Saddam's gang of hard-core Ba'athists was priority one for the military in Iraq. The "thunder run" had been swift, the city had been taken sooner and with far more ease than expected, but most of the bad guys had skipped town. Few on the Pentagon's deck of fifty-five most-wanted Iraqis—not the Ace of Spades himself, nor his two sons—had been captured or killed as yet.

Safely ensconced in a briefing room in the base, the man in the headdress was agitated when he spoke. More than agitated. He was downright terrified. The interpreter pointed this out to the base commander, who didn't read too much into it. For him, it was expected. These people had lived under a monstrous and ruthless dictatorship for decades. Squealing on one of their tormentors wasn't exactly a casual undertaking.

The interpreter wasn't so sure.

The base commander was disappointed to find out that the regime member being shopped by the man in the headdress wasn't on the Pentagon's most-wanted list. In fact, no one had ever heard of him. They didn't seem to know anything about him at all.

The man in the headdress didn't even know his name. He only referred to him as the *hakeem*.

The doctor.

And even nestled in the safety of the forward operating base, he could only utter the word in a cowed, hushed tone.

He didn't have a name to give them. He didn't have much in terms of hard detail, except that before the invasion, men in darkened, official-looking cars were often seen driving into his compound in the middle of the night. The fearless leader himself had been to see him on a few occasions.

He couldn't even really describe him, except for one chilling detail that intrigued all those in the room: The hakeem wasn't Iraqi. He wasn't even an Arab.

He was a Westerner.

And there were certainly no Westerners on the deck of cards.

For that matter, only one person on the list was not part of the military or the government. Curiously, she was also the only queen in the deck—biologically speaking, anyway. The lowest-ranked card in the deck was a woman, a scientist named Huda Ammash, affectionately nicknamed Mrs. Anthrax, the daughter of a former minister of defense and rumored to be the head of Iraq's biological weapons program.

The elements were all there. Doctor. Close to Saddam. Westerner. Terrified local. It was enough to get the ball rolling.

Intel was requested and delivered that very night.

Plans were drawn up.

By first light, Rucker and his men had secured the outer cordon with ground forces and armored vehicles. The target location, as pinpointed by the man in the headdress, was a three-story concrete house in the middle of the Saddamiya district of Baghdad. The area hadn't always gone by that name. It had once been a hard neighborhood. Saddam had grown up on its mean streets, attended school there, and that was where he'd forged his unique take on life. After taking over the country, he'd brought in the bulldozers and had the whole area flattened before redeveloping it as a closed community of imposing modernist concrete and brick houses set behind arcaded walkways and virtually walled off from the rest of the city. It took on his name and became home to those he deemed worthy. The battalion had been in charge of the area since the troops had taken Baghdad and had treated it with caution, given the obvious aversion to the invading forces from the loyalists who still lived there.

The weapons squads took up their positions, the snipers were in place. The assault was ready for initiation.

Rucker had, as per the newly adopted standard procedure in these cases, used the "cordon-and-knock" approach. Once the perimeter was secured, troops had advanced to the house and made their presence known. An interpreter, using a bullhorn, informed those inside that they had ten minutes to come out of the house with their hands up.

Ten minutes later, all hell had erupted.

∾∾∾

As MEDEVACS TENDED TO the wounded, Rucker gave the order to "prep the objective," to minimize further casualties during the inevitable re-entry attempt. Two OH-58D Kiowa choppers flew in and rained down 2.75-inch rockets and machine-gun fire onto the house, while the ground troops unleashed more Mark 19s and a couple of more potent, shoulder-mounted AT-4 antitank missiles.

Eventually, the house fell silent.

Rucker sent his men back in, only this time, two Humvees charged in ahead of them, their .50-caliber machine guns smoking. He soon realized the objective was more than well prepped. His men made their way in with little difficulty, finding several dead bodies and only encountering three solitary and shell-shocked Republican Guards, who were swiftly taken out.

Relief washed over him when he heard the shouts of "Clear" over the radio. His advance troops had confirmed overall control of the site.

Rucker made his way into the hakeem's house as the dead bodies were being lined up for identification. He looked at their dirty, bloodstained faces and frowned. They were all clearly local men, Iraqis, foot soldiers long abandoned by their commanding officers. He called for the man with the headdress to be brought in. The man was spirited in under heavy guard and allowed to check the dead. With each one, he shook his head, his fear more visible with each negative identification.

The hakeem was nowhere to be found.

Rucker scowled. The operation had required considerable resources, three of his men were wounded, one of them seriously, and it looked as if it was all for nothing. He was about to order another sweep when a voice he recognized as belonging to Sergeant Jess Eddison crackled over the radio.

"Sir." Eddison's voice had an unsettling quiver in it that Rucker hadn't heard before. "I think you need to see this."

Rucker and his XO followed a squad leader to the inner vestibule of the house, from where the grand, marble-clad stairs ascended to the bedroom areas above. A door off to its side led to the basement. Using torches to light up the windowless passage, the three men made their way carefully down the steps and met up with Eddison and a couple of PFCs from the Second Platoon. Eddison directed his flashlight's beam into the darkness and led them down the hall.

What they found wasn't exactly a standard rec room.

Unless your name was Mengele.

The basement covered the whole footprint of the house as well as its outer courtyard. The first few rooms they found weren't particularly distressing. The first was an office. Its contents seemed to have hastily been cleared out. Shredded papers littered the floor, and a small stack of burnt books lay in a mound of black ash and bindings in a corner. Next door was a large bathroom, followed by another room with sofas and a large TV set.

The room they entered after that was much larger. It was a full-fledged operating room. The fittings and the surgical equipment were state-of-the-art. Its relative cleanliness belied the squalid state of the rest of the house. Presumably, the guards manning the house hadn't ventured in there. Maybe by choice. Or maybe by fear.

Its floor was wet with a bluish liquid. Rucker and his team followed Eddison, their boots squeaking against the damp stone tiles. The passage led to a lab where, lined up on a white Formica drawer unit along the room's long wall, sat a row of clear vats filled with a green-blue solution. A few of them were shattered in what seemed like a random, hasty cover-up. The others were intact.

Rucker and his squad leader moved in for a closer look. Tubes fed into the liquid, and suspended in the undamaged vats were human organs: brains, eyes, hearts, and some smaller body parts that Rucker didn't recognize. A worktable nearby was littered with petri dishes. They had meticulously marked labels that were indecipherable to their untrained eyes. Next to them sat a pair of powerful microscopes. Cables that would have connected to computers led nowhere. All the computers were gone.

Off to one corner, Rucker found another room, long and narrow. Stepping inside, he found several large, stainless-steel fridges lined up side by side. He thought about whether to check them himself, or to wait for a hazmat team. He decided there wasn't a risk, given the lack of locks or markings, and opened the first of the fridges. It was filled with neatly stacked vats containing a thick red liquid. Even before he saw the labels marked with dates and names, Rucker knew the vats contained blood.

Human blood.

Not the small, medical pouches he was used to.

This was blood by the barrel-load.

Eddison led them through to the part of the basement that he had initially signaled them about. A narrow corridor led to another area that must have been excavated under the courtyard, though Rucker couldn't be sure, the dark maze confusing any sense of direction he may have enjoyed aboveground. It was, for all intents and purposes, a prison. Cell after cell lined either side of the passage. The interiors of the cells were decently furnished with beds, toilets, and sinks. Rucker had seen far worse. It felt more like a windowless hospital ward, if anything.

If it weren't for the bodies.

There were two in each room.

Shot in the head in a final, desperate act of insanity.

There were men and women. Young and old. Children, at least a dozen of them, boys and girls. All wearing identical white jumpsuits.

The last cell would mark Rucker to the end of his days.

On its bare, white floor lay the supine bodies of two young boys. Their heads had recently been shaved clear. They stared up at him with unblinking eyes, small, round punctures cratering their foreheads, acrylic-like pools of blood, thick and shiny, framing their hairless skulls. And on the wall of the cell, a crude drawing, carved into the wall as if with a fork or some other blunt instrument.

The etching of a desperate soul, a silent scream to an uncaring world from a horror-stricken child.

A circular image of a snake, curled on itself, and feeding on its own tail.

Chapter 1

∽∾ ∾∽

Glancing back at the remains of the mosque, Evelyn Bishop spotted him, half-hidden behind a shrapnel-encrusted wall, standing alone, the ever-present cigarette held between thumb and forefinger. The sight jarred her back to a distant past.

"Farouk?"

Even after all this time, it was unmistakably him. His eyes smiled tentatively back at her, confirming it.

Ramez—the diminutive, hyperactive ex-student of hers, now an assistant professor in her department and, handily for access to this part of the country, a Shi'ite—looked up from the cavity under the mosque's outer wall. Evelyn told him she'd be right back and made her way over to where the man stood.

She hadn't seen Farouk since they'd worked together on sweltering digs in Iraq twenty-odd years earlier. Back then, she was the tireless *Sitt* Evelyn, Lady Evelyn, young, vibrant, passionate about her work, a force of nature, running the excavations at the palace mound of Sennacherib in Nineveh and at Babylon, sixty miles south of Baghdad. He was simply Farouk, part of the digs' local entourage, a short, paunchy, balding chain-smoker, a dealer in antiquities and a "facilitator," the kind of fixer that any undertaking in that part of the world seemed to require. He'd always been courteous, honest, and efficient, a quiet, self-effacing man who always delivered what he promised with a humble nod and never shied away from a troublesome request. But from the stooped shoulders, the furrows lining his forehead, and the few surviving wisps of gray where thick, black hair had once ruled, it was clear that the years hadn't been overly generous to him. Then again, Iraq hadn't exactly been experiencing a golden age of late.

"Farouk," she said, beaming. "How are you? My God, how long has it been?"

"A very long time, *Sitt* Evelyn."

Not that he was ever a fountain of ebullience, but his voice was, she thought, markedly subdued. She couldn't pin down the look on his face. Was the aloofness simply due to the intervening years, or was it something else?

A hint of unease crept through her. "What are you doing here? Do you live here now?"

"No, I only left Iraq two weeks ago," he replied somberly, before adding, "I came to find you."

His answer threw her. "To find me . . . ?" She was now certain that something was definitely wrong. That his eyes were darting around nervously in between sharp drags on his cigarette added to her concern. "Is everything alright?"

"Please. Can we . . . ?" He beckoned her away from the mosque and led her around a corner to a more discreet, sheltered corner.

She followed him, eyeing the ground warily, ever alert for the small cluster bomblets that littered the whole region. Watching Farouk's furtive glances at the village's main road down the hill, it was clear to her that he was on the lookout for an entirely different threat. Through the small alleys, Evelyn glimpsed the activity down the slope—trucks unloading relief supplies, makeshift tents being erected, cars making their way through the chaotic scene at a snail's pace, all of it punctuated by the occasional distant explosion, a constant reminder that although the thirty-four-day war was officially over and the cease-fire was in place, the conflict was far from resolved—but couldn't see what he was worried about.

"What's going on?" she asked. "Are you alright?"

He glanced around, again making sure that they weren't being watched, then flicked his cigarette away and pulled out a small, tattered brown envelope from his jacket pocket.

He handed it to her and said, "I brought these for you."

She opened the envelope and pulled out a small stack of photographs. They were Polaroids, slightly bent and worn.

Evelyn raised her eyes at Farouk quizzically, although her instincts were already telegraphing her what the pictures would show. She'd barely started flipping through the first few photos when her worst fears were confirmed.

〜〜〜

SHE'D MOVED TO LEBANON in 1992, just as the country was emerging from a long and ultimately pointless civil war. She'd decamped to the Middle East shortly after graduating from Berkeley in the late 1960s. She'd been working on a series of digs in Jordan, Iraq, and Egypt when a teaching position opened up at the American University of Beirut's Archaeology Department. Coupled with the potential to participate actively in the excavations of the newly accessible downtown area of the city, an alluring possibility considering its Phoenician, Greek, and Roman history, it was an opportunity she couldn't pass up. She applied for and got the job.

Now, a decade and a half later, Beirut was firmly and irrevocably home. She knew she'd live out her years here and die here, and the thought didn't displease her. The country had been good to her, and she'd more than returned the favor. A small cabal of enthusiastic and passionate students would attest to that, as would the city's revitalized museum. During the reconstruction of the downtown area, she'd butted heads with the developers and their bulldozers and tirelessly lobbied the government and the international monitors of UNESCO. She'd won some battles and lost others, but she'd made a difference. She'd been an intrinsic part of the rebirth of the city, of the whole country. She'd experienced the optimism as well as the cynicism, the selflessness and the corruption, the generosity and the greed, the hope and the despair, a whole cocktail of raw human emotions and instincts, unveiled and exposed with little consideration for modesty or shame.

And then this disaster.

Both Hezbollah and the Israelis had grossly miscalculated, and predictably, innocent civilians paid the price. That summer, barely a few weeks earlier, Evelyn had watched the Chinooks and the warships ferrying out the trapped foreigners with a lump in her throat, but it had never occurred to her to join them. She was home.

In the meantime, there was a lot of work to do. Classes were scheduled to resume in just over a week, one month later than normal. The summer term's courses had had to be rescheduled. Some faculty members wouldn't be coming back. The next few months would be an organizational challenge, with, occasionally, a curious distraction to take in, such as the one that had brought her here, today, to Zabqine, a sleepy town in the rolling hills of south Lebanon, less than five miles from the Israeli border.

The town itself was only there in name. Most of its houses had been reduced to mounds of gray rubble, twisted iron rods, and melted glass. Others had simply been obliterated, swallowed up by the black holes of laser-guided bombs. The bulldozers and trucks had moved in swiftly, clearing away the debris—more macabre landfill for some beachfront hotel development. The bodies of those who had died under the pancaked floors of their homes had been buried, and defiantly, the town was now showing tentative signs of life. The survivors, those who had managed to leave before the onslaught, were moving back, living in makeshift tents while figuring out how to rebuild. The power supply wouldn't be back for a long time, but at least a water tank had been trucked in to provide drinking water. A small line of villagers waited their turn there patiently, plastic containers and bottles in hand, while others emptied supplies from a couple of UNIFIL trucks that had brought in food and other basic supplies. Kids ran around, playing—of all games—war.

Ramez had driven her down to the village that morning. He was from a nearby town himself. An elderly local man, the only villager to have stayed in Zabqine during the bombing—it had left him half-deaf—had led them up the carpet of shattered masonry to the remains of the small mosque. Even though Ramez had described it to her, the sight that greeted her when they finally reached the hilltop was still unsettling.

The mosque's green dome had somehow survived the bombs that

had wrecked the rest of the small, stone structure. It just sat there, propped up bizarrely on top of the debris, a surreal installation that only war can conjure up. The shredded strips of what once was the mosque's red carpet fluttered eerily from the bare branches of nearby trees.

In pulling down the mosque's walls, the bombs had ripped the earth open, revealing a crevasse under its rear boundary, and exposing a previously hidden chamber underneath. The biblical frescoes on its walls, though faded and eaten away by time, were unmistakable. It was a pre-Islamic church, buried under the mosque. According to the Bible, the coast was well traveled by Jesus and his followers and was dotted with relics from biblical times. The church of St. Thomas, close by in Tyre, was built on what was thought to be the oldest church anywhere on record, a first-century edifice built by Saint Thomas upon his return from Cyprus. But Islam had swept over the region in the late seventh century, and many places of worship had been supplanted and taken over by the new faithful.

Poking around a Shi'ite shrine for the remnants of another, earlier faith wasn't going to be easy, especially not now, with the war still a fresh, gaping wound, and with emotions running even higher than they normally were.

Evelyn had imagined the day would be challenging.

But not in this way.

❧❧❧

A GALE OF DISAPPOINTMENT swept through her. She looked at Farouk with undisguised sadness in her eyes. "What are you doing, Farouk?" she asked softly. "You know me better than this."

The Polaroids in Evelyn's hands showed hastily taken images of artifacts, treasures of a bygone age, relics from the cradle of civilization: cuneiform tablets, cylinder seals, alabaster and terra-cotta figurines, pottery vessels. She'd seen many similar shots since American troops had stormed into Baghdad in 2003 and international outrage had erupted over their failure to secure the city's museum and other sites of cultural importance. Looters had run amok, accusations of inside jobs and political machinations were made, withdrawn, and reinstated, and estimates of the number of stolen objects had rocketed up and down with breathless unreliability. One thing was certain: Treasures dating back thousands of years had undeniably been stolen, some had been returned, but most were still missing.

"Please, *Sitt* Evelyn—" Farouk pleaded.

"No," she cut him off harshly, pushing the Polaroids back into his hands. "Come on. You're bringing me these—what? You really expect me to buy them or help you sell them?"

"Please," he repeated softly. "You have to help me. I can't go back there. Here." He was hectically going through them, looking for something. "Look at this."

Evelyn noticed his yellowed fingers were shaking. She studied his face, his body language—he was clearly frightened, as he should be. Smuggling ancient artifacts out of Iraq carried some rather severe penalties, penalties that could prove fatal depending on which side of what border one was apprehended on. But something was nagging at her. Admittedly, she didn't know this man intimately and hadn't seen him in years, but she thought she had a pretty good handle on understanding people and what they were made of, and for him to stoop to participating in the pillaging of his country, a country she remembered him caring about deeply . . . Then again, she hadn't lived through several bloody overthrows and three major wars, and all the horrors in between. She reined in her judgmental instincts and had to admit she had no idea of what his life must have been like since she last saw him. And what desperate measures people resorted to in order to survive.

He pulled a couple of shots from the pack and his eyes settled on her again. "Here."

She watched him as she drew a calming breath, nodded, and turned her attention to the photographs he was handing her.

The first shot showed several old codices lying flat on what looked like a table. Evelyn examined it more closely. Without being able to look inside the books, it was hard to tell how old they were. The region had such a rich history, pretty much a continuous parade of civilizations stretching over several thousand years. A few telltale details, however, hinted at their age: They had cracked leather covers, some of them gold-tooled and others stamped with geometric designs, mandorla medallions, and pendants. Ridges running over the lacings across their spines were also clearly visible, all of it placing the books as pre–fourteenth century. Which made them potentially very, very attractive to museums and collectors.

She moved on to the second shot and froze with a chill of recognition. She brought the photograph up closer, studying it intently, her fingers brushing over it in a futile attempt to make it clearer, her mind trying to swim through the deluge of memories that the image had triggered: It showed an ancient codex, sitting innocently between two other old books. Its tooled-leather cover cracked and dusty. The leather envelope flap of the back cover was extended out. A distinctive feature of medieval Islamic books, it was normally tucked in under the front cover when the book was closed, used as a bookmark as well as to preserve and protect its pages.

Taken at face value, there was nothing remarkable about the old book, except for the symbol tooled into its cover: the ringlike, circular motif of a snake feeding on its own tail.

Evelyn's eyes shot up to meet Farouk's gaze. She couldn't fire off the words fast enough. "Where did you find these?"

"I didn't. Abu Barzan, an old friend of mine, did. He also deals in antiquities. He has a small shop in Al-Mawsil," Farouk explained, using the Arabic name for the town Mosul, a couple of hundred miles northeast of Baghdad. "Nothing illegal, you know, only what we were allowed to sell, under Saddam." Exporting the most valued antiquities, preinvasion, was the exclusive turf of Ba'ath Party officials. The rabble—the rest of the population—were left to fight over the crumbs. "Saddam had informants everywhere, as you know. Now it's different, of course. Anyway, my friend came to see me in Baghdad, around a month ago. He goes around the north, to old villages, looking for pieces. He's half-Kurd, and when he's there, he conveniently forgets his half-Sunni side, and they open their houses to him. Anyway, he'd come across these pieces—you know how it is now. It's a huge mess. Total chaos. Bombs, killings, death squads . . . People running around scared, doing what they have to do to keep out of danger and put bread on the table. Selling what they can, especially now that they can sell them openly. But there aren't many buyers, not inside Iraq anyway. Anyway, Abu Barzan had this collection he was trying to sell. He wanted to leave the country, settle somewhere safe—we all do—but it takes money. So he was asking around, quietly, looking for a buyer. He knew I had some good contacts outside the country. He offered to split the proceeds with me."

Farouk lit up another cigarette, glancing around furtively as he did.

"Anyway, I thought of you when I saw the Ouroboros," he added, reaching out and tapping the snapshot of the codex. "I called around to see if anyone knew where you were. Mahfouz Zacharia—"

"Of course," Evelyn interjected. She'd kept in touch with the curator of the National Museum of Antiquities in Baghdad. Especially post-invasion, when the whole looting scandal had erupted. "Farouk, you know I can't touch these. We shouldn't be having this conversation."

"You have to help me, *Sitt* Evelyn. Please. I can't go back to Iraq. It's worse than you imagine. You want this book, don't you? I'll get it for you. Just help me stay here, please. You can use a driver, can't you? An assistant? I'll do anything. I can be useful, you know that. Please. I can't go back there."

She winced. "Farouk, it's not that easy." She shook her head faintly and glanced at the desolate hills sweeping away from the mosque. Along a small stone wall, row upon row of brown tobacco leaves, threaded onto wires months ago to dry in the summer sun, lay there, rotten and grayed, covered in the same thick dust that smothered the entire region. Overhead, the faint buzz of an Israeli drone rose and died with the breeze, a constant reminder of the simmering tension.

Farouk's face darkened. His breathing was now shorter and faster, his hands agitated. "You remember Hajj Ali Salloum?"

Another name from the past. An antiques dealer too, if Evelyn's memory was correct—which it usually was. Based in Baghdad. His shop was three doors down from Farouk's. She remembered them being close, though staunchly competitive when it came to clients and sales.

"He's dead." Farouk's voice was quivering. "And I think it's because of this book."

Evelyn's expression clouded as she struggled for words. "What happened to him?"

A sharper fear flickered in his eyes. "What is this book about, *Sitt* Evelyn? Who else is after it?"

Consternation flooded her voice. "I don't know."

"What about Mr. Tom? He was working on it with you. Maybe he knows. You need to ask him, *Sitt* Evelyn. Something very bad is happening. You can't send me back there."

The mention pricked Evelyn's heart. Before she could answer him, Ramez's voice echoed through the mounds of rubble around them.

"Evelyn?"

Farouk shot her an anxious glare. She craned her neck to see Ramez appear, making his way over from the mosque. She glanced back at Farouk, who was looking down through the alleyways, towards the main street. When he turned back to face her, the blood seemed to have drained from his face. He shot her a look of such terror that she felt her heart constrict. He pushed the small stack of photos and the envelope into her hands and just said, "Nine o'clock, downtown, by the clock tower. Please come."

Ramez reached them, clearly wondering what was going on.

Evelyn fumbled for words, unsure about what to say. "Farouk's an old colleague of mine. From the old days, in Iraq." Ramez seemed clearly aware of the unease hovering over them. Evelyn sensed Farouk was making a move and reached out to him reassuringly. "It's okay. Ramez and I work together. At the university."

She was doing her best to telegraph to him that her colleague wasn't a threat, but something had visibly spooked Farouk, who just nodded furtively at Ramez before telling her with an insistent, pleading voice, "Please be there." And before she could object, he was already scrambling up the path, away from the town center, heading towards the mosque.

"Wait, Farouk!" Evelyn sidestepped away from Ramez and called out after him, but to no avail. He was already gone.

She turned back to Ramez, who seemed mystified. She suddenly remembered that the Polaroids were still in her hand, in plain sight for him, and he'd noticed them. He looked a question at her. She stuffed them in the envelope and pocketed it quickly while conjuring up a disarming smile.

"Sorry about that. He's just . . . It's a long story. Shall we get back to the chamber?"

Ramez nodded politely and led her back up the path.

She followed him, her eyes distant, the pit of her stomach garroted by Farouk's unsettling words, her mind too overwhelmed to register a fleeting image from the town below: two men, standing by the edge of the road, a hard, stone-dead look in their eyes—not uncommon given the setting or the context, an expression she'd gotten used to seeing since the war—and yet, somehow disconnected to the activity around them, looking up in her direction, before one of them got into a car that drove off rather abruptly, the other catching her eye momentarily before moving off and disappearing behind a collapsed house.

Chapter 2

❧

"Do you have him yet?"

He'd left Baghdad over four years ago, and yet, despite his natural talent for foreign languages and his best efforts, his Arabic vocabulary and accent were still influenced by his years in Iraq. Which is why the men who were assigned to work for him—led by Omar, the man who had just called—all came from the east of his new adopted homeland, close to its border with Iraq, where they'd been facilitating the smuggling of weapons and fighters in both directions. The two languages were broadly similar—think of California Valley–speak vs. East London cockney—but the variance between them was enough to spawn inaccuracies and generate misunderstandings.

Which wouldn't do.

He prided himself on accuracy. He didn't tolerate imprecision, nor did he have much patience for unreliability. And he could tell from the man's discomfited tone, from the very moment he'd been interrupted and picked up the call, that his patience was about to be sorely tested.

There was a hesitant pause before the cold answer came back over his cell phone. "No."

"What do you mean, no?" the hakeem rasped as he angrily flicked off his surgical gloves. "Why not? Where is he?"

Omar wasn't easily cowed, but his tone was now tinged with some added deference. "He was being careful, *mu'allimna.*"

On either side of the border, the men assigned to him always called him that. *Our teacher.* A lowly servant's self-effacing moniker of respect. Not that he'd taught them much. Only to make sure they did what they were asked and did it without asking any questions. It wasn't so much teaching as it was training, with fear as the prime motivator.

"We didn't really have the right opportunity," Omar continued. "We followed him to the American University. He visited the Archaeology Department. We waited for him outside the building, but he must have used another exit. One of my men was watching the sea gate and saw him sneaking out and getting into a taxi."

The hakeem frowned. "So he knows he's being followed," he said gruffly.

"Yes," Omar confirmed reluctantly, before adding, "But it's not a problem. We'll have him for you by tomorrow night."

"I hope so," the hakeem countered acidly. "For your sake." He was trying hard to keep his rage in check. Omar hadn't failed him yet. The man knew what the stakes were, and he was ruthlessly good at his job. He'd been seconded to the hakeem with clear orders to look after him and make sure he got everything he needed. And Omar knew failure wasn't tolerated in the service. The hakeem took some solace from that. "Where is he now?"

"We followed him to Zabqine, a small town in the south, close to the border. He went there to meet someone."

This instantly piqued the hakeem's interest. "Who?"

"A woman. An American. Her name's Evelyn Bishop. She's a professor of archaeology at the university. An older woman. She must be in her sixties. He showed her some documents. We couldn't get close enough to see what they were, but they must have been pictures of the collection."

Interesting, the hakeem mused. The Iraqi dealer's hardly in town for a few hours and the first thing he does is head straight out to see a woman who happens to be an archaeologist? He archived the information for further consideration. "And . . . ?"

Another hesitant pause, then Omar's tone dropped lower. "We lost him. He spotted us and ran. We looked for him all over the town, but he disappeared. But we're watching the woman. I'm outside her apartment right now. They were interrupted, there's unfinished business between them."

"Which means she'll lead you to him." The hakeem nodded quietly to himself. He raised his hand and rubbed his face with it, massaging his furrowed brow and his dry mouth. Failure would certainly not be tolerated here. He'd waited too long for this. "Stay on her," he insisted coldly, "and when they meet up, bring them both to me. I want her too. Do you understand?"

"Yes, *mu'allimna*." The reply was crisp. No hesitance there.

Which was just how the hakeem liked it.

He clicked off and replayed the conversation in his mind for a beat before stowing the phone in his pocket and getting back to the business at hand.

He washed his hands and slipped on a new pair of surgical gloves, then walked over to the bed where the young boy lay, strapped in, hovering at the edge of consciousness, his eyes narrow, ceramiclike white crescents peeking out from under heavy eyelids, tubes emerging from various spots on his body drawing out minute amounts of liquids and sucking the very life out of him.

Chapter 3

❧

It was past six in the evening by the time Evelyn made it back to the city and to her third-floor apartment on Rue Commodore.

She felt exhausted after a day that had marked her on many levels. After Farouk had slipped away, Ramez—who, in what Evelyn took for a remarkable display of self-restraint, hadn't asked her about him or even tried to casually slip it into conversation—had been able to get them a face-to-face with the mayor of Zabqine, who understandably had more pressing matters on his mind than discussing the excavation of a possible early-Christian temple. Still, Evelyn and her young protégé had charmed him, and the door was left open for a further exploratory visit.

Which was quite a feat, given that her mind was totally elsewhere the whole time they were with him.

From the moment Farouk had shown her his tattered envelope of Polaroids, the memories they'd awakened inside her had consumed her every thought. Once at home, she'd taken a long, hot shower and was presently sitting at her desk, staring at a thick file that had followed her like a shadow with each relocation. With a heavy heart, she pulled its cloth straps open and started to flick through its contents. The old photographs and faded, yellowed notebook sheets and photocopies lit up a part of her that had been smothered in darkness for a long time. The pages flew by, one after the other, conjuring up a jumble of emotions that swamped her, taking her back to a time and a place she'd never been able to forget.

Al-Hillah, Iraq. Fall, 1977.

She'd been in the Middle East for just over seven years, most of that time spent on digs in Petra, Jordan, and in Upper Egypt. She'd learned a lot on those digs—it was where she'd first fallen in love with the region—but they weren't hers. Before long, she was yearning to sink her teeth into something she could call her own. And after a lot of hard research and some relentless lobbying for funding, she'd managed to swing it. The dig in question would concern the city that had fascinated her for as long as she could remember and yet had been underserved by archaeology of late: Babylon.

The history of the fabled city went back more than four thousand years, but as it was built of sun-dried mudbrick, not stone, not much of it had survived the ravages of time. The little that had was eventually carted away by the various colonial powers who had ruled over the troubled area over the last half century. With Mother Nature, the Ottomans, the French, and the Germans picking away at it like vultures, the ancient cradle of civilization didn't stand a chance.

Evelyn had hoped, in however small a measure, to try to rectify that injustice.

The digs had started in earnest. The working conditions weren't too harsh, and she'd gotten used to the heat and the insects by then. She'd been surprised at how helpful the authorities had been. The Ba'athists had taken control of the country five years earlier after a decade of coups d'état, and she'd found them pragmatic and courteous—*The Exorcist* had been filming nearby when she first got there, and Saddam's bloody takeover was years away. The area around the dig itself was poor, but the people were kind and welcoming. Baghdad was only a couple of hours' drive away, which was handy for good food, a decent bath, and some sorely missed social interaction.

The find itself had come about by fluke. A local goatherd who was digging for water had discovered a small trove of cuneiform tablets, among the oldest examples of writing, in an underground chamber near an old mosque in Al-Hillah. Being close by, Evelyn had been the first on the scene and decided the area merited further exploration.

A few weeks later, while doing soundings inside an old garage adjacent to the mosque, she found something else. This find wasn't nearly as ancient or valuable. It wasn't a spectacular find, by any means: a series of small, barrel-vaulted, underground chambers, tucked away for centuries. The first few rooms were bare, aside from some austere wooden furniture and some urns, jars, and cooking utensils. Interesting, but not exceptional. Something in the deepest chamber, however, grabbed her attention far more viscerally: A large, circular carving of a snake eating its own tail had been tooled into the main wall of the chamber.

The Ouroboros.

It was one of the oldest mystical symbols in the world. Its roots could be traced back thousands of years to the pig dragons of the Hongshan culture in China and to ancient Egypt and, from there, on to the Phoenicians and the Greeks, who gave it its name, Ouroboros, which meant the "tail-devourer." From there, the image was found in Norse mythology, Hindu tradition, and Aztec symbolism, to name but a few. It also held a firm place in the arcane symbolism of alchemists over the centuries. The self-devouring serpent was a powerful archetype that represented different things to different peoples—a positive symbol for some, a portent of evil for others.

Further exploration of the chambers yielded more curious discoveries. What had been thought to be cooking utensils in one of the chambers turned out to be something rather more esoteric: primitive laboratory equipment. The shards of broken glass, upon closer examination, were actually pieces of flasks and beakers. Remnants of cork stoppers and pipes were also found, along with more jars, and pouches made of animal skins.

Something ominous about the chambers captivated Evelyn's curiosity. She felt as if she had stumbled into the locale of an unknown clandestine group, an unknown cabal who wished to meet away from curious eyes, watched over by the sinister tail-devourer. She spent the next few weeks exploring the tunneled rooms more carefully and was rewarded by a further discovery: a large, earthenware jar, sealed with animal skin, buried in a corner of one of the dark rooms. The Ouroboros, similar to the one on the wall, was tooled into it. In it, Evelyn found paper folios—the material had supplanted parchment and vellum in the area since the eighth century, long before reaching Europe—that were richly covered with texts and elaborately decorated with mesmerizing geometric patterns, scientific renderings of nature, and colorful, if bizarre, anatomical studies.

As Evelyn flicked through the various images of the symbol in her file—etchings, woodcuts, and other prints—she came across a bunch of old, faded photographs. She put the file aside and perused the pictures. There were several shots of the chambers, and others of her with the team at the dig, one of whom was Farouk. *How he's changed*, she thought. *How we've all changed.* She stiffened as her fingers fell upon a shot that sent a little tremor though her. It showed her much younger self, a bright-eyed and ambitious thirty-year-old woman, standing with a man of roughly her age. They were side by side at the site of a desert dig, two adventurers from a bygone age. The shots weren't exactly high-resolution clear—they were small prints she'd had developed at the time and were weathered after sitting in her folder for almost thirty years. The sun had been beating down savagely that day, and both their faces were obscured by sunglasses and safely tucked away under the protective shadows of their safari hats. Regardless, her eyes quickly filled in the details of his features. And even after all these years, the sight of him still made her heart turn over.

Tom.

She gazed deeper into the picture, and the noise of the chaotic city outside receded into silence. The image brought a bittersweet smile to her face as conflicting emotions swirled inside her.

She'd never understood what had really happened all those years ago.

Tom Webster had appeared unannounced at Al-Hillah, a few weeks into her find. He'd introduced himself as an archaeologist-historian with the Haldane Institute, a research center that was affiliated with Brown University. He told her he'd been in Jordan when a colleague had mentioned Evelyn's inquiries about the Ouroboros. Research in the dark ages, before the Internet, involved the use of libraries and picking the brains of experts by actually talking to them—and often, shockingly, face-to-face. He said he'd driven overland to see her and find out more about her discovery.

They'd spent four weeks together.

She'd never felt as strongly about any man since.

Their days were spent examining the chamber, studying the writings and the illustrated folios from the chamber, and following leads to libraries and museums in Baghdad and elsewhere in Iraq, seeking out scholars and historians.

The calligraphy of the texts placed their origin firmly in the Abbasid era, sometime around the tenth century. Carbon dating one of the folios' leather straps had supported their assumption on that front. The texts were beautifully written and illustrated and dealt with a variety of subjects: philosophy, logic, mathematics, chemistry, astrology, astronomy, music, and spirituality. But nothing explained who had written them, nor was there any mention of the tail-devourer symbol's significance.

Evelyn and Webster worked together with a shared passion, and their inquiries showed a brief spark of promise when they uncovered information about an obscure group of the same era, the Brethren of Purity. The Brethren's precise identity was a matter of conjecture. Little was known about them beyond that they were Neoplatonic philosophers who met in secret every twelve days, and whose shrouded legacy included a remarkable compendium of scientific, spiritual, and esoteric teachings garnered from different traditions that was considered to be one of the oldest encyclopedias on record.

Certain aspects of the writings found in the chamber, however, matched the writings left behind by the Brethren, both in style and in content. None of the writings from the chamber, however, dealt with the spirituality of its occupants. Although rooted in Islam, the Brethren's writings also included teachings from the Gospels and from the Torah. The Brethren were seen as freethinkers who didn't ascribe to any specific creed, seeking instead to find truth in all religions and valuing knowledge as the true nourishment of the soul. They strove for a reconciliation, a fusion of the sectarian divisions that plagued the region, in the hope of creating a broad, spiritual sanctuary for all.

Evelyn and Webster had speculated about whether the cabal from the underground chamber could have been an offshoot of the Brethren, but there was nothing to prove or disprove that theory. One aspect of that theory, though, fit rather nicely: The Brethren were thought to have been based in Basra and in Baghdad. Al-Hillah sat between them.

Throughout their time together, Evelyn had been surprised by Webster's unflagging interest, and she'd been taken aback by his unbounded energy and drive in elucidating the little mystery she'd unearthed. Also, for someone she'd never heard of, he seemed to know an awful lot about the Ouroboros and about the history of the region.

She was also pretty sure that he'd fallen in love with her, just as she had with him. Which made his sudden departure all the harder to stomach. Especially given what he'd left her with. And the lie she'd had to live with ever since.

Her face clouded over with grief as memories of that painful separation came rushing back. A passive acceptance, one she'd nurtured over many years, took control and pushed the melancholy feeling away and yanked her back to her present predicament.

A few illustrated pages from the cabal's chamber, alluring in their beauty and their mystery, stared down at her from frames on the wall opposite her desk. She tore her eyes off them and pulled out the stack of Polaroids Farouk had left with her. She pulled out the one showing the ancient codex, and a chill crawled down the back of her neck as she remembered his unsettling news.

Someone she knew was dead. Because of it.

Where had Farouk's friend found it? And what was in it? All those years ago, their search, hers and Tom's, had come up blank. Why would this book be of any more importance?

She remembered Farouk's last question: *Who else is after this book?*

Given the turmoil around her, this was the last thing she needed right now. But there was no escaping it. She didn't want to go to meet Farouk, but she knew she couldn't disappoint him. He was counting on her. He needed help. He was scared. The more she remembered the fear that gripped his face, the more apprehensive she became of that meeting.

Another thought kept haranguing her.

She had to let Tom know.

If she could reach him, that is. They hadn't exactly kept in touch. In fact, she hadn't seen him or spoken to him again after he'd left Iraq.

Not even when she'd found out she was pregnant.

She put down the picture and pulled out her personal organizer. It was a large-size, leatherbound Filofax that had been with her for decades and could barely close for the paperwork, cards, and notes that had been stored between its battered covers over the years. She rummaged through its pockets and sleeves until she found the old card. It had his name, Tom Webster, printed in a stark, copperplate type on its front, along with the institute's name and logo. She'd resisted using it, and with time it had gotten relegated to a remote corner of the Filofax and of her mind.

Thirty years. It was a pointless call to attempt.

Farouk's plea rang in her ears. *You have to ask him*, Sitt *Evelyn*. Something inside her tore and made her give it a shot.

It took a few moments for the signal to bounce off a few satellites before the familiar ringing of a U.S. landline was shortly followed by a woman's voice that, in an overly friendly tone, informed Evelyn that she was through to the Haldane Institute.

Evelyn hesitated. "I'm trying to reach an old friend," she said eventually with a wavering voice. "His name's Tom Webster. He left me this contact number for him, but . . . well, it's been a while."

"One moment, please." Evelyn's heart contracted as the phone operator checked her records. "I'm sorry," the operator came back, somewhat inappropriately chirpy. "I don't show anyone here by that name."

Evelyn shrank back in her chair. "Are you sure? I mean, could you check again, please?"

The operator asked Evelyn to confirm the surname's spelling, ran it again, and came up with nothing. Evelyn heaved a doleful sigh. The operator must have caught it, as she then added, "If you like, I can check our personnel records and get back to you. Perhaps your friend left some forwarding details."

Evelyn gave her her name and her Beirut cell-phone number, thanked her, and hung up. She hadn't really expected to reach him there, it had been far too long for that, but the bubble of excitement still left her feeling tense and restless.

She checked her watch. It was almost seven. She frowned. She'd agreed to meet Mia for a drink at her hotel. The timing couldn't have been worse. She thought of calling her and canceling it, but she couldn't bear the thought of sitting alone for two more hours, captive to the memories rattling around in the attic of her mind, waiting to go out on a rendezvous that she was dreading more by the minute.

She decided a drink with her daughter, surrounded by good music and some distracting faces, might help nurse her through the wait. She just had some ducking and avoiding to do, on a particularly trouble-some subject. At least until she understood what was going on.

She closed the file and laid it down on her desk, stuffed the Polaroids and her cell phone into her handbag, and headed for the hotel across the street from her apartment.

Chapter 4

〜〜〜

The telex machines were history. The middling Chinese restaurant was gone, replaced by a gleaming new Benihana. The circular and eponymous News Bar was also long gone—supplanted by the equally imaginatively named Lounge, complete with dark Wengé paneling, piped Café del Mar compilations, and passion-fruit mojitos—as was Coco, its resident parrot, who, with his eerily faultless imitation of an incoming artillery shell, sent many an uninitiated visitor scurrying for cover.

The hotel's fifteen minutes of fame stretched out over most of the 1980s, when it was the favorite haunt of "the pack" in Beirut. Dan Rather, Peter Jennings—they'd all stayed here. At a time when rival militias had turned West Beirut into the modern era's standard-bearer of urban chaos, before the honor was usurped by Mogadishu and then Baghdad, the Commodore was a sanctuary of filet mignon, electricity, working telex machines, and a bar that never ran dry, thanks to a dauntless hotel manager and some hefty protection payments. Truth be told, the manager probably did his job too well: Most of the reporters who were in town to cover the fighting rarely ventured away from the cushy safety of the hotel, filing their eyewitness reports from the front desk rather than the front line.

Those days were, mercifully, long gone—for the most part, anyway. And the face-lift that had brought the city back to life didn't pass by the hotel, now known as the Meridien Commodore. Despite the fancy makeover, it was still the hangout of choice for the visiting news media, even sans Coco. The pack was loyal, a loyalty that was much in evidence since the sudden eruption of the brief but brutal war that had hogged the headlines around the globe all summer. The Commodore was back to its former glory, fueled by alcohol, adrenaline, and the best broadband connection in town, again displaying that intangible knack of making its guests feel as if they were part of an extended Sicilian family—which was comforting to Mia Bishop, given that her experience in war zones was nonexistent.

Not that it was something she was particularly keen to redress.

She hadn't exactly chosen genetics as a ticket to adventure.

∞

"I know it's probably none of my business, but . . . are you sure you're okay?"

After chatting with Evelyn about how her own work was progressing, and trading anecdotes and observations about the myriad aftereffects of the war that would color their lives for the foreseeable future, Mia finally popped the question. It had been gnawing at her from the moment they'd sat down, and although she felt uncomfortable asking, she felt even less comfortable not offering her mom an opening if she needed one.

Evelyn shifted slightly at the question, adjusting her position on the deep sofa, then took a lingering sip from her wineglass. "I'm fine," she confirmed with what seemed like a forced half-smile, before her eyes wandered and lost themselves in the soothing glow of the wine. "It's nothing."

"You sure?"

Evelyn hesitated. "It's just . . . I saw someone today. Someone I hadn't seen for a long time. Fifteen years, maybe more."

Mia flashed her a loaded smile. "I see."

Evelyn caught her drift. "It's nothing like that, believe me," she protested. "It's just a local fixer who helped out on our digs. In Iraq. Pre-Saddam. I was down south with Ramez—you met him, didn't you?"

Mia nodded. "I think so. Last week, in your office? Small guy, right?"

He was the only colleague of Evelyn's that she'd met. She'd only been in Beirut for three weeks, flying in on one of the first planes to land at the airport since it had reopened after its runways were blitzed by Israeli warplanes in the opening day of the war.

Her introduction to the bizarre world of postwar Beirut had been pretty swift: The massive Airbus had lurched to an abrupt stop seconds after touching down, then veered off the tarmac sharply, revealing a bulldozer and a cement truck that were nonchalantly repairing a huge bomb crater in the middle of the runway. Mia could still picture the workers' casual wave to her and the rest of the shaken passengers on board.

Beirut was open for business, craters in the runway or not. And she could finally get going on the big Phoenician project she'd been gearing up for all year, albeit a few months later than scheduled.

She'd been approached while working with a small team of geneticists in Boston who had undertaken the prodigious task of tracing the spread of mankind across the globe. That project, which involved collecting and analyzing DNA samples taken from thousands of men living in isolated tribes on all of the continents, had confirmed with breathtaking finality that we were all descended from one small tribe of hunter-gatherers who lived in Africa around sixty thousand years ago, a discovery that didn't go down too well in more "sensitive" circles. Mia had joined the team just after getting her postgraduate degree, which was shortly before their central findings were announced; since then, the work had been somewhat anticlimactic and repetitive, consisting mostly of collecting more and more samples to beef up the overall picture. She'd thought about moving on to other cutting-edge areas of research, but the most interesting work in genetics was being hampered by the presidential aversion to stem cell research. So she stayed put—until the offer popped up.

The man who'd made the approach was a representative of the Hariri Foundation, a charity with seriously deep pockets set up by the billionaire former prime minister of Lebanon, before his assassination in 2005. The proposal the charity's rep put forward was vague, but compelling: Simply put, he wanted her to help them figure out who the Phoenicians were.

Which kind of threw her.

Surprisingly, and despite that they were mentioned in many ancient texts written by those they interacted with, little was known about the Phoenicians firsthand. For a people who were credited with inventing the world's first alphabet and whose role as "cultural middlemen" sparked the revival in Greece that led to the birth of Western civilization, they didn't leave much behind. None of their writings or literature had survived, and everything known about them had been pieced together from third-party reports. Even their name was attributed to them by others, in this case the ancient Greeks, who called them the *Phoinikes*, the red people, after the luxurious reddish purple cloth they made using a highly prized dye they extracted from the glands of mollusks. There were no Phoenician libraries, no troves of knowledge, no papyrus scrolls squirreled away in alabaster jars. Nothing from two thousand years of enigmatic history that came to a brutal end when their city-states eventually fell to a series of invaders culminating with the Romans, who, in 146 BC, burned Carthage to the ground, spread salt over its ruins, forbade resettlement in the city for twenty-five years, and obliterated the last major center of Phoenician culture. It was as if any trace of them had been wiped off the face of the earth.

But the name stirred great passions in Lebanon itself.

Following the civil war of the 1970s and 1980s, some Christian factions in Lebanon had effectively hijacked it, using it to create a subtle distinction between themselves and their Muslim countrymen by painting those as later migrants from the Arabian Peninsula after the rise of Islam who had a less worthy claim to the land. Every argument in the region, it seemed, ultimately boiled down to four simple words: "We were here first." Tensions had escalated to a point where the word *Phoenician* had become taboo in official circles. There wasn't a single mention of it to be found anywhere in Beirut's National Museum, where exhibits' tags now sported more politically correct terminology such as "Early Bronze Age."

Which was a shame—as well as, quite possibly, a distortion of history. Hence the project.

Mia was aware that she was stepping into a political minefield. The project's aims were altruistic enough: If it was possible to use DNA samples to establish that all of the country's inhabitants, Christian and Muslim alike, were descendants of one culture, one people, one tribe, it could help defuse long-held prejudices and inspire a feeling of unity.

Two local experts had been hired to work with Mia: a highly respected historian who taught at the university, and a geneticist to assist her. The former was Christian, the latter, Muslim. But as Mia soon found out, tribal allegiances were of paramount importance to the people of the region, and redefining history wasn't necessarily welcome.

Still, with the big three-oh closing in on her, no husband or kids to worry about, a social diary as bleak as a liquor store in downtown Kabul, and an intriguing and generously funded project to call her own, it was really a no-brainer, even more so since it was an opportunity for her to get to know her mother.

To really know her.

So she'd signed on the dotted line and packed her bags—then proceeded to unpack just as swiftly and watch CNN for two months until the fighting stopped, the cease-fire was finally agreed to, and the blockade was lifted.

∽⌒∽

"It's LITERALLY under the mosque," Evelyn was telling Mia. "Could be one of the earliest chapels on record; it's pretty amazing. I'll take you down there if you like. Ramez is from a small town near there and he heard about it."

"And this guy just showed up there, out of the blue?"

Evelyn nodded.

Mia studied her mom. Something in the firm honesty in the woman's voice assured Mia that her mom wasn't just being coy, but the nervous flutter was still there. "Can't imagine what they're going through out there," Mia commented ruefully. "Was he looking for work?"

Evelyn winced with discomfort. "Yes. Sort of. It's . . . complicated."

She didn't seem to want to go into it any deeper. Mia decided to leave it at that. She acknowledged Evelyn's reply with a slight nod and a reciprocal half-smile and took another sip of her own. A pregnant silence hung between them for a moment, then a waiter glided over, filled Mia's glass from the almost empty wine bottle in the ice bucket, and asked if they wanted another.

Evelyn sat up, snapping out of her reverie. "What time is it?"

She checked her watch as Mia shook her head at the waiter. As he walked away, Mia noticed a man with close-cropped, jet-black hair, deep-set eyes, and a pockmarked face, standing at the bar, smoking, and glancing sideways at them—a cold glance, maybe just a touch too focused—before turning away. She hadn't been in Beirut long, but she knew that in this town, men took more notice of her than she was used to, with the appeal of her winsome features amplified by the distinctly foreign air of her paler, slightly freckled skin and her honey-blond hair. She would have been disingenuous if she'd denied enjoying the flirtatious glances, and in this case, she would have shrugged off the man's glance as a compliment, especially if the guy were cute, only not even this guy's mother would have thought of describing him as "cute," and there was nothing remotely flirtatious about his look. In fact, his shuttered glance creeped her out. Which, again, wasn't a first, not in this town— the flip side to her exotic-foreigner appeal was that a lot of people were angry, and suspicious, particularly of foreigners, since the brutal war had erupted around them unexpectedly. But somehow he didn't fit, he didn't look as if he was in here to have a good time, the expression on his face was just too stone-cold, too remote, like an android's, and—

Evelyn cut through Mia's little fog of paranoia by suddenly getting up. "I've really got to go. I don't know what I was thinking," she chided herself as she collected her jacket and her handbag from the sofa. She turned to Mia. "I'm sorry, I really can't be late for . . . I'm supposed to meet someone. Can we get the bill?"

Mia could see the urgency etched into her mom's face. "Go. I'll take care of it."

Evelyn moved to rifle through her handbag. "At least let me—"

But Mia reached out and put her hand on hers, comfortingly, stopping her. "Don't worry about it. Just go. You can get the next one."

Evelyn gave her a smile that was loaded with such intense signals— gratitude, concern, unease, and maybe even, Mia suddenly thought with an unexpected tightening in her chest, fear—and hurried off.

Mia watched her weave through the first few drinkers standing around their corner and disappear into the cloudy haze of the crowd. The bar was buzzing with its customary loud, big-drinking, and even-bigger-smoking clientele. She sat back, sinking into her seat, not sure about what to think, and as she cast her eyes around the room, she caught sight of the android at the bar making his way out as well.

He seemed rushed.

Too rushed.

The realization tripped a fuse inside Mia's already unsettled mind. She tried following him with her eyes and lifted herself off the armchair, craning her neck after him, but he was already lost in the sea of people crowding the bar and blocking her view of its entrance.

Malignant thoughts came flooding out from the dark recesses of her imagination, and the room suddenly seemed to recede and shift out of focus. The two—or was it three?—glasses of wine didn't help. She settled back into the chair, dazed and rattled, calming herself down. And then she saw it.

Evelyn's cell phone.

Tucked into the side of the sofa, one end sticking out, barely visible.

Her mind zapped into a fast rewind—and in her mind's eye, she remembered seeing her mom taking it out of her handbag when they'd first sat down and putting it down on the sofa, by her side, as if willing it to ring somehow.

Mia didn't hesitate.

She just grabbed it and bolted after her.

Chapter 5

〜〜

Mia made it out of the hotel lobby and into the street just in time to see a gray Mercedes taxi disappearing down Rue Commodore. Through its rear windshield, she could just about make out the back of Evelyn's head. Several taxi drivers who hung around outside the hotel angling for fares came up to her, offering their services, and in the muddle, another car slid past her, a black BMW sedan with four men in it—and through its front passenger window, Mia glimpsed the android from the bar, talking into a cell phone while staring intently ahead, his granite-black eyes laser-locked on Evelyn's taxi.

There was now no doubt about it in her jumbled mind: Evelyn was being followed.

This can't be good.

A thought cut through Mia's sauvignon glaze for a nanosecond— call her on her cell phone, warn her—before she remembered that her mom's cell phone was right there, in her own hand.

Brilliant.

She looked left, right, adrenaline coursing through her and clearing her mind, the urgency and absurdity of what she was thinking battling it out for control, the cacophonous, confusing offers of the taxi drivers crowding her mind even more—then she grabbed the driver closest to her, shouting, "Where's your car?"

In broken English, he told her his taxi was just there and gestured towards another Mercedes—there had to be more of them in this town than in Frankfurt, Mia had thought when she first arrived—that was parked a few cars back and across the street from the hotel.

Mia pointed at the receding BMW. Two other cars had now slipped in behind it. "You see that car? We have to follow it. We have to catch it. Okay?"

The driver didn't seem to get it and shrugged while sliding an amused glance at his pals—

But Mia was already hustling him over to his car. "Come on, let's go, *yalla*," she insisted forcefully, "we have to follow that car, do you understand? Follow? The car?" She was gesticulating wildly and enunciating the syllables slowly, as if that would magically make her foreign words comprehensible.

Something, though, did the trick, as the driver seemed to get the message that whatever she was rambling on about was pretty urgent. He led her to his car and ushered her into the backseat while he slid behind the wheel, and within seconds the car was barging out of its parking spot and into the chaotic evening traffic.

ᑳᕽᐁ

MIA WAS LEANING far forward, practically sitting on top of the driver as the taxi stop-started its way across the narrow, congested streets of West Beirut. They drove all the way down Rue Commodore, Mia rapiering looks at each intersection to make sure Evelyn's taxi hadn't turned off into another direction, finally catching a glimpse of the distant Mercedes as it veered right and headed up towards Sanayeh Square.

The black BMW, trailing by a car or two, followed suit.

Mia's head was spinning. She was struggling to get through to the driver, trying to get him to maintain a delicate balance between making sure he didn't lose Evelyn's car and not making it obvious to the android and his pals that they were tailing them—not an easy thing to communicate when you're basically miming your instructions through a rearview mirror.

Concurrently, a barrage of questions was pummeling her mind. Why was her mom being followed? Who was following her? Were they just keeping tabs on her? After all, this was a "secret police" kind of place, and with the recent war, foreigners were suspect, weren't they?—though what threat a sixty-year-old woman could possibly pose escaped Mia. Or were they out to harm her? Kidnap her? There hadn't been any kidnappings of foreigners in Beirut since the Wild West days of the 1980s— Mia had done her homework after the rep from the foundation had first approached her—but the whole region was careening out of control, extremists on all sides of the great divide were dreaming up new ways of inflicting pain and causing outrage every day, and nothing, really, was unimaginable.

All right, now you're being ridiculous. Calm down. She's an archaeology professor, for God's sake. She's been living here for years. It's probably just some routine formality. You'll give her back her phone, she'll be off to her rendezvous, and you'll be back at the hotel in time for Jon Stewart.

She didn't buy it.

This just felt very, very wrong.

Flashing over the evening in her mind, and despite that Mia didn't really know her mom that well, she'd still registered the discomfort and feigned reassurance in her voice the second they'd first sat down that evening.

In fact, it was a small miracle that their bond was anywhere near as strong.

Mia had really been raised by her mother's sister, Adelaide, and Adelaide's husband, Aubrey, in Nahant, a tiny island north of Boston linked to the mainland by a causeway, since the age of three. She only got to see her mom at Christmas, when she visited, and during the summers, when Mia would travel to whatever sweat-hole she was digging up.

Shortly after Evelyn had given birth in Baghdad, it had become apparent to her that bringing Mia up in Iraq was going to be far from ideal. Being a single mother in the Middle East, at the time, was an invitation for whispered disdain. The political situation wasn't great either. A year after Mia's birth, Saddam Hussein had grabbed power in a bloody coup, plunging the country into fear and paranoia. Iraq had severed diplomatic relations with Syria, and skirmishes along its border with Iran led to a ten-year war that started in 1980. Evelyn's digs were a source of pride for the new regime, and so she was safe. But the conditions around her grew bleaker by the day, and before long, she was on a plane to Cairo.

Egypt embraced Evelyn, and the work was hugely rewarding. The schools and the health care were another matter. Evelyn struggled through her first year there, juggling motherhood with her digs, trying to provide a decent life for Mia while knowing that sooner or later, she'd have to make a choice. A cholera epidemic that hit the country when Mia was three convinced her that she couldn't keep her there. Medicine was scarce, children died, and Evelyn had to get Mia to a better, safer place.

The thought of leaving the region had gutted Evelyn. Her sister, Adelaide, provided her with a difficult compromise. She and her husband had one child, a girl who was five years older than Mia. Complications during the birth meant that Adelaide couldn't have more children, even though she and her husband desperately wanted them. They'd been considering adopting when Evelyn visited that Christmas. And one evening, as the snow blanketed the beach outside their house, Adelaide made the suggestion. They were a caring, solid couple—both were college professors—and Evelyn knew they could provide Mia with a loving home and a sister.

They'd been true to their word and had given Mia a great home. She'd gone on to college, and as was often the case with the onset of adulthood, she'd drifted away from Evelyn.

And then this project had come up.

Mia's DNA snooping was closely linked to the more traditional research and stones-and-bones sleuthing of historians and archaeologists. The project had a couple of local Phoenician experts on board, but a lot of the information she needed was second nature to Evelyn. And so they'd hooked up the day of her arrival in Beirut, more as tentative friends than as mother and daughter.

Mia would have liked to warm up to her, but Evelyn was hard work. Whereas she had an explorer's instinctive curiosity about people's lives, she rarely invited them into her own. Mia shared the fascination, but was far more forthcoming—too much so, if you believed her mother. And so Mia had initially found Evelyn distant and aloof, and her initial feeling was that they'd collaborate cordially and that would be it. But after a few long drives to distant archaeological sites, and a couple of *arak*-fueled dinners in traditional mountain *tekhshibis*, Mia was pleasantly surprised to discover that the efficient and coldly rational excavator that was Evelyn Bishop was powered by a big, human heart.

A big, human heart that was now being shadowed by men with uncertain intentions.

∽∽∽

KEEPING HER UNEASE IN CHECK, Mia concentrated on the road ahead. For a moment, she lost sight of the Merc, then it reappeared half a dozen or so cars ahead, rushing across town, its stealthy shadow close behind.

Evelyn's taxi led the way off the Ring and descended towards the downtown area. Gutted during the civil war, the heart of the old city had been rebuilt with no expense spared and was now teeming with shopping arcades and restaurants. The Merc and the BMW made it through before traffic closed in around Mia's taxi, with cars from three different directions converging on the intersection just ahead of them in a frenzied free-for-all and cutting them off.

Mia urged her driver on with frantic gestures and manic pleas, bullying and badgering him as he bolted and chopped his way forward while dodging the maze of fenders and bumpers crowding them. A dozen curses and some threatening hand gestures later, they finally burst onto the open road ahead.

The traffic got much busier as they got closer to the pedestrian zones, and a hundred yards or so ahead, Mia spotted Evelyn getting out of her taxi and disappearing into a bustling arcaded street.

"There, that's her," she exclaimed, pointing at the distant figure—only to have her surge of adrenaline brusquely cut off by the realization that her taxi was now stationary again. Between it and Evelyn was a solid sea of other stopped cars, densely packed and three across, held in check by a lone, Moses-like traffic cop while cars lumbered and fought their way across from an intersecting street.

Mia's eyes raced left and right, trying to gauge the best move, then she spotted the android and another man stepping out of the BMW—which was also mired in the blocked traffic—and slipping through the cars, heading in Evelyn's direction. The area was swarming with people—dinner in Beirut was never before nine o'clock, often later, and on a mild October night like this, the eateries and the wide pedestrian piazzas of the downtown area were a popular draw, staying open until well after midnight. The choice before Mia was suddenly no longer theoretical: Tailing Evelyn from the relative safety of a car with a reasonably chunky driver to boot was one thing; actually reaching her, and possibly drawing out her pursuers, was something entirely different.

She had no choice.

She reached into her pocket, thrust a ten-dollar bill in the driver's hand—U.S. dollars were the currency of choice in Lebanon—and with her heart in her mouth, she bolted out of the car and cut through the snarled traffic, hoping her instincts were way off the mark and wondering what she'd do if they weren't.

Chapter 6

Evelyn's mind had been swirling with questions ever since Farouk had bailed on her in Zabqine. True to his word, he was standing there, puffing away nervously, waiting for her by the clock tower that stood at the center of the Place de l'Étoile.

A little over a hundred years old, the tower had seen the worst of the civil war and had remarkably survived despite sitting right on the notorious Green Line that divided East from West Beirut. Almost fifteen years after each crenellation of its exquisite Ottoman craftsmanship had meticulously been restored, it now stood sentinel over a city that was once again seething with anger and outrage. Lebanese flags and highly charged antiwar banners fluttered from its sides, while graphic images of the horrors of the recent fighting loomed over its base.

Farouk had chosen well. The piazza was brimming with people, some of them taking in the display in stunned silence, others striding past carrying shopping bags or chatting on their cell phones with detached insouciance. It was easy to go unnoticed in the crowd, which was exactly what he needed. Having the Parliament building across the square, with the handful of armed soldiers posted there, was also a plus.

He stubbed his cigarette out just as Evelyn reached him and, after casting an apprehensive glance over her shoulder, led her away from the tower and down one of the radiating, arcaded streets.

Evelyn dispensed with the small talk and jumped right in. "Farouk, what's going on? What did you mean by Hajj Ali's being dead because of these? What happened to him?"

Farouk stopped at a quiet corner by a shuttered art gallery. He turned to her, his fingers trembling as he pulled out and lit another cigarette. A shadow fell across his face as he seemed to struggle with some evidently painful memories.

"When Abu Barzan—my friend in Mosul—when he first showed me what he was trying to sell, I immediately thought of you for the book with the Ouroboros. The rest . . . they were very nice pieces, there's no doubt, but I knew you wouldn't be interested in being a part of anything like that. But you have to understand, the other pieces, they're the ones that are more obviously valuable, and, as I said before, I needed to get some money, as much as I could, to get away from that cursed place for good. I tried to contact some of my clients who were, shall we say, less conscientious, but I don't have many of those. So I also told Ali about it. He had some good contacts, a different clientele than mine, ones who ask fewer questions. . . . And I was in a rush, I had to find a buyer before Abu Barzan did, even if I had to split my share with a third party like Ali. Half of something was better than nothing, you see, and if Abu Barzan managed to sell them before I did, I'd end up with nothing. When I told Ali about them, I gave him photocopies of the Polaroids that Abu Barzan had given me." Farouk shook his head, as if berating himself for a terrible mistake. "Photocopies of all the pictures."

Farouk took a long drag on his cigarette, as if steeling himself for the more difficult part of his tale. "I don't know who he showed them to, but he came back not even a week later saying he had a buyer, at the agreed price, for the whole lot. The whole lot. I wanted to keep the book outside the sale—I knew how interested you were at the time in anything with that symbol on it, and I thought it might entice you to help me with selling the rest, or at least, help me find a job here in Beirut—so I told Ali to tell his buyer that he could have all the other pieces in the Polaroids, everything apart from the book, but that we'd give him a small discount to make up for it. Ali agreed that it seemed to be a reasonable counteroffer, the two alabaster figurines alone were worth far more than we were asking for the whole lot, and the book, well . . . surely it wouldn't be missed." He swallowed hard. "I couldn't have been more mistaken.

"I didn't hear anything for a week or so, then one morning his wife called me up. She was frantic. She told me some men had come for him, at his shop. She said they weren't Iraqis. She thought they were Syrian, and that they might even be"—he rubbed the bridge of his nose, as if the word itself was enough to conjure up physical pain—*"mukhabarat."*

Mukhabarat.

A ubiquitous term in the region, commonly uttered in careful, hushed tones, and one of the first words Evelyn had gotten to know when she'd first hit Baghdad all those years ago. In the literal sense, it simply meant "information" or "communications," but no one used it in that context. Not anymore. Not since it became the shorthand name for the secret police, the ruthless "information purveyors" no tyrant could rule without. Not that such internal security agencies were limited to the Middle East. In the disturbingly brutal new world order of the twenty-first century, pretty much all countries—except for, maybe, Liechtenstein—were wielding them with abandon, and they all seemed to treat their victims with an unrepentant savagery that made Ivar the Boneless's demented practices seem lame.

"They kept her outside while the two men talked to him," Farouk added dolefully, "then she heard some shouts. They wanted to know where the pieces were. They hit him a few times and then they dragged him out of the shop, bundled him into a car, and drove away. They took him, just like that. It's a common occurrence in Iraq these days, but this wasn't political. Before they left, Ali's wife overheard them talking about the pictures. The photocopies I gave him. They were the buyers, *Sitt* Evelyn—or, more likely, they were there on behalf of the eventual buyer. And one of them told the other, 'He just wants the book. We can sell the rest ourselves.' *Just the book, Sitt* Evelyn. You understand?"

Evelyn felt a searing nausea rising in her throat. "And they killed him?"

Farouk couldn't quite bring the words out. "His body was found that evening, thrown in a ditch by the side of a road. It was . . ." He shook his head, wincing, clearly haunted by the thought, and let out a pained breath. "They'd used a power drill on him."

"What did you do?"

"What else could I do? Ali didn't know about Abu Barzan. I didn't tell him where the pieces came from. Although I knew him well, times are desperate right now, we live in a state of constant fear and paranoia, and I'm ashamed to admit that I didn't trust him enough to tell him about Abu Barzan so that he wouldn't deal with him behind my back."

Evelyn saw where this was leading. "Which means Ali could only tell them about you."

"Exactly. So I ran. I packed some things as soon as I put the phone down and I left my house. I had some money there—we all keep whatever we have at home, the banks aren't safe anymore. Not a lot, but enough to get me out of Baghdad, enough to bribe the men at the border posts. So I took it and I ran. I hid at a friend's house, and that night, after Ali's body was found, I knew for certain that they'd be looking for me. So I left the country. I took buses, paid for rides on trucks, anything I could find. First to Damascus—it was the less obvious route than through Amman, and it's closer to Beirut, which was where I wanted to reach. To see you. I asked at the university, and they said you were in Zabqine for the day. I couldn't wait. I had to see you."

Evelyn hated the question she just had to ask. Despite feeling sick to her stomach over the horrific fate that had befallen Ali, and her deeply felt grief for Farouk—not just for his ghastly current predicament, but also for the nightmare he must have lived through during the last few years—she couldn't push the image from the Polaroid out of her mind.

She put her warring emotions in check. "What about the book? Did you see it? Do you know where it is?"

Farouk didn't seem to mind. "When Abu Barzan came to see me, I asked him to show me the collection, but he didn't have anything with him. It was too dangerous for him to travel with them. Too many roadblocks and militias. I imagine he must have kept them in his shop, or at his home, somewhere safe. He only needed to move them once he had a buyer, across the border into a safer place to conclude the deal, in Turkey or Syria—Turkey would be more likely, it's not that far from Al-Mawsil—without having to risk coming through Baghdad."

More questions were swamping Evelyn's mind. "But how did he get it? He didn't say where he found it?"

Farouk didn't answer. He was looking beyond Evelyn, and all of a sudden his eyes lit up with fear. He grabbed her hand. "We have to go. *Now.*"

For the briefest of moments, his words didn't register with her. They just seemed to hang in midair, a detached parallel conversation that wasn't meant, couldn't be meant, for her, a conversation she was witnessing remotely. Then she felt her head turn, almost by reflex, beyond her control, following his alarmed glare, and noticed two stocky men, the same two men she seemed to remember from an earlier sighting, moving forcefully through the crowd, their mouths set in tight lines under thick black mustaches, their eyes like dark slits in a pockmarked helmet and just as devoid of life, and heading straight for them.

Then Farouk almost yanked her arm out of her socket and they were moving rapidly through the unsuspecting crowd.

Chapter 7

ᕫᕬ ᕫᕬ

Adrenaline flooded Mia's veins as she advanced cautiously through the bustling arcade, desperately scanning the crowd for any sign of her mother while trying not to draw attention to herself. She had lost precious seconds cutting through the surge of traffic and skirting around the blocked BMW, and by the time she finally made it to the pedestrian zone, the android and his buddy were nowhere in sight.

Reaching the end of the covered passage, she had no choice but to give up the relative cover of the colonnade and step out into the openness of the piazza, which sloped gently down towards the clock tower. The air around her was charged with a disconcerting blend of indomitable festivity and lingering sorrow. Hoping she wouldn't get spotted, she slipped between the rows of diners, her palms wet with apprehension, her eyes searching for any sign of Evelyn or her pursuers.

The crowd momentarily opened up before her, and her heart froze as she spotted her mom, around a hundred yards or so up ahead, talking to a man Mia didn't recognize. Relief washed over her for an instant— Evelyn was right there, talking to someone she clearly knew, everything was going to be just fine—before she saw the man suddenly react to something and grab Evelyn before they ran off together.

The urgency of his reaction jolted Mia. Quickly casting a glance

around the piazza, she spotted the android and his buddy, halfway between her and Evelyn, not quite running but moving as swiftly as they
could without attracting too much attention.

A fear the likes of which she'd never experienced in her sheltered,
academic existence spiked through her and nailed her to the ground.
She felt like calling out for help, but there was no familiar face to turn
to, no cops to enlist, and no time to think.

She cast aside her fear, summoned her legs back to life, and tore off
after them.

～⌒～

FAROUK AND EVELYN HURRIED down the pedestrian plaza, slicing through
the crowd, moving with no particular escape route or plan in mind,
both of them darting terrified glances back at their relentless pursuers
while struggling to stay ahead.

"Farouk, stop," Evelyn yelled out, her voice ringing with irritation
and panic. "There are people all around us. They can't do anything
here."

"They don't seem to mind," he fired back without slowing down.
He would have taken the risk—maybe—had the Parliament building's
soldiers been within reach, but by the time he'd spotted the two men
chasing them, they were already between them and the soldiers, and
there was no way he and Evelyn could circle back to get to them.

Something suddenly caught his eye in the crowd ahead of them. Another man, same tightly drawn mouth, same icy stare in his eyes. Walking calmly towards him and Evelyn, his hand moving to the inside of his
jacket where Farouk was sure he glimpsed the handle of a holstered gun.

Farouk saw a side street open up to the left and dived into it. It ran
uphill for a hundred yards or so and led to a mosque that was at the
edge of the pedestrian area.

Evelyn stumbled through the turn and righted herself quickly. Her
breathing was now labored, her legs were already hurting, and it was
clear she couldn't keep this up much longer. She was in reasonably good
shape for someone her age, but she hadn't run like that for, well, ever.

They kept going, leaving behind the bustle and bright lights of
the piazza, their footfalls echoing in the tunnel of darkness that now

surrounded them. A thought suddenly struck her. Farouk didn't know where he was going. He didn't know Beirut well, if at all, and it didn't make sense that he should be leading her. Evelyn knew the downtown area pretty well, but she wasn't familiar with that alley, and surely it made more sense to stay with the crowd. Plus, going uphill, even up a soft incline such as the one they were now on, wasn't helping.

"Farouk, listen to me," she called out, breathless, "we need to find some cops, someone who can protect you—"

"No one can protect us," Farouk snapped, his voice cracking with desperation, "not from them, don't you see? We've got to find a taxi, a car, something—"

His voice cut off as, from behind them, the staccato claps of three sets of urgent footsteps sliced through the night and bounced off the walls around them. The man with the holstered gun had joined his two buddies, and the three of them were reeling Farouk and Evelyn in now that they didn't have to worry about drawing attention to themselves.

Evelyn was finding it harder and harder to keep going with every step and was just about ready to give up when a narrow side street opened up to their right, running alongside the rear wall of the mosque. It led down to Rue Weygand, a major avenue that was busy with evening traffic—and taxis.

The sight invigorated her and seemed to have the same effect on Farouk. "Come on," he screamed out, as they cut right and hastened down the deserted alley, gasping for breath as they rushed towards the bright lights and possible salvation up ahead.

They were halfway down the street when Evelyn saw a lone car turn into it and head for them.

It was a black BMW.

Farouk beelined for the car and started waving at it frantically, yelling out the local equivalent of "Help!" but Evelyn slowed right down, suddenly fearful. She could make out a man silhouetted inside the car, backlit by the bright street behind him. He looked as if he was holding up a phone to his ear.

Something told her he wasn't there by chance.

"Farouk," she cried out to him, "wait."

Farouk lurched to a halt and turned to her, out of breath and confused. Evelyn was still eyeing the car suspiciously when it suddenly stopped in the middle of the alley, its engine still running ominously. Then the driver flicked the high beams on, flooding the street with harsh, cold light.

Evelyn took a couple of steps backwards, shielding her eyes from the blinding light, then the noise behind her drew her attention. She turned to see the three men who were chasing them burst into the alley, clearly lit by the car's headlights. They stopped when they saw her. One of them had a phone in his hand, the clamshell type, and he snapped it shut and pocketed it. He looked around to make sure they were clear and nodded to his buddies. Evelyn heard the car's doors click open. She spun around and saw the driver emerge from the car.

She looked at Farouk. He was standing there, as frozen in fear as she was, while the four predators closed in on them, the black BMW with its door wide open purring in the background like a hungry wraith waiting to be fed.

She started to scream.

Chapter 8

❦

Mia heard her mother's screams just as she reached the mosque wall. She looked down the backstreet and saw two men struggling with Evelyn. They were halfway down the alley, about sixty yards from Mia. She squinted from the car's headlights, and she thought she recognized its distinctive BMW grille.

Evelyn was kicking and screaming as the android's buddy tried to muzzle her with his hand. She bit him, then lashed out at him with her handbag, which only fired him up even more. He grabbed hold of it and tore it out of her hand, flinging it to the ground before striking her with a ferocious backslap that sent her reeling back.

Nearer to Mia, Farouk had his back against the outside wall of the mosque that ran down the alley. He looked like a cornered, proverbial deer, all lit up by the car's headlights. Two other men—the android and another she hadn't seen before—were converging on him. The android's hand was up in front of his face, his finger extended in a harsh, threatening gesture.

Mia's entire body went rigid. Her flight instinct wanted her to duck back behind the safety of the wall and keep out of it. Any fight instinct she might have had was pummeled into submission by common sense: The odds were overwhelmingly against her, and given that she wasn't Batgirl, there was nothing she could think of to do.

Well, maybe one thing.

Basic. Primal. Not particularly creative or adventurous.

Maybe dangerous.

Definitely dangerous, come to think of it, but she had to do something.

So she screamed her head off.

First, "Mom," then, "Help."

The frenzy halfway down the alley suddenly froze as if some great TiVo in the sky had its cosmic pause button hit. All the heads turned to Mia, the kidnappers glaring at her with expressions of angry surprise on their faces, the man Evelyn was with dropping his jaw in bewilderment, and Evelyn's eyes locking with Mia's in a brief glance of desperation and gratitude Mia would never forget.

The freeze-frame didn't last long, and springing back to life, the two men on Evelyn doubled their efforts to get her into the backseat of the car, the android leaving Farouk to his buddy and rushing towards Mia.

She took a few hesitant steps back before the flight instinct kicked in big-time. She bolted back towards the mosque, summoning every last atom of energy from her burning legs, still screaming her lungs out. Darting a quick glance over her shoulder, she spotted Evelyn's friend slipping away from the thug who was coming at him and pushing him aside before breaking off in the opposite direction, cutting to the unguarded passenger side of the car.

The android angrily yelled something at her in Arabic that chilled her veins, and she could hear his crisp footsteps closing in behind her as she rounded the mosque's wall and almost crashed into two Lebanese army soldiers who came tearing around the bend. They seemed to be coming from the mosque's main entrance, where Mia could see a small sentry box. She grabbed one of them and, struggling to catch her breath, pointed back towards the android, who suddenly appeared at the alley's mouth.

The android lurched to a stop, startled, at the sight of the soldiers.

"My mother. They're kidnapping her. Please, help her," Mia blurted, scouring the soldier's eyes for any sign of comprehension. He stared at her suspiciously before coldly motioning for her to move aside and, with one hand already reaching for his handgun, shouted something out to the android that sounded like an order. The android raised a firm but calming hand and yelled back at him in a tone that threw Mia—the guy was almost berating the soldier as if he were his drill sergeant. More alarmingly, she noticed his other hand going behind his back. Mia turned to the soldier in confused panic and was relieved to see that the soldier wasn't having any of it. He shouted back at the android as he raised his gun—then his chest opened up in an explosion of blood and he was thrown back against the mosque's wall just as two deafening gunshots reverberated in Mia's ears.

Mia tore her eyes off the fallen soldier and spun to see the android adjusting his aim just as the other soldier grabbed her and pushed her down against the wall while taking aim with his other hand. Several shots burst out of the android's gun and bit loudly into the wall by Mia, spitting out shards of stone that cut into the ground around her. The soldier next to her let off a few rounds that must have missed, as she saw the android fire off a couple of more shots before doubling back and disappearing down the alley.

The soldier sprang to his feet and rushed to his fallen partner. Mia willed herself off the ground and staggered over to join him. The sight made her stomach lurch. The wounded soldier seemed dead. His face was splattered with blood, his eyes blankly staring into nothing. The surviving soldier spat out some angry words before gesturing to Mia to stay put and rushing off after the android. Mia stared at him blankly and took another look at the bloodied corpse on the ground. Still dumbstruck and in shock, she wasn't going to stay behind on her own. She stumbled off after him.

She heard a screech of tires as she entered the alley. The soldier was about ten yards ahead of her, his gun raised, but he didn't stand a chance. The BMW was already bearing down on him. He loosed off a couple of wild shots before the big car ploughed into him, flicking him over its hood like a rag doll. He spun in the air and crashed into its windshield, spiderwebbing it before bouncing heavily onto the car's roof and trunk and landing with a dull thud on the ground.

She was next.

She ducked behind the wall just as the BMW burst out of the alley. Its bumper clipped the corner of the wall inches from Mia in a thunderous explosion of steel and stone, then the car swerved right and charged off towards the mosque. As it rushed past, Mia caught a glimpse of the men in the car, the android and the driver in front, her mother crammed in between the two thugs in the backseat.

There was no sign of Evelyn's companion.

Mia stumbled out from behind the wall. The street was deathly quiet again, as if nothing had happened. She didn't know where to turn. She spotted the second soldier, lying down the alley from her. Beyond him, she saw her mom's handbag, its contents strewn on the ground around it, and, a bit further away, a lone shoe of hers. Mia made her way over to the soldier, suddenly aware that her whole body was violently shaking. He lay there, on the ground, contorted in unnatural bends, a rivulet of blood snaking out of the corner of his mouth. He looked at her with pained eyes and blinked.

Her legs collapsed from under her, and she knelt down beside him and cried.

Chapter 9

⌒⌒⌒

The next hour or two went by in a blur.

Sitting in an austere interview room in the Hobeish police station on Rue Bliss, Mia felt sick to her stomach. It didn't help that the room, with its bare concrete-block walls, was cold and damp. She was shivering intensely, though that was probably more from the shock and the fear.

She tried to remain focused on the only thing that really mattered right now: getting her mom back. But she wasn't sure the two detectives sitting across the table from her or the agitated cops darting confusingly in and out of the room were getting the message.

She'd left the bloodied soldier and blundered zombielike down to the main road at the end of the alley and just stood there, tears streaming down her face, facing the oncoming traffic with her arms up. Something about the haunted look on her face must have connected with the people driving by, as one car after another soon stopped to help. Before long, the cavalry appeared in the form of several Durangos filled with armed Fuhud policemen, a kind of paramilitary überforce. The quiet backstreet quickly morphed into a noisy, chaotic zoo. The soldier who'd been shot was already dead. The one who'd been rammed by the car was still hanging on, and an ambulance soon arrived and took him away. Evelyn's handbag and her shoe were retrieved. Mia was questioned and shuffled from one cop to another—she tried to explain about her mom forgetting her phone and handed it over to them along with her own, that last request slightly unsettling her—before she was eventually packed into one of their jeeps and whisked off to the station under armed guard.

She shifted in the cold, metallic chair and took a small sip from a bottle of water someone had brought in for her. "Please," she murmured. Her throat felt as if it had been rubbed down with sandpaper. Her desperate screams still rang in her ears. She swallowed and tried again. "Listen to me. You have to find her. They took her. You have to do something before it's too late."

One of the detectives facing her nodded and answered her in broken English, but it wasn't what she wanted to hear, just more of the same evasive and condescending platitudes. More worrisome, his partner, a wiry, ferretlike man who had quietly been rifling through her mom's handbag and spreading its contents on the table, now seemed to be keenly interested in some pictures that he'd found in a brown envelope in the bag. As he studied them, he glanced up at Mia with a look she didn't really like. He nudged his taller colleague and showed him the photographs. Mia couldn't understand what the men were saying— she couldn't even see what was in the photos—but the suspicious glances were now coming her way from both men.

Her shivering was cutting deeper than before.

The two detectives discussed something among themselves and seemed to be in agreement on their next step. The ferret collected Evelyn's things and stowed them back into her handbag, while his platitude-spouting friend gestured to Mia to stay put, explaining to her as best he could that they'd be back shortly. Her reactions were still running on a slight time delay, and before she could really object or question what they were concerned about, they were already heading out of the room. After they shut the door, she heard a key turning in the lock before it clicked ominously.

Great.

She slumped in her chair and shut her eyes, hoping she could blink the nightmare away and start her day over.

ᴄᴏᴄᴏ

AN HOUR LATER, the two detectives were facing her across the table again, only they were now joined by a pug of a man in a gray suit, no tie, and an annoyed expression wrinkled across his pink-pale face that indicated he'd been dragged from the solitary comfort of his home. Her mind was a bit clearer now—she'd been offered a cup of Turkish coffee, a thick, syrupy local specialty that had taken some getting used to, but that she'd grown to like over the last few weeks—and she'd perked up when her new visitor had introduced himself as John Baumhoff and informed her that he was with the American embassy.

The conversation that followed was far less promising.

Baumhoff tapped his fingers on the Polaroids, which he'd laid out across the table for her to see. "So you're saying you know nothing about these?" he asked her again, in a voice that was a touch too high-pitched for his gender.

Mia sighed and made a concerted effort to calm herself. "I've told you what happened. I don't know anything about these things, these relics, whatever they are. We were having a drink. She forgot her phone. I thought she was being followed. I tried to warn her. These men stuffed her into their car and took her away—"

"Killing a soldier and seriously wounding another in the process," Baumhoff interjected, with a knowing glance at the detectives standing behind him, who nodded in solemn agreement.

"Yes, exactly," she flared up, "which is why you need to find her, goddammit. She's probably already locked up in some hellhole while you're all sitting here playing canasta with these Polaroids."

He studied her through tired and jaded eyes, then reached out and collected the photos, picking them up one by one with his lethargic, puffy fingers. "Miss, um"—he seemed to have already forgotten the name he'd written down on the notebook in front of him—"Bishop," he continued with his nasal drawl, "if your mother has indeed been kidnapped, there's little we could have done anyway."

"You could have put up roadblocks," Mia protested, "you could have alerted the army, God knows they're everywhere. You could have done something."

Baumhoff glanced at her wryly. "We're not back home, Miss Bishop. It doesn't work like that out here. If they want someone, you can be pretty sure they'll get him. Or her, in this case. They know all the side roads. They know where they'll be safe. They've got it all worked out ahead of time. The thing is"—he shrugged—"this isn't Iraq. There hasn't been a foreigner kidnapped here for, oh, at least fifteen years, if not longer. It just isn't done anymore. Apart from the occasional political assassination, this is a surprisingly safe city, particularly if you're a foreigner. Which is why," he added, pausing to reconsider the photos in his hands, "I've got to agree with these folks in that this is probably something else. Some kind of trouble your mother got herself into." His eyebrows arched up and he sucked in his lips and opened his palms quizzically, as if waiting for her to fill in the blanks or come clean somehow.

Mia looked at him, bewildered. "What are you talking about?"

He studied her for a beat—his little cynical mannerisms were really grating on her now—then held up the stack of photographs. "These," Baumhoff said. "They're stolen goods, Miss Bishop."

Mia's jaw dropped. "What?"

"Stolen," Baumhoff repeated. "From Iraq. You must have read about the little war going on over there."

"Yes, but . . ." Mia's daze came back in a rush.

"Thousands of relics of all kinds have been stolen from museums there. They're still trickling through, finding their way into the hands of collectors who don't care too much about their origin. They're worth a lot of money . . . if you can smuggle them out, and," he said pointedly, "if you can find the right buyer." He gave her a knowing glance.

Mia's face clouded as she struggled for words. "You think my mom had something to do with this?"

He gestured at the photos. "They were in her bag, weren't they?"

"How do you know they were stolen?" Mia fired back. "They could be legitimate, couldn't they?"

Baumhoff shook his head. "There's been a ban on exporting any Mesopotamian relics ever since that whole mess started. I can't say for sure that these are stolen, I haven't yet had time to have them checked— I won't know until I make inquiries with our people there tomorrow— but the odds are, they're smuggled. Which could explain what happened tonight. It's not a good crowd to mess with."

Mia flashed back to her chat with Evelyn at the Lounge. "Wait a second," she said excitedly. "She said someone came to see her that day. A guy who worked with her years ago. In Iraq."

This piqued the detectives' interest, and they asked Baumhoff for some clarification. Mia filled the three of them in on what Evelyn had told her, and they noted it with interest. Baumhoff shrugged and tucked the Polaroids into his attaché case. "Alright. Well, it's late, and there's nothing more I can do here. They're going to need to keep you here overnight until an administrative officer can take a formal statement from you in the morning," he informed her casually as he got out of his chair.

Mia went ballistic. "I just witnessed my mom being kidnapped and you're leaving me here?"

"They won't release you before they get that statement," Baumhoff reported glumly. "It's part of the French bureaucracy they inherited, and it can't be done this late. You'll be fine here. They're going to let you stay in this room overnight, it'll be more comfortable for you than a cell, believe me. They'll get you some food, and a pillow and some blankets. I'll be back in the morning."

"You can't leave me here," she burst out at him, clambering to her feet. The ferret spread out his arms in a calming gesture and blocked her off. "You can't do this," she insisted.

"I'm sorry," Baumhoff said with clinical detachment, "but a man's been killed, another's fighting for his life, and, like it or not, you're part of it. We'll clear it all up tomorrow. Don't worry. Just try and get some sleep."

And just as he gave her a parting, helpless half-smile, a cell phone warbled somewhere in the room.

Baumhoff and the detectives instinctively went for their phones before quickly realizing that the ringer wasn't any of theirs. The ferret—no surprise there—was the first to sniff it out. He reached into Evelyn's handbag and pulled out two cell phones, Evelyn's and Mia's own. Mia didn't recognize the ring tone. It was Evelyn's phone.

The ferret instinctively hit the call button and picked it up. He was about to say something into the phone, then stopped. He stared at it for an instant and glanced up at Baumhoff. The embassy's man shot him a quick and low "Give it to me." The ferret turned to his partner for direction. The taller detective nodded and said something clipped that obviously allowed it, before Baumhoff, anxious not to lose the call, grabbed the phone and pressed it to his ear.

"Hello," he ventured with a forced, casual tone.

Mia watched Baumhoff's face tighten with seriousness as he concentrated on the call. She could hear faint echoes of the voice on the other end of the line—it was definitely a man's voice, and sounded American. Baumhoff listened for a moment, then said, "No, Ms. Bishop isn't available right now. Who is this?"

Mia heard the caller answer briefly, and when it wasn't to Baumhoff's liking, he then said irritably, "I'm a colleague of Ms. Bishop. Who is this please?"

The man on the phone said a few more words, which caused Baumhoff to take on a surprised expression. "Yes, of course, she's fine. Why would you think otherwise? Who is this?" His patience eroded quickly, and he suddenly raised his voice huffily. "I need you to tell me who you are, sir."

The room froze into silence for a second or two, then Mia saw Baumhoff frown and move the phone away from his ear. He stared at it with an annoyed expression, then looked up at the detectives. "I don't know who that was. He hung up, and there's no caller ID number showing." He used hand gestures to confirm what he meant.

He glanced at Mia. She gave him a look that said she was clueless about it too. The ferret reached for the phone. Baumhoff handed it back to him, nodded, and turned to Mia. "I'll be back in the morning."

And with that, he was gone.

Mia glared after him, but it was pointless. The detectives walked out, locking the door behind them. She paced around the room, staring at its grim, bare walls. The anger that had swept through her and cleared away her physical discomfort was subsiding, and with it, the fatigue and the nausea came rushing back.

She slumped down to the floor and shrank back against the wall, clasping her face in her hands.

Her no-brainer was turning into *Midnight Express*.

Chapter 10

⤋⤌

Pain seared through Evelyn's head with each bump in the road.
The trunk of the car was lined with several folded blankets, but that didn't help much. Not only was the road surface rough and riddled with potholes that felt like veritable crevasses at times—more of a mountain trail than a paved road, Evelyn imagined in her fleeting moments of lucidity—the journey itself felt like an unending series of tight bends that veered left and right and climbed up and down hills and mountains, tossing her body around without warning like a bottle adrift in a storm, and squashing her against the insides of the trunk with each change of direction.

Her suffering was intensified by the duct tape across her mouth and the cloth sack around her head. The sensorial isolation would have been bad enough without the long and winding road from hell. She could hardly breathe, struggling to suck in faint wisps of the dank, stale air through her nose. She worried about what would happen if she got sick. She could suffocate on her own vomit, and they wouldn't even hear her. The thought sent a bracing shot of anxiety through her veins. Her bones ached from the constant battering of the ride, and the zip-tie nylon cuffs around her wrists and ankles chafed against her thin, wrinkled skin.

She wished she could find relief by losing consciousness. She could feel herself spiraling into the darkness, but each time, just as she was on the verge of blacking out, another bump would send a jolt of pain quaking through her and jar her awake.

The car hadn't traveled far from the downtown area when it had pulled into a deserted lot behind a heavily damaged building in the southern outskirts of the city. Evelyn had been dragged out of it, tied, gagged, hooded, and stuffed into the trunk of a waiting car with practiced efficiency. She'd heard her abductors discuss something briefly, their words unclear in her confused and muffled state, then the doors were slammed shut and the car had lurched onto its journey. She couldn't begin to guess how long she'd been in here, but she knew that hours had already passed.

She had no way of knowing how much longer it would take.

Her mind was besieged by a tangle of blurred images. She saw herself running mindlessly through the downtown arcades, out of breath, her legs burning from exertion. Following Farouk. His terrified face.

Farouk. What happened to him? Did he get away? He wasn't in the car with her. She thought she remembered seeing him slip away from their kidnappers and run down the alley, past the car. Right after someone had screamed out her name.

Mia. She didn't dream it, did she? Was her daughter really there? She flashed to the surreal image of Mia, standing there, frozen in shock, yelling out from the far end of the street. She was reasonably sure that had actually happened. But how? What was she doing there? How did she get there so quickly? She remembered having drinks with her. Leaving her at the hotel. Why was she in that alley? And, far more important, was she safe?

A fist of grief punched through her and throttled her heart. There had been deaths. She was sure of it. The gunshots rang in her ears. The soldier, mowed down by the car. The deafening, horrifying thuds, the body slamming against the windshield like a crash-test dummy, shattering it. She tried to concentrate, tried to remember more clearly, but every bump shook her to her roots and sent her thoughts scattering.

She tried to let herself go, to force the blackout, but it wouldn't come. The discomfort and the pain were unyielding. With a burgeoning horror, she started to focus on the specifics of her journey. Hours. It had taken hours. That didn't sound good. Not in such a small country.

Where were they taking her? She plowed through dissonant memories, back to newspaper reports she remembered from years ago, from the "dark days" of Lebanon. The kidnappings. The journalists, the random hostages who had been plucked off the streets. She remembered how they'd described their journeys—wrapped in duct tape like mummies, stuffed into crates, hidden in trucks. A growing sense of dread gripped her as she visualized their captivity cells. Bare. Cold. Chained to radiators that didn't work. Surviving on scraps of vile food. And then the scariest thought of all came rocketing blindingly out of the darkness.

None ever knew where they were held.

Years of captivity. The most efficient intelligence services in the world. Not a clue. No informants. No ransoms. No rescue attempts. Nothing. It was as if they'd been wiped off the face of the earth, only to reappear years later—if they were lucky.

The car must have then hit a serious pothole, as her head snapped back and bounced up against the sheet metal of the trunk's lid. The burst of pain was enough to finally send her over the edge and into the merciful peace of a dreamless sleep.

Chapter 11

Farouk gazed blankly into the chaotic patchwork of shelters and makeshift tents. He could feel the suffering and the despair in the stillness around him, even in the oppressive darkness that was only broken, here and there, by the faint glimmer of a gas lantern. It was eerily quiet, except for the muted sounds of scattered radios that wafted through the trees. Most of the refugees had finally succumbed to sleep.

The garden square of Sanayi' was one of the rare patches of greenery in the concrete maze that was Beirut—*green* being a generous term, given how parched and unkempt its grounds were, even in normal circumstances. With the onset of the war in the south of the country, hundreds of refugees had made it their home. As had Farouk, since arriving in the city where he had no one to turn to. Not anymore, that is.

He took a final drag from a cigarette before stubbing it out on the ground beside him. He patted his pockets. The pack of smokes he found was empty. He crumpled it and tossed it away and shrugged to himself. He pulled the lapels of his jacket up against his neck and shrank back against the low wall that ran along the edge of the square.

This was what his life had come down to. Alone in another war-torn country. Homeless. Squatting on a patch of dried-out mud. His morning was looking even less promising than that of the wretched souls piled across the wasteland before him.

He wrapped his shaking hands around his head and tried to shut the world out, but the rush of the last twenty-four hours wouldn't go away quietly. He rubbed his face, cursing himself for remembering Evelyn's interest, for interfering with a sale that was all but agreed, for instigating this whole disaster . . . then stared out into the shadows, wondering what to do next.

Leave? Go back home, to Iraq? Go back . . . to what? A demolished country, ravaged by a brutal civil war. A land of mass kidnappings, death squads, and car bombs, a place of unmitigated chaos and suffering. He shook his head. There was nothing to go back to, and nowhere else for him to go. His country was gone. And he was here, now, a stranger in a strange land, his only contact and friend taken away.

Because of him.

He'd dragged her into this, and now they had her.

The thought was like a dagger to his heart. He shook his head again and again. How could he have let that happen? It was his fault, there was no escaping it. He saw them, he knew they were coming for him, and yet he still led them to her, got her taken in his place. He shivered as he remembered Hajj Ali's tortured body. His old friend—*Sitt* Evelyn—in the hands of those monsters. The thought was too horrific to imagine.

He had to try to help her. Somehow. Let people know what he'd gotten her into. Help them find her, point them in the right direction. Warn them about what they were dealing with. But how? Whom could he talk to? He couldn't go to the cops. He was in the country illegally. He was trying to sell stolen goods. Even with the best intentions, the cops wouldn't take too kindly to an illegal Iraqi smuggler.

He thought of the young woman in the alley. If it weren't for her, he'd have been taken along with Evelyn. He'd be . . . he imagined the power drill, its spinning tip digging into his skin. He pushed the thought away and focused on the woman again. At first, he thought it was pure luck. Just some stranger who wandered into the wrong street at the wrong time. But then he remembered the woman screaming out. He thought she might have said "Mom," which puzzled him. Was she her daughter? Regardless, why was she there? Had Evelyn arranged to meet her there, or was it just a coincidence?

It was academic either way. He didn't know who she was or where to reach her. He hadn't stuck around after his escape. He didn't even know what had happened to the girl. For all he knew, they'd taken her too.

A face crept out from the jumble in his mind. The man Evelyn was with, in Zabqine. Ramez—that was his name, wasn't it? What had Evelyn said? They worked together. At the university.

He could find him. He'd been to the Archaeology Department. Post Hall, on campus. Ramez had seen him with Evelyn. He could tell him what he knew. She might even have told him what Farouk had told her. He'd be worried about her. He'd listen.

That was it. It was the best he could do. Thinking it through even further, the idea grew more appealing. He needed money. His cash had almost run out, and his plight was now much more desperate. It wasn't about settling into a better life somewhere more sane than his homeland. It was about survival, plain and simple. He had to disappear, and that would take money. He had to find a buyer for Abu Barzan's collection. He hadn't spoken to Abu Barzan since leaving Iraq. The bastard could have found a buyer himself by now, and if he had, then Farouk would be left with nothing to sell. Evelyn's colleague had to have contacts in that world. Wealthy Lebanese collectors. Maybe Farouk could interest him in helping to sell the pieces. Give him a cut. The divide between rich and poor was a veritable canyon in this town, and most people weren't exactly flush these days. Money was tight. And even the virtuous and the principled had to eat and pay the rent.

A shroud of fatigue descended over him. He slid down to the ground and shriveled up into himself, hoping for sleep to overcome him. He would go to the university in the morning. Find Ramez. Talk to him. And maybe—just maybe—this could all end better for them than it had for his friend Ali.

He didn't believe it for a second.

Chapter 12

Tom Webster put down his cell phone and looked out the floor-to-ceiling window of his office on the Quai des Bergues. It was a crisp early evening in Geneva. The sun was setting behind the craggy peaks of the Alps to the west, reflecting off the lake and bathing its still water with a fiery golden pink glow. The snow hadn't arrived yet, but it wouldn't be long now.

The call had left him with a feeling of deep unease.

He replayed the brief conversation in his mind, examining every nuance, going over every beat of what he'd heard. First came the pause once the call was answered. There was a definite hesitance there. Then the garbled words, in a language he was reasonably sure was Arabic. And then the man who'd finally spoken into the phone, claiming to be a colleague of hers. There was something distinctly formal about his tone. His insistence on knowing who was calling Evelyn was a definite signal that this was not the casual pickup of a friend's phone.

She's gotten herself sucked into this. Then, a more troubling thought: *Is she alright?*

The message he'd received from the phone operator at the institute had taken him by surprise. It had been . . . how long?

Thirty years.

He wondered what had prompted Evelyn's call, after all that time.

He had his suspicions.

The two events—the call from one of his scouts in Iraq, out of the blue, a little over a week ago, and Evelyn's call to the Haldane switchboard—had to be connected. That much was obvious. But he hadn't anticipated any problems going forward. He and his partners always operated pretty much off the radar. They had to be careful, of course—discretion was paramount to their work—but there was no reason to expect any complications.

He tried to rationalize the call and calm his worries, but he couldn't escape them. This didn't bode well. A long time ago he had learned to trust his instincts, and right now they were clamoring for attention. He needed to know what was really going on. Then he'd need to call the others. Let them know what was happening. And come to a unanimous agreement—as the three of them always did—as to how to handle the situation.

He checked his watch. Beirut was two hours ahead. The time difference meant that he wouldn't be able to get any answers for a few hours. He'd need to stay up and make some calls just before daybreak. Which he didn't mind.

As with the others before him, this was what he had devoted his whole life to.

And if his instincts were right, it now involved Evelyn.

Again.

He exhaled deeply and turned to his desk. The codex was lying there. He'd taken it out of the safe earlier. It just sat there, innocently. He stared at it, then picked it up and shook his head faintly.

Innocent.

Hardly.

The book had entangled him, and others, in its tantalizing web for centuries. It was irresistible, and for good reason. It was worthy.

He shrugged, opened it to its first page, and thought back to how it had all begun.

Chapter 13

∽✦∽

Tomar, Portugal—August 1705

Sebastian felt the chill of dampness seep out from the walls and smother his bones with its deathly embrace as he followed the guard down the narrow, winding steps.

He kept his eyes low, away from the flames of the guard's torch. In the swaying, golden light, he noticed that a groove had been worn into the center of the treads. It had thrown him at first, before he'd realized it had been carved into the stone by the repeated passage of shackles.

Many prisoners had languished here, in Tomar. And many more would.

He followed the guard down a long, narrow passageway. Rough, wooden doors with forbidding steel locks lined it on either side. The guard finally stopped outside one of them. He fumbled with a large ring of keys and unlocked it. It shuddered on its hinges as it swung outwards. The opening was like the mouth of a cave, a doorway to a tenebrous abyss. Sebastian looked at the guard. The sweating man nodded with unsettling disinterest. Sebastian steeled himself, pulled a torch down from its wall mount, lit it against the guard's, and stepped inside.

Despite the hellish surroundings, the silhouetted figure, huddled against a dark corner, was instantly familiar. Sebastian froze at the sight as a feeling of infinite sadness descended on him.

"It's alright," the old man told him. "Come."

Sebastian couldn't move. His feet felt as if they were bolted to the cold stone floor.

"Please," the old man whispered again, his voice coarse and dry. "Come. Sit with me."

Sebastian took a hesitant step closer, then another, his eyes unwilling to accept the heart-wrenching sight facing him.

The battered, demolished man raised a chained, twisted arm and beckoned him over. Two of the fingers, Sebastian noticed, weren't moving at all. The thumb was gone altogether.

Isaac Montalto was a good man. He'd been a close friend of Sebastian's father. Both were learned men, teachers and tutors to the elite, and had spent years working together in the great city of Lisbon, studying and translating Arabic and Greek texts that were long forgotten. A small invader had put an end to that. The virus, an unremarkable flu by today's standards, had ravaged the city mercilessly that winter, taking Sebastian's family with it. The baby boy had survived—his father had acted swiftly and placed him in the care of his friend Isaac, at his home in nearby Tomar, when the first signs of the illness had appeared in the family. Isaac and his wife had cared for the baby as best they could those first few weeks, before Isaac's wife had gotten sick herself. The old man had no choice but to put Sebastian into the care of the friars at the monastery of Tomar. Isaac's wife also hadn't made it through that winter, but Isaac and Sebastian had survived.

Being a widower, Isaac hadn't been able to keep the baby with him. The friars at the monastery would raise him, along with other orphans. But Isaac was never far away. He was a friend and a mentor, keeping a watchful eye as the baby grew into a boy and into the young man he was now. He'd waved him off with a heavy heart when the boy had been selected to pursue his duty to God at the cloisters of the Cathedral of Lisbon. But that was three long years ago. And now he was here, a victim of the Inquisition, a pale, battered reflection of the man he used to be.

"Isaac," Sebastian said, his voice filled with sorrow and remorse. "My God . . ."

"Yes," Isaac whispered with a pained chortle, his eyes narrowing with the pain in his chest. "Your God . . ." He swallowed heavily and nodded to himself. "He must be very proud. To see to what great lengths his servants are willing to go to ensure his word is followed."

"I'm sure he never intended anything like this," Sebastian offered.

Somehow, a hint of a smile found its way into the old man's eyes. "Careful, my dear boy," Isaac cautioned him. "Such words could land you in the next cell."

The madness of the Inquisition had infected the Iberian Peninsula for over two hundred years. As with its more famous analogue in Spain, its main thrust in Portugal was to root out converts from other faiths— Muslims and Jews—who, despite claiming to have embraced the Catholic faith, were still secretly following their original beliefs.

It hadn't always been that way. The Reconquista—the retaking of Spain and Portugal from the Moors that began in the eleventh century—had resulted in a tolerant, multiracial, and multireligious society. Christians, Jews, and Muslims had lived, worked, and thrived together. In cities like Toledo, they had collaborated on translating texts that had been stored for centuries in churches and mosques. Greek learning that had long been lost to the West was rediscovered, and the universities of Paris, Bologna, and Oxford were all based on their efforts. It was where the Renaissance and the scientific revolution had truly begun.

But this religious tolerance had displeased Rome. The questioning of man's blind faith in God and in one set of strictures had to be stopped. The monarchs of Spain used this intolerance to make their move. The Inquisition was set up in 1478, with Portugal following suit just over fifty years later. As was the case in all conflicts that were based on religious differences, the true motivation behind it had a lot more to do with greed than with faith. The Reconquista and the Inquisition were no different. They were essentially land grabs.

The enforced baptisms had begun straightaway. The peninsula had to be cleansed—and pilfered. The Jews and Muslims who remained in Spain and Portugal were given a choice of conversion or expulsion. The converts became known as Neo-Christos—new Christians. Many of those who elected to stay were landowners and successful traders. They had a lot to lose. And so they accepted the cross, some of them grudgingly embracing their new faith, others refusing to give up the religion of their birth or its rituals, following the strictures of their faith in the confines of their homes, and, in the case of some of the more determined Marranos, actually attending covert synagogues.

The prisons of the Inquisition soon overflowed to other public buildings. Those taken in for questioning were stretched on the rack and had their arms and legs wrenched off. The inquisitors also seemed to have a soft spot for the soles of their victims' feet. Some were beaten with cudgels while others were cut open, the cuts smeared with butter, then held over open fires. Falsified court decisions and forged denunciations led to forced confessions. Those who confessed voluntarily were allowed to pay a fine and repent in an *auto da fé*, "act of faith" public ceremony of penance; those who confessed on the rack had their property confiscated and were sentenced to imprisonment, often for life, or burned at the stake.

The Neo-Christos sent envoys to Rome to beseech—and bribe—the pope and his cronies to rein in the inquisitors. The king spent even more in keeping Rome on his side. And while the money flowed to the Vatican, the Marranos continued to live in fear, having to decide whether to leave the country and lose everything, or risk facing the torture chambers.

Isaac had decided to stay. And the torture chamber that stalked him for years was to become his final home.

"I didn't know, Isaac," the young man told him. "I didn't know they were after you."

"It's all right, Sebastian."

"No," he flared up, his voice faltering with emotion. "They say they found books in your possession. They say they have written evidence, admissions from some who know you and who confirm their accusations," he lamented. "What can I do, Isaac? Please. Tell me something, anything that I can use to overturn this horrible injustice."

Sebastian Guerreiro had followed the path of his lord with an open heart. He hadn't expected it to lead to this. He had been in the service of the Inquisition for just over a year. The grand inquisitor himself, Francisco Pedroso, a charismatic and forceful man, had selected him for duty. But with each passing day, with each witnessed horror, the questions in the young man's mind had multiplied until he was finding it impossible to reconcile the teachings he had so embraced with the actions of his mentors.

"Shh," the old man replied. "You know that nothing can be done. Besides, the accusations are true. My faith was handed down to me by my father, as it was to him. And even if they weren't, thirty hectares of Tomar soil would make them so." Isaac cleared his throat and looked up at Sebastian. His eyes, glistening with life, belied his shattered body. "That's not why I asked for you to be brought here. Please. Sit with me." He patted the straw-hewn ground beside him. "I need to tell you something."

Sebastian nodded weakly and joined him.

"I was hoping I wouldn't have to ask you this for many years, Sebastian. It's something I was always planning to do, but"—he sighed heavily—"I don't think I can wait any longer."

Surprise and confusion flooded Sebastian's face. "What is it, Isaac?"

"I need to entrust you with something. It could be a monstrous burden to bear. One that could get you killed or see you end up in gilded surroundings like these." Isaac paused, seemingly studying the young man's response, before adding, "Should I continue, or am I mistaken in my faith that you are still the Sebastian you always were?"

Sebastian caught his scrutinizing gaze, then dropped his eyes to the ground in shame. "I am as you remember me, but I am not certain that I am worthy of your trust," he said ruefully. "I have seen things, Isaac. Things no man should allow to happen, and yet I have stood back and said nothing." He glanced up at Isaac, wary of the older man's castigating stare. He saw only warmth and concern radiating back from the prisoner. "I have shamed my father's memory. I have shamed you."

Isaac reached out, his mutilated hand trembling as it landed on the young man's arm. "We live in evil times. Don't blame yourself for the vile actions of those who have it in their power to do otherwise."

Sebastian nodded, his heart still suffocating with regret. "No burden would be too great, Isaac. Not after what I have been party to."

Isaac seemed to weigh one last time his decision to tell Sebastian. "Your father wanted you to know," he finally said. "I promised him I would tell you when the time was right. And I fear that if I don't tell you now, I may never get that chance. And then it would all be . . . lost."

Sebastian's eyes lit up. "My father?"

The old man blinked a nod. "We found something, he and I, many years ago. Here, in Tomar. In the crypts of the monastery." He fixed

Sebastian with a fervent stare. "A book, Sebastian. A most wondrous book. A book that once might have contained a great gift."

Sebastian's brow furrowed. "'Once'?"

"The monastery, as you know, holds a veritable trove of knowledge in its crypts, chests, and crates of old codices and scrolls dating back centuries, spoils of foreign misadventures and crusades, all of them waiting to be translated and catalogued. It's an arduous and endless task. Your father and I were fortunate enough to be invited to work with the monks on translating them, but there are so many of them, and a lot of them are mundane records of disputes, personal correspondences of trivial importance . . . banalities.

"In a dusty crate, one book captured our interest the instant we saw it. It was lost among more worthy books and old scrolls. It was partially damaged by water at some point in its long history, and its last pages and its back were missing. Its cover, however, was relatively unscathed. On it was a symbol we had never seen before, that of a snake, coiled into a circle, feeding on its own tail.

"The book was written in an old Arabic, one that was rather difficult to translate. Its title, though, was clear." He paused to clear his parched throat and darted a wary glance at the doorway, making sure they were not overheard. "It was named *Kitab al Wasifa*—the book of prescriptions."

The old man leaned in conspiringly. "Your father and I decided to keep the book's existence secret from the monks. We smuggled it out of the monastery one night. It took us months to translate it properly. The Naskhi script it was written in was ancient. And although it was Arabic, it was scattered with Persian words and expressions, which wasn't unusual when dealing with scientific documents, but it made it harder to read. But we did read it. And the four of us—your parents, myself, and my dear departed Sarah—we made a pact. To try its teachings ourselves. To see if it worked. And if so, to let the world know of our find.

"At first, it seemed to hold its promise. We had stumbled on something marvelous, Sebastian. Then, gradually, with time, we became aware of the flaw. A flaw which, if it wasn't overcome, meant that no one could ever know about our discovery, as that would lead to a different kind of upheaval, one that would turn the world on its head in a way no sane man would want. And so, it had to remain our secret." His face winced with sadness. "And then fate intervened, with pitiless cruelty."

The old man's thoughts seemed to drift back to a painful time, to the winter when he'd lost his wife and his friends. His years had seemed bleak ever since.

"What was in the book?" Sebastian asked.

The old man looked at him, then, with a vehement glow in his eyes, he simply whispered, "Life."

❧

ISAAC'S REVELATION wrestled Sebastian's mind and pinned it mercilessly to the ground for days. He could think of nothing else. He couldn't sleep. He drifted through his work inattentively. Food and drink lost its taste.

He knew his life would never be the same.

He finally managed to find an opening in his duty roster when his absence wouldn't raise suspicions and traveled to the hills outside Tomar. He knew Isaac's land well. It had been seized since the old man had been incarcerated, its vineyards left to rot untended while the Inquisition's court schemed its way to its inevitable verdict.

Sebastian rode out to the hillock Isaac had painstakingly described. He reached it as the last of the day's light clung obstinately to the darkening sky. The blossoming olive tree was easy to find. *The tree of sorrow,* Isaac had called it. In another place, at another time, it would have been the opposite, Sebastian thought.

He dismounted and took twenty paces towards the setting sun. The stone outcropping was there, exactly where Isaac said it would be. Sebastian's nerves throbbed with anticipation as he knelt down and, using a small dagger, started to dig into the dry soil.

Within moments, the blade struck the box.

His hands dug into the ground, feverishly clearing the soil around the small chest before lifting it out carefully, as if it would crumble under his grasp. It was a simple metal box, perhaps three hands wide and two hands deep. A sudden flurry of crows took flight farther down the hill, cawing as they circled overhead before disappearing into the valley beyond. Sebastian glanced around, making sure he was alone, then, his skin tingling with excitement, he pried the box open.

In it, as Isaac had described, were two items. A pouch, wrapped protectively in an oiled leather skin. And a small, wooden box. Sebastian put the box down and unwrapped the skin, exposing the book and its tooled cover.

He stared at it, his eyes drinking in the curious, mesmerizing symbol on its tooled cover. He opened it. The first pages were made of smooth, strong, and burnished paper. They were filled with beautiful, richly rendered, full-length illustrations of the human body and of its inner workings. Numerous labels of writing swamped them. Other pages were covered with careful and precise Naskhi script, in black ink, with elaborate rubrications throughout. He tore his attention away from the pages and turned it over and saw what Isaac had spoken of. The back cover of the book was missing. Its torn binding indicated that some of its last pages were also lost. The last couple of pages that remained were shriveled and rough, the ink washed away long ago and leaving behind nothing more than an unintelligible, bluish smearing.

With a burning ache in his heart, Sebastian understood.

A key part of the book was missing. At least, that was what Isaac and Sebastian's parents had hoped, once the flaw had revealed itself: that the missing pages would hold the secret, the key to overcoming it. But they couldn't be sure. The flaw was, perhaps, insurmountable. Perhaps there was no cure. In which case the book was of great danger, and the whole venture was doomed to failure.

He put the book down and picked up the small box. It also had the symbol carved into its lid. Hesitantly, he unhooked its copper clasp and opened it.

The box's contents were still there.

And on that lonely hill, Sebastian knew what his destiny would be.

He would continue their work.

He would try to overcome the flaw.

Even though doing that, he knew, would place his life at great risk.

∽∽∽

TRACING THE BOOK'S ORIGIN wasn't easy. Sebastian's father and Isaac had worked on it for years. The most they'd been able to ascertain was that the book was part of several crates of codices and scrolls that had made their way to Tomar after the fall of Acre in 1291.

The texts had been collected by the Templars during their forays into the Holy Land, when the knights were known to have explored the mysticism and knowledge of their Muslim enemies, long before the order had been suspended by Pope Clement V in 1312. Following the arrests of the Templars in France, their possessions across Europe were ordered to be transferred to the Knights of the Order of St. John of the Hospital—the Hospitallers. Provincial councils, however, were allowed to judge the Templars locally, and in Spain, the Tarragonese Council, led by Archbishop Rocaberti, a friend of the Templar warrior-monks, convened and decreed the innocence of the Catalan-Aragonese Templars, as well as those of Mallorca and of the Kingdom of Valencia. The order would be dissolved, but the brethren would be allowed to remain in their monasteries and to collect a pension for life.

James II, the king of Aragon, who didn't want the Templars' riches to end up in the coffers of the increasingly powerful Hospitallers, created a new order, the Order of Montesa, and effectively folded the old Templar order into it. The members of the new order, now known as *montesinos*, would submit to the rule of the established Order of Calatrava, which was also Cistercian and followed similar ordinances to those of the Templars. They would keep their belongings, and they would protect the kingdom from the Granada Muslims, the last remnants of Islam in the Iberian Peninsula.

In Portugal, the king, Dinis, hadn't forgotten the Templars' great contribution in defeating the Moors. He cunningly championed the order's legacy. After calmly confiscating all their belongings, he waited for Clement V's successor to be voted in, then convinced the new pope to allow the creation of a new order that he would name, simply, the Order of Christ. The Templar order basically just changed its name. The Castilian-Portuguese Templars weren't even interrogated, much less tried. They simply became members of the new order, also accepted to follow the rule of the Order of Calatrava, and carried on unscathed.

The castle of Tomar had been the headquarters of the Templars in Portugal and remained so under the new order. A towering edifice of startling architectural beauty that has lost none of its splendor, it was famous throughout the peninsula for its elaborate Gothic, Romanesque, and Manueline carvings and motifs and for its distinctively Templar round church, where many of the Templar masters were buried. Over the years, a convent and cloisters had also been added, and it became known as the Convento de Cristo.

Isaac had told Sebastian that the Templar records showed that the chest that had housed the damaged codex had come from the Levant. Further detail of its provenance was hard to pin down, as Portuguese Templar documentation was difficult to unearth. A concerted effort had been made to bury any written evidence that the Templars had brazenly morphed into the Order of Christ. The Portuguese Templars—and, eventually, the Order of Christ—had also absorbed most of their French brethren who had managed to escape King Philip the Fair's persecution. Their distinctly French surnames had to be cloaked to avoid potential challenges from the Vatican.

Still, there were crypts and libraries that Sebastian's father and Isaac hadn't been able to access. Sebastian, on the other hand, as an officer of the Inquisition, could. And so the young man began, with great care and discretion, to explore the hidden archives of the Church, in the hope of learning more about the codex's clouded origin.

He spent hours at the archives of Torre do Tombo in Lisbon. He visited the old Templar churches and castles at Longroiva and Pombal, wading through ancient records of donations, concessions, disputes, and codes of law, searching for clues that would either elucidate the contents of the missing pages or tell him where he might find another copy of the book. He rode out to the castle of Almourol, built by the Templars on a small island in the middle of the Tejo River and rumored to be haunted by the ghost of a princess who yearned for the return of her lover, a Moor slave.

He found nothing.

He kept Isaac informed of his movements, but the old man was getting progressively worse. An infection had settled into his lungs, and Sebastian knew he would not survive the winter. But his inquiries caught the attention of his superiors.

He was soon summoned to appear before the grand inquisitor. Francisco Pedroso knew of the young man's visits to the dying Marrano and had heard of his inquiries across the land. Sebastian excused his trips as the overzealous pursuit of heretic texts, making sure he didn't taint anyone with his actions. He also shrugged off his visits to Isaac's chamber as the final, vain attempts to save the man's soul.

Through bloodless, aged lips, the sinister priest told Sebastian that God kept a close eye on all of his subjects, and he reminded the young man that speaking on behalf of victims was regarded as more criminal than the accused.

Sebastian knew that his efforts in Portugal had come to an end. From here on, he would be watched. Any misstep could lead to the dungeons. And with the death of Isaac that winter, he realized there was nothing left for him in the land of his birth.

His parents' legacy, and Isaac's, had to be safeguarded. More than that, their work needed to be completed, their promise fulfilled.

On a brisk spring morning, Sebastian guided his solitary horse across the Ponte Velha and into the eucalyptus forests of the surrounding mountains. He was headed for Spain and to the Templar commanderies at Tortosa, Miravet, Monzón, Gardeny, and Peñíscola. If need be, he would continue his search at the very seat of learning and translation, in Toledo.

And when those inquiries would yield little result, he would follow the trail of the snake-eater back to its source, across the Mediterranean, by way of Constantinople, and all the way to the very heart of the old world and to the veiled secrets it sheltered.

Chapter 14

The wailing dawn prayer call from a nearby mosque seeped in through every pore of the concrete-block wall of the interview room and yanked Mia out of her sleep.

She checked her watch groggily and frowned. She'd only just managed to overcome the discomfort of her bedding—two prickly blankets that she'd folded up and laid out on the tiled floor—and block out the noisy racket of the call-outs and bookings that rocked the station throughout the night.

Things brightened up marginally a couple of hours later, when a lone cop with a pleasant demeanor appeared at the interview room's door bearing a fresh bottle of water and a piping hot *man'oushi*—a thin, pizza-like pastry topped with a rich mix of thyme, sesame seeds, and olive oil. In an act of supreme courage, she asked to use the toilet again, knowing full well that a second visit to the station's facilities and their medieval vileness might require years of therapy—and quite possibly some antibiotics—to overcome. She was brought back to her makeshift cell and locked in for several galling hours, which she spent pacing around and trying to rein in her darkest thoughts, until, around lunchtime, the door creaked open and ushered in hope in the form of Jim Corben.

He introduced himself as one of the embassy's economic counselors, and asked if she was alright. The ferret and Inspector Platitude were with him, but she could immediately tell that a completely different set of dynamics was at play here. Corben had presence, and the detectives were very much aware of it. His posture, his handshake, the firm tone of his voice, the confident eye contact—two different species of man, she thought when comparing him to Baumhoff, and that was before she got into the gaping physical chasm that separated the two embassy men. Baumhoff was totally outclassed on that front—porcine, balding, pasty-skinned fiftysomething versus trim, cropped-haired, slightly tanned, and midthirties. Her impressions were also unreservedly tainted by the fact that just after asking her if she was alright, Corben had uttered the magic words that cut right through her despair and almost brought tears to her eyes, six little words that she'd never forget.

"I'm here to get you out."

It took a second or two for the bliss of it to sink in. Then he took charge and ushered her out the door. The detectives didn't object or say a word, even though she hadn't yet given a formal statement. Corben had obviously laid down a higher law, and they simply stood aside and watched her go. She followed Corben, in a daze, through the back of the police station, out a back entrance, and into the brightness of the sun-soaked outside world without so much as a form to fill out or a release to sign.

He led her briskly to his car, a charcoal gray Grand Cherokee with dark-tinted windows and diplomatic plates that was parked among the Fuhud's patrol cars and SUVs, and helped her in before jumping behind the wheel. He negotiated his way out of the station's lot and, with a quick nod to the guard manning the gate, slipped into the midday traffic.

Corben glanced in his rearview mirror. "There are a couple of reporters outside the station. I didn't want you to get caught up in that."

"They know about me?"

Corben nodded. "There were a lot of witnesses last night. But don't worry. So far, we've managed to keep your mom's name out of it, and you haven't been mentioned anywhere either, which is how I'd like to keep things, at least as far as you are concerned. The guys at the station have their orders. They know what to say and what to keep to themselves."

Mia felt as if she were coming out of hibernation. "Mentioned—you mean in the news?"

"Your mom's kidnapping made the morning papers. Right now, they're just talking about a nameless American woman, but they'll get her name later on today, the embassy's going to have to make a statement. We're trying to play it down, but it's picking up steam. The government isn't too keen on publicizing it either. It's bad press for the country, and things are a bit sensitive right now, as I'm sure you know. They're going to spin it as a deal for stolen relics that went bad, smugglers fighting over the spoils, that kind of thing."

"That's bullshit," Mia protested. "My mom wasn't a smuggler."

Corben shrugged sympathetically, but he didn't seem convinced. "How well did you know her?"

Maybe it was because she was exhausted and hungry, or maybe it was because there was some remote validity to his insinuation, but Mia didn't really know what to think anymore.

"She's my mother," she shot back regardless.

"You didn't answer my question."

Mia frowned. "I've only been here for three weeks, alright? I was in Boston before that. So I can't say we've been two peas in a pod, but she's still my mother and I know what she's like. I mean, come on. Have you met her? She's messianic when it comes to archaeology." She heaved a tired sigh, then added, "She's a good person."

A good person. She knew how vacuous that sounded, but, bottom line, she believed it.

"What about your dad? Where is he?"

A distant sadness clouded Mia's face. "I never knew him. He died shortly after I was born. A car crash. On the road to Jordan."

Corben glanced at her and nodded, seeming to process her words. "I'm sorry."

"It's alright." She shrugged. "It was a long time ago."

She stared quietly out her window. People were out in the streets, getting on with the routines of their lives. A pang of envy tugged at her heart. She coveted their insouciance—before remembering that they probably weren't as carefree as they seemed, given what they'd just been through, and the fragility of the country. She didn't know what was going on behind their affable façades, and it made her think that maybe when it came right down to it, when it came down to the crisis points that define who people really are, maybe we didn't really know as much about others as we thought we did. With a twinge of guilt, she found herself wondering if maybe Baumhoff and Corben could possibly be right. She didn't really know her mother that well. She didn't know what was really going on in her life. And that was where gut feelings and hard truths could easily diverge.

The car slowed and stopped, caught up in traffic in the narrow, single-lane road. She turned to Corben. "You can't seriously think she could have been trading in looted relics?"

He met her gaze straight on. "The way I understand it, they were after her specifically, and unless she's the first in a campaign targeting foreigners, which our intel suggests is highly, highly unlikely, it's the only angle we have to work with right now."

Mia's spirits sank visibly as she digested his words. Corben studied her thoughtfully. "Look, it doesn't matter why they took her. The fact of the matter is, someone's got her, someone's grabbed a woman, an American woman, off the street, and the reason behind it only matters if it'll help us get her back. 'Cause that's what we're after, that's the endgame. Getting her back. The rest we can deal with later." A gentle reassurance had crept into his voice.

Mia managed to find a half-smile. Her eyes brightened with his resolve, and she nodded appreciatively.

"I know you're tired," he added, "I know you're probably desperate to get back to your place and jump under a shower and wash the whole experience off, but I really need to talk to you about what happened last night. You were there. What you tell me could be crucial in helping us find her. Time is always against us in these situations. Do you think you can handle that right now?"

"Absolutely," she nodded.

Chapter 15

An acrid, bitter smell speared Evelyn back to consciousness.

She jolted upright, shaking its sting away. Her eyes shot open, only to be assaulted by the fierce neon lighting in the room. It seemed to be coming at her from all sides, as if she were sitting in a white box. She squeezed her eyes back shut.

Slowly, hints of awareness broke through her daze. For one thing, she wasn't stuffed in the car's trunk anymore. She was sitting on a hard, metal-framed chair. She tried to shift her position and felt a burning pain from her wrists and ankles. She tried to move them, but couldn't. She realized she was cuffed into place.

She sensed movement around her, and warily she opened her eyes. Inches from her face, a blurry hand was pulling away. Its fingers held something, a small cylinder of some kind. As she regained her focus, she realized it was a capsule. She thought it must be smelling salts. She caught a final whiff of it as she followed the hand up. A man was standing there, facing her.

The first thing Evelyn noticed were his eyes. They were an unusual blue, and utterly devoid of any emotion. The word *arctic* came to mind. They were fixed on her, scanning her with detached curiosity, alert to every twitch in her body.

They never blinked.

She guessed that the man was in his fifties. He had a handsome, distinguished face. His features—the brow, the cheekbones, the chin and nose—were prominent, aquiline, and yet, finely sculpted. His skin was slightly tanned to a rich, golden hue. He sported a full head of undulating, salt-and-pepper hair, which he wore suavely gelled back, and he was tall, easily over six feet. What stood out mostly in her mind, though, was how slim he was. Not in a bulimic, waiflike manner. Just skinny, which his height only accentuated. He clearly looked after himself well and had his appetite on a tight leash and didn't seem any weaker for it. His posture exuded confidence and influence, and his cold eyes presaged a steely, uncompromising disposition, which she found unsettling.

For some reason, her instincts were telling her he wasn't Arab. Which was confirmed by his accent, when he finally decided to speak up. Not to her. To someone she hadn't noticed, behind her.

"Give her some water," he ordered calmly, in an Arabic that was definitely not indigenous but that, oddly, had an Iraqi tinge to it.

Another man appeared beside her and brought a bottle of cold mineral water up to her mouth. His features were dark and brooding, his eyes dead, like those of the men who'd grabbed her in Beirut. Her captor seemed to have a veritable private goon squad at his disposal. She stored the thought as she gratefully took in a few gulps, before this dark man pulled back and disappeared from view again like a ghost.

The man facing her moved to a low cabinet that ran along the wall and pulled open a drawer. She couldn't see what he was doing, but she heard what sounded like a plastic packet being ripped open. With rising trepidation, she cast her eyes around the room. It was windowless and painted a harsh, acrylic white, all around. The shiny, white drawer cabinet ran the full length of the wall. The room seemed impeccably kept and meticulously efficient—harshly efficient, Evelyn suddenly thought. A reflection, she realized, of its master.

Several other worrying thoughts abseiled into her mind.

First and foremost was that she wasn't blindfolded. Her kidnappers in Beirut—well, that was self-evident. They weren't about to waltz through the crowded downtown arcades in balaclavas. But here . . . This was different. And this was no hired henchman. This man was clearly in charge. And that he didn't mind showing her his face did not bode well at all.

Next was his attire. He was wearing a sports shirt and khaki chinos, under a dark blue blazer. That wasn't the problem. The problem was the white doctor's coat he wore over them. In the white room. With the long white unit of drawers and cabinets. And with, she now noticed as she glanced up, the kind of stark lighting you normally find in an operating room.

Evelyn swallowed hard.

She didn't dare look behind her, to the rest of the room, but her mind filled in the surgical equipment that she imagined was lurking behind her back.

"Why did he come to see you?" the man asked with his back turned. His English had a European accent. If she'd had to guess, she would have said Italian, or possibly Greek. But she had more pressing concerns at the moment.

Her instinct was to ask him who the hell he was and why he'd had a bunch of murderous thugs pluck her off the streets, haul her into the back of a car, and bring her here, but she reined in her indignation. Her mind raced back, processing the events that had led to her being here. She knew it had to do with Farouk, with his murdered friend. With the pieces from Iraq. And, if she remembered correctly, quite possibly with the Ouroboros. Which meant that the man in the lab coat probably knew exactly what he was after. And pissing him off would therefore be the wrong move right now.

"Why am I here?"

He turned to face her. In his hand was a syringe and a rubber strap. He nodded to the man behind her, who pulled over a chair and a small table for him and set them facing Evelyn. The man in the lab coat sat down and calmly placed the needle and the strap on the table. He turned to her and, casually, reached out and clamped his hand around her jaw. His grip tightened harshly, painfully, around Evelyn's face, but she didn't flinch and his voice didn't waver. "If we're going to get along," he told her, "we need to establish some ground rules. Rule number one is never to answer a question with another question. Understood?"

He kept his eyes locked on her until she nodded. He released his grip, a faint smile breaking across his thin lips.

"So," he went on, "and I would very much prefer not to have to repeat myself again—why, exactly, did he come to find you?"

Evelyn felt her skin crawl as she watched him reach over and roll up her sleeve. She could smell a subtle, musky aftershave on him. Annoyingly, it wasn't half-bad.

"I'm assuming you're talking about Farouk," she replied, saying it in a way so as not to make it sound like a question.

A smile flitted across the man's lips. For such a handsome face, it was disconcertingly threatening. "I'll allow you that one." He tucked her sleeve into place. "And, yes, I am talking about Farouk."

She studied him, unsure about where to begin. "He needed money. He was trying to sell some pieces from Iraq. Mesopotamian artifacts." She paused, hesitating, then ventured, "Am I also allowed to ask questions?"

He pursed his lips thoughtfully. "Let's see how we get along first," he told her, his eyes fixed on her while he tapped two fingers on her forearm and beckoned a vein to reveal itself.

Chapter 16

The hotel wasn't far from the police station, and it made sense for them to have their chat there.

The bar—sorry, *Lounge*—was virtually empty at that hour. Mia consciously steered Corben away from the corner where she'd been sitting the night before with Evelyn, leading him to the patio terrace instead. October was a balmy, pleasant month in Beirut—not as stiflingly hot as the high summer months, and too early for the winter rain. Perfect for a chat in an outdoor café. Not so perfect when the chat meant reliving the most traumatic night of your life a mere few hours after the event itself.

She walked Corben through the events leading up to the kidnapping, starting with Evelyn's preoccupied mood and her mention of meeting someone "from her past," an Iraqi fixer from many years ago, his coming to see her "out of the blue," how it was "complicated," and—and this made her shiver with unease—the pockmarked android at the bar. With clarity slowly returning to her frazzled mind, she flashed forward to the man who was being kidnapped along with Evelyn and wondered aloud if that wasn't perhaps the Iraqi fixer.

As she spoke, Corben listened to her with total concentration, alert to every nuance in her story. He scribbled a few things in a small black notebook and interrupted her several times, peppering her with questions about specific details that she surprised herself by remembering.

Not that she felt they'd be of much use. The visuals scorched into her memory—the android's face, the car's grille, the man Evelyn was meeting—none of them felt distinctive enough. If one of the thugs had had a nasty scar running down one cheek or a hook for a hand, maybe. But nothing made these guys stand out from the crowd, not in this town. She couldn't imagine that any of it was helpful to Corben and felt downcast as the chances of his being able to whisk her mom back to safety seemed to recede into the dark corners of her mind.

She mentioned Evelyn's forgetting her cell phone and suddenly realized her own phone hadn't been returned to her. She also remembered the odd phone call that came in to Evelyn's phone when she was in the police station, the one Baumhoff had picked up. The incident intrigued Corben, who asked her to be as specific as she could about what she'd heard and observed. He also made a note to recover her phone for her as well as to get hold of Evelyn's, and to check with Baumhoff about the call. It seemed to be relevant, which buoyed her spirits somewhat.

Corben asked her about the Polaroids, and she reiterated what she'd told Baumhoff and the detectives, that she'd never seen them before, that Evelyn hadn't shared them with her. The last part of her story—the soldiers' appearance, the shoot-out, and the car—was more painful to talk about. Corben was patient and empathetic throughout. His eyes exuded support and concern, and he helped her through it until she was done.

He didn't look particularly comforted by what he'd heard. She saw him slide a glance around the room, and up at the back of the hotel over the patio, as if sizing it up.

Mia could see the concern creasing his brow. "What is it?"

Corben seemed to weigh his words carefully. "I want you to change hotels."

"Why?"

"I think we need to take some precautions. Just in case."

"In case of what?"

He frowned, as if he preferred not to get into it but had to. He spoke slowly and calmly. "The guy at the bar saw you sitting with her, having a long chat. Then you show up in the alleyway and interfere with their plan. It seems to me like there's a good chance they were also after

Evelyn's contact, otherwise they wouldn't have bothered grabbing him, and from what you tell me, it looks like he was able to break free and get away. Now if that's the case, they didn't get everything they wanted, and it's because of—or rather, thanks to—you. But they're not going to be happy about it, and they're going to want to know why you were there. What your relationship to Evelyn is. And whether or not you're part of whatever it is she's mixed up in."

Mia felt a chill slide down the back of her neck. "Are you saying they might come after me?"

"They don't know what you know until they talk to you," Corben speculated. "Which isn't going to happen, so don't worry about it," he quickly assured her. "But we're going to have to be careful."

"Careful? What do you mean, *careful*? These people don't seem to have a problem with grabbing people off the streets." Mia felt the walls of the terrace closing in on her.

"Look, I'm sorry, I don't mean to frighten you, but you're right. These guys aren't messing around," he confirmed gravely. "I'm going to have a couple of our men watch over you, but we're not in control out here. Depending on how things pan out over the next couple of days, you might want to think about putting your research project on hold for a while and leaving the country until things are sorted out."

Mia stared at him with mute dismay, then shook her head in disbelief, flummoxed by the turn of events. "I'm not going anywhere. My mom's been kidnapped, for God's sake." She searched his face for a smile, a nod, something, anything to reassure her that the torrent of violent scenes her imagination was spewing out was just a paranoid overreaction. None was forthcoming. This was real.

She felt as if she were going to be sick.

His voice broke through her daze. "You said she lives across the street from here?"

"Yes." She nodded. "That's kind of why I picked this place."

"Okay. I need you to show me where that is. Let's go over there now. I'll have a quick look around, then we'll come back here and pack your stuff up."

Corben got out of his chair and put his hand out to help her up. Mia stood up and felt her legs go all rubbery. She clung to his arm while she regained her composure.

He gave her a reassuring smile. "You're going to be fine. It's all going to be fine. We'll get her back."

"I'm going to hold you to that," she murmured back, thinking she wasn't going to let him out of her sight until this thing was well and truly over and she and her mother were safely ensconced in another continent.

Chapter 17

⤸⤸

The man in the lab coat sat back, his hawklike eyes scrutinizing Evelyn. He seemed confused by something.

"And so, this man," he questioned acidly, "who's desperate to sell some antiques, travels across two rather daunting borders to come and find you, even though—by your own admission—you haven't seen him in over twenty years, you're not a client of his, nor have you ever brokered pieces for him in the past. You see what I'm getting at?" He paused thoughtfully. "It really all comes right back down to my very first question, which is, why did he come to see you?"

Evelyn felt a chill slide down her spine. *There's no point in lying or in skirting the issue,* she thought. *He knows.* Unsure whether she was doing herself a favor or digging her own grave, her voice faltered. "He knew I'd be interested in one of the pieces."

His expression softened, as if a difficult barrier in their little chat had been overcome. His brows rose questioningly. "Which piece would that be?"

"A book," she answered somberly.

"Ah."

He nodded slowly and sat back, looking satisfied. He steepled his fingers in front of his mouth. "And why did he think you'd be interested?"

Evelyn cleared her throat. She told him about what happened in

Al-Hillah in 1977. Getting called to the accidental discovery. The underground chambers. The remnants of what she believed was a secret society of some kind. She also told him about the Ouroboros. In the chamber, and on the book that Farouk was selling.

As she did, she studied her inquisitor's face. Although he was clearly wholly intrigued by her story, she could tell that he already knew about the symbol. He asked if she had looked into this cabal, wanting to know what she had uncovered about them. She told him about the Brethren, about the similarities in the documents and the discrepancy in the locales. The truth was that there wasn't much to tell. Her research had hit a wall. It was as if the cabal from the underground chamber had simply vanished.

Evelyn went quiet. She'd told him everything she knew, except for one thing. She'd kept Tom out of it. She wasn't sure why she didn't want to mention him. Tom hadn't specifically asked her not to mention his interest to anyone. But she knew. She knew he hadn't been truthful with her. She knew he hadn't told her why he was really there, what had really brought him out there, what he really knew about this long-lost cabal. And right now, sitting with her wrists and ankles cuffed to a metal chair in a windowless chamber, she knew that the man facing her was after whatever it was Tom was chasing all those many years ago. And that, therefore, if the man facing her ever found out about Tom, he'd be more than interested in extending him the same invitation that he'd inflicted on her.

Thinking about it, she felt a slight stab of anger. Of betrayal. What did Tom really know? And—more to the point—did he know that others were also interested in the cabal? Others who were, shall we say, less than amiable? If Tom had told her everything he knew, would she have been any safer? Would she have done anything differently? She wasn't sure it would have made any difference. It was all so long ago.

Despite her misgivings, and after all those years, she still felt an urge to protect him. Which was something she couldn't quite explain. It was just . . . there. An instinct that defied her self-preservation instincts.

Oddly, it made her feel better, knowing she was keeping something back from her inquisitor. Knowing she was resisting him in some way. A small victory, of sorts.

Unfortunately, he seemed to sense it. Something crossed his face, then he asked, "And so you gave up on it and moved on to new areas of research?"

"Yes," she confirmed flatly.

He studied her. She held his gaze with as candid an expression as she could muster, hoping the anxiety rushing through her wasn't breaking through, before dropping her eyes and looking away.

"Who else knows about your find?" he asked.

The question, though expected, rattled her. She tried to stifle the unease. "No one." *That came out too defensively,* she suddenly thought. Plus it was blatantly wrong, and he'd know that, for sure. "I mean, the people I worked with on the dig, the other archaeologists and the volunteers, of course," she clumsily added. "And I asked around at the university in Baghdad, and with other contacts." She wasn't sure if that first "No one" had come out too quickly.

The man in the lab coat stared at her with a disturbingly penetrating gaze. It was as if he was inside her mind, she could feel him rummaging around in there, and she wanted him out. He finally nodded and leaned over. "May I?" He picked up the rubber strap.

Evelyn flinched. "What are you doing?"

He held up his hands in a calming gesture. "I'm just going to draw some blood from you. It's nothing to worry about."

She moved her arm left and right to try to impede him. "No, please, don't—"

He lashed out and grabbed her by the jaw again, only this time his grip was as tight as a vise. His eyes hardened to cold steel as he leaned menacingly forward to within inches of her. He hissed out his words slowly. "Don't make this any harder on yourself." He held her there for a breathless moment, letting the point sink in, then unclamped her and went about wrapping the rubber strap around her arm, above the elbow.

Evelyn just sat there, shocked into silence, and watched him do it.

He held her arm open and tapped it with his long, thin fingers. A vein pulsed out welcomingly. He reached over and picked up the syringe. Without even glancing at Evelyn, he pricked the needle carefully into the vein. With an efficient touch, he flicked the rubber strap off her arm to allow the blood to flow back into it. He gave it a moment, then started pulling back on the plunger slowly, sucking out her blood.

Evelyn felt the nausea rising in her throat. She looked away, to the far wall across the room, trying to block out the unpleasant sensation.

"This wasn't a bad start," he noted casually. "Unfortunately, I'm going to need to ask you some more pointed questions. To start with, I need to know who else knows of your interest in this lost group. I also need to know exactly what our little dealer friend told you, as far as where he got the artifacts from and, more importantly, where he's keeping them. And finally, I need to know where to find him. Now before you answer any of my questions, I would ask you to be as forthcoming and as detailed as you possibly can. The options at my disposal for inflicting pain on you are too numerous to mention, and I would very much prefer you not to have to explore them. Besides, I really don't want to damage you. You seem to be in reasonably good health. A lifetime of physical work that's not too intense such as yours is probably the best regimen to follow. You could be very useful to my work. But I do need some answers, and if I have to entice the truth out of you forcibly, I suppose some localized damage won't really affect the usefulness of the rest of you."

Evelyn didn't know what to make of his words, which rang concussively in her ears. *The usefulness of the rest of you?* What the hell did he mean by that? Her mind struggled under a brief assault of horrific implications before she went light-headed as the blood was being sucked out of her. The minutes stretched until she finally felt the needle slipping out of her arm.

The man in the lab coat got up, held the syringe up to the light, gave it a small shake, and seemed satisfied by his work. He capped the syringe and set it on his worktable. He picked up something else and came back and sat down. Evelyn saw that he'd brought back another syringe, a smaller one, along with a small glass vial that held a liquid the color of pale straw. He also had a small ball of cotton dabbed with alcohol, with which he dressed the small hole in her arm. He then reached for the small syringe and the vial and drew the liquid into the syringe.

"I already know you haven't been completely forthcoming on the matter of who you've shared your little fascination with. Our eyes and our voices can betray so much more than we imagine, if one knows what to look for." He squirted out any air bubbles left in the needle and turned to her. A glaze of cruelty shimmered in his eyes as they settled on her again. "I do," he warned, before reaching over, pinning down her arm, and emptying the syringe into her, adding, "and this is a small taster of what you can expect if I feel you're not being entirely truthful with me again."

Fear tightened around Evelyn's heart like an iron fist as she watched the liquid disappear into her body. She looked up at her captor, her mind swamped by panic, her eyes searching his impassive face for clues, her breathing coming short and fast. Her mouth opened to form a question, but it was cut short by a strange burning sensation that flared up around the needle's entry point. It held there for a moment before it started to spread in both directions, making its way down to the tips of her fingers and up towards her chest, and as it traveled in her blood, it quickly increased in intensity, growing from a prickling pain to a scorching, excruciating torment until it felt as if every vein in her body were on fire, as if her entire cardiovascular system were a pipeline of burning fuel.

She was shaking now, her body rigid with pain, her vision blurred, her lips quivering, bubbles of sweat coalescing on her forehead and trickling down her face.

She felt as if she were being fried from the inside out.

The man in the lab coat just sat there and watched. He held the vial up, in front of her face, and seemed genuinely impressed by it. "Interesting little substance, this. It's called capsaicin. We get it from chili peppers, although biting into an enchilada's not quite the same as having this concentrate pumped into your blood, is it?" His wry smirk went all fuzzy as she blinked away her tears and shuddered from the searing pain.

"The chili pepper's such a great little fruit," he went on matter-of-factly. "It tells us a lot about human nature. I mean, think about it. The reason it burns so much when you bite into it is, in evolutionary terms, a defense mechanism. It's how the plant wards off animals and avoids getting eaten. Which works fine for all the other animals, but not for us humans. No, we're different. We take this little red fruit and we don't stay away from it. We seek it out, we farm it, and we derive pleasure from it. Perverse pleasure. For one thing, we actually add the stuff to our food. Willfully. By choice. We enjoy the pain it causes us. But that's nothing compared to the perverse pleasure we get from using it to cause pain to others. Did you know that the Mayans used to punish wayward girls by rubbing it into their eyes, and, when the girls' virginity was in question, onto their genitals? The Incas used to position themselves upwind from their enemies and make massive bonfires of chili pepper before battles. Even today, the Chinese use it to torture Tibetan monks. They tie them up around raging fires and dump chili in the flames. It makes their burns much more intense, to say nothing of what it does to the monks' eyes. Pepper spray or chili con carne? It's the blowfish of fruit. And you know what's most surprising? We're now discovering it's got huge potential as a painkiller. A painkiller. Talk about human ingenuity."

His words were wasted on Evelyn. She could see his mouth moving and hear snippets of sentences, but her brain was swamped and had lost its ability to process them. The wave of pain raced through to every neuron in her body, ravaging her down to her very core. She tried to cling to something hopeful, some image or thought that would somehow counterbalance the pain, and her mind latched on to Mia's face, not the screaming face from the alley, but the beaming, smiling face she was more used to. She was on the verge of blacking out when, just as suddenly as it had swept through her, the burning started to recede. She took some deep breaths, tensing up for another wave of pain, waiting for it, fearful of its return, but it didn't come back. It just died out like a flame.

The man in the lab coat was watching her with grim interest, as if she were a caged test animal. His arctic eyes didn't register the slightest glimmer of concern. Instead, he casually slid a glance to his watch and nodded almost imperceptibly to himself, as if making a mental note of her reaction and how long it had lasted.

His last words to her before he'd administered the injection swooped into her mind. He'd called it a small taster of what she could expect.

She shuddered at the thought.

Not just a taster.

A *small* taster.

She couldn't even begin to imagine what a full course would feel like.

He watched her regain her senses and nodded to the ghost behind her. Without a word, the ghost gave her another sip of water, then receded into the shadows. The man in the lab coat tilted his head and leaned in for a closer look.

"I believe you have things to tell me?" he asked crisply.

Chapter 18

◠◠◠

Mia felt an unfamiliar vulnerability as she and Corben exited the hotel and crossed Rue Commodore. It was an odd sensation. Every pore in her body was tingling with discomfort, and she found herself scanning the faces in the busy street suspiciously, searching the surroundings for hidden threats, even eyeing the clutch of waiting taxi drivers with unease.

She stuck close to Corben as he stopped by his parked car and retrieved a small leather pouch from its glove compartment. Glancing at him, she noticed that he was also keenly focused on the people and movements around them. She didn't know whether to take solace from that or whether to feel even more worried. Instinctively, she inched a bit closer to him as they headed back down the sidewalk towards the entrance of Evelyn's building.

When Evelyn had first arrived in Beirut, the city was still dusting itself off after years of what the locals stoically referred to as "the troubles." The central government was only there in name, and basic amenities such as electricity and phone lines were hard to come by. Living across the street from the Commodore was as good as it got. The hotel's uninterrupted supply of services to its guests also extended to its camped-on neighbors. The university managed to secure Evelyn a decent apartment on the third floor of a gray stucco building literally across the street from the hotel, and she'd called it home ever since. It might not have had the best view in town—not the sea and its flaming sunsets, nor the monumental mountain range to the east—but at least she didn't have to huddle by a little gas lamp to read after those same sunsets had burnt themselves out behind the horizon. Plus the hotel's barmen could shake up a pretty decent martini, and the wine list was decent and fairly priced.

Mia had visited her mother there several times over the years. The apartment had become a holiday home for her until she'd gone to college. She'd been there a couple of times since taking up her posting in Beirut, but somehow it hadn't felt the same. She knew it wouldn't feel the same on this visit either.

As they reached the building, Mia pointed it out to Corben. He cast a casual glance up and down the street before leading her through the glass-and-iron doorway, which was open, and into the ground-floor lobby. The building was a typical 1950s, six-story structure with solid balconies running along its façade. It had a modernist, Bauhaus feel to it—which also meant that it didn't have the electronic buzzers and other security trappings found on more recent constructions. The doors into the lobby would be locked at night, but were kept open during the day. A concierge was typically to be found sitting outside, playing backgammon or smoking a hookah while inevitably discussing politics, but he wasn't around.

They got into the elevator, an older model with a creaking metal grille that had to be manually shut before the cabin would move, and rode it up to the third floor. The landing was dark with only a small, high window giving out to an internal well, but there was a light switch on a timer that Mia clicked on. There were two apartments per floor, and Mia directed Corben to the one on the left. He stood by the door and examined the lock for a brief moment. He looked across the landing towards the other apartment's front door, then beckoned Mia over to it.

"Do me a favor and stand over here, will you?" He positioned her so her back was turned to the door.

"Like this?"

"Perfect." He listened for a beat and, satisfied that they were alone, walked back over to the door to Evelyn's apartment.

Mia didn't quite get his little request. She watched as he unzipped his small leather pouch, from which he pulled out some thin instruments. He then casually started to pick the front door's lock.

Mia turned her head cautiously and noticed that he had placed her so that the back of her head was blocking the peephole in the door behind her. She looked back at Corben, staring at him with curious amazement. "I thought you said you were an economic counselor," she finally whispered.

He glanced sideways at her and gave her a nonchalant shrug. "That's what it says on my business cards."

"Right. And breaking and entering is part of what business degree exactly?"

He screwed up his face in a final tweak of concentration, and the lock clicked open just as the overhead light clicked itself off. He flashed her a hint of a self-satisfied grin. "It was an elective."

She smiled, rousing slightly from her unease. Any relief was welcome at this point. "And here I was thinking no one ever remembered anything they studied in college."

"You've just got to pick the right courses, that's all."

She looked at him uncertainly, then the realization dropped into place. "You're CIA, aren't you?"

Corben didn't rush to answer.

She studied his silence, then added glumly, "Why do I suddenly feel like things have gotten a lot more serious?"

His expression darkened alarmingly. "You already know it's serious." The words, and the way he said them, carved themselves into her mind. He seemed to sense her dread, as he then added reassuringly, "You're in good hands. Let's just take things one step at a time." He looked for a nod of acceptance, which she eventually managed.

He slowly pushed the door open. It led into a small entrance hall, beyond which the living room was visible. He glanced inside. The apartment wasn't overly bright, being on a narrow street and surrounded by taller buildings, and it was morbidly quiet.

He stepped in and motioned for Mia to follow him.

The living room was spacious and had a window and a pair of sliding glass doors that led onto a balcony that overlooked the street. It was as she'd always remembered it, comfortably furnished with deep sofas and Persian rugs. It bore the clutter of a lifetime of travel and exploration: framed manuscripts and etchings on the walls, relics and artifacts on small stands scattered along shelves and sideboards, and stacks of books everywhere. She cast her eyes across the room, drinking in its rich layers. Everything about it spoke of Evelyn's full life, of her devotion to her chosen path. It had that cozy, slightly musty, cocooning feel to it and reeked of personal history, all of which made Mia's last home, her sparse rental back in Boston, feel positively bleak. Her current accommodation—the room at the Commodore—didn't even bear mention.

She wandered around the big room in a blur, dazed by the memories that swamped her mind. She paused in front of the framed manuscripts, drawn to their unusual depictions of the human body and the swirls of lettering surrounding them, then saw Corben moving farther into the apartment. She followed him and saw him emerge from her mom's bedroom, glance into the guest bedroom and the bathroom, and head back out, past Mia, towards the living room.

Mia hesitated at the door, then entered her mom's room. The afternoon light wafted in through the net curtains, suffusing the room with an inviting softness. She hadn't been in there for years. As soon as she stepped inside, an unmistakable scent came rushing at her, vivid and warm. She felt as if she were ten again, padding into the room late at night, curling into her mother's bed, cuddling up beside her. She took hesitant steps over to the dressing table. Pictures of her, at all ages, were pasted all around its mirror. Her eyes settled on one of them that showed her, in her early teens, with Evelyn, smiling among the ruins at Baalbek. She remembered that day well. She felt an urge to take it with her, but felt bad at the thought and left it there.

She felt a sudden sadness at being an uninvited guest in her mother's sanctuary, and a spasm of worry about her mother radiated through her. With a heavy heart, she left the room and headed back to the living room. Corben was there, checking out Evelyn's shelves. Wrapping her arms around herself for comfort, Mia edged over to the window at the side of the balcony and looked down into the busy street, watching the people idling by, willing Evelyn to reappear among them, safely and in one piece.

What she got instead was a navy blue Mercedes E-series sedan that glided unobtrusively past the building and pulled over slightly beyond the hotel.

Chapter 19

Corben sized up the room with an expert eye and realized another visit—a longer, more thorough one—would be necessary, as soon as he could get Mia settled somewhere safe.

He would also need to look in Evelyn's office on campus as soon as possible. The local detectives would be checking out both places soon—they didn't move as swiftly here as they did back home, which, on this occasion, suited him perfectly. He had a window of opportunity and he knew he had to make use of it.

It had all come about unexpectedly, and yet, ironically, he could just as easily have missed out on it altogether. He wouldn't normally have gotten involved with a situation like Evelyn's kidnapping, at least, not once he had ascertained that there wasn't a political angle to it, which was pretty obvious to him from the outset. That he was here now, in her apartment, was due to something entirely different. He'd positioned himself, within the embassy and among his CIA colleagues, as the Iraq specialist. As such, anything having to do with that country would inevitably wind up on his desk. He'd made sure that everyone there knew it. Which was why Baumhoff had—in a cavalier manner, initially—told him about Evelyn's kidnapping that morning and shown him the Polaroids.

The trail that had begun in that underground lab in Iraq had gone cold for more than three years. He'd changed countries and worked on several other assignments since then, but he'd kept a careful eye on that elusive ball, hoping that when a clue, a hint, something, popped up, he wouldn't miss it. And now, his diligence and commitment had paid off. With a bit of luck, maybe—just, maybe—the trail was warming up again.

Life turned on a dime. He'd been around long enough to know just how true that was.

He saw Mia standing by the window and headed over to the oak desk that sat in the far corner of the room. It was stacked with files, textbooks, and course materials. Corben was more interested in the laptop that sat to one side. As he unplugged it, he noticed Evelyn's thick, weathered personal organizer. It was open to a two-page spread that encompassed that week. A slightly tattered, old-fashioned business card was lying on it. He picked it up. It was the card of some archaeologist out of Rhode Island. He used it to mark the page the organizer was open at, which he then closed and placed on top of the laptop. He'd want to go through that too.

He noticed an old jacket file under the organizer. Something about it drew his eye, and he pulled it out.

Its position on the desk suggested that Evelyn had been going through it just before leaving her apartment the night before. The first image, the woodcut of a snake-eater that leered out at him when he opened the file, sent a jolt of adrenaline through his veins.

The trail had suddenly heated up considerably. And right at that moment, a sudden outburst from Mia snuffed out his excitement with brutal efficiency.

"It's them," she blurted out, turning to Corben, her eyes alight with fear. "They're here."

Corben rushed over to the window and looked out. Mia was pointing out three men who were walking down the sidewalk, towards the entrance to the hotel. The blood had drained from her face.

"They're already coming after me!" she exclaimed.

"They're the guys you saw last night?"

Mia nodded. "The one in the middle's the creep from the hotel bar. I think the one to his left was with him when they were chasing Mom downtown. I'm not sure about the last one."

Corben took stock of the three men. His trained eye caught barely discernible hints in their body language that pegged the middle one, the one with the jet-black hair, as the gang's leader. They moved fluidly along the narrow sidewalk one after the other, sliding discreet glances around the street, acutely aware of their surroundings. He scanned their bodies for signs of weapons, and even from the third-floor window, his practiced eye could make out a bulge under the lead man's jacket.

Mia's eyes were glued on them. "They're just going to walk into the hotel and look for me? They can do that? In broad daylight?"

"They can if they have Internal Security IDs. Which they could well have. Every militia was given its own quota of agents. They could be tied to any one of them." A more worrying scenario was playing itself out in his mind as he reached for his cell phone and punched a number on his speed dial.

He had a dozen or so local "contacts"—a sampling of ex–militia members mostly, who had their own "circles of trust," as well as a few officers of the Lebanese military intelligence, past and present—that he could call for muscle, if and when he needed it. Each contact had his own sphere of influence and was useful in a specific area.

After two rings, a man's voice answered.

"It's Corben," he announced flatly into the phone. "I need some backup at the Commodore. I've got three guys moving in, maybe more. They're armed." He looked out, then added, "Hang on."

Corben and Mia stood there together in silence, watching the killers close in on the hotel. Corben's muscles tightened. The moment of truth was seconds away.

Down below, the three men reached the hotel's entrance.

They didn't walk into it. They didn't even look at it.

They just kept going, past a couple of parked cars, past Corben's Grand Cherokee, and crossed the street.

His alternate scenario was right on the mark.

They were heading straight at them.

Chapter 20

Mia watched the killers cross the street, and with a reeling horror she realized they were coming to Evelyn's building. Her whole body seized up as she watched them disappear from view, hidden by the projecting balcony. She wasn't about to step outside to monitor their progress. She turned to Corben.

"How did they know we were here?" she asked.

"I don't think they're here for you. It's too soon for that. They're here to search this apartment." He pulled the phone back to his ear. "You need to get someone here quick. We're in the apartment building right across the street from the hotel. Third floor. It's Evelyn Bishop's place. Hurry up, they're just coming into it now," he barked into it, before clicking it shut. He tucked Evelyn's file firmly under his jacket and belt, in the small of his back, and grabbed Mia by the arm. "Come on," he urged as he led her to the front door.

They hurried out onto the landing, only to come face-to-face with a woman who was stepping out from the neighboring apartment. The woman froze at the sight of two strangers rushing out of Evelyn's apartment. She hesitated, then started to say something in Arabic, but Corben snapped at her abruptly, cutting her off. "Get back inside, lock the door, and stay clear from it. Do you understand?"

The woman's eyes darted from him to Mia and back in alarmed

confusion. "Do it now," Corben ordered again, stepping forward and herding her back into her apartment. The woman nodded furtively and disappeared behind her front door, snapping its dead bolt into place as directed.

The elevator's "in use" light went amber, followed by a loud click and the hum of the motor cranking up. The cabin was making its way down from the top floor to the lobby. The killers would soon be here.

Corben moved to the edge of the staircase, which was adjacent to the lift shaft, and listened for a quick beat. He stepped back, looked up the stairs, and grimaced. He didn't like that option. Access to the roof could be locked. Neighbors could come into play. Too many unknowns.

"What?" Mia asked. "What do we do?"

"Inside." He hurried her back into Evelyn's flat.

Corben carefully closed the door and spun its dead bolt shut. He saw that Evelyn also had a chain lock and raised his hand to pop it in place, then thought better of it and left it alone. He knew it would give away that someone was in the apartment, which was the last thing he wanted.

He also knew he only had seconds to come up with a plan.

He shot a focused glance at the big sliding glass doors opening onto the balcony, and at the window, made his decision, and turned to Mia. "Shut those curtains. As tight as you can. I don't want any light coming in. And shut the bedroom doors too."

She did as ordered, plunging the living room into a suffocating darkness. As she did this, Corben had grabbed an armrest cover off the sofa and was going around the lamps and the chandelier in the living room, crushing the bulbs in his fingers with cold efficiency. He did the same to the lamp in the entrance hall.

Mia shut the bedroom doors and hurried back out to find Corben in the kitchen, rummaging through the drawers. He pulled out a couple of kitchen knives and checked their blades. He chose the one that seemed most solid among the lot and stowed it under his belt, to one side.

Mia watched him, stunned. "Please tell me you have a gun tucked away in an ankle holster or something," she half-joked.

"They're in the car," he replied grimly. Being an American was viewed with a sharply increased degree of suspicion in the tense city, and "economic counselor" was getting to be right up there with "cultural attaché" as shorthand for CIA. A telltale bulge from a handgun—which people in this town were more likely to spot than the citizens of, say, Corleone—was definitely taunting fate. Which is why the Glock and the Ruger stayed in a locked compartment in the Jeep unless it looked as if the situation really called for one, or both. This hadn't looked like that kind of situation.

Notch up another one for hindsight.

Corben scanned the kitchen. It was tucked off to one side, away from the living room, and had a glass door that led out to a small balcony. A tall, freestanding fridge, an older, heavier model, was next to the door, with Formica counters and cabinets along one wall. He crossed over to the edge of the room and looked out. He noted that the kitchen's balcony door had no curtains or blinds. Which didn't really matter. He'd already decided it would be their fallback position. He pulled out Evelyn's file and handed it to Mia. She glanced at it curiously and looked him a question.

"Stay here and hang on to this for me," he told her. "Close the door behind me and keep it shut until I get back." He headed out, stabbing a finger at the balcony door. "And keep that door open."

Mia tried to object, but the words dried up in her mouth.

Corben saw how shaken she was and paused. "We'll get through this," he added firmly, his eyes hard with conviction. She managed a reluctant, scarcely perceptible nod before he rushed out of the room.

Mia closed the door, her heartbeat pounding loudly in her ears. She turned and looked down the kitchen, at the balcony beyond, then her eyes dropped to the file in her hands.

She stared at it for a moment with nervous curiosity, then opened it.

Outside, Corben moved fleetly through the darkness and reached the front door. He looked through the peephole just as the elevator outside gave off a barely audible snap as its door-locking mechanism released. He knew there wasn't any risk of them spotting any movement behind the lens or coming from under the door, as the room behind him wasn't lit.

He heard the metal grille inside the elevator creak open, and two of the men he'd watched in the street stepped out. He realized the third man was still downstairs, keeping watch. These men were pros.

They knew what they were doing. He tensed up even more with the thought.

He observed them as the pockmarked man Mia had described from the bar hit the light switch and glanced around the landing.

Satisfied that they weren't about to be interrupted, they turned to face the door to Evelyn's apartment. Corben flexed his fingers and felt his muscles tighten as each killer pulled out a 9mm automatic, rolled a silencer into place, and chambered a round. The pockmarked man nodded to his underling to go ahead.

Corben breathed in deeply and slid back to one side of the door. He'd be hidden behind it as it opened. He leaned right back, pressed against the wall. He closed his eyes for the briefest of moments, getting them more accustomed to the darkness around him.

The door squealed lightly with an exploratory tug. There was no sound of keys slipping into the lock. The killers evidently didn't have them. Corben gritted his teeth and waited for it. A second later, a half dozen successive coughs from one of the silenced automatics were echoed by the loud bursts of bullets chewing through the wood of the door and obliterating the door lock. Corben raised a hand to shield his face as splinters and shards of steel ricocheted around the small hallway. A faint smell of charred wood and gunpowder drifted up to his nose.

He stiffened as the door creaked open and swung slowly towards him, and watched with rapt attention as a silencer appeared, hovering in midair. It glided deeper into the entrance hall, followed by the rest of the gun and the jacketed arm of the first of the killers.

Corben went for it, and everything suddenly raced into fast-forward.

Chapter 21

◦◦◦

With rapierlike agility, Corben lunged at the man and grabbed him by the wrist, yanking him into the room while using his back to slam the door shut behind him.

He twisted on himself and used the man's own momentum to spin him around and slam him into the back of the door, thereby blocking it. A wild round went off from the silenced gun, the spark from its muzzle lighting up the intruder's twisted face, which was bloodied from his encounter with the door. Corben knew he didn't have more than a second or two before the pockmarked man outside reacted and tried to barge through. He kept one hand gripped on the killer's wrist, pinning the gun against the door, and used the other to drive a crushing punch to his lower back, striking him in the kidney.

The man gasped out heavily under the blow. His hand lost its hold of the gun, which clattered across the floor. Corben felt the man's muscles slacken and grabbed his chance, sidestepping away from the door in the opposite direction while pulling the killer fully across the door just as several bursts of gunfire bit through the wood and raked through the intruder. He held on to the man's arm and felt his body shudder and writhe from the bullets cutting through him, then let go. The man's body collapsed onto the floor in a heavy thud and just lay there, motionless, emitting a wheezing gurgle, blocking the door.

Corben caught his breath and skulked by the door, listening intently in the deathly silence. The man outside called out, "Fawwaz?"

"He's dead, asshole," Corben shouted back, "and you're next. I've got his gun."

Which wasn't exactly true. Not yet, anyway.

Corben scowled and waited tensely for an answer, but nothing came back. Thin shafts of light from the landing were streaming in through the bullet holes in the door, casting a soft, ethereal glow on the entrance hall and the dead body. Corben looked around, searching for the gun, his mind running through his options. None of them was particularly promising. Abruptly, the little light there was vanished. The timer in the landing had just kicked in, and the killer outside made no effort to switch it back on. Instead, Corben heard him yell out another name, "Wasseem," followed by a barked order that echoed eerily down the stairwell. The pockmarked shooter outside was probably telling the third man to come up and join in.

The more, the merrier.

Not.

Corben urgently scoured the darkness for the dead man's weapon. He couldn't find it at first, then spotted it on the far side of the hallway from him, facing the door and anyone coming in. Getting it would be risky. Corben would be completely exposed if he attempted it.

As he mulled whether to go for it, he heard rapid footfalls echoing up the stairwell and knew it would be seconds before he'd again be facing the killers' two-to-one advantage—with the two sporting automatics, as opposed to his meager kitchen knife. He realized he had to make a move. He bolted from the wall and dived for the gun just as the killer outside kicked the door in. The dead man's body was blocking the door. The killer outside shoved the door inwards, pushing his friend's corpse farther back into the room while reaching in and unleashing a barrage of gunfire that exploded all around Corben. Corben's fingers reached the fallen gun just as several bullets bounced off the floor beside him. He managed to grab it and leapt out of the room, more shots splattering the jambs of the doorway inches from him.

He rushed through the darkened living room and ducked for cover behind Evelyn's desk as several bullets crunched into its oak carcass. He peered out and unleashed a brief volley of his own, forcing the killer to duck behind the doorway. They were no more than fifteen feet apart. The living room was bathed in darkness, making it hard for either of them to get a clear shot at the other. Corben, at least, had the advantage of knowing the layout of the apartment. It would buy him a few extra seconds, which he needed if he was going to make it back to Mia.

Corben stole a glance at the gun he'd picked up. Even in the bare glimmer of light that was coming through from the edges of the curtains, he could tell that it was a SIG-Sauer, and more specifically a P226. Hardly the sleekest of designs, but a supremely accurate and reliable handgun. Corben processed the choice of weapon: These weren't standard-issue Makarovs, which were a dime a dozen in the area. These guys—and whoever sent them—had access to, and funding for, some serious steel. He made a quick mental calculation of the shots he had left. Given that its double-column magazine held fifteen rounds, plus one in the chamber if one was really hell-bent on getting the maximum bang for one's buck, and assuming the magazine was full before the corpse had shot up the door, which was a reasonably safe assumption, Corben guessed he could have maybe a half dozen rounds left.

At best.

He heard some clicks—the killer was trying the light switches, to no avail. The door scraped open and more footsteps entered the apartment. The third killer was here. Corben heard a brief, heated exchange between the two men—getting up to speed and planning their next move, no doubt—and decided to use that momentary distraction. Careful not to waste precious bullets, he loosed a couple of shots and rushed out from behind the desk, scurrying across the darkened room, and landing behind the large sofa that backed up to the balcony. Several muffled shots shattered the side table to his right and obliterated two picture frames that were on it. He didn't return fire. He waited instead, straining his ears to hear if either of the intruders would step into his killing zone. They were too experienced for that and stayed tucked away behind the wall of the doorway. He could hear one of them reloading. Undeterred, he inched his way farther until he was facing the small hallway that led to the kitchen. He took a couple of deep breaths and sprinted across the open ground to it. Several shots cut through the air around him, but he kept going and ducked behind the wall as more shots bit into it. He returned fire and charged down the hallway to the kitchen, flinging the door open and slamming it shut behind him.

Mia had her back against the counter, riven with fear. Corben saw that she was clasping the file tightly across her chest. Her face lit up at the sight of him still in one piece and seemingly uninjured. She looked as if she had a mountain of questions for him, but now wasn't the time for them and she knew it.

Corben stuffed the gun under his belt and grabbed hold of the large fridge. His face contorted and he grunted as he rattled it across the tiled floor, using it to block the kitchen door. He had it halfway across when bullets from the hallway tore through the door, either finding the back of the fridge or exploding against the back wall of the kitchen. Mia screamed as one of them hit the balcony door and punched a spiderweb of cracks through it. Corben yelled out to her, "Stay clear of the door," and with a final grunt, he shoved the fridge into place. More shots came at them and pinged against it, but it held, shielded him and Mia from their onslaught.

The shooting paused, and heavy thuds came pounding the door from the hallway. The killers were trying to push it open, and the heavy fridge, though tough to budge, was giving way, inch by inch. Corben grabbed a chair and levered it between the edge of the fridge and a fat radiator, buying them some extra seconds, and without pausing for breath, he took the file from Mia and tucked it into the small of his back while shouting, "Come on."

They dashed out onto the balcony. It was a small, narrow rectangle with clothes wires hanging across it lengthways. Corben knew from scoping it out that it backed up onto a mirror-image service balcony of the neighboring apartment. The two balconies were separated by a wall of thick glass blocks that went right up to the stuccoed parapet, which had a metal railing mounted on it.

He led Mia to the edge of the balcony. "Climb over," he urged her, "I'll give you a hand."

She didn't seem particularly thrilled by the prospect.

He darted a look back inside the kitchen. The fridge was teetering inwards with every loud shove of the door, the chair straining against the radiator. "Come on," he insisted, "just climb over to the other side and don't look down." Advice that people in those situations always seemed to give, but that, of course, no one ever followed.

Not one to mess with tradition, Mia peered over the edge and glanced straight down. The courtyard at the rear of the building, a wasteland of crates and discarded building materials three floors below, seemed to drop even deeper.

Another jarring thud from inside convinced her.

She gritted her teeth and swung one leg over the parapet.

Chapter 22

Hugging the partition wall, Mia lifted herself and shifted her weight so that she was now sitting on the railing, with neither leg touching the floor.

Corben held her hand as she inched her way across the smooth metal railing, actually managing not to look down.

"That's it, keep going," Corben egged her on, moving with her as she slid farther across, slowly and carefully, her knuckles white as they gripped the railing underneath her.

A sudden, loud crash from the kitchen unsettled her—the chair snapping out of its tight hold. Mia lost her grip and slid backwards. She screamed as she let go of the railing and tried to grab the wall she was straddling, but the glass blocks were too smooth to hang on to.

Corben lunged outwards and caught her. He pulled her upright and gave her a final push, sending her onto the neighboring balcony, where she landed with a thud and out of breath.

He stole one last glance into the kitchen before climbing over the railing and clambering across. The balcony door facing him was mercifully open. As he joined Mia, they heard the fridge scraping its way furiously across the kitchen floor under the bull-like shoves of the two killers. Corben hurried Mia inside, and they raced through the small apartment. There was no sign of the woman they'd met, which was just as well. She must have been cowering in a bathroom or under a bed, which is where Corben hoped she'd stay until they were all well out of the building.

He released the dead bolt on the front door and flung it open. The landing was quiet—the killers were still deep inside Evelyn's apartment. He motioned to Mia and they rushed down the stairs. They had almost reached the first floor when they heard shouts and loud footfalls chasing down after them. Punctuating the renewed threat, several muffled rounds rocketed down the stairwell, sparking against the railing and hammering the limestone steps under their feet.

Corben and Mia flew down the stairs and rocketed out of the lobby and onto the sidewalk. Up the street was Corben's Jeep and the hotel. Beyond the hotel was the killers' parked Mercedes. Corben didn't think he and Mia would have time to climb into the car and drive off before the killers hit the street, but he had a good chance of reaching his weapons cache, which would make a serious difference. With Mia at his side, he started to rush towards the Jeep, then spotted a man with the same hard expression striding towards them. The man's hand was already reaching for the bulge under his jacket. The killers had left a fourth man guarding their car.

Mia had noticed him too. "Jim," she cautioned.

Corben darted a glance down the street, mapping out their options. "This way." He took her hand and they headed in the opposite direction, down the street, away from the hotel and the Jeep and its locked weapons cabinet.

They hurtled down the narrow sidewalk, jostling through startled pedestrians who called out angrily after them. Mia saw Corben peering over his shoulder and followed his gaze. She caught a glimpse of the android and another killer as they emerged from Evelyn's building and joined one other man. All three were now rushing down the street after them. Her eyes rocketed wide as she spotted the android looking right at her. His fierce glare hit her like a punch to the gut.

He recognized her from last night. She was sure of it.

She felt a wobble in her legs at the realization, but mustered whatever willpower she had left and kept moving.

Corben was reasonably familiar with the area, and he knew their options were limited. The street was lined with stores and apartment-building entrances, neither of which would provide any cover. He knew the three killers wouldn't back off, nor would they have any problem with gunning him down and grabbing Mia in plain sight. He also knew he had two or three rounds left in the handgun, which wouldn't go a long way against stopping them. His eyes scanned the gaps and doorways for a miracle, and he spotted a dip in the sidewalk that announced an entrance ramp. A car emerged from the cavernous mouth of the underground garage, turned, and drove up the street, past them.

"In there," he shouted to Mia as he took her hand and led her in.

They hastened down the curving ramp, their shoes slapping hard against the bare concrete surface and echoing like thunderclaps against the smooth walls around them.

They reached the main parking area, which was dotted with a forest of columns. Cars were tucked into the narrow bays between them. There was no sign of any attendant around, no stash of keys to raid. Corben scowled. They were boxed in.

The neon lights clicked off, plunging the underground garage into darkness. Corben turned to Mia, pointing at the other end of the space. "Go down to that far corner and hide under a car. Don't make any noise, no matter what you hear."

She caught her breath. "What are you going to do?"

"I'll hold them off here. They'll be exposed coming down the ramp, and if I can get one of them, I think the others will back off. Now go."

He watched her scamper off into the dark recesses of the garage, then slipped between the cars and positioned himself behind a big sedan that was directly facing the ramp. He pulled out the automatic and cradled it in both hands and aimed it at the entrance, which was back-lit from the street above. He silently hoped he hadn't made a mistake in his mental count of spent rounds, and if he had, he hoped it was in his favor. His heart was still trying to pound its way out of his chest. He took in several deep breaths through his nose, blocking out the stench of oil and grease around him, calming himself, preparing himself for the shot.

He heard a clatter of footsteps hurtling onto the echoey ramp and suddenly dying out. The garage was bathed in silence. He knew the killers were now stealing down towards them. He flexed his fingers, then clamped them back onto the gun's handle as he lowered himself into position.

A long, narrow shadow scuttled down the wall of the ramp, followed by two other dark, ghostly forms that merged into it. From the angle of the shadows on the wall, Corben knew the killers were crouched low. His entire body went rigid as he adjusted his aim and brought his finger back from the trigger guard and prepared to fire. Every shot had to count, and even then, the odds were stacked against him.

His pulse throbbing in his ears, he watched as the distorted shadow glided down the ramp wall and suddenly stopped. He ratcheted down his grip on the gun by a touch then retightened it, keeping the feel in his fingers on edge. He tried to edit out the sounds drifting down from the street and focus on any noise that would clue him into the killers' progress, but there wasn't any. He imagined what they would do, which depended on how desperate they were. Rushing in would probably lead to their overwhelming him, but they'd take a hit or two. Unless the gun he'd appropriated wasn't fully loaded to begin with, which wasn't even worth contemplating. He pushed the doubts away and concentrated on the shadow.

It didn't move. It just stayed there, ominous, stalking him, taunting him.

Then he heard a sudden rush of footsteps and tensed up, his eyes scanning the wide opening like radars, his gun darting left and right across the narrow kill zone—a split second of adrenaline overload before he saw the shadow racing up, not down, the wall. The killers were retreating, and they were doing it in a rush. He kept his position, on high alert in case they were trying to draw him out, then he heard the distant wail of a siren getting closer.

The backup. They'd made it.

He bolted out from behind the car and charged up the ramp. He made it to the street in time to see the killers' Merc pulling out of its parking space and tearing off into the distance. From behind him, two Fuhud cars came racing down and pulled up outside the Commodore. Cops armed with M16s poured out of the vehicles and secured the street while three officers charged up the steps and disappeared into the hotel.

Corben exhaled deeply, tucked away his gun, and headed back down the ramp to inform Mia that they were safe.

For now.

Chapter 23

Mia moved through her hotel room in a daze. Her mind was under siege, the twin barbarians of fear and fatigue at the gates. She was determined to keep them at bay a little longer. She needed to pack up and get the hell out of here. The hotel was definitely no longer safe.

She wasn't sure anywhere else was, for that matter. These men she'd crossed twice now in less than twenty-four hours, these psychos—they didn't seem to have a problem finding the people they were after, nor did they seem to suffer from stage fright. They showed up brazenly, in plain sight, and went about their dirty deeds as if they had an all-access pass to the city. And she'd messed up their plans. Twice.

Not something she wanted to dwell on right now.

She tried to calm her nerves and focus on the task at hand. Corben had told her to just grab the essentials, but she didn't have that much to pack anyway—the bulk of her stuff was still waiting to be shipped over once she'd felt more at ease in the city and settled into an apartment. He'd given her fifteen minutes to get it done, and that was twenty minutes ago.

She was cramming her laptop and some paperwork into a backpack when Corben returned. He was carrying a laptop and a big, leather personal organizer, both of which she knew were her mother's and thought she remembered spotting on her desk.

"You all set?" he asked.

She nodded.

He led her out. She gave the room a final parting look and followed him as they made their way down to the lobby and exited the hotel.

Cops and Fuhud officers were all over the street. Cars were slithering through the makeshift roadblock, the cops waving them on after a perfunctory glance. Curious locals were milling about in front of shops and on their balconies, taking in the disruption and—a local tradition, this—trading murky conspiracy theories that the shooting was already generating.

As they walked to Corben's Jeep, Mia slid an uneasy glance towards the entrance to Evelyn's building. She saw several officers gruffly keeping people at bay as some paramedics brought out a stretcher. The dead shooter's body—she assumed it was that—was covered with a tattered old blanket that would have given Gil Grissom a heart attack. Forensics were clearly not a major priority right now.

She climbed into the passenger seat of Corben's car and watched as he exchanged some words with a couple of the hard-faced men in civilian gear before sliding into his seat. She noticed them get into a dusty black Range Rover parked nearby. As the one closest to her got into the car, his jacket swung open and she spotted a holstered handgun under it.

Corben slammed the car into gear, and the big Jeep pulled out and raced down the street. Mia scanned the surroundings warily and saw that the Range Rover was close behind. It followed them down the one-way street for two blocks. She noticed Corben check his rearview mirror, and she looked back to see the Range Rover slow down abruptly and stop at a slight angle, blocking off the street behind them. Corben gave a small, satisfied nod and just drove on. An effective and simple way, she guessed, to make sure no one was following them.

"Where are we going?" she asked.

"My place," he answered flatly. "Until we know what we're dealing with here, I don't trust any of the hotels."

The plan threw her. "You're sure your place is safe?"

There was no hesitation in his voice. "Put it this way. It's off the radar. And for those who have it on their radar, it's off-limits and they know it."

" 'Off-limits'?"

He thought for a moment before answering. "The only people who might know what I really do are other intelligence agents, and there are understandings in place, between governments. Red lines. Clearly defined. You don't just cross them without risking serious repercussions. The order would have to come from pretty high up, and that's not what this is about." He paused, then added, "You'll be safe there. Right now, this isn't about you. They were after your mom, they wanted to check out her apartment. They didn't necessarily see you clearly enough to realize you were also at the scene of the kidnapping, but we have to play it safe. If they have informants inside the police force, which they probably do, they'll make the connection. Let me get you out of harm's way while I check things out. You need to get some rest anyway. I'll go to my office and make some calls, talk to our people. Then we'll figure out the next step."

Mia was too punch-drunk and weary to question his judgment any further. She just nodded to herself and stared ahead.

She remained silent for the rest of the drive. He clearly had a lot on his mind, and she wasn't ready to discuss things. Not here, not now. Not in her present state of mind. She needed to catch her breath, allow the flood of adrenaline from the last hours to drain, and clear her mind. Then she'd want to talk about things. And that would take time.

⌒≈⌒

FAROUK WAITED PATIENTLY in the shadows outside Post Hall. Before him, students and staff ambled in both directions along the narrow drive that fronted the Ottoman-era stone building where the university's Archaeology Department was housed.

He kept watch over the entrance, leaning against one of a few parked cars that were lucky enough to have campus passes, sheltered under a dark canopy of thick cypress trees. Scattered cigarette butts littered the ground by his feet. He'd been there for hours, and the cavernous growls from his stomach were getting more frequent.

He'd seen the reports of Evelyn's kidnapping in the morning papers and had approached the building with caution. To his surprise, it hadn't seemed any different to how it was on his earlier visit, the day before, when he'd been looking for Evelyn. He remembered that Evelyn's name wasn't mentioned in the papers, which explained the lack of reporters or camera crews, but not the absence of additional security—at least, there was none that he could see. Although he'd watched the two Fuhud detectives enter the building and then leave perhaps an hour later, he still didn't feel comfortable walking into the building, as he had done the previous day, to find the assistant professor. He preferred to wait outside where he could keep an eye on the approaches and avoid any more nasty surprises.

His patience finally paid off when Ramez, Evelyn's elfin colleague, made his appearance around lunchtime.

Farouk scanned the lane in both directions. He couldn't see anything that gave him cause for alarm. With his heartbeat ringing in his ears, he emerged from his cover and walked towards him.

❧❧❧

LESS THAN FOUR BLOCKS AWAY, Omar snapped his cell phone shut and looked out the navy E-class Merc's windshield. The traffic on Rue Bliss was, surprisingly, flowing decently. The street, still furrowed by the old tramway rails, was usually a nightmare to navigate. It was a couple of miles long and bordered the whole length of the university. The campus wall ran along one sidewalk, only bisected by a couple of entrance gates. The other sidewalk was lined with hugely popular cafés, pastry shops, and ice cream parlors. Customers' cars were double- and triple-parked with breathtaking insouciance—standard practice in Beirut—causing jams and the occasional brawl with metronomic reliability.

The chaos, in this case, was useful. It provided good cover for a casual chat. Which was why Omar was there.

He'd been denied free access to the old woman's apartment. He'd lost a man in the chaos that followed. Worst of all, the hakeem wasn't happy.

He knew he had to make amends.

Omar glanced into his side mirror. Several cops were standing by the entrance of the Hobeish police station.

He spotted his contact exiting the building.

The man looked down the street, in his direction, and saw the Merc. Omar flicked him a discreet, barely noticeable wave out the window. The ferret caught it, nodded casually to his colleagues as he walked past them, and made his way over to the parked car.

∽∾∾

MIA TOOK IN her new accommodations with a heavy heart. She finished off the *shawarma* lamb sandwich they'd hastily picked up on their way to the apartment and crossed to the kitchen with a sleepwalker's heavy step, still coming to terms with the events that had brought her here.

The apartment had two bedrooms, one more than Corben, who was single and lived alone, needed, but then smaller apartments were hard to find in Beirut, and rents were relatively cheap. He'd given her a quick tour—kitchen, bathroom, guest bedroom, clean towels—before leaving her here and heading out to the embassy. He'd said he'd be back in a few hours.

She felt strange being here. Staying with a man she hardly knew. Scratch that. A man she didn't know at all. Normally—assuming, that is, that she was there because she was kind of seeing the guy, or interested in him in some way—she would have killed time by poking around, checking out the books on his shelves, the CDs by his stereo, the magazines on his coffee table. Old-world moves, for those of us without iPods or pages on Facebook that told you everything you needed to know and dispensed with the need for physical snooping. She might even have sneaked a peek inside the wardrobes in his bedroom, the side table by his bed, or the cabinet in his bathroom. It was shameful, but somehow expected. Basic human curiosity. You did it to get an idea about what made the other person tick. If you were lucky, it put a smile on your face and drew you closer to that person. On less fortunate occasions, it creeped you out and sent you running for the hills.

This wasn't either.

She didn't feel the urge to explore, even though the guy was a CIA agent. Imagine the possibilities. An Aladdin's cave of gadgets and intrigue was beckoning from the recesses of her imagination, but she wasn't listening. She hardly gave his apartment a cursory glance, and what she saw barely registered. Not that there was much to register. It was sparsely furnished, and the little there was had that distinctly single-male, dark-leather-and-chrome look. Everything in it seemed to be there for a reason. Nothing was superfluous or added for effect. It wasn't necessarily a reflection of any blandness on his part. She guessed that guys like Corben, guys who did what he did, traveled and lived light. She didn't think he kept mementos of favorite regime changes on his shelves, or photo albums of infiltrations and informants on the coffee table.

She threw the sandwich wrapper in the bin, washed her hands, and leaned back against the counter. The hunger was satiated, but she still felt awful. She was coming off her adrenaline high, and the exhaustion was kicking in big-time. She felt a wobble in her legs and closed her eyes for a moment to push it back. She filled herself a big glass of water, guzzled it down, and made it to the living room, where she curled up on the sofa.

Within seconds, her body had shut down without a fight, sending her crashing into a dreamless sleep.

Chapter 24

Keeping an embassy in Beirut had been a major headache for the State Department for over thirty years. Although the pain had abated of late, anyone who worked there knew it was only a temporary respite.

The old building on the busy corniche, overlooking the Mediterranean, was due to be replaced in the mid-1970s by a purpose-built facility. The civil war that began in 1975 put an end to that plan. Ambassador Francis E. Meloy was kidnapped while being driven across the city's Green Line and assassinated in 1976, and by the time the fighting took the first of many breathers a year later, the city had been carved up by rival factions and the area the new embassy was being built in was no longer considered safe for Americans. The project was shelved, its abandoned concrete shell still standing to this day.

The embassy staff soldiered on in the old building until a suicide car bomb—the first major use of the terror weapon, and a herald of many further devastating attacks against U.S. interests around the world—ripped its front half right off in April of 1983. Forty-nine embassy staff were killed, including eight CIA agents, one of whom was the agency's Near East director, Robert Ames. Their deaths effectively wiped out the Agency's capabilities in the country and paved the way for the string of high-profile kidnappings that followed. It took years to build up a presence there again, only for five of its agents—the team that had only recently started to delve through the mess that was Lebanon in the 1980s—to get blown out of the sky over Lockerbie, Scotland, in 1988 while on board Pan Am Flight 103.

What was left of the diplomatic mission squatted in the nearby British embassy—a seven-story apartment building that was bizarrely veiled by a massive, tentlike antirocket net from top to bottom—for a few tense months before relocating to two villas in Awkar, in the lush, forested hills just north of the city. The area was under Christian control, but it didn't prove to be any safer. Another car bomb ripped through that compound the following year, killing eleven. The State Department threw in the towel and closed its mission down for a couple of years, but with fighting finally subsiding in the early 1990s, the staff returned to Awkar while awaiting the construction of a new, highly fortified compound east of the city, close to the Ministry of Defense, a project that had yet to materialize.

Corben had driven straight to Awkar after leaving Mia at his apartment.

He checked in briefly with his colleagues on the second floor of the consular annex. The CIA station chief, Len Hayflick, and the four other agents in the Beirut team had their offices there. They had their hands full. Beyond the ongoing assignments, such as tracking down Imad Mughniyah, the man thought to be behind the truck bomb that blew up the marines' compound in 1983 and killed 241 servicemen, and monitoring burgeoning militant groups such as Fatah al-Islam, Lebanon was "in play" again. An undeclared, dirty war was in full swing. It was the bread and butter of the agency, but while there were big opportunities, there were even bigger risks. Still, the Bishop kidnapping needed to be handled with urgency, and Corben had quickly maneuvered to snag the assignment once Baumhoff had shown him the Polaroids.

Corben spent the afternoon in his office working his phone and his databases. There was nothing new on the kidnapping. No calls had come in, no one had claimed responsibility, no ransom demands had been made. Not that it surprised him, but he still half-expected some fringe group to claim it for their own and try to use it for some kind of leverage. The United States wielded a big stick in the region, but it could also bestow great favors if merited or, in this case, coerced. No such favor was requested.

A follow-up call to a Fuhud officer he'd conferred with briefly after leaving Mia in her hotel room informed him that the dead man from the apartment didn't have any identifying papers or tags on him. They would be running a close-up of his face in the next day's papers, but Corben didn't think anyone was going to be claiming him anytime soon. He made a couple of other calls to contacts of his in the Lebanese intelligence services and sounded them out without giving too much away about his involvement beyond looking for a kidnapped American national. Nothing new had come up, no fingers pointed one way or another. He made sure they would contact him if anything broke.

He recovered Evelyn's cell phone from Baumhoff and scrolled through to its received-calls log, but the last caller wasn't ID'd, confirming what Baumhoff had told him. No one had called it since. He accessed the dialed-calls log. She'd called a bunch of local numbers over the last few days, but the most recent call was the one that immediately piqued his interest. A U.S. number. Rhode Island, according to the area code.

He remembered the business card that had been sitting on her open organizer on her desk and pulled it out. The number matched. It belonged to someone called Tom Webster, at the Haldane Institute for Archaeology and the Ancient World. Corben made a quick calculation of the time difference and realized it was still early on the East Coast. It was unlikely anyone would be there at this hour. He opened a browser window on his computer and got onto the institute's Web site. It informed him that it was a privately funded research center devoted to the study and promotion of the archaeology and art of the ancient Mediterranean, Egypt, and Western Asia, affiliated with Brown University. There was no sign of anyone by the name of Webster in its listings. He jotted down "Tom Webster," "Haldane, Brown U," and "privately funded" in his notebook and made a mental note to call it later.

He walked the phone over to the communications office and handed it to the chief geek there, technical operations officer Jake Olshansky, asking him to work his magic and see if he could trace the shy caller who had called Evelyn's phone. He also requested a log of incoming and outgoing calls going back two weeks and asked the young techie to see if he could also pull up similar logs for Evelyn's home landline, assuming she had one. He picked up Mia's phone from Baumhoff and had a quick look through it, but nothing on it jumped at him. He asked Olshansky to run a quick log off its SIM card and made a mental note to pick it up on his way out to bring back to her. He also gave him Evelyn's laptop—his own attempt to boot it up had been thwarted by password-protected access, but he knew Olshansky would find a way in without too much trouble.

Back in his office, he turned his attention to Evelyn's personal organizer again. It was overflowing with cards and notes, an active, busy life's cache of information. His first trawl through it didn't kick up anything useful. The calendar entries of the last week, and of the last two days in particular, didn't appear to mention anything about the man from her past that Evelyn had come across. He put the organizer aside, saving it for later. He knew he'd need more time to go through it in detail.

The profiles he pulled up for Evelyn and Mia didn't kick up any surprises—not that there was much there. Nothing about either of them hinted at anything other than two women who lived quiet lives and never strayed on the wrong side of the law, not even for an unpaid parking ticket. He found some fairly vocal comments Evelyn had made during the struggle over the downtown area between the developers and the conservationists, but it wasn't overly confrontational and he quickly dismissed its relevance.

Corben sat back and ran through the events since Mia's drink with Evelyn the night before. He latched onto the ease and the confidence with which the goon squad was operating. Beirut had come a long way since its lawless dark ages, and a well-armed, well-trained hit team couldn't just operate with impunity without having some kind of "official" link or sanction from one of the handful of main local militias, which meant, inevitably, a "big brother" connection to one of the government intelligence services—Lebanese or Syrian. Identifying the dead shooter could immediately point to which clan the goon squad was working for, but that didn't seem likely. Hired guns were cheap to come by, and tracks were easily covered. Every militia, every agency, had someone on tap on the inside to make things happen or, more often, disappear.

He needed to know where the threat was coming from. Even an accent would have gone a long way in identifying where the shooter hailed from and, possibly, lead him to his target, who he knew had hired the hit team. Sadly, the shooter's vocal abilities had been seriously compromised by, well, death. Corben also knew these guys had already screwed up twice. A third time was unlikely. He'd have to be more than careful from here on.

Corben reached for the file he'd taken from Evelyn's desk and went through it. Possibly more information was tucked away on the hard drive of her laptop, but given how dated the sheets and the photographs in the file seemed, he suspected that it was where he should focus. He read Evelyn's notes more thoroughly and examined the photographs again. From his days in Iraq, he knew that Al-Hillah was a short drive south of Baghdad.

He imagined the underground chamber she had discovered and thought back to the lab he'd investigated.

Both in Iraq, within a hundred miles of each other.

Both featuring the Ouroboros.

Coincidence sat right up there with altruistic politicians, free lunches, and a democratic Middle East in his fantasyland hall of fame.

He went over the notes from his chat with Mia. He focused on the words *Iraqi fixer*, and drew a circle around them. He mulled it over, then took another look at the Polaroids from Evelyn's handbag. An idea was coalescing in his mind, and he gave it some space. Everything seemed to fit. A man from Evelyn's past in Iraq, this "fixer," appears unannounced. Shortly after, she disappears. In her handbag are shots of highly prized Mesopotamian relics. He was pretty sure the fixer had come to see her to offer her the goods, the book in particular. She had a previous connection to the snake-eater—a connection he needed to know more about. But he knew his target was still alive and well and operating with the same ruthless abandon he'd displayed in Baghdad. He knew that same ruthlessness had dispatched men to kidnap Evelyn and search her apartment.

He was close.

He could feel the hakeem, out there, chasing after his elusive dream. He needed to flush him out, and the obvious route involved the Iraqi fixer. Clearly, he had what the hakeem was after. He was the key to tracking down the pieces, and he was still out there, probably in hiding. The question was, how to find him? Before the hakeem did.

The fixer had to be lured out—assuming he hadn't skipped town already, which was a distinct possibility, given how precarious his presence here seemed to be. Corben thought about it and reached for a second look at the file he'd taken from Evelyn's flat. Several old snapshots were in it, mementos from the dig in question, and some of them showed Evelyn standing with men who were clearly Arab workers. There was a good chance that one of them could be the missing fixer, but Corben didn't know what he looked like.

Mia, on the other hand, did.

He mulled it over. He'd need to talk to her about it. He preferred not to involve her—she'd been through enough already in less than twenty-four hours—but the stakes were high, and she was already caught up in it. He just had to make sure he handled it with great care. Which wouldn't be easy, given whom he was dealing with.

His desk phone buzzed and interrupted the state of play unfolding in his mind. He checked the caller ID display as he reached for the handset. It was the ambassador.

Chapter 25

⌒∿⌒

Despair settled onto Evelyn like a thick winter mist as she stared at the walls of her cell.

Outwardly, the small room was better than what she was expecting. It wasn't anything like the grimy, decrepit, rat-infested hellholes her recall had conjured up from the accounts she'd read of the kidnapped hostages back in the 1980s. This room felt more like something you'd find in your average Middle East hospital. Well, maybe not any hospital. More like a mental ward.

The walls, floor, and ceiling were painted white. The bed, though narrow and bolted to the floor, had an actual mattress on it, as well as the added luxury of a pillow, sheets, and a blanket. There was also a toilet and a small sink, and both worked. The lighting was on the harsh side, courtesy of two neon ceiling fittings that buzzed annoyingly at the very edge of her hearing threshold. Two features, however, undermined any sense of relief that she could glean from the relative civility of her accommodation. The only opening to be found wasn't on any of the walls. Instead, it was a small, mirrored observation porthole—using one-way glass and allowing her captors to look in, she guessed—in the thick, metal door to the room, a door that, she also noticed, lacked a handle. Beyond that, the room was as unsettling as any cesspit she'd read about, but in a different way. Its relative comfort alluded to an extended stay, and its clinical, cold austerity was even more subtly threatening than the cells she'd read about. A palpable malice was in these walls, and she could feel it in her pores.

The burning pain that had seared through her veins was all gone now. She rubbed her bare arms slowly, still thrown that there was no aftereffect from the—what had he called it? She couldn't remember. She thought back with anger at how the words couldn't come out fast enough once she started to tell him what she knew. She felt weak, helpless, and, worst of all, humiliated. She'd faced adversity and difficult situations many times since moving to the area all those years ago, and she prided herself on her inner strength and the resolve she knew she could draw upon when needed. The last few hours had bulldozed clear through any perceptions she had of her own courage. Her captor had effortlessly reduced her to a cowering, terrified wreck, and the thought burned through her as fiercely as the demonic liquid he'd brutally injected into her.

The worst part of it, the most frustrating and maddening part of it all, was that she didn't even know what she was caught up in.

The discovery of Al-Hillah had ultimately led to nothing. The trail had abruptly ended in the very chamber where it had begun, and with it had ended their affair.

After Tom had left, after the cyclone in her mind had settled, she had chided herself for allowing herself to be swept up by him, for avoiding the signs. But then again, he had been maddeningly tough to read. Throughout their brief liaison, she had sensed a deep-seated unease, a conflict deep within him that she just knew he was struggling with. She had no doubt that he'd been keeping things from her, and her being here in this cell proved it. At the time, she'd felt—she'd hoped, anyway—that it wasn't the kind of dreary deception one would expect: a wife somewhere, a mundane life he was briefly escaping from. This seemed to cut deeper. But when she'd dared to bring it up, he'd skirted around it and moved the conversation on with deft charm. She knew his feelings for her were genuine—he'd said so himself. Of course, she knew that men lied, but deep down, she knew she wasn't wrong about him, and her instincts had proven more than reliable over the years. She remembered, even today, the honesty that shone through his eyes when he'd told her how he felt about her, but his ability to move on with such clinical commitment was something she'd never gotten over.

She could still hear his parting words as if he were standing beside her now, whispering them into her ear.

I can't stay with you. We can't be together.

It's not someone else. I wish it were that simple. But it's not something I can talk about. Just know that if there were any way in the world that we could be together, I would do it.

And with that, he was gone.

Leaving her with the unenviable task of moving on with her life and forgetting about him, leaving her to deal with a separation made even more intolerable by the simple fact that it was unexplained and—in her eyes, anyway—unjustified. And leaving her to deal with raising his child, a child he knew nothing about. A child she'd lied to for years. A little girl whose father, she'd told her, had died.

She'd lived with the lie for thirty years, and even after all this time, just thinking about it now triggered a clawing tightening in her chest. It was a hard thing to do, but she knew Mia would have gone out looking for her father if she'd thought he was out there somewhere, and Evelyn hadn't wanted that. He'd been very clear about things. There was no need to expose Mia to a painful disappointment.

At least, she'd managed to keep that from the hakeem. Above all else, she couldn't let him know that Mia was Tom's daughter. He hadn't yet made the connection; he hadn't asked that question. If he had, she shuddered, she probably would have told him. And that would have set him off after Mia too, which was something she couldn't bear to imagine.

Small victories. It was all she could cling to right now.

Something beyond her cell door caught her attention. A noise. Harsh, labored movements, footsteps shuffling on the stone floor.

She edged to the door and tried to peer out through the mirrored porthole, but all she saw was the harsh reflection of her own face. She plastered her ear to the door and listened intently. She heard a door being unlocked, followed by some movement and a cry that sent shivers down her spine, a young boy's cry, a pained, pleading yell. The haunting sound was swiftly followed by an angry man's bark, ordering him to shut up—*"Khrass, wlaa"*—and a sound that Evelyn was sure was a slap, quickly followed by a pained yelp from the boy's voice, as if he'd just been hit. She could just about make out some whimpering before she heard the door slamming shut, and the lock sliding into place.

She waited a minute or so for the man to move off, counting down the seconds, her heart in her throat, wondering if she should try to make contact with the other prisoner. Another thought occurred to her: What if others were being held here? She had no way of knowing. The man who had led her back to her cell had put a black cloth cover over her head, only removing it once she was in. She had no idea of what lay beyond that door. And the thought, the possibility, that others were being held here scared her even more.

She decided to risk it.

"Hello? Is anyone there?" Her whisper echoed in the silence around her.

There was no answer.

She repeated it again, this time a bit louder, more desperate. Still, no one answered her.

She thought she heard a low whimpering in the distance, but she couldn't be sure. Her heartbeat was pulsing loudly in her ears, confusing matters.

She waited a few more minutes and tried again, but nothing more than a deathly silence came back. Shivering, and dispirited, she sank down to the floor and cupped her face in her hands, trying to make sense of the nightmare swirling around her.

Her mind hurtled back to the face of the man in the lab coat as he watched and listened to her story. His interest was visibly piqued when she mentioned Tom. He asked her all kinds of questions about him, wanting to know everything about the man. He was riveted and took notes, nodding ponderously as she spoke. Her instincts had been right. She should have kept Tom out of it, but, realistically, there was little she could have done to keep quiet. The flames racing through her body had seen to that.

Mia was safe, for now—at least, she hoped she would be—but Evelyn knew her captor would spare no effort in finding Tom Webster. And along with that unnerving thought, another one, even more unsettling, surfaced as she wondered if her daughter would be able to get anyone to help look for Evelyn half as diligently, and if she'd ever see her again.

Chapter 26

The ambassador's office was located at the back of the main villa, as far away as possible from the entrance to the compound and sealed off from the outside world by bombproof doors and thick, mirrored bulletproof glass. Marines and Lebanese army troops patrolled the pine forest to the back of the compound as well as the entry gate.

The precautions were obviously necessary, but no one had any illusions about their ultimate effectiveness. If a decision was made—more than likely, in one of the region's capitals—to hit the embassy as part of some perverse political game plan, no barricade would be able to prevent it from happening. Everyone working here knew it, starting with the person at the center of the crosshairs, the ambassador himself. Corben had experienced how differently men dealt with being in that charmed position. The current ambassador, to his credit, took it with admirable stoicism.

Corben walked in to find the ambassador sitting with a man he didn't know, who was quick to stand up and introduce himself as Bill Kirkwood. The man had a firm handshake, a sharp gaze, and a personable demeanor. He was tall, on par with Corben, and seemed to be in reasonable shape. Corben guessed Kirkwood was probably a few years older than he was, placing him somewhere around forty.

"Bill flew in from Amman this afternoon," the ambassador informed Corben. "He's here about the Evelyn Bishop situation."

Which surprised Corben. A little too quick, for his liking. "What's your interest in this?" he asked Kirkwood.

"I met her a few years ago. I'm with the cultural heritage division at UNESCO, and Evelyn was out here batting for us against the developers of the downtown area. She's quite a whirlwind, not someone you easily forget," Kirkwood added with an affable smile. "We've been funding some of her work ever since."

Corben looked a question at the ambassador, unsure about where this was headed.

"Bill's concerned," the ambassador informed Corben, "from a personal as well as a professional point of view," then turned to Kirkwood, leaving him to elaborate.

"Well, my primary interest is, of course, Evelyn's well-being. That's paramount. She's someone we respect and care about, and I need to make sure everything is being done so that we can get her back quickly and safely," Kirkwood clarified. "Beyond that," he added with some hesitance, "yes, there's an obvious concern about one of our most respected and visible professionals being tainted with something the papers will pounce on like relic smuggling—which, from what I understand, is how the Lebanese government would like to spin this." He paused for a moment to slide a questioning glance at the ambassador, before adding, "And I can only assume we're not too disinclined to go with them on that."

"We need to weigh the pros and cons of how it comes out," the ambassador replied with the composed defensiveness of a seasoned pro. "Lebanon is in a very fragile state right now. An American, especially an older woman, getting plucked off the streets for no reason—it would undoubtedly be seen as a terrorist, anti-Western act. And the timing couldn't be worse. These people are desperate to regain the image of peace and normalcy they'd only just managed to bring back after all the years of mayhem. And with what happened this summer, the country's now in desperate need of foreign investment, more than ever. The prime minister and the interior minister have both called me up on this already. They're panicking. I don't need to tell you a lot of it's about perception when it comes to raising funding, and if this were to spiral out and inspire copycats . . ."

"Whereas a smuggler caught up in some kind of dirty deal is not a reflection of political instability and therefore much easier to brush off," Kirkwood observed, somewhat wryly, before turning to Corben. "You see what we're dealing with here."

"I can't imagine it would reflect well on your organization to have her paraded as a smuggler," Corben countered.

Kirkwood considered his comment for a beat and nodded guiltily. "Of course, it wouldn't. I won't deny that we're also keen to avoid any tainting by association. The organization doesn't exactly enjoy whole-hearted support on Capitol Hill. We've only just managed to rejoin it as a nation, and that wasn't easy to pull off." The United States had, in fact, been one of the thirty-seven founding members of UNESCO, the United Nations Educational, Scientific, and Cultural Organization. The organization, which opened its doors in 1945 shortly after the end of the war, was set up to promote peace and security by encouraging collaboration among nations through, well, education, science, and culture. Over the next four decades, as it grew to include over 150 countries as members, its policies—primarily its foreign policy, which was deemed worryingly "leftist"—diverged from the United States' own agenda. The rift reached a head when the United States finally withdrew from the organization in 1984. It only rejoined in 2003 in a bipartisan token gesture from President Bush, but you didn't have to dig deep to realize that the organization was still viewed with the same skepticism and contempt in official circles in Washington as was its big brother, the UN.

"This needs to be handled with utmost care," the ambassador affirmed, "both in terms of getting Evelyn Bishop back and in terms of what we tell the public."

Corben studied the two men for a moment. "As far as getting her back, you know that's our priority too. As far as the media is concerned, well . . . this isn't political. We're pretty sure of that." He turned to Kirkwood. "I do think it has to do with Iraqi relics, but Evelyn Bishop's role in that context remains unclear."

"Do you know what these relics are?" Kirkwood asked.

Corben hesitated briefly. He didn't want to say any more than he had to, but he had to tread carefully. "Statuettes, tablets, seals. We've got some Polaroids," he informed them.

"May I see them?"

The question somewhat surprised Corben. Kirkwood was drilling deeper than he would have expected. "Sure. They're in my office."

Kirkwood nodded. "Okay. So we think she got involved with these guys in some way. But was she a willing partner in the transaction, or was she out to stop it from taking place? Do you see what I mean? That's the angle we need to adopt. She got wind of it somehow, she tried to stop them or turn them in, and they grabbed her. Knowing her, it's probably what really happened."

"It would certainly work for everyone," the ambassador noted.

"The thing is," Corben observed, "she didn't contact anyone about this. If she really was out to stop them, she would have called someone—and given the smugglers a reason to silence her. Which is what my real concern is here. If this is actually what happened, and they're out to silence her . . . they're not going to come to us with any demands. We need to get through to them and offer them something for her safe return. Assuming they haven't gone too far already." He looked at them grimly.

"I assume you're going to put the word out through your channels, get the message out that we want her back, no questions asked," the ambassador asked.

"I've already got that going," Corben assured him. "But our contacts are much weaker since the summer. The country's divided right down the middle. One side won't talk to us at all, and the other one isn't of much use in this case."

"I have a lot of contacts in the area," Kirkwood told Corben. "I'd like to work with you on this. There may be a different set of people I can reach out to than the ones you have access to. We have a lot of contacts when it comes to Iraqi antiquities. And it can be seen as a neutral, UN-led effort, rather than coming directly from the Great Satan," he added, using the region's favorite epithet for America.

Corben looked at the ambassador, who was clearly comfortable with the request. Corben wasn't. He always worked alone. It was as much a part of his job description as it was a personal choice. And although he didn't relish having someone looking over his shoulder, Corben couldn't exactly refuse. Besides, Kirkwood could prove helpful. The UN did have extensive contacts in the area. And, after all, finding Evelyn would undoubtedly lead to the hakeem. Which was the endgame, though it wasn't something he was too keen to share with either man before him.

"Not a problem," Corben agreed.

Kirkwood surprised him with his next question. "I hear there was another woman involved. What do we know about her?"

"Mia Bishop," Corben informed him. "She's her daughter."

Chapter 27

⌒⌒⌒

The living room was basking in the soft glow of dusk as Mia stirred out of her slumber on Corben's sofa. Blinking her eyes open, she was momentarily confused by the unfamiliar surroundings, then it all came rushing back. She sat up slowly and mopped the languor off her face with her hands. She waited for her senses to reboot, then pushed herself to her feet and padded over to the French doors and out onto the balcony.

The buildings across the street were uniformly gray and looked as tired and weary as she felt. Many of the balconies had been glassed in illegally, turning outdoor terraces into interior space, and shrapnel scars and bullet holes pockmarked virtually every façade. A forest of television aerials sprouted from the flat roofs, and telephone and electricity wires cobwebbed overhead, a constant reminder of the patched-up, makeshift feel of the place. From a strictly aesthetic point of view, this wasn't an attractive city, not by any means. And yet, somehow, defying expectation and logic, it charmed anyone who visited it. Including Mia.

She was drying herself off after a quick shower when she heard some noise coming from the front door. Her whole body went rigid. She listened intently, then quickly wrapped herself in a towel and crept up to the bathroom door. She inched the door slightly ajar and peered through the narrow slit. She couldn't see the front entrance. Her mind flew into overdrive. Should she barricade herself in the bathroom? Bad idea. It didn't have any windows. Should she scuttle over to one of the bedrooms, which had access to a balcony? Not hugely useful, given that the apartment was on the sixth floor of the building and that she didn't feel like doing another high-wire act. She was running out of options when the dead bolt clicked noisily and the door juddered open. Every hair on her body went stiff for a nanosecond, before Corben's voice rang out through the flat.

"Mia?"

She shut her eyes and breathed out in relief, chiding herself for letting her imagination run amok. "I'll be out in a sec," she replied, making a concerted effort to sound as unflustered as possible.

She got dressed and found Corben in the kitchen. He had brought back her cell phone. She switched it on and saw that she had a couple of messages. That Evelyn was the abducted woman in the news was starting to leak out. The first message was from the project supervisor at the foundation. The second was from Mike Boustany, the local historian who was working with her on the project and whom she'd gotten to know quite well. She needed to call them both back and let them know what had happened, but decided it would keep until the morning. She also knew more concerned friends and colleagues would be calling as the news spread, so she set her phone to a low ring, opting to screen her calls. The only call she'd take, if it came in, was from her aunt in Boston. She wanted to discuss things with Corben more thoroughly first. He had also picked up some food on his way back, and she felt ravenous.

They laid out the foil containers of lamb *kafta* skewers, hummus, and other mezes on the coffee table in the living room and sat cross-legged on cushions, digging into the food and sipping cold Almaza beers. Eating was, in Beirut as in the rest of the Mediterranean, an elaborate feast of delicately prepared dishes as well as a cardinal social ritual. Mia succumbed to the therapeutic charms of the food and the beer, and, for a while, the casual conversation between her and Corben—mostly about the meal—flowed easily, and she enjoyed the respite from the recent frenzied insanity and, she realized, his company, even though there was a guarded superficiality to what they talked about. She didn't mind. Casual conversations, right now, were a welcome break, but as their plates emptied and the dusk's golden light faded to black, so did the pretense

of anything convivial about their ambrosial meal. The thousand-pound
gorilla that had quietly been stalking them from the dark corners of its
cage had clawed its way out and was now clamoring for attention.

She'd used the time alone to go over everything that had happened,
everything she'd seen or heard. She felt she was missing a lot. "Jim," she
finally ventured, after a pregnant lull. "What is this really all about?"

She caught a small evasive skip in his eyes before they came back to
meet hers. "What do you mean?" he asked.

"I don't feel I'm even close to understanding what's really going on."

Corben's face clouded. "I'm not sure I know much more than you
do. We've been kind of thrown into the deep end without warning, and
so far, all we've been doing is reacting to events as they happen."

"But you have an idea," she persisted. She felt her face flush. She
wasn't used to pressing someone like that, not in such a situation, but
then, she'd never been in a situation like this. Not that she imagined
many people had.

"What makes you say that?"

"Come on, Jim."

"What?" he protested, spreading his hands questioningly.

"Well, the file, for one thing."

"What file?"

She gave him a clearly dubious look. "The one you took from my
mom's flat. I had a look at it when I was in her kitchen."

"And . . . ?"

"And of all the stuff in her apartment, it's the one thing you zeroed
in on. There's this symbol all over it, the snake that's curled around in a
circle, like it's eating itself. The same symbol I saw on the cover of one
of the books in the Polaroids they showed me at the police station, the
ones that were in her handbag." Mia paused, scrutinizing his face, gauging him. She couldn't read anything in his reaction, or rather, in his lack
of one, but then, she didn't expect anything less from an intelligence
operative. But she was on a roll and felt a nervous energy crackling
through her. She pressed ahead. "Then there's the gangland level of violence. I mean, Christ, I know smuggling museum pieces isn't exactly a
white-collar crime, and I'm no expert when it comes to the underworld
or to what passes for normal on the streets of Beirut these days, but it
all feels pretty hard-core to me—grabbing people off the street, killing

others, shooting up apartments . . ." She trailed off, summoning up the courage to venture even further. "Then there's your involvement."

Corben's brow furrowed. "My involvement?"

Mia gave him a sly but nervous half-smile. "I didn't think the CIA was really into recovering stolen loot from museums."

"An American national's been kidnapped," Corben reminded her. "That's Agency territory." He took a final, casual sip from his bottle and put it down coolly, before his eyes settled on her again.

As inscrutable as the Sphinx, she thought, her mind sidetracking, thinking about how maddening it would be to face him across a poker table or, worse, to live with someone as sealed in. "If you say so, but . . ." She shrugged and didn't sound convinced, not that she was trying to. "Come on, Jim." She searched his eyes for a connection, a will to open up. "She's my mom. I know you guys have this whole 'need to know' thing going on, and I get that, but my mother's life and maybe mine are in the balance here."

She held his gaze as he clearly weighed whether to give in. She could almost hear his brain whirring, going through the worrying details of what they were involved in, and selecting what, if anything, to share and what to keep in the vault. After a brief silence, he pursed his lips and nodded almost imperceptibly, then got up and walked across the room. He brought back his briefcase and sat down again. He opened the combination lock and pulled out the file, and set it down squarely on the coffee table in front of him, resting his hands on it.

"I don't have a full picture of what's going on, alright? But I'll tell you what I know." He patted the file. "Your mom had this out on her desk, an old file which at face value doesn't seem related to her current work. It's on her desk the same day she meets with someone from an old dig in Iraq. I think he might have given her the Polaroids that were in her handbag. Maybe he came to see her about selling them, maybe he hoped she could hook him up with some buyers. Maybe she was interested in them herself. Because of this." He opened the file and pulled out a photocopy, one of the images of the Ouroboros, and slid it over to Mia. "As you rightly noted, the excavation in the file has to do with this snake symbol, the same one that's on the book."

It was an old, black-and-white image of the coiled snake, taken from a centuries-old woodcut. Mia studied it more closely than she had before.

The beast in the image was more than a snake. It had exaggerated scales and fangs, more akin to a dragon. Its eyes were cold and stared blankly ahead, as if the act of devouring itself were the most natural, and painless, of acts. It was a sinister image that harked back to a primal fear, a yellowed, weathered copy that reeked of malice.

She looked up at Corben. "What is it?"

"It's called an Ouroboros. It's very old, it's been used at different times by different cultures."

"What does it mean?"

"It doesn't seem to have one specific meaning. I think it's more of an archetypal, mystical symbol that meant different things to different people, depending on where it was used. I found many instances of it, from ancient Egyptian myths to Hindu legends, and later with alchemists and gnostics, and that was without spending too much time on it."

Mia was finding it hard to draw her eyes away from the image. "The relics aren't important. Whoever's got her is after that book."

"Possibly. This might tell us more." He tapped a finger on Evelyn's file. "I haven't yet had time to go through it properly. Either way, it's not really the issue. It's only relevant in that it's why she was kidnapped. And right now, the best lead we have for finding her is the guy who I think brought these to her, this man from her past, the Iraqi fixer you said she mentioned. He knows more about what's going on and about who else is involved in this. We don't know anything about him, but . . ." Corben paused, hesitating. Mia could see that something in him didn't want to continue, but, after a brief moment, he said, "You could well be right in that he was the same guy who was with her when she was kidnapped. And if he was, well, you saw him. You can identify him. And I'm hoping that if he's the same guy, then maybe"—he turned the file so it was now facing her the right way—"just maybe, there's a picture of him in here somewhere. And that would help us a lot."

She looked at him uncertainly, feeling somewhat shortchanged by his answer, then nodded and opened up the file again. Much as she felt drawn to the materials in it—the sheets of notes, handwritten in ink with a graceful, classic penmanship that she knew well from the letters her mom had sent her when she was growing up; the photocopies of documents and pages of books, in English, Arabic, a few in French, with sentences underlined and notes scribbled in the margins; the maps of

Iraq and of the broader Levant, with markings and arrows and circled notes; all of it with many, many question marks—she flicked through them after no more than a cursory glance, looking for the photographs she needed to examine.

She came across a batch of old snapshots, scattered between the pages, and studied them closely. She recognized a younger, slimmer Evelyn in some of them, decked out in khaki field pants, mesh hats, and big tortoiseshell sunglasses, and found herself imagining the exciting, unconventional life her mother must have led at the time: a single woman, a Westerner, traveling to exotic, sun-drenched locations, meeting different peoples, immersing herself in their cultures, working with them to explore the hidden treasures of their past. A driven life, to be sure, and more than likely a fulfilling one, but one that had to come at a price, which in Evelyn's case seemed to be a wistful loneliness, a guarded solitude.

Her fingers paused at a shot of Evelyn standing alone with a man. His features were too obscured by the sunglasses, the shade of his hat, and the downward, slightly turned angle of his face. She felt a prickling at the back of her neck. She knew that shot. She'd been given a copy of it when she was seven, which she kept safely tucked into her wallet, always close. The man in the photograph was her father. Evelyn had told her it was the only picture of him she had. They'd only spent a few weeks together. It saddened Mia that she didn't even know what he really looked like.

She stared wistfully at the photograph, then a troubling realization crept into her mind. Her father was there. He had been with Evelyn when she'd found the underground chambers.

And he'd died a month later. In a car crash.

A sharp pain spiked inside her heart. For a second, it felt as if it stopped beating altogether, and she felt the blood draining from her face.

Corben seemed to spot it. "What is it?"

She handed him the picture. "The man in the picture." Her words came out as if emerging from a fog. "He was my father. He was there."

Corben studied her, waiting for more.

"He died a month later. In a car crash." Her eyes were alight with questions. "What if he was killed? Murdered. Because of this."

An uncertain look crossed Corben's features. He shook his head. "I don't think so. There's nothing here that indicates that Evelyn had any trouble over this before. If his death was related to all this, then she would have been under threat too. Which doesn't seem to be the case, I mean, she lived a pretty open life."

He handed her back the picture. She took another lingering look at it, then nodded. "I guess you're right," she conceded.

"I'll take a look anyway, just to cover all the bases. What was his name?" Corben asked.

"Webster," Mia said. "Tom Webster."

⤳⤳⤳

The name pummeled Corben like a shotgun blast.

Tom Webster.

Evelyn had tried to reach Tom Webster last night. And mediums didn't usually call the switchboards of academic institutions to reach the deceased.

He wasn't dead. At least, Evelyn didn't think so. He was alive. And she'd lied to her daughter all these years.

Adrenaline surged through Corben. This was important. He had to put a high-priority trace on the name. He needed more information from Mia about where he had supposedly died, what else Evelyn had told her about him, although, given that she'd lied to her about his death, Corben didn't think anything Mia could tell him about her long-lost father would turn out to be true.

It could wait.

He watched Mia as she put the shot to one side and moved on, checking out a few more shots until her eyes fell on something that seemed to snare her interest.

"The man from the alley. I think that's him," she said.

Chapter 28

The hakeem adjusted the glass slide under the microscope and tapped a few buttons on his keyboard. Another magnified image came up on the flat screen. He studied it carefully, as he had done with all the data that the tests had thrown up.

She's clean, he thought. Evelyn's blood work hadn't flagged anything unusual. No foreign substances, no tampering. Her readings were in line with what he would expect to find in a reasonably healthy woman of her age.

He stared through the cells on the screen and revisited her words. There was no doubt in his mind that she had told him everything she knew. He was working off a solid base.

Tom Webster. He couldn't get the name out of his mind.

Could he be one of them?

The possibility electrified him. He ran it through his mind, again and again. It seemed too far-fetched. So many years had passed. . . But what other explanation was there? Every time he tried to dismiss the idea, to put another spin on it, his initial suspicion came back, slicing through his doubts with Occam-like sharpness and implanting itself firmly in his consciousness. Why else would he appear like that, unannounced, at the first sign of the discovery, and then disappear when the trail seemed to die out? No, there was no other rational explanation.

He had to be one of them.

Tasked with protecting their secret.

Keeping an eye on archaeological digs in the region, making sure that no one stumbled across something that they had gone to great lengths to suppress. Something they'd kept—something they'd hoarded greedily, he scowled—to themselves for centuries.

His pulse quickened.

He thought back to her pathetic tale of lost love and replayed her story in his mind. The man—Tom Webster, the name was branded onto his consciousness, not that he believed it to be his true name—had swooped in and out of her life with clinical efficiency. The discovery had led nowhere, or so he'd led her to believe. What had he really uncovered, what hadn't he shared with her? He'd then pulled a disappearing act, leaving her with an unborn child and a numbing spiel about why he couldn't be with her, for reasons he couldn't share with her.

Déjà vu.

He'd heard—read, actually—something along those lines before.

Many years ago. Back home, in Italy.

In Naples.

It was part of what had triggered his journey.

Yes, of course, he knew it was something some men said. When they lost interest. When they wanted to move on to new conquests. Chapter one of the idiot's guide to dating. A he's-just-not-that-into-you kind of thing. Normally, his cynical, jaded view of humanity would have supported that take on it.

Not this time. This felt different.

It fit.

And the very idea that this Tom Webster could actually be part of something he wasn't sure even existed, something he doggedly wanted to believe, against all rationale, was out there . . . He smiled inwardly.

This is real. Just as I always suspected.

The principe *was right.*

A wave of exhilaration coursed through him, coupled with an anger at the way fate dealt its hand. Evelyn had discovered the chamber in 1977 and left the country three years later. He'd arrived in Iraq a couple of years after that.

He cursed his misfortune.

If he'd been there at the time of the discovery of the chambers, he might have heard about it. He might have met this Tom Webster. And he might already possess what he was searching for.

Fate. Timing. The right place at the wrong time. But maybe this was a chance to make up for it.

He needed to find this Webster. The number Evelyn had for him was in her organizer, in her apartment. Omar and his men should have brought that back from the woman's apartment, but that effort had been thwarted—he'd have to have a serious talk to someone about that. He knew he could easily find the number using the Internet, but he didn't expect it to yield much. Webster probably didn't want to be found. He'd surely covered his tracks.

The hakeem also needed to get his hands on that slippery antiques dealer. He had to get his hands on the book, which he knew could be the key to everything. But this woman and her story . . . she was, indeed, a godsend. Not that he actually believed in such inanities.

But there were complications he needed to better understand.

The woman's daughter, for one. She'd risked her life by interrupting his men and allowed the dealer to escape. Then there was the issue of the man who was with her at the archaeologist's apartment. The hakeem had dispatched Omar and his men to go over it and bring back anything of interest—and anything bearing the sign of the snake. Not only had her daughter been there too, but the man she was with was clearly a professional. A well-trained player who'd outgunned Omar—who wasn't exactly a slouch when it came to that kind of wet work—and killed one of his men. From what Omar had told him, he was American. Who was he, and what was he doing there with her? Was he a new player in this game—another one? Was he also one of them? Was it all suddenly coming alive? Or was he there for other, more trivial reasons, without knowledge of what the game was really about?

The hakeem tried to rein in his exhilaration. He'd waited for so long, tried so hard. He had devoted his life to this pursuit. And now, he felt with growing certainty, it was all coming together.

Finally.

He had to know who these new players were.

But until then, he had to tread carefully.

He would use his contacts to check up on Webster, though he suspected the man would be difficult to trace. Omar would call his contacts in the Lebanese police and intelligence services. Find out what he could about the American. Most pressing, the hakeem had to find the antiques dealer. He couldn't lose sight of that. He glumly realized that there were no guarantees that the man would be found. Omar had really screwed up on that front, though the hakeem knew his man would do everything necessary to make up for his mistake.

His spirits rose as a realization broke through the questions swamping his mind. If the archaeologist wasn't just another deluded victim, if this Webster did really harbor strong feelings for her . . . The hakeem might just be able to use her to draw him out.

The lure of the damsel in distress.

It always worked in the movies.

He just had to make sure that her cry for help was loud enough.

Chapter 29

❦

Mia pulled the shot closer.

The face belonged to a man who was standing aloofly, slightly apart from a group of sweaty, smiling workers. She concentrated, trying to marry it to the terror-stricken man who had been moments away from being stuffed into a car and carted off—along with her mother—to some unknown fate.

She held it up. "This guy here." She handed it to Corben and pointed out the man she thought she recognized.

Corben examined it, then flipped it over. Names were written on the back of the photograph in pencil, in the same elegant hand as the notes in the file. He flipped it over again and back, assigning the names to the faces. "Looks like his name's Farouk."

"Just Farouk?"

"That's it." Corben pulled out his notebook and wrote it down. "No family name."

Mia looked at him, deflated. "Is that enough?"

Corben put down his notebook. "It's something." He studied the face in the photograph, as if committing it to memory. "Go through the rest of them, will you? Maybe there's another shot of him in there."

She did so, without success. Still, at least they had a face and a name, which, presumably, Corben's people could build on.

Mia set the photos down. Her thoughts kept getting drawn back to Evelyn. She'd been gone for almost twenty-four hours now. Mia had heard the cliché about the first forty-eight hours being the most critical in any missing person's investigation—not from anyone actually in law enforcement, but from countless TV shows and movies. Still, it didn't seem counterintuitive—clichés became clichés for a reason—and if it was true, half the window of opportunity to finding Evelyn was already shuttered.

"How are you going to find him?" she asked.

"I don't know. We don't have much to go on. There's her organizer, although there's nothing listed in this week's diary entries. Now that we have a name, I need to go through it again, see if there are any contact details for him. We have her cell phone. We need to go through its log, see if any of the numbers on it are his. Same with her laptop, although it's password-protected, so it could take a little while to break into."

She nodded soberly and picked up Farouk's picture again. She swept her eyes over it, frustrated and feeling helpless, then a conflicted thought blossomed in her mind.

"He saw me, I'm sure of it," she said in a tentative voice, still looking through the picture, remembering that night. "He saw me when I got to that alley."

Corben glanced at her uncertainly. He knew that already.

"He'll recognize me. Which means he'll trust me if he sees me again. Maybe we can use that. Maybe there's some way we can lure him out."

"What, with you as bait?" Corben asked somewhat incredulously. "We're trying to keep you out of the spotlight, remember?"

Mia nodded. Still, she felt it was a strand she wanted to pull at some more. He'd seen her, and he should trust her. That had to be useful, in some way. Her mind traversed back to her conversation with Evelyn. What had her mom said? Her colleague. He was with her.

"There's an archaeology professor. Ramez. He works with my mom. A young guy. He's the one who took her down south yesterday, to check out that crypt. She said he was with her when this man—Farouk—showed up."

"You didn't mention him back at the hotel," Corben noted.

She scrunched her face apologetically. "I'm sorry, I should have. But

I was thinking, maybe he knows something. Maybe Evelyn told him something about what was going on."

Corben processed it for a beat. "You know this guy?"

"I met him once when I went to her office, on campus."

"Okay, good." Corben logged the name into his notebook. He checked his watch and frowned. It was past nine. "He won't be at the university this late." He reached into his briefcase and pulled out Evelyn's organizer, then had another idea, picked up his phone, and hit a speed-dial key. He got up and crossed to the glass doors leading out to the balcony. Mia heard him connect with someone and ask him to check Evelyn's cell phone for a "Ramez." He waited a few moments, then said, "Hold on," and crossed back to the table. He scribbled a number down in his notebook, shot a quick "Got it" to whoever it was he had called, and redialed quickly. Mia could hear it ringing, but no one seemed to be answering. Corben let it ring a few more times—cell phones in Beirut, annoyingly, hardly ever had a voice-mail service—then put the phone down with a frustrated look. "He's not picking up," he informed Mia.

"You don't think he's also been . . . ?" She hesitated to vocalize the rest of her question, suddenly sensing she was letting her imagination loose again.

Worryingly, his look didn't dismiss the suggestion outright. "No, I think I would have heard something. He's probably just tired of fielding calls from people who will have heard about your mom's kidnapping and know he works in the same department."

She frowned with concern. "Can you get his home address?" she asked, surprising herself with her tenacity before wondering if her question had an irksome teaching-your-grandma-to-suck-eggs ring to it.

Corben didn't seem to mind and checked his watch again. "I don't want to flag him to the local cops, not at this hour. And there's no reason he'd be on our database for us to have that kind of information on tap ourselves. I'll try calling him again in a few minutes."

Mia studied him as he processed the information. His face was still almost hermetically unreadable, but she could definitely sense some concern there. She flashed back to standing with him outside her mom's front door and raised her eyes to meet his. With a slight hardening in her voice, she ventured another question.

"Outside Mom's apartment. You said I already knew this was serious. And of course, it was, I know that, but the way you said it . . ." She paused for a moment. She knew she was right, and the conviction within her came through with blinding clarity. "You still haven't told me everything. There's more to this, isn't there?"

He sat back and ran a hand through his hair, giving the back of his neck a small rub, then looked at her and seemed to reach a verdict. He leaned in, reached into his case, and pulled out his laptop. He flipped it open and powered it up, then placed his index finger on the small fingerprint scanner before tapping some keys. The screen lit up. He navigated through it in silence, found the folder he needed, and turned to her.

"This is classified," he informed her with a raised finger before pausing to take a breath, seemingly still debating whether he was making a mistake in sharing this with her.

He turned the screen to face her. It showed a photograph of what looked like a wall inside a narrow, cell-like room. Something circular, the size of an open umbrella judging by the scale of the light fixture overhead, was scratched into the wall. Mia recognized it instantly.

"I was stationed in Iraq in the first years of the war," he explained. "One of our units got some intel about a doctor who was close to Saddam, but by the time they raided his compound, he was gone."

A barrage of questions rose within Mia, but Corben wasn't through.

"What they did find in his compound was pretty horrific. There was a huge lab in its basement. State-of-the-art operating chamber, the works. He was running experiments there, experiments that . . ." His voice drifted off for a moment as he chose his words, and a fleeting look of pain crossed his face, a pain Mia could hear in his voice. "He was experimenting on humans. Young and old. Male, female. Kids . . ."

Mia felt her blood chill as horror and concern for her mother consumed her in equal measure.

"There were holding cells in the compound, but everyone in them had been executed shortly before they were raided. We also found dozens of bodies buried in a field not far from the house," he went on, "dumped in mass graves, naked. Many of them had been operated on. Some were missing body parts. There were stashes of organs, gallons of blood, stored in fridges. Some of their wounds, where he'd cut them open, weren't sutured. He didn't bothering closing them up once he'd taken out what interested him. There were other . . . more disturbing discoveries in the lab that I'll spare you. He just used them like guinea pigs and tossed out what he didn't need. It seems Saddam supplied him with them, along with everything else he needed." Corben paused, as if to purge the images from his mind and collect himself. "This"—he pointed at the image of the Ouroboros on the laptop's screen—"was carved into the wall of one of the holding cells."

Mia felt a sudden wetness on her mouth and realized she'd unconsciously caught her lower lip with her teeth and bitten into it hard enough to draw blood. She released her bite and dabbed her lip with her finger, then rubbed the droplet away. "What kind of experiments was he running?"

"We're not sure. But given Saddam's interest in finding efficient ways to commit mass murder . . ."

Mia's eyes rocketed wide. "You think he was working on a biological weapon?"

Corben shrugged. "The secrecy surrounding his work, the dead bodies, Saddam's championing him . . . put it this way. I don't think he was looking for a cure for cancer."

Mia stared at the shot of the cell again. "But why the carving on the wall?"

"We don't know. We managed to track down some people in Baghdad who came across him. I spoke to a dealer in antiquities, as well as a guy who used to be a curator at the National Museum. It seems this man, the hakeem as they called him, was fascinated by Iraqi history, turn of the millennium specifically. They said he knew a lot about it and had traveled extensively in the region. Once they felt comfortable opening up a bit more, they separately told me he'd asked them to look for any local references to the Ouroboros in ancient books and manuscripts."

"Which, presumably, they did."

"You bet," Corben confirmed, "but they didn't find anything. So he asked them to look some more, and to widen the search, even outside Iraq's borders. And to keep looking. Which they did. They said he was completely obsessed with it, and they were both terrified of him."

"And they found nothing?"

Corben shook his head.

"And now he wants this book . . ." Mia connected the dots in her mind. "So this . . . this doctor. He's still out there."

He nodded.

A devastating sense of dread choked Mia's heart. "And you think he has my mom?" The words almost dried in her throat as she uttered them, willing the answer to be negative.

Corben's somber look told her it wasn't, but she knew that already. "His trail went cold north of Tikrit a few weeks after the discovery of the lab, and we haven't had any leads since. Given that Evelyn had a connection to the Ouroboros through the chamber she found, and given the ruthlessness of whoever seems to be after the relics," he said gravely, "I think it's more than likely that either he's got her or she's being held by someone who's linked to him in some way."

Mia felt the air vacate her lungs. Her mom's situation seemed horrible enough when she thought they were just—just—dealing with a gang of smugglers. This . . . this was too horrific to imagine.

She stared out into nothingness, her mind short-circuited by Corben's grim revelation. The room seemed to darken around her, and everything in it shifted slightly out of focus. She sensed Corben picking up his phone and heard dialing tones at the periphery of her consciousness, followed by the same unanswered ringing tone as before and his phone snapping shut. It took a moment for her to emerge from her daze and register that he must have been trying Ramez's number again.

A question drifted out of the fog. She turned to Corben. "Given all the fuss about WMDs and what you know about this man, I'd have thought you'd have a massive team of people on the case, working it with you. Surely, getting him is a huge priority, isn't it?"

"It was," Corben said glumly. "It's not anymore. We cried wolf about WMDs once too often, and the word itself has become poison. We deserve as much, I guess, but no one wants to hear about them anymore, and if anything, the priority's to disengage from Iraq, not commit more resources."

"But he's a monster," Mia protested, clambering angrily to her feet.

"You think he's the only one running around out there?" he

countered with calm frustration. "There are plenty of other mass murderers out there, from Rwanda, Serbia, you name it—they're living quietly in leafy suburbs of London or Brussels under assumed names, no one's bothering them. The only people after them are investigative reporters. That's it. They're the new Simon Wiesenthals, and there aren't that many of them, just a handful who care enough to devote their time and risk their lives tracking these butchers down. They're the only ones making a difference. Once in a while, they'll out one of them in a story that might get a few columns not too far from the front page, and some prosecutor will maybe pay attention and look into it if it creates enough of a stink, but generally, these guys get away."

Which was true. Saddam and his decapitated brother-in-law were rare exceptions. The norm was that deposed dictators were often able to enjoy exile in blissful, unrepentant comfort while their underlings, the thugs who had overseen or actually participated in the killings, vanished into lives of placid anonymity.

"There isn't a concerted, official effort to bring any of these people in," Corben added. "Life moves on. Politicians step down, others take their place, and the crimes of the not-so-distant past are quickly forgotten. No one in the State Department wants to hear about this right now. The Iraqis themselves aren't in a position to go after him, they've got bigger problems to deal with. And I can't exactly see the Lebanese government getting involved given the mess their country's in."

Mia couldn't believe it. "You're working on this alone?"

"Pretty much. I can draw on the same Agency resources if and when I need them, but until I have a definite, and I mean definite, lock on this guy, I can't call in the troops."

Mia stared at him, stupefied. The news was getting bleaker by the minute, and the images he'd seeded in her mind refused to fade. "He experimented on kids?"

Corben nodded.

A realization thudded heavily into the pit of her stomach. "We have to get her back. But we also have to stop him, don't we?" She felt tears welling up, but she bit them back.

His eyes were on her, and something warmer flickered in them. He nodded thoughtfully, taking in her words. "Yes."

"We need to find Farouk. If we can get to him before that"—she paused, unsure about how to refer to the hakeem, then chose—"monster does, and if he has this book, then maybe we can trade it for Mom."

Corben's expression brightened. "That's what I'm hoping."

He picked up his phone and hit the redial button.

Chapter 30

❦

Ramez stared worriedly at his phone as it vibrated with a low buzz that sent it skittering sideways across the coffee table in brief, tortuous spurts.

With each grating buzz, the phone's LED screen lit up, casting a temporary, ghostly blue-green glow across the darkened living room of his small apartment. His eyes blinked to attention each time, transfixed by the bright display. The words PRIVATE CALLER—shorthand for a withheld number—stared alarmingly back, taunting him, before the display flicked back to blackness. His body went rigid every time the phone sprang to life, as if the device were hardwired straight into his skull.

Mercifully, after about eight spurts, it stopped buzzing. The room was plunged into darkness again, a bleak, lonely darkness that was occasionally interrupted by the reflections, from the headlights of passing cars in the street below, that scuttled across its mostly bare walls. It was the third time the anonymous caller had tried to reach him in the last hour, and the assistant professor wasn't about to answer. Given that he hardly ever received such calls—withheld numbers were, oddly, a frowned-upon social faux pas in Lebanon—he knew what it had to be about. And it terrified him.

His day had started out like any other. Out of bed at seven, a light breakfast, a shower and a shave, and a brisk, twenty-minute walk to the campus. He'd read the morning papers before leaving home, and he'd spotted the story about the woman's kidnapping downtown, but he had no idea it was Evelyn. Not until the cops had shown up at Post Hall.

He was their first port of call in the department, and the news had sucker punched the breath right out of him. With every word he uttered, he'd felt himself getting drawn deeper and deeper into a tar pit of trouble that he was keen to avoid, but knew he couldn't. They were trying to find Evelyn, and he had to help. There was no way out.

They'd asked if he knew anything about her interest in Iraqi relics, and the man who had appeared in Zabqine immediately came to mind. They'd perked up at the mention of Farouk, and he'd given them his name—his first name, as he didn't know the man's full name—and description. From their guarded comments, he'd gathered that his description fitted one they had of a man who'd been seen with Evelyn when she was kidnapped.

The encounter with the detectives had already spooked him enough. Seeing Farouk emerge from behind some parked cars and approach him outside Post Hall a few hours later made him jump out of his skin. At first, he didn't know what to make of it. Was Farouk working with the kidnappers? Was he here to grab Ramez too? The assistant professor had shrunk back defensively at his approach, but the Iraqi fixer's supplicating and woeful manner had quickly convinced him that the man posed no threat.

Presently, sitting there in his darkened living room, he picked through that worrying conversation, every word of it still ringing with frightening clarity. They'd found a quiet spot to talk, at the back of the building. Farouk had opened by saying he needed to tell the police what he knew about the kidnapping, to help Evelyn, but he couldn't go to them himself. He was in the country illegally, and, given what he'd seen in the papers, the stolen relics were already a point of contention. Ramez cut in by telling him the cops had already been to see him and informed Farouk that he himself had given them his description—admittedly, in the hope of helping find Evelyn.

The news made Farouk panic. They had his name, his description, and it looked more and more as if they were after him for smuggling relics. His eyes took on a haunting, cornered gleam as he asked Ramez to help him. He was in desperate need for money, and, yes, he was trying to sell the valuable relics—he had initially hoped that Ramez would help him in that, but that was moot. All that mattered now was survival. He filled Ramez in on what he knew, what he'd seen—the men who came after him in Iraq, the book, the drill marks on his friend Hajj Ali Salloum—and with each of his revelations, the assistant professor's blood curdled with dread.

Farouk asked Ramez to act as a go-between. He wanted Ramez to talk to the cops, make a deal on his behalf: He'd go in and help them as much as he could with finding Evelyn, but he didn't want to end up in a Lebanese prison, nor did he want to be sent back to Iraq. More than that, he wanted their protection. He knew the men who kidnapped Evelyn were really after him, and he knew he wouldn't survive for long out on his own.

Ramez demurred, not wanting to get involved, but Farouk was desperate. He pleaded with him, asking the assistant professor to consider Evelyn's situation, to do it for her sake. Ramez finally said he'd think about it. He gave Farouk his cell phone number and told him to call him the next day, at noon.

Which would be noon, tomorrow.

Not ten o'clock.

Not tonight.

Ramez's eyes were still glued to his cell phone as his weary mind tried to divine who had been calling him. If it was Farouk, he didn't want to take the call. He still hadn't made up his mind about whether he would help him. On the one hand, he felt he owed it to Evelyn, and, beyond that, he had to. He couldn't exactly withhold such crucial information from the investigating cops. On the other hand, Beirut wasn't exactly famed for its rigorous observance of legal process, and Ramez, above all else, wanted to stay alive.

If it wasn't Farouk calling, Ramez didn't even want to begin to think of who it could be. A wave of paranoia surged through him as he imagined men with power drills about to burst in and take him away. He shrank back into the sofa, his arms wrapped around his knees, his chest heaving, the walls of the small room closing in around him.

It was going to be a long night.

Chapter 31

⏥

Mia watched Corben click his cell phone shut. He turned to her and shook his head. He checked his watch and frowned thoughtfully.

"I don't like leaving this till morning," he said, "but I don't think we have much choice. If they're onto him, then we're already too late. If they're not, then I'd rather not alert them to him at this hour. I'll call the guys at Hobeish first thing in the morning," he added, referring to the police station where Mia had been held, "and take it from there."

"We could go to the university, early," Mia suggested, "and get to him first thing."

Corben did a double take. " 'We'?"

"You don't know what he looks like. I can point him out to you," she protested.

"I can just ask for him at the department."

"I've met him. He'll feel more at ease if he sees a familiar face," she insisted, her voice alive with nervous energy. "Besides, I don't want to stay here alone. I'll feel like a sitting duck." She paused, catching her breath. "I want to help, okay?"

Corben looked away, clearly weighing his options and seemingly not liking any. After a moment, he turned to her cheerlessly. "Okay," he relented. "Let's see what he has to say and take it from there." He went to the fridge and pulled out two more beers and offered Mia a bottle.

She took it and crossed over to the balcony. She stood there and sipped at it, staring pensively into the night. The lights from the densely packed buildings were burning brightly, crowning the city with a pale, whitish aura. She wondered where Evelyn was at that very moment and thought about Farouk and Ramez. Where had they bunkered down for the night? Beirut was a crowded city, and it knew how to keep its secrets. No one really knew what went on behind closed doors, but in this city, Mia suspected, the lurking malevolence was in a class of its own.

"I don't get it." She turned to Corben. "This symbol, the coiled snake. What's he looking for, exactly? If it's really this book that he's after, why does he want it? He can't just be some maniacal collector."

"Why not?"

"He seems willing to go to some pretty extreme measures to get hold of it," Mia noted. "It's got to have some serious significance to him, don't you think?"

"He's a bioweapons scientist. These guys are into viruses, not relics that are hundreds of years old," Corben reminded her. "I can't imagine its relevance to his work."

"Unless he's looking for clues to some ancient plague," she half-joked.

Corben didn't dismiss it out of hand. Instead, his face clouded, then the faintest of smiles flitted across his lips. "Now there's a merry thought to sleep on."

She felt a ripple of concern. An outright dismissal would have been better.

They left it at that, finished their beers, and put the food away in a leaden silence. She watched Corben as he went about the nighttime routine of spinning the dead bolt on the front door and switching off the lights. She found herself wondering about what made someone take on a life like that: solitary, dangerous, mired in secrets, trained to manipulate and predisposed to mistrust. From what she could gather, he seemed like a pragmatic, clearheaded guy who wasn't suffering from a righteous, save-the-world delusion. She couldn't deny that his action-adventure hero side was alluring—she hadn't exactly met men like him in the sedate academic waters she usually navigated. But there was also something dark, unknowable, and guarded about him that, while also somewhat attractive, was also a bit scary.

"Can I ask you something?"

He turned, curious. "Sure."

She smiled, slightly uncomfortable with the moment. "Is Jim your real name? I mean, I read somewhere that you guys always seem to use Mike or Jim or Joe as cover."

He breathed out a small chuckle and winced. "It's actually Humphrey, but . . . it doesn't exactly go with the job profile."

She wasn't sure for a second—then he smiled. "It's Jim. You want to see my passport?"

"Yeah, right," she mocked. "All of them." She paused for a breath, then her face grew serious. "Thanks. For everything today."

He winced uncomfortably. "I'm sorry I took you there. To your mom's apartment."

Mia shrugged. "We got to her stuff before they did. Maybe that'll count for something."

It was close to eleven by the time her head finally hit the pillow in the guest bedroom. She found it hard to fall asleep and just lay there, staring at the unfamiliar, impersonal surroundings, wondering how it had all gotten so complicated so quickly. She'd been warned about coming to Beirut when the offer had first come up, mostly by people who only remembered the city from the endless news reports about the civil war, the bombings, and the kidnappings, people who weren't familiar with the country's phoenixlike, if tenuous, return from the ashes—at least, the one that had been cut short a couple of months earlier. She could have pulled out from taking up her posting—she didn't need an excuse, war being a pretty convincing reason for anyone to give a country a wide berth—but she'd felt drawn to exploring new directions and experiencing a more exciting life than the one most of her peers seemed more than happy to settle for.

She tried to subdue her churning mind, tossing and turning and fluffing her pillow and moving it around, but it was a losing battle. She was too awake.

She sat up and listened. She couldn't hear anything coming from outside her bedroom. Corben had to be asleep. She considered taking another shot at taming the beast of insomnia, then decided against it and climbed out of bed.

She went into the living room. A pale glare from a streetlamp cast long shadows across the walls. She took quiet steps into the kitchen and poured herself a glass of water. As she headed back into the living room, her eyes fell on Evelyn's file, lying there on Corben's desk.

Beckoning her.

She flashed back to the quick peek into it that she'd stolen back in her mom's kitchen and decided it merited more than that.

She walked over to the desk and opened it.

The images of the Ouroboros immediately snared her attention.

She sat down on the sofa and worked her way through the photographs from the digs and the photocopies of images taken from books, taking a good look at them this time while putting the handwritten notes aside.

As she went through them, she pulled out the different incarnations of the beast that her mom had compiled and laid them out on the coffee table. They were markedly different: Some were rudimentary, which Mia presumed were the oldest ones. One looked Aztec; a couple of them had a distinctly Far Eastern look about them, with the snake looking much more like a dragon; others were more elaborate and figurative, married to the imagery of the Garden of Eden or of Greek gods.

She settled on the version that was of most interest, the one that had been tooled into the book from the Polaroids and carved into the wall of the underground chamber. The image disturbed her, as it had done before. She put it aside and started going through Evelyn's notes.

Evelyn had evidently spent many hours researching this, but at some point, she'd obviously given up. Confirming this, Mia noticed that many of the sheets were dated, the earliest in 1977, the last of them in 1980. She quickly gathered that the underground chamber Evelyn had discovered was in a town called Al-Hillah, in Iraq. Curious, Mia pushed herself to her feet, retrieved her laptop from her bag, and fired it up. She found an unprotected Wi-Fi connection within range, camped onto it, and opened her browser. She did a quick search, easily finding the town's location, south of Baghdad, on a map. She committed it to memory and moved on.

She read about the manuscripts that Evelyn had found hidden in the chamber. According to her notes, the style of the writings were reminiscent of those of a secret society of the same era, a group of highly sophisticated gnostics called the Brethren of Purity, who were also based in southern Iraq. There were several pages of notes that dealt with this line of research, with afterthoughts and additional markings and arrows linking sentences scribbled across them. Mia jotted the name of the society down, making a mental note to look into it. Some words were circled or underlined. Her eyes picked out the mention *Offshoot of Brethren?* with a prominent question mark.

Turning the page, a circled blurb drew her attention. It said, *Other writings match, but no mention of rituals or liturgy here. Why?* In the margin of the opposite page, next to more scribbled notes and dates, Evelyn had written *Beliefs?* and *Heretics? Is that why they were hiding?* with more big, emphatic, multiple question marks.

Mia read the page more closely. Evelyn had found common ground between the writings of the Brethren and the writings from the chamber. One glaring difference, however, was that nothing left behind in the chamber covered its occupants' spiritual beliefs.

The next pages laid out Evelyn's research into the Ouroboros. Mia went back to some of the photocopies of the various images, which also had notes scribbled across them.

There seemed to be as many interpretations of what the symbol stood for as there were cultures that had adopted it. Some saw it as a representation of evil, while others—far more, Mia noted—saw it as a benign, hopeful symbol. Mia found this somewhat disconcerting, at odds with the twinge of unease she felt when she saw the snake.

Evelyn had collected dozens of references to it throughout history, from ancient Egypt and Plato all the way to the nineteenth-century German chemist Friedrich Kekulé, who discovered the ring-shaped molecular structure of benzene after, so he claimed, dreaming of a snake who had seized its own tail, and, most recently, to Carl Jung, who had studied its archetypal grip on the human psyche and its particular significance to alchemists. There was even, Mia noted with a bittersweet knot in her throat, a Phoenician version of it, a tail-eating dragon carved into one of their temples.

Throughout, Mia picked up on a recurring theme, one that was at odds with her instincts. It was a theme of continuity: It spoke to the cyclicality of nature, the endless circle of life, death and rebirth, the primordial unity of all things. She went back to a sheet that showed an almost pastoral rendition of a winged Ouroboros in a garden with a cherub in its center.

Mia stared at it, processing what she'd read. Something didn't sit well. She thought back to her chat with Corben, about the hakeem's possible motives. The symbol didn't tally with anything worrying, but then, it didn't need to, did it? The swastika was, after all, a symbol of good luck in the Far East ever since the Stone Age. Hitler saw it otherwise and turned it into something monstrously different. Could this be the same thing? Corben kept saying the man was insane. But what if he was really searching for a lost virus, a poison, a plague. Somehow, the pieces' relevance seemed portentous, their importance malevolent. And yet, most of what she'd read about the tail-devourer symbol seemed to have an opposite feel. She couldn't see anything fearful in what was mostly regarded as a symbol of continuity. She questioned whether her initial reaction was more primal, whether it had to do with the instinctive apprehension that the archetype inspired in most people, regardless of its intended symbolism. Perhaps that, coupled with the context in which she had experienced it—on the run, hiding out from killers with bullets whizzing around her—helped explain it. But it left some unanswered questions. Was the tail-devourer something to be feared? What was its significance to the hakeem, if not something sinister? Did the members of the cabal who met in the underground chamber have something that the hakeem was so desperately after?

She thought back to the date, tenth century, and went back to her laptop. She ran a search on the scientists of the era. Some of the big names she remembered—Avicenna, Jabir ibn Hayyan—popped up immediately. She surfed from one site to another, gathering tidbits of interest and logging into her account at the Britannica online edition along the way.

Mia's mind was nestled in a comfort zone she was well used to as she worked her way through the research material on the screen before her. The more she read, though, the more that comfort eroded. Nothing in what she found seemed to shed any light on what the hakeem was after.

It wasn't for a lack of great minds working in the area at the time of the Brethren. She trawled through a couple of biographies of Al-Farabi, who was widely considered second only to Aristotle in his grasp of science and philosophy, earning him the moniker of Second Teacher. She read about Al-Razi, who would be known to the Europeans, much later, as Rhazes, the father of what we now refer to as plaster of paris, who was already using it to set broken bones in the tenth century; and Al-Biruni, who traveled extensively in the Far East and wrote extensive treatises about conjoined twins. More relevant to Mia's thinking, though, was Ibn Sina, or Avicenna, as he became known in the West. The most influencial physician of his time, Avicenna had become an accomplished philosopher and poet by the age of eighteen. By twenty-one, he'd written long, expert tracts about all the sciences known at the time. He differed from his predecessors in that he was more interested in the potential of chemicals to treat disease. In that vein, he'd studied illnesses such as tuberculosis and diabetes in great detail, and his masterwork, the fourteen-volume *Canon of Medicine*, was so authoritative and advanced that it remained the standard medical reference text in Europe until the 1600s—well over five hundred years after he wrote it.

All these men had achieved great advances in many disciplines. They studied the human body, identified diseases, and proposed cures. But nothing linked any of them to the Ouroboros, nor did she find anything in their work that had a nefarious aspect to it. They were simply interested in mastering the forces of nature.

If anything, these scientist-philosophers were interested in bettering mankind, not destroying it.

She picked up the photographs of the underground chamber and studied them again. She tried to imagine what went on there and considered it with new eyes. There was actually nothing sinister about it. She followed that line of thought and picked up a sheet from the file on which Evelyn had sketched out a plan of the chambers and marked it with what they'd found. They'd found no bones there, no traces of dried blood, no cutting tools or sacrificial altars. Evelyn seemed to have reached the same conclusion. At the bottom of the sketch, scribbled in her distinctive script, she'd written and underlined the word *Sanctuary*, followed by another question mark.

A sanctuary from what? Whom, or what, were they hiding from?

The battery in Mia's laptop died out, and as it did, a deep-seated tiredness swamped her. She put the file away and found her bed again.

This time, it didn't take her long to drift off into sleep, but as she did, one lingering, confused thought seemed determined to ride roughshod over any hopes of a peaceful rest: the idea of an ancient terror being resuscitated to unleash havoc on this world, presaged by the haunting image of the tail-devouring snake, which had inexorably wormed its way into the deepest recesses of her mind.

Chapter 32

ᴄᴏ᙭ᴏ ᴄ᙭ᴏ

Paris—October 1756

The false count navigated wearily through the hot, suffocating ball-room, his head pounding from the haughty chatter, the garish laughter, and the incessant, relentless music, his eyes assaulted by the sparks from the spinning Catherine wheels and the gloriously outlandish costumes of giraffes, peacocks, and other exotic animals that paraded before him.

It was on nights like these that he missed the Orient most. But he knew those days were long, long gone.

He cast his tired eyes around the great room, feeling every inch the impostor that he was. Papier-mâché animal heads sitting precariously on powdered wigs stared down at him and tall feathers tickled at his nostrils as, all around him, the guests at the Palais des Tuileries mingled and danced with abandon. Pearls and diamonds ensnared his gaze every-where he turned, shimmering under the light of hundreds of candles that carelessly soiled the carpets with mounds of molten wax. It wasn't his first ball, nor would it be his last. He knew he would suffer many more evenings like tonight's *bal de la jungle*, the jungle ball—more dreadful displays of unbridled pomp, more throwaway conversations, more unabashed flirtations. It was all part of the new life he'd created for himself, and his presence was expected—anticipated, even—at occasions like these. He also knew the pain wouldn't end here: In the days and nights to come, he would have to endure endless, giddy retellings, in countless salons, of the evening's public glories and of its more private, salacious goings-on.

It was a price he had to pay for access, and access was what he needed if he was ever to succeed, although, with each passing year, that success seemed more and more remote.

It was, truly, an impossible task.

Often, as tonight, he would find himself wandering, lost in his thoughts, trying to remember who he really was, what he was doing here, what his life was really about.

It didn't always come to him that easily.

More and more frequently, he was finding it hard to keep his creation at bay and not fully lose himself in his false persona. The temptation hounded him at every step. Each day, he passed scores of poor folk in the streets, men and women who would give their right arm for the life he enjoyed—the life they believed he was enjoying. He wondered if he hadn't struggled enough, if he hadn't hidden enough, if he hadn't been alone long enough. He felt tempted to abandon his quest and relinquish the role that had been entrusted to him in that dungeon in Tomar all those years ago, and to embrace his outwardly fortunate position, settle down, and live out the rest of his days in pampered comfort and—more important—in normalcy.

It was a temptation that was getting harder and harder to dispel.

∽∾∽

His journey to Paris had been anything but straightforward.

He'd managed to slip away from Naples, but he knew he wasn't safe anywhere, certainly not in Italy, and that di Sangro would not rest until he found him. He had seen it in the prince's eyes; he also knew the prince had the money and the manpower to track him down. And so he set out to muddy his trail, establishing new identities wherever he went before moving on and leaving behind confusing fabrications as to their backgrounds and their movements.

He had carefully seeded deceptions in Pisa, Milan, and Orléans on his way to the great city, taking on new names as he traveled forth: the Comte Bellamare, the Marquis d'Aymar, the Chevalier Schoening.

More names would—some justly, others falsely—come to be associated with him in the years to come. For now, however, he was comfortably settled into his Paris apartments and his new persona, that of the Comte de St. Germain.

Paris suited the count. It was a huge, bustling city—the largest human settlement in Europe—and it attracted plenty of travelers and adventurers, the boisterous as well as the discreet. His appearance there would be diluted by those of countless others. Here he could meet other travelers, men who, like him, had been to the Orient and who may have come across the symbol of the tail-eater in their travels. It was also a city of learning and discourse, and a repository of great knowledge, with rich libraries and untold collections of manuscripts, books, and relics, including the ones that were of particular interest to him: those pilfered from the Orient during the Crusades, and those confiscated after the suppression of the Templars almost five centuries earlier. The ones that could house the missing piece of the puzzle that had ambushed his life all those years ago.

He arrived in Paris at a time when the great city was in transition. Radical thinkers were challenging the twin tyrannies of monarchy and Church. The city was bubbling with contradiction and upheaval, with enlightenment and intrigue—intrigue that St. Germain put to good use.

Within weeks of his arrival, he managed to befriend the king's minister of war and with his help, he insinuated himself into the king's orbit. Impressing the aristocrats wasn't hard. His knowledge of chemistry and physics, gleaned from his years in the East, were enough to regale and hoodwink the debauched buffoons. His familiarity with foreign lands and his mastery of numerous languages—his French in Paris was as impeccable as his Italian was in Naples, to add to his fluent mastery of English, Spanish, Arabic, and his native Portuguese—were cautiously wielded if and when his notability needed an additional boost. He was soon comfortably ensconced in the king's coterie of pampered acolytes.

With his credentials established, he was able to resume his quest. He smooth-talked his way into the great houses of the nobility and into the most private of collections. He ingratiated himself with the clergy in order to delve through the libraries and crypts of their monasteries. He also read extensively, immersing himself in the travelogues of Tavernier, the studies of pathology of Morgagni, the medical treatises of

Boerhaave, and other great works that were appearing at the time. He'd studied Thomas Fuller's *Pharmacopoeia Extemporanea* and Luigi Cornaro's intriguing *Discourses on the Temperate Life* in great detail—the man had died a vibrant ninety-eight-year old. And while he gained a great wealth of knowledge from these works, he was no closer to a solution to his impossible quest.

The symbol of the tail-eater was nowhere to be found, nor did there seem to be any medical or scientific clues to overcoming the critical deficiency of the substance.

He hovered between enthusiasm and despair. New leads would excite him, and then, with each dead end, the doubts about his mission would resurface and further undermine his resolve. He wished he could share his burden with someone else, draft someone to help him and perhaps even take over from him, but after seeing how even the vaguest smell of it had turned di Sangro into an obsessed predator, he couldn't bring himself to risk approaching anyone else.

Many nights, he'd wonder whether ridding himself of the substance and of its demonic formulation would release him from its slavery. He managed to go without it a few times, but never for more than a week or two. And then a renewed sense of destiny would overcome him, and he'd resign himself to the only life he knew.

ᜰ

"I BEG YOUR PARDON, my dear sir."

The woman's voice jarred him out of his tortured daze.

He turned to see a bizarre herd of jovial revelers standing before him. Their expressions ranged from giddy to confused. An older woman nearing sixty in a ballooning sheep's costume gingerly inched forward from among them. Something about her sent shards of distress cutting through him. She studied him with a curious, perplexed expression on her round face before extending her hand and introducing herself as Madame de Fontenay. The name drove the shards in deeper. He masked his unease as he gave her a slight bow and took her hand.

"My dear count," she asked, flustered with nervous excitement, "would you have the kindness to tell me whether a close relative of yours was in Rome around forty years ago? An uncle, perhaps, or even"—she hesitated—"your father?"

The false count smiled effusively with practiced insincerity. "Quite possibly, madame. My family seems encumbered with an insatiable will to travel. As for my father, I'm afraid I couldn't tell you for certain. It was hard enough for me to keep up with his touring when I was a child, and I'm afraid I am completely in the dark as to his movements before my birth." The small herd chuckled loudly and far more generously than St. Germain's remark merited. "Why, if I may," he added, "do you ask?"

The curious look in her eye hadn't dulled. "I knew a man at the time. He paid me court, you see. I still remember our first encounter," she reminisced. "We sang a few barcaroles of his composing together, and . . ." A serene glimmer lit up her eyes as her mind seemed to wander back to that time. "His features, his hair, his complexion . . . even his carriage. He had the impress and the nobility that one only finds in the great." She seemed genuinely startled. "I see the same, all of it, in you."

St. Germain bowed with false modesty. "You are far too generous, madame."

The woman waved away his words. "Please, Count. I beseech you to think about it and let me know if I was indeed in the presence of a relation of yours. The similarity is simply too uncanny to discount."

St. Germain moved to put an end to his discomfort. He beamed at his inquisitor. "Madame, you are most kind to pay me such a compliment," he gushed. "I will not rest until I have conjured up the identity of my illustrious relation who so impressed you." He gave the woman a concluding half-bow, his body language coaxing her to move on, but she would not budge. She just stood there, transfixed by him.

"Most intriguing," she muttered to herself, before asking, "I am told you also play the piano divinely, Count. Perhaps you were taught by the man I remember."

He smiled at her, but his smile was having trouble reaching his eyes. He was about to answer when he noticed a familiar face watching him from beside the little menagerie. The woman—Thérésia de Condillac—seemed to be enjoying his little quagmire.

"Ah, there you are," she finally exclaimed as she stepped forward, a knowing gleam in her eye. "I've been looking everywhere for you."

Courteous bobs and bows and hasty introductions were exchanged before the woman hooked her arm into St. Germain's and—with the briefest of apologies—brazenly whisked him away from his stymied tormentor.

"I hope you don't mind my taking you away from such an ardent admirer, monsieur," she commented as they disappeared into the crowd.

"I'm not sure I would have used the word *ardent*. *Senile*, perhaps?"

"You mustn't be so unkind, Count." She laughed. "Judging from her rosy countenance, she might well lead you to some half brothers you weren't aware of."

They made their way to the gardens, which were lit up by torches and more spinning Catherine wheels. Wisps of smoke from the pyrotechnics hung low, obscuring the nearby riverbank. Elephants, zebras, and an array of monkeys, brought in from the royal menagerie at Versailles, were on display in the sprawling gardens, symbols of omnipotence to their royal owners, who were blissfully oblivious to the metaphors of slavery and oppression the less fortunate associated with the caged animals.

They found a quiet bench that sheltered under a chestnut tree and overlooked the quay, by the river's edge. They'd met a few weeks earlier, at Thérésia's uncle's house. St. Germain had sought the man out after hearing of his reputation as a keen orientalist who had a substantial collection of manuscripts from the region. They'd met again in the salon of Madame Geoffrin—coincidentally, he'd first thought, although, as the evening had progressed and her questions had become more personal, he'd been less certain of that. Not that he minded. Thérésia de Condillac was a much desired woman. She was blessed with a radiant femininity and was a childless, moneyed widow who didn't lack suitors and who didn't shy away from their advances.

They watched the army of revelers from a distance and exchanged pleasantries, occasionally at the expense of the more garishly costumed guests. Thérésia's costume was as minimalist as St. Germain's in its ambition: It consisted simply of a shawl of white feathers, which, thrown over her simple white ball dress, imbued her with the ethereal—and distinctly un-jungle-like—guise of a dove. St. Germain, wigless and head to toe in black, looked even less like the panther he claimed to be.

"My uncle tells me you've become a regular visitor to his house," she eventually mentioned. "He's most impressed by your knowledge of the Levant. He yearns to return to Constantinople, you know."

He turned to her. She seemed to be studying his face for his re-sponse. "I can understand his missing it. There is great comfort to be had from its"—he paused as he took in the surreal scene in the distance—"simplicity." And then, suddenly, as if to mock his very words, a fleeting image in the distance jolted him.

Through the mist from the fireworks, among the crowd of pastiche gorillas and ostriches, a pair of eyes materialized, staring straight at him, the eyes of a young man, his cheeks and forehead painted over heavily with streaks of gold and brown, his head covered by a curly blond wig that was pierced by animal ears, a thick mane of fur draped around his neck. He was peering out from among the throng like a tiger eyeing its prey through the thick blades of an African savanna.

The predator was there for only the briefest of moments before a small gaggle of guests obscured him. An instant later, after they'd passed, he was gone.

St. Germain blinked his eyes and scanned the distance, but there was no sign of the tiger. With the din from the crowd and the orchestra still pounding his senses, he asked himself if he'd even seen it in the first place. He shook the image away and focused on his companion again.

Thérésia seemed to notice his eyes wander, but didn't react to it. "Possibly," she just replied. "Then again, I suspect it may have more to do with his craving for some *mariage à la cabine*," she joked, refer-ring to a form of temporary marriage that was practiced there, *kabin*, in which Christian women could be hired by the month. "Which," she added with a pique of seriousness in her tone, "is something that I imag-ine would appeal to you too, if I'm not mistaken."

Her candor caught him out. "I imagine it would appeal to most men," he replied.

"Yes, but something about the impersonal, noncommittal nature of it—it seems particularly suited to you."

Her comment went to the heart of him. Not that it was unexpected. He'd cultivated the reputation of someone who valued his independence and his privacy and who, while he enjoyed the occasional intimate dalli-ance, had no appetite for attachment. But the way she said it, that slight knowing, sardonic edge in her voice, in her eyes—it was as if she could see through him. Which unsettled him.

"I'm not sure if I should take that as a compliment or as a rebuke," he countered cautiously.

"I'd say it's neither," she said playfully. "Just a passing comment from an intrigued observer."

"An observer? Am I to take it that I'm being studied, like one of these poor beasts?" he asked, waving at the nearest cage. Against his better judgment, he found himself scanning the crowd again for any sign of the prowling tiger. There was none.

"Hardly, my dear count," she reassured him. "Although I imagine anyone intrigued by you would find it intolerably frustrating, given your fondness for evasive replies to even the most basic of questions. I wonder, does anyone really know you, in the true sense of the word?"

He smiled at her question. He wanted to answer that he didn't really know himself, not anymore, and—oddly—he felt an urge to actually say those very words to her. But his instinctive shutters came back down at the mere hint of the thought. "Where would my allure be if I were an open book?" he said instead.

"Oh, I think your allure can withstand some measured disclosure. I just wonder if it's really a fear of scaring off your admirers, or rather, a fear of letting anyone in?"

He didn't rush to answer. Instead, he just held her gaze and basked in it, unsure about how to react.

After that dinner at Madame Geoffrin's salon, he'd inquired, discreetly, about Thérésia. She had a reputation of enjoying the company of men—men of her choosing—but lately, something had changed. She hadn't been romantically linked to any of her suitors for months. St. Germain wasn't conceited enough to think it had anything to do with him. Her retreat from promiscuity had taken place well before they'd first met. And while he'd had advances, too many to remember—the aristocracy in Paris was particularly debauched—this felt different. It felt less frivolous, somehow. More substantial.

Which was a problem.

St. Germain desperately wanted to be with her. There was something undeniably desirable about Thérésia de Condillac, but the very reasons he felt drawn to her were the same ones that made her too dangerous to invite into his life.

"I think you paint my life with far more flourish than it deserves," he finally replied.

Thérésia leaned in closer. "Why don't you tell me what secrets lurk in that impenetrable fortress of yours and let me be the judge of that?"

St. Germain shrugged. "I wouldn't presume to bore you with the banalities of my tiresome existence. But . . ." His voice drifted off. As alluring as her face was, he couldn't stop his eyes from sidetracking off into the distance, where, through the parade of gaudy costumes, he spotted the tiger again. As before, the man stood there, immobile behind the haze of moving revelers, staring unwaveringly at him. And, as before, he disappeared from view almost instantly.

A surge of unease swept through him. He suddenly felt exposed, endangered.

This time, Thérésia reacted to it. "Is everything alright, Count?"

St. Germain's tone didn't waver. "Of course. It's just that it's late, and I'm afraid I must excuse myself." He took her hand and kissed it.

She seemed slightly confounded by his leaving and gave him a wry smile. "Pulling the drawbridge up again, Count?"

"Until the siege is lifted," he replied as he gave her a half-bow, then walked away, feeling her gaze following him as he melted into the crowd.

ॐ

HE MOVED HURRIEDLY through the guests, his eyes darting left and right, his mind reeling from the surreal, beastly costumes that swirled around his every step, and headed straight for the main gate. He could feel his pulse racing in his ears as he exited the palace and waved to his coachman, who stood with a few other drivers by a small bonfire. The man ran off to fetch his carriage, and moments later they were heading east, down the Rue St.-Honoré, towards St. Germain's apartment on the Île de la Cité.

He sank back into the comfort of the coach's velour seat and shut his eyes. The rhythmic clatter of the horse's hoofbeats soothed him. He thought back and chided himself for the stab of panic that now seemed somewhat unwarranted. He wondered if his instincts hadn't been perturbed by Thérésia's presence, and somehow, thinking about her pushed away his unease and helped settle his tired mind. He realized he had to see her again. It was unavoidable. He turned towards the window and let the cool night air rush over his face.

The carriage turned right on Rue de l'Arbre Sec, and they were soon driving across the Pont Neuf. St. Germain had chosen the older Cité district over the other, newer neighborhoods of the city and had rented smart rooms that overlooked the river and the quays of the right bank. He found the flowing water comforting, despite the skim of floating detritus that befouled its surface. The breeze, which came down the Seine most days and nights, also helped lessen the stench from the household garbage and human waste that was habitually thrown straight out into the streets in the distasteful tradition of *tout à la rue*.

St. Germain looked out to his left as they crossed the bridge. It was a crisp autumn night, and the moon, which was almost at its fullest, suffused the city in a cool silvery glow. He loved the view from the bridge, especially after nightfall, when the tradesmen and the peddlers had packed up their wares and the strollers had turned in. The northern quay that stretched upstream was crowded with idle skiffs and sailboats and dotted by irregular bonfires. Farther on, the slate roofs of the row of buildings that squatted across the Pont Notre Dame shimmered in the moonlight, the faint light of taper candles twinkling from their windows. And beyond, the sublime Notre Dame loomed over the island, its spireless twin towers stretching up impossibly into the canopy of stars above, an edifice to the greatness of God that was, with each passing day, gaining acceptance as further proof of the genius of man.

They reached the western tip of the island and turned onto the Quai de l'Horloge, a narrow lane with a row of houses on one side and a low wall overlooking the river on the other. St. Germain's rooms were in a whitewashed building at the far end of the terrace. They were still fifty yards or so away from its entrance when he heard the coachman call out to his horse and pull on the brake. The carriage lurched to a premature halt.

St. Germain leaned out of his window, calling out to his driver, "Roger? Why are we stopped here?"

The coachman hesitated before answering. "Up ahead, *Monsieur le Comte*. Our path is blocked." His voice had an unfamiliar tremble in it.

St. Germain heard the neigh of a horse and looked down the road. The streets of Paris were lit that month, and in the dim glow of a suspended oil lantern, blocking the lane perhaps thirty yards ahead of the stopped carriage, were three horsemen. They just stood there, side by side, immobile.

He heard more hoofbeats approaching from the direction of the bridge and spun around to look back. Another horseman was coming down the quay, and as he passed under another lantern, St. Germain glimpsed the gold and black tiger's streaks painted across the rider's face, more threatening now under a flowing black cloak.

St. Germain turned in alarm at the horsemen blocking his route. His eyes scrutinized the darkness, filling in the shadowy features of the middle rider from the dark recesses of his memory. He'd barely managed to fully form the image when the familiar voice came bellowing out across the night.

"Buona sera, Marquese." Di Sangro's voice was just as St. Germain remembered it. Dry, sardonic, and raspy. "Or perhaps you'd prefer me to call you *gentile conte?*"

St. Germain rapiered a glance back at the approaching rider cutting off his retreat, whose masked face suddenly came alive in his mind's eye. He realized why the young man had unsettled him and remembered glimpsing him before, in a Paris café in recent weeks, as well as where they'd first met. In Naples. Years earlier. Briefly, upon visiting di Sangro's palazzo.

He was di Sangro's son. The deferential teenager, though, was gone, replaced by a young man who reeked of menace.

St. Germain slid a glance at his coachman, who was looking to him nervously. "Drive, Roger," he ordered him fiercely, "go through them."

The coachman yelled and whipped the horse, which burst into a gallop and charged forward. Looking out the window, St. Germain saw the horses blocking their path rear slightly backwards before one of the riders brought up something that glinted ominously in the moonlight. It took a split second for St. Germain to realize it was a crossbow, and before he could shout it down, the rider took aim and fired. The small arrow sliced the air with a sharp whisper and struck the coachman squarely in the chest. He let out a pained moan before slumping to one side and tumbling off the advancing carriage.

The riders spread out and edged forward, yelling and waving their arms at the confused horse that weaved erratically from side to side but kept charging ahead. The carriage rattled down the uneven paving, with St. Germain hanging on to the edge of its window, his mind racing through possible moves just as he glimpsed the rider on di Sangro's other flank raise another crossbow and fire at the horse.

From the sharp, pained whinny of the horse, St. Germain knew the arrow had buried itself deep into its flesh. The horse reared up, sending the carriage careening sideways unevenly. A wheel must have gotten hooked on the edge of a paving stone because St. Germain found himself hanging onto the window ledge as the light carriage bounced upwards and rolled heavily onto its side, sliding a few yards before grinding to a halt.

St. Germain shook himself back to consciousness and unfolded himself, his senses alert to the movement outside. The street had gone silent, the only noise disturbing the deathly stillness coming from the hooves of his attackers' horses as they slowly closed in around him. With his back to the blocked door under him, he curled his legs and kicked the opposite door open, then pulled himself out, aching and bruised from the tumble. He dropped to the ground and glanced up the street. The body of his coachman just lay there, immobile. St. Germain felt his anger swell up as he straightened his bruised body and stood up.

Up ahead, the three riders were now joined by di Sangro's son. *"Bravo, ragazzo mio,"* di Sangro congratulated him. *"Sei stato grande"*— you did well. He then turned to face St. Germain.

The four of them now stood there before him, bearing down on him, backlit by the grim lantern that swayed feebly overhead.

Di Sangro prodded his horse forward a few steps, his eyes locked on his prey. "That's quite a life you've made for yourself, *Marquese*. Paris will be sad to lose you."

"And Paris's loss will be Naples's gain, is that it?" St. Germain spat back.

Di Sangro smiled and dismounted. "Maybe not all of Naples's, but certainly mine." His son followed suit, while the other two riders remained on their mounts. The prince stepped closer to St. Germain, scrutinizing him as if for the first time. "You look well, *Marquese*. Extremely well, in fact. Could it simply be that this filthy Paris air suits you so?"

St. Germain said nothing. His eyes darted tensely from di Sangro to his son and back. The resemblance was strong, especially in the eyes, even more so now that the boy had turned into a man. Di Sangro himself had noticeably aged in the intervening years: heavier, paler, the skin on his face and neck sagging and lined. He cursed himself for not making the connection sooner, for not realizing who the young man was the minute he first laid eyes on him in that café. He'd always expected di Sangro to catch up with him at some point, and he'd had several years of peaceful, if guarded, anonymity. He knew his life in Paris was now over, but, more immediately, he needed to do something if he was going to have any chance of setting up another existence.

His mind frantically processed his options, but there weren't many. A thought, however, blazed through the bleak scenarios like a beacon, a simple realization that colored his reactions in the various confrontations with di Sangro that he'd played out in his mind over the years: Di Sangro needed him alive. The threats of revelation or death were hollow: He knew di Sangro would do his best to keep him alive and use all the methods at his disposal, however grisly and for as long as it took, to wring the truth out of him.

It was, however, a double-edged sword. Alive was only an attractive option as long as he was free. Captivity, and torture, were far less desirable. Especially given the doubts he harbored about how long his resolve would resist.

He was boxed in. The two riders had stationed themselves to either side of their master, blocking both routes of escape. Behind him was the wall of the building, its entrance door beyond shuttered up since sundown. And facing him, behind di Sangro and his son, was the low wall and the river.

St. Germain took a deep breath and pulled out his sword. "You know I can't go with you," he told di Sangro flatly. "And there is nothing here for you."

Di Sangro smiled coldly and waved at his men. "I don't think you have much choice, *Marquese*." He drew his sword and held it up to St. Germain, as did his son. From the corner of his eye, the count noted that the riders with the crossbows had also reloaded.

St. Germain edged sideways, keeping the prince and his son at bay with the tip of his sword. Much as he felt tired and weary from the burden he had carried across the continents, this wasn't the release he was looking for. He couldn't accept the idea of capture, not by this man. He was ready to resist it with his every breath, although he knew that if he died, the secret, as far as he knew, would die with him. He wondered if that would be, on balance, a good thing—or did he owe it to the world to keep the knowledge alive, even if it was in the hands of a maniacal and selfish man such as di Sangro?

No, he had to stay free. He had to stay alive. He wasn't ready to die. And, he now also realized, he couldn't keep it to himself anymore. It was too dangerous. If he managed to get away this time and continued with his quest, he had to enlist others, regardless of the dangers involved. He just had to choose better.

A fierce determination raced through his veins, and he lunged ferociously at the two men. As their swords clashed noisily in the deserted street, he noticed that di Sangro had slowed a bit since their last encounter, but his son had more than taken up the slack. The young man was a gifted swordsman. He countered St. Germain's swings with surgical efficiency and seemed to predict the count's moves unerringly. The prince edged back, content with acting as a barrier to St. Germain's escape, as his son took over, lunging and swinging his blade at the count. The son's cloak had slipped off his head, and in the feeble light of a nearby suspended lantern, the tiger markings streaked across his face now looked positively demonic, heightening the predatory scowl in his eyes and unnerving St. Germain.

The son's blade was now slicing the air faster and more viciously, with St. Germain struggling to parry and block the onslaught. As they stomped through the central gutter and its filthy slush, St. Germain scuttled to his side to avoid another big swing and his shoe caught on a paving stone, throwing him off-balance. Di Sangro's son grabbed the opening and bolted forward, lunging at St. Germain. The count recovered his footing and darted to his right, but couldn't fully avoid the blade, which cut into his left shoulder and sent a burning pain searing through him. He raised his sword back in time to deflect his attacker's next swing and stepped back to regroup.

They circled each other like jungle cats, their eyes locked on each other, the clanging of their swords now replaced by their labored breathing. A leering smile curled up the sides of the young man's fine lips, and he slid a glance at his father, who gave him a pleased and approving nod. St. Germain saw an unguarded cockiness in the young man and a mirrored pride in his father as he felt the blood trickling down the inside of his sleeve. The wound was going cold, and with it, the pain would be getting more intense and the muscles would stiffen. He had to move fast, even though he knew he wasn't going to defeat all four men.

He knew where he had to strike.

He summoned all the energy he could muster and struck out at the prince's son with renewed vigor, lashing his blade at him from all sides and forcing him back a few steps until he was trudging through the central gutter and its pile of sludge. The young man seemed taken aback by St. Germain's determined attack, and as he fought back the deluge of demented lunges and swings, he shot a doubting glance at his father, as if looking to him for reassurance. St. Germain saw the split second of weakness and attacked. His blade plunged into the young swordsman's side, making him howl with pain.

The prince's son stumbled backwards with a shocked, almost disbelieving look as he touched his wound and brought up his bloodied hand. Di Sangro saw his son stagger through the filth and raced forward to him, calling out his name, "Arturo." His son shook his pain away and stayed him by holding up his hand and turned to St. Germain. He raised his sword, but his legs faltered as he took a step forward.

Di Sangro yelled out, *"Prendetelo,"* to his men—get him—and rushed to his son's aid. St. Germain watched as the two riders dismounted and converged on him, cutting off both ends of the street. Their crossbows blinked at him through the darkness. He looked behind him—the low wall edging the lane was within reach. He bolted and, reaching it, flung his sword over and clambered onto it. Flames of pain shot through his shoulder as he pulled himself onto the ledge. He righted himself and stood up.

Below him was the Seine, cold and littered with detritus, only this time, the water, flowing slowly and shimmering under the moonlight, wasn't comforting. It made him dizzy. He sucked in some night air and turned back to face the street. Di Sangro saw him standing there. Their eyes locked for a brief moment, and St. Germain saw the pain, the anger, and the utter desperation radiating from di Sangro, who then yelled out, "Don't be foolish, *Marquese*—"

But before the prince could do or say anything else, St. Germain just turned away, closed his eyes, and stepped off the ledge, letting himself drop into the river.

He hit the water hard and sank deep into its murky darkness. Tumbling over himself, he was momentarily disoriented and couldn't tell which way was up. His arms flailed as he spun over himself aimlessly, his ears throbbing from the changing pressure, his lungs aching for air. He tried to calm himself, but the cold was biting into him and he could feel his head going woolly. As he spiraled down, he caught a glimpse of what he thought could be a reflection on the surface and decided to head for it, but the weight of his clothes was pulling him down. He reached down and managed to pull off his sodden shoes, but his clothes were locked in place by rows of buttons, layer upon layer of the finest material, breeches, shirt, cravat, waistcoat, and justaucorps that now clung tightly to his skin and inhibited his movements.

He felt as if the devil himself were reaching up and dragging him down to his death, and in that brief moment, he felt a perverse relief at ending it all, here and now, but something made him fight to stay alive and he thrashed away with his limbs, pushing against the water desperately until he made it back to the surface.

He broke through and found himself floating down the Seine among scattered pieces of timber and rotten fruit. He had drifted away from the Île de la Cité and was in the middle of the river, moving slowly back in the direction of the Tuileries. He fought against the tide, swallowing up big gulps of filthy water and coughing it up, his drenched clothes still weighing him down, his arms hitting blindly against floating debris and garbage. He fought as he'd never fought before, struggling to stay alive, to stay afloat, all the time trying to edge closer to the right bank, to dry land. Inch by inch, the bonfires of the homeless, scattered along the quays to his right, drew nearer, and by the time he grabbed a rusted iron ring that stuck out from the stone pier along the riverbank, he'd lost all track of time.

He dragged himself out of the water and lay on his back, sucking in grateful gulps of air, letting his drained body regain some semblance of life. He didn't know if it was minutes or hours later, but it was still dark when he heard a voice he thought he recognized calling out to him. He thought he was dreaming when, moments later, Thérésia's angelic face came beaming down at him from among the stars, muttering words that he couldn't quite comprehend.

He felt his battered body being lifted under the shoulders by a man, and aided by Thérésia, he soon found himself wrapped in a thick blanket and ensconced in the cushioned comfort of a great carriage that whisked him away from the rats and the brigands and burrowed into the dark streets of the city of light.

ᮎᮧᮎᮧ

As THEY DROVE to Thérésia's apartment, questions swamped St. Germain, and his confused mind struggled to process the answers she gave him.

She told him that she had noticed that something seemed to have unnerved him at the ball, and that as he had headed out of the palace, she had spotted a man dressed as a tiger shadowing him. She had left the ball soon after them, having lost interest, and her coachman had told her that the man had indeed followed the count out and trailed his carriage. She had headed off after them, sensing trouble, and had witnessed the fight from the bridge, too afraid to intercede. After St. Germain had jumped into the river, she'd thought he had drowned. Her coachman had spotted him floating down the middle of the river and, ultimately, brought her to him.

The words didn't fully register with St. Germain, but he didn't mind. For now, he was happy to be alive and happy to be with her. Deep down, he knew this would only be temporary, but he didn't want to think about that right now. He just let himself drift away into the comfort of her arms and tried to shut the world out for as long as he could.

She took him to her apartment, in the newly fashionable Marais district, and had her maid draw up a hot bath. She helped him out of his clothes and into the tub, and later, after she'd dressed his wound and fed him, they put out all the candles save for a solitary one by the bed and made love with ravenous abandon.

He woke up with the first hints of sunlight and watched her sleeping by his side. His shoulder still hurt, but at least the wound had stopped bleeding. He ran his hand gently down to the small of her back, relishing the smoothness of her skin under his fingers, and dreading the inevitable reinvention that he'd soon have to undertake.

Watching her breathing peacefully by his side, his mind escaped to a sunnier life where he didn't have to live a lie, and where he could take pleasure in the ever-dwindling time he had left. He found himself asking himself the same question that had been tormenting him of late, wondering again about the validity of the quest he had devoted his life to, about whether it was time to finally give it all up and retreat into a blissfully mundane existence.

As he pondered the journey of his life, he also found himself doubting what he would ultimately achieve even if he did succeed in finding what he was looking for.

Finding it was one thing.

Announcing it, revealing it to the world, and making sure that it was available and shared by all . . . that was a far more insurmountable challenge.

The world wasn't ready for it, so much was certain. Powerful forces would be aligned to smother it, to keep it from altering—and empowering—mankind. Immortality—spiritual, individual immortality, that is—was a gift only religion was allowed to bestow. Nothing else could be allowed to alleviate the dread of the specter of death's inevitable and irresistible invitation. The gift he was pursuing was sacrilegious, unthinkable. The Church would never allow it. Who was he to overcome such venomous hostility?

Confusion flooded his mind. Countering his weariness and his feelings of despair was the observation that, despite everything, the future held promise. With every passing year, he felt the winds of change blowing through the cities of men around him. Salons and coffeehouses were brimming with new ideas that were challenging ignorance, tyranny and superstition. Religious dogma and persecution were being undermined. Rousseau, Voltaire, Diderot, and others were feverishly working while warding off the suppression of their works by the ever-present Jesuits. People were finding themselves lifted and inspired by the words of great thinkers who believed that man was essentially good, and that happiness in this earthly life, achieved through social fraternity and advances in sciences and in arts, was a far more sensible and noble aspiration than hoping to reach paradise through penitence.

They were beginning to dare to value their lives more than their afterlives.

But there was still a lot to overcome. Poverty and sickness, chiefly. Premature death lurked around every corner, and the most brilliant minds were still trying to understand what the human body was made of and how it worked. This would be a huge distraction to their work, and it could have disastrous effects. And beyond all that was the seemingly intractable issue of man's greed, his innate propensity to covet and amass. As St. Germain had witnessed, firsthand, in di Sangro.

St. Germain looked at the sleeping silhouette by his side. He reached out and stroked her naked shoulder. He studied her face, radiant even in sleep, and saw promise and inspiration in its finely sculpted lines, and it tormented him. Something deep within him tore.

He felt exhausted.

Perhaps it was all unattainable. Perhaps it was time to be selfish.

Perhaps it was time to give up.

The thought brought him comfort. But there were more pressing problems to solve.

Either way, he'd have to leave. He had the ability to travel and reinvent himself. He'd undertaken a couple of sensitive missions for the king, who, in another misguided attempt to assert himself, had instituted *le Secret du Roi*, the "King's Secret," a covert network of agents he would send abroad to pursue objectives that were mostly opposed to his publicly announced policies, such as seeking peace with the British. St. Germain could make use of the system to slip away and resettle in secret.

With a heavy heart, he knew it was the only option.

As if reading his mind, Thérésia stirred beside him and stretched awake. Her face beamed with a luminous smile as she curled her body into his.

She seemed to read the expression on his face, and her face darkened for a quiet moment, before she asked uncertainly, "You're going to leave Paris, aren't you?"

He couldn't bring himself to lie, not to her. He simply nodded without taking his eyes off her.

She held his gaze, then leaned in and gave him a languorous kiss. When she finally pulled back, she simply said, "I want to go with you."

He looked at her and smiled.

Chapter 33

❦

The campus was barely stirring to life as Ramez moved cautiously down the quiet, tree-shaded lane that led to Post Hall.

He'd hardly slept. He'd watched his clock tick the interminable hours away, minute by minute, and by the time the sun had finally deigned to make its appearance, he couldn't take the confinement anymore. Hesitantly, he'd emerged from his apartment and made his way to the university, looking over his shoulder, scanning the street as he hurried along, alert to anything that looked even remotely out of the ordinary.

The building itself was deserted this early in the morning. The most conscientious of the staff didn't come in before seven thirty, which wasn't for another half hour. He paced around his office, looking out onto cypress trees outside, stealing anxious glances at the cell phone on his desk, tormented by indecision—and by fear.

As he heard the first of his colleagues trickling into the department, he decided to put an end to the ulcerous pain that was knotting up his chest and grabbed his phone.

❦

THE FERRET WATCHED intently as the taller detective spoke on the phone. Reading between the lines, he realized what was going on. His suspicions were soon confirmed once his partner hung up. The man who'd called worked with the kidnapped American professor at the university. He'd been contacted by the Iraqi antiques smuggler they were looking for, who wanted to make a deal before coming in. He was scared.

The taller detective had told him to stay put; he and his partner would be there shortly.

He told the ferret to get ready to head out to the university with him and picked up his cell phone to make a call. He wasn't exactly bolting out the door at the news. That was good.

The ferret guessed he'd be calling the American agent to give him the news. He had to move fast. They weren't paying him to stand idle.

He had to let them know. Then he had to delay things at the station long enough for them to get there first.

He told his partner he needed to take a quick leak, then left the room. He found a quiet corner in an interview room, made sure he wouldn't be overheard, and speed-dialed Omar's number.

〜

THE BRIEF CELL-PHONE RING echoed through the apartment and roused Mia from an almost comatose sleep. She sat up and rubbed her eyes, feeling groggy. She wasn't sure what time it was. The room was completely dark, the outside world ruthlessly blotted out by roller shutters. She noticed some sunlight creeping in from under the bedroom door and realized it was morning.

She was surprised at how deeply she'd been gone, given the circumstances. She ran her hands through her hair, pulled on her pants, and stumbled out of the bedroom to find Corben in the kitchen. He was already dressed and was talking into the phone while stuffing some files—including the one he'd taken from Evelyn's apartment—into his briefcase.

His body language, focused and urgent, sent a spasm of dread down Mia's spine.

He saw her and tilted the phone upwards, away from his mouth. In a low but firm voice, he said, "We've got to go." His steely expression filled in the rest. They had to go *now*. Her questions would have to wait.

She'd hardly managed to get her shoes on before they were heading down in the elevator to the underground garage. Corben filled her in as they hurried into his Cherokee, and within minutes they were rushing towards the university.

"They're sending a couple of men over," Corben concluded, "but I'd rather have Ramez in our custody than in theirs when that call comes in."

He checked his watch. Mia checked hers. "So this Farouk's supposed to call him at noon?"

Corben nodded. "We've got about four hours."

Mia's mind was racing ahead questioningly, a surge of adrenaline flooding her senses. "So why wasn't he picking up his phone last night when you tried calling him? What if it had been Farouk? What if he's changed his mind, or something's happened to him?"

Corben shrugged. "I guess we'll know in four hours' time."

"He should've picked up his phone," she insisted.

Corben turned to her. "This is good. At least he's made contact."

Mia took in a deep breath and settled back in her seat, trying to subdue the methodical, analytic scientist inside her, but there were too many unknowns, too many possible variants, for her to switch off. "What if Farouk's watching him? You don't want to scare him off."

"If he's watching, he'll see you," Corben reassured her. "And that should give him some comfort, maybe even encourage him to come out."

Mia nodded to herself and turned away, looking ahead as the street tore past. She didn't like the silence. It allowed her to take stock of what she was actually doing, and with that came apprehension. She thought again of her mom, of what she must be feeling. She tried to calm herself by thinking forward and imagining a best-case, uneventful scenario—they pick up Ramez, Farouk calls, he's brought in, and either they act on his information to track down the hakeem and free Evelyn, or they get the smuggled pieces and trade them for her freedom, and everyone lives happily ever after. But her mind refused to cooperate, insisting instead on fleshing out outcomes that were far less rosy and, despite her best efforts to block them, involved a lot of suffering and a disturbing number of deaths.

Corben made a right turn at the bottom of Rue Abdel Aziz onto the tail end of Bliss and turned into the circular driveway of the main entrance to the university. The Medical Gate, as it was known, was shrouded in darkness at all times of day by the sweeping canopy of a gargantuan, ancient banyan tree. He pulled right up to the cast-iron gate. Vehicular access to the campus was tightly controlled due to the local penchant for car bombs, but Corben's Jeep had the diplomatic 104 plates that indicated it was affiliated to the U.S. embassy and enjoyed special privileges. Sure enough, the guard manning the gatehouse spotted the plates and, after a cursory glance inside the car, waved them in.

They pulled into a parking spot under a row of stately cypress trees up the road from Post Hall. Mia felt her nerves tingling as she followed Corben out of the car. She noticed him look around as if to make sure no one was watching before he opened the SUV's tailgate. The trunk was bare, aside for a latch in its carpeted floor, which Corben unlocked. He gave the surroundings another quick once-over before opening the concealed lid. Neatly strapped into place and tucked away inside the compartment was a small armory: shotgun, submachine gun, a couple of automatics, and several boxes of rounds. The tingle grew more pronounced as Corben pulled out one of the handguns, rammed a full magazine in, and tucked it into his belt underneath his jacket.

He slammed the lid shut and seemed to spot the apprehension in her expression. "Just in case," he reassured her.

"Good idea," she muttered, unsure whether to feel relieved that he was armed this time.

They walked past a couple of students who were hanging out before class and entered the old stone building. There was no receptionist in the lobby—the Archaeology Department was small, with no more than a dozen or so full-time staff. Mia knew that Evelyn's office was on the upper floor and led Corben past the empty lecture hall and the entrance to the campus museum and up the stairs.

They checked the rooms as they walked down the corridor until they came to Ramez's office. His door was open. The assistant professor's face lit up with alarm when he spotted them, then his expression turned to confusion as he seemed to recognize Mia.

"I'm Evelyn's daughter." She smiled, trying to put him at ease. "We met here before, remember? In her office?"

"Of course." His eyes were still fearful as they darted from her to Corben and back. He wanted to mouth some more words, but Corben didn't give him that chance and took over.

"I'm with the American embassy," Corben informed him flatly. "We're trying to find Evelyn, and we're hoping you can help us. The Fuhud detectives you called up told me about the man who came to see you yesterday, Farouk. We really need to talk to him to see if he can help us secure her release."

"He's going to call me at noon." Ramez's voice quivered uncomfortably.

Corben pointed at the cell phone on the desk. "That one?"

Ramez nodded. "They said they were coming here. They said they'd tell me what to say."

"I'd prefer it if you came with us to the embassy," Corben said. "You'll be safer there. Just until we bring Farouk in."

Ramez's eyes widened at the mention, and he took an instinctive step backwards. "Safer?"

"Just a precaution," Corben assured him. "We don't know how well connected these guys are, but they seem to know what they're doing. They're also looking for Farouk. I can't guarantee your safety anywhere else." He paused, clearly letting the warning sink in.

From the grim expression on Ramez's face, it seemed to have sunk him with it.

"We should go," Corben told him soberly as he stepped to the desk and picked up the phone. He handed it to Ramez, who took it, looked at it for a moment, and slipped it into the front pocket of his jeans. "I'll let the detectives know you're with us." He saw some lingering anxiety in the assistant professor's eyes. "You'll be fine. Let's go."

Ramez glanced at Mia. She gave him a small nod and a supportive half-smile. He shrugged and nodded back with grim acceptance.

Corben led the way as they exited the building and walked back to the car. He scanned the quiet surroundings—the university's campus was an oasis of tranquillity even during the worst of times—as he ushered Ramez into the backseat. Moments later, the big gates parted again and the big gray Cherokee rejoined the noisy streets of Beirut.

Corben waited for a couple of cars to pass before cutting across Rue Bliss in the opposite direction and heading up the big, open intersection that fronted the university's entrance. He glanced in the mirror at Ramez and reached for his cell phone to call the Fuhud detectives.

The assistant professor was staring nervously ahead, his face riven with unease—and just then, something else rushed into the mirror, a dark shadow accompanied by a strained engine growl and an earsplitting screech of tires, and a split second later, something rammed the Cherokee full force from behind.

Chapter 34

⌒⌒

Corben's hands tightened against the steering wheel as the Jeep lurched forward from the collision, the power of the impact launching Mia and Ramez against their seat belts as they screamed in panic.

Corben flicked a glance through his mirror and saw the car, a large, dark Mercedes that he recognized from outside Evelyn's apartment, fall back a bit as the Cherokee disengaged briefly from its attacker, the momentum of the hit propelling it forward, but before he could floor the pedal to try to outrun them, the charging car screamed forward and rammed the back of the Cherokee again, hitting it at a slight angle this time and sending it swerving wide and out of control. The parked cars to their right flashed past in a blur before the Cherokee's front bumper clipped one of them and spun on itself, plowing into the small gap between two of the cars, its air bags popping open and slamming into Corben and Mia as the big SUV bulldozed through the cars in an orgy of mangled steel and exploding rubber before skidding to a lung-wrenching stop.

Less than five seconds had passed from the moment of the first impact.

Dazed, his vision blurred and his ears ringing, Corben heard the attacking car screeching to a halt somewhere nearby, off to his left. He knew they had seconds to live if they didn't move with lightning speed.

He couldn't see anything out of the windshield, which had spider-webbed, but his own window was open and he saw the doors to the attackers' car swing open and armed men emerging, one of them, the pockmarked man he recognized from the chase outside Evelyn's apartment, spewing out loud orders in Arabic. Corben shot a glance at Mia, who looked shell-shocked but seemed unhurt, next to him, an air bag pinning her against her seat, and pulled out his gun. Without flinching, he put a bullet in his air bag, then one in hers. They flattened with a sudden outpouring of air. Crouching low, he swung his arm towards his window and loosed a few rounds at the hit men, sending them scattering for cover as he yelled to Mia, "Get out, that way, go!" and stabbed a finger towards her door.

Mia unclipped her seat belt and tugged at the door latch desperately. The door wouldn't open, its frame bent from the collision. "It's stuck," she shouted back as she pushed, putting her weight into it. "It won't open!"

"Get it open now or we're dead," Corben yelled as he fired out his window again, peppering the street around them with bullets, buying them a few more seconds. "Ramez, get out of the car, away from the street," he ordered. He edged upwards for a peek over the headrest of his seat, towards the back of the car, and saw the tips of Ramez's fingers poking up from the back, shivering nervously. "Ramez," he shouted again, but the assistant professor didn't answer him, instead muttering something angrily in Arabic that Corben couldn't make out.

Mia slammed her shoulder into the door and it groaned open a couple of inches. She kicked and pushed at it until it was wide enough for them to climb out. "Okay," she screamed.

Corben herded her out frantically, yelling, "Get out and stay low," as he fired a few more rounds before crawling across the seat behind her, head down, and slithering out of the car headfirst onto the sidewalk. "Ramez," he shouted as he pounded on the back door. He craned his head up to look into the car, but had to duck down, cursing, as a volley of bullets crunched into the other side of the car and splattered against the wall behind him.

He heard the leader of the killers shout something out in Arabic—"We need him alive, don't kill the professor"—and a second later Ramez screamed back in Arabic, "I'm coming out, don't shoot!"

Corben yelled, *"No!"* as he heard the opposite passenger door creak open. He spun to Mia, ordered her, "Stay down," clenched the gun in both fists, and took in a deep breath before springing upwards, finger on the trigger, only to find Ramez, his hands raised, stumbling away from the Cherokee, towards two of the killers who had now emerged from their cover. The sight down the nozzle of Corben's handgun found one of them and he loosed a couple of rounds. The man snapped backwards and yelped in pain as his shoulder erupted in a red puff of blood. Corben swung across to fire at the other man but hesitated for a split second as Ramez was in his line of fire, and before he could find the shot, the pockmarked leader of the hit team swung out from his cover and fired back. Corben ducked down as the rounds hammered their way into the car's bent panels like rivets while others sizzled past, skimming the stranded SUV's roof and biting into the wall beyond.

Mia and Corben huddled against the Cherokee and crouched low, with their backs against the car, Corben scanning left and right, mind racing frantically, Mia watching him with her heart in her throat.

He heard some more hurried orders in Arabic—"Finish them off, hurry, we have to move"—and tensed up as he peeked over the doorsill and glimpsed two of the killers converging on the Cherokee, one from either side, while Ramez was being shoved into the big sedan by the leader. Corben took in a big gulp of air, raised a cautioning finger at Mia, and waited a split second, listening carefully to the rushing, approaching footsteps before rolling to his side, towards the back of the beached SUV, and, staying low, raising his gun to fire from under the vehicle at the feet of one of the killers who was now less than ten feet away. He steadied his grip and ripped out three quick shots and saw bursts of blood erupt from the man's ankles before he toppled over, screaming in agony.

The move took the other killer by surprise. He freaked out, unleashing a ferocious barrage of bullets at the SUV, cursing maniacally at the top of his voice as the rounds tore through the metal and the seats and exploded any remaining windows, before the gang's leader ordered him back to the car with a fierce yell. The crazed shooter kept cursing out loud and firing as he retreated to the sedan.

Corben felt his jaw muscles tighten as he waited for him to turn and climb in, figuring that would give him the opening to take him out. Sure enough, the wild firing stopped a couple of seconds later. Corben visual-ized him getting into the car, and just when he imagined the man would be most vulnerable, half into the car, he darted out from behind the SUV and fired, only the car's door was already swinging shut, and more worrying, the man whose ankles he'd obliterated was turning to face him and raising his submachine gun at him. Corben quickly dropped to one side and fired off four rounds into the writhing man's chest and skull before watching the Merc tearing down the street until it disap-peared from view around a corner.

Corben got up, the staccato beating of his heart pounding deafen-ingly in his ears. He stepped out into the street and checked the downed killer. There was little doubt that the man was dead. He looked around him, taking in the otherworldly, deathly silence after the ear-shattering chaos of only seconds ago, and called out to Mia, "You okay?"

Mia emerged from behind the SUV, covered in dust and with dead-ened eyes, but otherwise intact. "Yeah," she said, nodding as she came around the battered car and joined him.

The whole experience had been mind-blowingly brief and intense, and she felt shell-shocked and yet, oddly, desensitized. The crash, the bullets—she felt strangely dissociated from it, as if it had happened to someone else. It was all such a blur, a confusing, manic storm, one that she'd somehow survived.

She saw the dead killer lying in the middle of the road and wanted to turn away, but couldn't, not immediately. Something made her get closer to it. She took a long, cold look at his body—one of his feet had been sheared right off at the ankle, a bloody mess splattered on the asphalt around it—and at his hard, lifeless face, before glancing up at Corben.

He looked at her, as if trying to suss out how she was feeling. Some-how, she didn't feel devastated. She didn't feel scared, she didn't feel like crying. She felt different.

She felt angry.

And right there and then, standing in the middle of that dusty road, with blood pooling under the dead killer and steam pouring out of the SUV's engine and stunned civilians emerging from every corner and converging on them in shocked silence, what she wanted most in the world was to make sure the bastards that did this, the bastards who had kidnapped her mother and killed those soldiers and had now also taken away Ramez, the pathological psychopaths who destroyed lives and rode roughshod over this city as if it were their little fiefdom, meting out pain and suffering with galling indifference, were stopped with—to use an expression for whose meaning she now had a whole new appreciation—extreme prejudice.

Chapter 35

Corben had just finished checking the dead killer's body for anything that would lead back to the hakeem, or for a cell phone—neither of which he found—when the Fuhud detectives barreled in.

With them there to arrange for carting off the dead body and the wrecked Cherokee, he was good to go. He didn't want to hang around there any longer than he had to, and he didn't have to. Filling in the detectives was a courtesy, to keep them sweet, but the clock was ticking. Farouk would be calling Ramez in less than four hours' time, and with Ramez in the hands of the enemy, Corben had to move fast.

He recovered his briefcase, and not holding out much hope, he checked the back of the Cherokee for Ramez's phone in case it had fallen out of his pocket in the chaos. It wasn't there. He dropped to one knee and swept his eye under the car too, but there was no sign of it there either. He made sure the weapons cache in the trunk was solidly locked, and after giving the two detectives a clipped briefing of what had happened and telling them to clear the area as quickly as possible and not to release anything to the press just yet, he turned down their offer of a ride and, instead, hailed a passing taxi to take him and Mia up to the embassy in Awkar.

MIA LOOKED BACK at the receding scene of the shoot-out through the rear windshield of the taxi as it drove off towards East Beirut and the hills beyond.

She was still dazed by what had erupted around her only minutes earlier, and a tangle of frenzied, jarring images flooded her mind. She settled back into the subdued normality of the comfortable car—the driver, who hardly spoke any English, had his radio on, piping mind-numbingly upbeat Arabic music around her, while Corben was on the phone with someone at the embassy—letting her mind settle down, until she found herself processing what had happened with more clarity. As the tightly packed, somewhat shabby stucco apartment buildings streamed by, she wondered where Ramez was being taken to. She pictured him in some grimy, windowless room somewhere—perhaps where Evelyn was being held too—and flashed forward to Farouk's imminent phone call. She felt a sudden upwelling of worry as she played out its implications in her mind.

She heard Corben end his phone call, and given that the taxi had been picked out randomly off the street and that the driver's failed attempt at casual conversation had clearly shown how virtually nonexistent his English was, she felt it was safe to talk. She turned to Corben.

"We need to find a way to warn Farouk," she urged him. "If he calls Ramez, he'll be walking into a trap."

"You're assuming they know he's expected to call him."

She hadn't thought it through, but it seemed to make sense to her. "Why else would they grab him? The timing's a bit too perfect for it to be just a coincidence, don't you think? I mean, Ramez calls in to say he's in touch with him, and boom, they show up and grab him?" The idea seeded her with more unease. She lowered her voice, feeling more aware of the driver's presence. "Last night, you said you didn't want to flag Ramez to the local cops. You must think the kidnappers have a mole at the station, right?"

Corben glanced at the driver. Mia followed his gaze. The driver seemed to be uninterested.

"I'd be amazed if they didn't," Corben said in a muted, unfazed tone.

"Which means they know Farouk's going to call him," she pressed, whispering conspiringly now. "You need to do something to warn him. What about putting something out on the news? Get the main local stations to say that Ramez's been kidnapped, maybe even give Farouk a signal to come in, to call the cops or—no," she quickly corrected herself, "to call you, to call the embassy directly."

"If he finds out that Ramez's been kidnapped," Corben countered, "he'll run. He'll be so scared he won't trust anyone. He'll just disappear. And if he does, we'll lose our only link to your mom."

"But he'll be walking into a trap."

Corben's expression suggested he had already thought of that. "Maybe we can use that."

Which took her aback. "What do you mean?"

Corben hesitated. "I mean we might have a chance to get Farouk and flush these guys out at the same time." He darted another glance at the driver. "Let's not get into it right now."

She got his drift. She still didn't think there was any risk in discussing it, but she relented and sat back in her chair and looked out her window, uncomfortable with the notion of using Farouk as bait.

The taxi cruised along the seafront, past the new marina where gleaming hundred-foot yachts mingled uncomfortably with rickety wooden fishing boats, and onto the highway that led to East Beirut. The city bubbled on regardless, turning a jaded eye to the not-so-infrequent acts of violence that would have caused huge outrage in other countries. As the fruit and vegetable vendors rushed by, something kept nagging at her, the question that wouldn't go away and that, once you got past the priority of getting Evelyn back, was really at the heart of everything that was happening.

She turned to Corben again. "What is he after? What the hell does he want with some moldy old book?"

"I don't know," Corben simply answered.

"But you must have researched it. You must have some theory about what it's about, what he's looking for, don't you?"

Corben slid another glance in the driver's direction, then looked at Mia. "Like I said. It's not necessarily relevant."

"Not relevant?"

"You're trying to apply your logic, your way of thinking, to what maniacs like this guy are about," he clarified. "But that's not how it works. We're talking about some very sick people here, guys who are certifiably insane. Saddam, his sons, his cousins . . . these guys lived in their own fantasy world. People's lives had no value for them. You know those kids who get their kicks plucking wings off butterflies or blowing up frogs with firecrackers? These guys are like that, only for them, humans are much more fun than frogs."

"Okay, I understand that, but I still don't get his interest in ancient relics."

"It could be anything," Corben replied. "Remember Mengele's experiments? Hitler's obsession with the occult? Maybe it's some cult from history that he feels connected to. The key word here is *insane*. Once you factor that in, anything's possible. There was a scientist working on a biological weapons program in South Africa a few years back, in the days of apartheid. You know what his pet project was? An ethno-specific bioweapon. He was developing a virus that would only kill black people. And that was after they'd started putting stuff in the water to make them infertile. And it's doable. Anything's doable when it comes to killing people. So you tell me. Is our guy after some ancient recipe for something, some virus, some old plague or poison that holds some poetic appeal to him? Or is he just some demented nut whose obsessiveness will help bring about his downfall? I'd go with the latter."

Mia thought about it for a moment. Maybe it wasn't that relevant after all. The point was to free Evelyn and, as a bonus, take down the hakeem. Still, it was bugging her. "Iraq, Persia, that whole area's got a rich history, medically speaking," she noted, "but that was a thousand years ago." Her brain was firing more efficiently now, and thinking about history and medicine nudged her into more comfortable and familiar territory, a theoretical, problem-solving mind-set that helped move her away from the harsh reality she'd been sucked into. She also found solace in the notion that perhaps this was where she could be useful.

"Do you know how old the book is?" she asked.

"No."

She frowned, deep in thought. An idea surfaced. "I've been working with a historian on my project out here. This guy—his name's Mike

Boustany—he's a walking encyclopedia when it comes to this region. Maybe if I showed him the Polaroids, he could give us an idea of how old the books are."

Corben grimaced. "I'm not sure we're ready to show them around. Not while this is in play."

"I'm sure he can be discreet if we ask him to." Mia could see that Corben wasn't convinced. "We need to explore every angle, don't we? Evelyn would want us to."

Corben held her gaze for a beat. "Sure, why not," he relented. "Knock yourself out. But I'd like you to think about something else. I want you to reconsider leaving the country." She opened her mouth to object, but he raised his hands to pause her. "I know you feel you need to be here, and that's normal. I wanted you here too, I thought you might remember something that could be important. But this is snow-balling out of control. I know you want to do everything you can to help get your mom back, but realistically, I don't think there's anything more you can do. These guys were prepared to kill you today. You need to think about your safety. We can keep you safe, but . . . I can't guaran-tee anything. I'm not saying you need to go far, but even Cyprus would be better than here. I just need you to think about that, alright?"

Mia felt a tightening in her chest. She knew she'd already used up whatever karmic goodwill she had coming to her in the last couple of days. Staying on was simply tempting fate, and, thinking about it, his suggestion, however deflating, made perfect sense to her. But then again, it wasn't about rational thinking. She couldn't leave. It was as simple as that. She knew she wasn't safe here; she wasn't even sure she had any-thing to contribute to finding her mom. But she was part of it. She felt connected not just to Evelyn, but to Ramez and Farouk and their struggle for survival. She felt connected to the city and to its people, and—there was no denying it—to the perverse and dangerous visceral elation that coursed through her when bullets were flying and when she was running for her life.

Beset by a confusing cocktail of dismay and relief, unsure about which instinct to follow, she looked at Corben. "Just do your best then," she finally muttered, not really wanting to debate the issue right now. "I can't ask for more."

"You got it." He paused, then nodded reassuringly. "We'll get her back."

She knew it wasn't a certainty. Far from it.

The odds were against it.

A deep sense of loss swooped down on her, and she turned and looked out the window as the city flew past her in a sun-drenched concrete blur.

Chapter 36

Corben found Mia a workstation in a small, unoccupied room by the press office, where she could make her calls and use the Internet.

He told her that given the urgency of Farouk's expected call and the live state of play, he'd have someone arrange for her to stay at a hotel or in an embassy safe house, and that he'd have someone watching over her in either case. He'd also have her stuff sent over from his apartment as soon as he had a chance to go there himself, but that in the meantime, to let him know if there was anything she needed.

He left her in the annex and crossed the courtyard leading to the main villa and the ambassador's office.

The thought of Mia discussing the Polaroids with her historian colleague flashed through his mind. It worried him slightly, but he didn't think it was avoidable. He would have preferred it if she'd agreed to leave the country. The hakeem and his men weren't pulling punches, regardless of the fallout. And aside from her being able to positively identify Farouk, Corben didn't really think she could bring anything more to the table. Still, he knew she'd be staying. And it aroused mixed feelings inside him.

Despite the context, he'd enjoyed her company. She was good-looking and smart, and she was American. It made a change from the local casual companions he'd been hooking up with since he'd been posted to this little corner of the planet. Beirut didn't lack in women—far from it, in fact, due to the huge number of men who left the country in search of a decent paycheck and a slightly reduced risk of death by shrapnel—and Corben was an attractive, available man. And with sexual electricity bouncing off the walls all across the city due to the constant—and in the case of the previous summer, realized—threat of war, his dance card was pretty well filled. But the job meant that his personal life had its limitations. Casual encounters never went beyond just that, and he knew nothing would have come out of being with Mia either, even if this thing hadn't erupted around them. Which suited him fine.

He wasn't exactly a nesting kind of guy.

He climbed the stairs that led up to the ambassador's office. Although he would have preferred not to waste time on such a meeting now, he had to brief his boss on the morning's events. He didn't really want to confer with anyone at the embassy at all, but he couldn't avoid the meeting. The shoot-out had been too visible, too glaring to be sidelined. So he was annoyed to discover that, as well as the head of station, the ambassador and Kirkwood would also be attending. He knew the next few hours were critical, and the last thing he needed was any unwarranted interference.

He was let in immediately, greeted the men, and took a seat facing the ambassador's desk.

He weighed his words carefully. Which wasn't a problem.

It was second nature to him.

He told them about Ramez's abduction, painting Farouk as a dealer-turned-smuggler who knew Evelyn and had sought her help in selling the relics. He left out any mention of the book, and of the connection to the hakeem, and surmised that some rival smugglers who were after the hoard had Evelyn and were after Farouk too. He told them about the call at noon, and about what he planned to do to try to get to Farouk first, in the hope of finding out who had Evelyn and having some leverage over getting her back.

None of this was ideal. He didn't really want any interference. Even less ideal was that he wasn't sure about Kirkwood. The man's abrupt arrival and his keen interest had triggered some warning bells inside Corben, ones he had long ago learned to trust. He sensed the man was keeping something from them.

Unfortunately, he didn't have time to look into it now.

～～～

FROM A WINDOW on the first floor, Kirkwood watched Corben head back to the annex.

He was already at the embassy when the call had come in informing the ambassador of the armed attack outside the university.

Another overt attempt, in broad daylight and in a crowded part of town this time.

Things were spiraling out of control.

He had to move with care.

Corben had walked him down to his office after their initial meeting with the ambassador the day before. He'd sensed that Corben wasn't going to be particularly open or forthcoming, but then he expected that, given what the man did for a living. Obfuscation and deceit were to be expected. These guys couldn't even share information with other law enforcement agencies. Still, Corben had agreed to let him check out the Polaroids, and seeing the photo of the codex had confirmed his suspicions. The two events—the call from the scout in Iraq, out of the blue, a little over a week ago, telling him about the book, and Evelyn's call to the Haldane switchboard, five days later—were connected.

He played things out in his mind and didn't doubt that whoever had kidnapped Evelyn Bishop was after the same thing he was. Someone else out there had, somehow, found out about it and was clearly willing to do whatever it took to get his hands on it.

Which complicated matters for Kirkwood.

He had some strong cards to play. But they involved trade-offs, and besides, he wasn't sure he'd be given a chance to play them.

He pulled out his mobile phone and, making sure no one was within earshot, hit a speed-dial key. It took a few seconds for the signal to bounce off a couple of satellites before the slightly crackly, foreign ring-tone whined through. Two rings and it was answered by a man with a beefy, throaty voice.

"How's it going?" Kirkwood asked.

"Fine, fine. It took a bit longer than expected to get across the border. So many people trying to get out of here. But it's fine now. I'm on the way."

"So we're still on schedule?"

"Of course. I should be there in a few hours. We're still meeting to-morrow night, as agreed?"

Kirkwood wondered whether a change of plans was merited, but decided to stick with what they'd agreed. The timing was probably right anyway, and besides, he didn't really see a shortcut that didn't present dangers or complications. "Yes. I'll see you there. Any problems, you call me immediately."

"There won't be any problems," the man answered cockily.

Kirkwood hung up, wondering if he'd made the right decision.

He looked out the window and thought back to Mia Bishop. He'd watched her earlier as she'd followed Corben into the annex.

The firmness in her step surprised him, given what she'd just been through. He wondered what was going through her mind, how she felt about being dragged into this. More important, he knew she was the last person to see her mother. How close were they? Did Evelyn confide in her? Was the young geneticist telling Corben everything she knew?

He needed to talk to her.

Preferably, without Corben present.

Chapter 37

༄ ༀ ༄

Corben hurried up the stairs to the third floor, headed for the communications office. It was past nine thirty, and Farouk's call was due in under three hours' time.

He'd already called Olshansky from the car and told him to start working on the tap.

The briefing hadn't gone too badly. They were letting him get on with things, which was all he needed right now. Kirkwood had sat back and hadn't asked any obtrusive questions.

He found Olshansky in his batcave, sitting in front of an array of three flat-screens. Muffled sounds and the occasional garbled voice were coming from the computer's speakers. The middle screen had a number of open windows. One of them was a rolling graphic display of a wave-form plotting the noise. Under it was what looked like an on-screen synthesizer, which Olshansky was manipulating using the keyboard.

"How are we doing?" Corben asked.

Olshansky didn't look up, his eyes riveted to the screens. "I've managed to download the rover into his phone, but so far, I think it's still stashed in someone's pocket. It's just garbled mumbo jumbo."

Olshansky's predecessor had hacked into the computers of Lebanon's two cell-phone service providers without too much difficulty. Having a few of its employees on the payroll probably helped. Corben was hoping to use that access to listen in on what was going on within the pickup range of the microphone on Ramez's cell phone, using a "roving bug," a remotely activated wiretap. The technology was alarmingly simple.

Most cell-phone users didn't realize that their phones weren't necessarily fully powered down, even if they were switched off. You just needed to set the alarm on your phone for a time when it's switched off and watch it light up to see that. The FBI, working with the NSA, had devised a surveillance technique—though it denied any existence of it—that allowed it to remotely download eavesdropping software onto most cell phones. This software would then enable the phone's mike to be switched on and off on its own, anytime, remotely and surreptitiously, effectively turning the phone into a bug, whether the phone was powered up or not. They didn't even need to have physical access to the phone to set it up. It was a clever evolution of an old and simple technique that was pioneered by the KGB, which involved upping the voltage on a landline just enough to activate the phone's mike even when it was on the hook.

Corben listened to the noise coming from Ramez's phone. It sounded like fabric rubbing against the phone's mike, as if the phone was in someone's pocket. In the background, some distant voices were barely audible.

"Can't you boost the voices?"

"I tried. The distortion's across the range. I can't isolate them." He shrugged at Corben. "This is as good as it gets right now."

ᴄᴏᴄᴏ

Ramez couldn't stop shivering. His chafed wrists pulsed against the plastic straps, the constant movement generating an irritating, burning sensation. At least, that's what he imagined was happening. He couldn't see out of the burlap sack covering his head.

They'd shoved it on seconds after stuffing him into their car, then—not that he'd resisted—they'd sadistically thrown in a couple of heavy punches to his face for good measure before pushing him down to the footwells of the backseat and pressing down on him with their shoes to keep him there.

The ride hadn't taken that long, and although being in that car—with his head covered in that stinking sack, the occasional stomp to the ribs, and the muffled sounds of the city wafting by—was horrific enough, he would have preferred it to drag on if it meant delaying his current situation.

They'd dragged him out of the car, into an echoey building and down some stairs, then thrown him into the chair and strapped him in. The maniac with the concrete knuckles couldn't resist landing another blow, which was all the more terrifying as, like those before it, it came unannounced, exploding onto his face through the stifling darkness of the sack.

He could hear occasional movement, footsteps around him, and there were voices a bit farther off, men's voices. The accent was unquestionably Syrian, which didn't bode well—not that anything else did. His mouth quivered as he tasted the sweat that trickled down his bruised face and mixed with the blood from his cut lip. The sack, which reeked of what smelled like an ungodly combination of rotten fruit and engine grease, wasn't entirely opaque. A few tiny pinpricks of light found their way in, not enough to see anything, just taunting him with a hint of the outside world without allowing him any advance warning of the occasional incoming blow that his captors seemed to enjoy randomly inflicting upon him.

His body went rigid as he heard footsteps coming right up to him. He could feel someone's presence, inches away, studying him. The silent shadow blocked out any light from outside, making Ramez's world even darker.

The man didn't say anything for a few maddening seconds. Ramez shut his eyes and tensed up, expecting another blow. The shivering wouldn't be cowed. Instead, it increased, and with it the burning in his wrists.

But the blow didn't come.

Instead, the man finally spoke.

"Someone's going to be calling you on your phone, in a couple of hours' time. A man from Iraq who came to see you yesterday. True?"

Dread flooded his senses. *How could they know this? I didn't tell anyone. I only called the police.*

The realization hit him like an anvil. *They have contacts in the police station. Which means no one's going to come looking for me.* It was a false hope anyway. In all of the city's grisly history, no kidnap victim had ever forcibly been rescued. They were either released or—in most cases—they weren't.

He didn't have any time to mull the bleak prospect as he felt the man grab his left hand and hold it firmly in place. His grip was rock solid. Ramez froze.

"I want you to tell him exactly what I tell you to say." The man's voice was unnervingly threatening, despite his calm tone. "I need you to convince him that everything's okay. He needs to believe you. He needs to believe everything's okay. If you do that for us, you can go home. We have no quarrel with you. But this is very, very important for us. I need you to understand how important it is. And to do that, I need you to know that if you don't convince him, this—"

With a startling suddenness, the man snapped Ramez's middle finger back, all the way back, ripping the bone off its cartilage until the finger touched the back of his hand.

Tears burst out of Ramez's eyes as he recoiled against the straps and howled with pain, almost blacking out despite the endorphins' hopeless rush, but the man was unmoved. He just held it there, pressed firmly backwards, and kept talking.

"—is what you can expect a lot more of before we allow you to die."

∽∽∽

OLSHANSKY ALMOST JUMPED out of his skin when the scream burst through the speakers of his system.

It went on for a few agonizing seconds before turning into a whimper and finally dying out. It even startled Corben, though he'd been expecting something like it. He knew what they would want from Ramez, and he knew they'd have to make sure he was scared enough to put in a convincing performance.

"Jesus Christ," Olshansky muttered. "What the hell did they do to him?"

"You probably don't want to know." Corben frowned. He heaved a frustrated sigh, imagining the scene unfurling in some underground rat hole.

The scream and the whimper were now gone, replaced by the same, annoying ruffle. Olshansky rubbed his face, shaking his head. He looked clearly shaken.

Corben let him have a moment of quiet. "What about the location?" he then asked, turning to the screen to his right. It showed a map of Beirut, overlaid by the boundaries of the different cell zones covering the city.

Olshansky collected his thoughts. "They're in this cell here," he said, pointing at the map. Cell-phone usage in Beirut was heavy, and each cell in the crowded city only covered an area of just under one square mile. But even with the enhanced triangulation at Olshansky's disposal, the hundred-meter diameter of the target zone was still a pretty big haystack in which to find the assistant professor.

Corben frowned. Ramez was in the southern suburbs of Beirut. Hezbollah territory. A definite no-go area for a lot of Lebanese. Virtually a whole different planet for an American, especially one with the dubious job title of "economic counselor." It was the one area where he didn't have a local contact.

"At least we know where they'll be coming from when the call comes in," Corben noted. He checked his watch again. He'd need to get back to the city pretty soon. He got up to leave. "Keep me posted if you get anything, clear?"

"You bet," Olshansky confirmed without taking his eyes off the screen. "What time's that call coming in?"

"Noon. I've asked Leila to come up," Corben added, referring to one of the translators on the payroll, "for when you manage to get something clear."

"Okay," Olshansky said in a hollow voice.

Corben was headed for the door when Olshansky remembered something. "By the way. Your caller with the stage fright? He's Swiss."

Corben stopped. "What?"

Olshansky still looked haunted. "The call on Evelyn Bishop's cell that came in without an ID that you asked me about?"

Corben had forgotten about the phone call he'd asked Olshansky to trace, the one that Baumhoff had taken on Evelyn's phone that night, at the police station.

"It came from Geneva," Olshansky continued.

Which surprised Corben.

"And check this out," Olshansky added. "Whoever was calling really values his privacy. The call was routed through nine international servers, each one hiding behind a mother of a firewall."

"But nothing that can resist your subtle ways, right?" Massaging Olshansky's überhacker ego was never a bad idea.

"Not this baby," Olshansky said glumly. "I managed to track it back to the Geneva server, but that's it. This is heavy-duty code we're talking about. I can't get in. Which means I can't pinpoint it any closer than that."

"Geneva."

"That's it." Olshansky shrugged.

"Well, let me know if you can narrow it down to something slightly more manageable," Corben replied flatly. "Might be tough to put the entire city under surveillance."

And with that, he walked out, the assistant professor's howl still ringing in his ears.

Chapter 38

The project supervisor at the foundation sounded mortified as Mia related what had happened. He apologized profusely, as if his own family were responsible for the attacks, and assured her that he fully understood her position and would support any decision she took.

She hung up, and her eyes settled on the computer screen before her. She realized she'd been in e-mail exile since having drinks with Evelyn. Corben had asked a secretary to log her into the press office's system, but as Mia reached for the keyboard, she decided she'd extend the exile a little longer.

She was, quite simply, overwhelmed. She glanced out the window at the lush forested hills behind the embassy, sorting out the confused, frantic scenes unfurling in her mind's eye, and inviting some of the tranquillity outside the window to seep into her. All she got instead was a recall of the Ouroboros, which she soon found herself doodling on the writing pad in front of her.

She gave up trying to duck it. She pulled a number off her cell phone and dialed it. Mike Boustany, the historian she'd been working with on the project, answered after the fourth ring, his dulcet tones replaced by urgent, heartfelt concern. He hadn't heard of Ramez's kidnapping yet, and it took him by surprise. He was even more shocked to hear that Mia was present at both.

He asked what was going on. Mia didn't feel compelled to hide any-thing from him. He stayed silent through most of it, clearly stunned by her experience.

"Maybe there's something you can help me with, Mike," she con-cluded. "What do you know about the Ouroboros?"

"The tail-eater? We've got some carvings of it, on some Phoenician temples. Is that what you mean?"

"No. The one I'm interested in is much more recent. Tenth cen-tury, maybe." She filled him in about its appearance in the underground chambers and on the book.

He knew a lot about the Brethren of Purity, but couldn't see a con-nection there to the Ouroboros. She wanted to go further, but felt she should avoid mentioning the hakeem and his house of horrors. Instead, she told Boustany about being a bit confused as to the symbol's sig-nificance and brought up what she'd read about the Arab and Persian scientists of the era.

Which was something he knew a lot about.

"What I don't get is this," she concluded. "Someone's willing to shed a lot of blood to get his hands on this book, but there's nothing sinister about what these scientists were trying to achieve. So what's in this book?"

Boustany chuckled softly. "Must be the *ikseer*."

"The what? What are you talking about?"

"Man's oldest craving. See, you're just looking at it from a rational point of view."

She frowned. "So I'm told."

"You've been reading up about the achievements of these scientist-philosophers that are easily demonstrable. But, as you know, they didn't limit themselves to one discipline. They were interested in everything known to man, they wanted to master the mysterious forces of nature and become the leading lights in all of the sciences. So they studied medicine, physics, astronomy, geology . . . their minds were hungry, and there was a lot to discover. They dissected bodies, postulated about how the solar system operates . . . And sooner or later, the one thing that hogged their attention was alchemy."

"Alchemy? These guys were scientists, not quacks."

Boustany's voice came back tranquil as a lake. "Alchemy was a science. We'd still be rubbing sticks for fire without it."

And with that, he took her back to the earliest days of the uneasy relationship between science and religion, and to the origins of alchemy.

Boustany explained how the ancient Greeks had separated science—which, at the time, consisted mostly of studies of astronomy and explorations of *khemeia*, which meant "the mixing together" of substances—from religion, to great effect.

"Science flourished as a rational vocation of academics and thinkers," Boustany told her. "This all changed when one of Alexander the Great's generals, Ptolemy, established his kingdom in Egypt. Alexandria—the city that had been founded by and took its name from the great conqueror—became a center of advanced learning, as exemplified by its legendary library. The invaders were impressed by the Egyptian mastery of *khemeia*, even though it was fused with their religion and their obsession with the afterlife. And so the Greeks absorbed both the science and the religion. *Khemeia* became intertwined with mysticism, and its practitioners were viewed as shady adepts of dark secrets—along with astrologers they became as feared as priests. They soon embraced that perception, reveling in their newfound status of sorcerers and magicians, and closed ranks, retreating behind a veil of secrecy. In an effort to feed their own myth, they shrouded their writings in a symbolism only initiates could understand."

Science and magic became indistinguishable.

And, as a result, science—serious science—foundered. This mind-set led to scientists working apart and not sharing their discoveries—or their failures. Even worse, it attracted quacks and charlatans, who dragged science further into disrepute. The allure of the ultimate chemical challenge—changing base metals into gold—became prevalent. It all spiraled out of control until two forces all but smothered science in Europe: the Roman emperor Diocletian's fear of cheap gold undermining his rule, which led to his ordering the burning of all known writings of *khemeia*; and the rise of Christianity, which ruthlessly stamped out heretical, pagan learning. The Christian Roman empire was thus cleansed of Greek learning. The East, however, would take up the mantle and run with it.

In the seventh century, armies of Arab tribes united and, driven by a new religion, emerged from the Arabian Peninsula and fanned out across Asia, Europe, and Africa. When they conquered Persia, they discovered the surviving remnants of Greek science. The writings intrigued them. *Khemeia* became *al-kheemia*, the Arabic prefix *al* meaning "the." Fate had entrusted Greco-Egyptian alchemy to Arab scientists. It would remain in their care for the next five hundred years.

And they would serve it well, embracing the knowledge handed down to them and greatly advancing it.

That golden age would wither away under the invasions of the barbaric Mongols and Turks. Eventually, the Crusaders would bring the remnants of Arabic scientific knowledge back to Europe. The Christians of the Iberian Peninsula, in particular, would spearhead the return of the lost Greek knowledge back to its European home as they reclaimed the lands of Spain and Portugal from the Moors. Through the efforts of translators working in Toledo and in other centers of learning there, the scientific advances of the East would find a new life in the West.

Al-kheemia would become alchemy, and centuries later, it would take on the more respectable name of chemistry.

"These philosopher-scientists achieved great things in the field we now call chemistry," Boustany informed her. "They created acids, mixed metals, and synthesized new substances. But one substance, in particular, was the most sought after for centuries."

"Gold," Mia said flatly.

"Of course. The tantalizing possibility of manufacturing gold never failed to seduce even the most levelheaded of these scientists. At some point in their careers, every one of them became obsessed with the one thing that their patrons, the caliphs and the imams, were most interested in: turning base metals into gold."

Mia mulled his words. She'd skimmed a brief bio of Jabir ibn Hayyan—whom the Europeans would later refer to as *Geber*—at Corben's apartment. His writings, cloaked in an unreadable code, were thought to be at the root of the term *gibberish*. He had been able to prepare strong acids, but he'd also worked extensively, and with success, on the transmutation of metals. Mia hadn't given it much attention since, even if it were remotely possible, not that she thought it was, she didn't think that it was, to use Corben's pet adjective, *relevant*, given the discoveries in the hakeem's lab.

"I don't think that's what this is about," she said.

"Why not?"

"There's something I haven't mentioned," she added somewhat hesitantly. "There's a guy out there who we think may be behind all this. He . . . he was running some weird medical experiments."

Boustany's voice disappeared for a beat. "On humans?"

"Yep."

Boustany went quiet, weighing her response. "So maybe this guy really is after the *ikseer*."

"Again with the *ikseer*. What the hell are you talking about?"

"An obsession as old as time itself. The *Epic of Gilgamesh*, which is one of the oldest written stories in recorded history, is about this." In the brief time she'd known him, the historian had developed this habit of teasing her. It was often endearing. Right now, she needed to know.

Boustany explained how for Avicenna and the other philosopher-scientists, the missing piece of the puzzle was the trigger, the catalyst that would stimulate the right mix of the base metals. Ancient tradition led them to believe the catalyst was a dry powder. The Greeks had called it *xerion*, which meant dry. The word became *al-ikseer* in Arabic. Hundreds of years later, the Europeans would refer to the undiscovered *al-ikseer* as the *elixir*. And, since scientists of the era were referred to as philosophers, and because it was believed to come from the earth, it also became known as the philosopher's stone.

"This mythical substance was believed to be so wondrous that these alchemists soon assigned other powers to it as well," Boustany added. "Aside from being the catalyst that would help create untold wealth, they also attributed to it the power to heal all illnesses. Eventually, conferring immortality was also believed to be within its powers. And so the notion of a potential *al-ikseer of life*—an elixir of life—took hold, and *al-kheemia* became a double-pronged quest for two intimately related goals: gold and eternal life."

The two became intimately linked in the alchemists' minds. Gold itself was incorruptible: It didn't age. Some scientists even found ways to ingest it as an elixir itself—usually in powdered form—and gold became more sought after for its perceived antiaging powers than for its timeless beauty or for its monetary value.

The notion of an elixir of life, Boustany went on, embraced the archetypal theory of aging, blaming it on the loss of some kind of vital substance. That was why our bodies effectively shriveled up and shrank before ceasing to function altogether. The Taoists called this substance the *ching* and described it as the vital breath of life. Aristotle, Avicenna, and countless others since also thought the body, in aging, lost its "innate moisture." The Viennese physician Eugen Steinach preached coitus reservatus to rejuvenate his patients—a method of preserving the vital fluid that we now call a vasectomy. Another surgeon, Serge Voronoff, believed that since reproductive cells didn't age as badly as the other cells in the body, they had to contain some kind of antiaging hormone. In a misguided attempt to transfer more of that magical elixir back into the body, he grafted monkey testicles into his patients' own testes with predictably dire results. Even the fervent belief in a rosy afterlife didn't seem to deter the desperate pursuit of longevity: In the 1950s, the aging Pope Pius XII kept six personal physicians on hand at all times. A Swiss surgeon by the name of Paul Niehans injected him with the glands of lamb fetuses. Niehans's impressive roster of clients at his clinic in Montreux, Switzerland, included kings and Hollywood stars.

"And so," Boustany concluded, "over the ages, alchemists and quacks concocted all kinds of potions and elixirs, fountains of youth that could replenish or replace this lost 'essence' of life. The hucksters' wagons have since been replaced by the supplements aisles in supermarkets and by the Internet, the snake-oil salesmen by pseudoscientists touting hormones, minerals, and other miracle cures and promising to restore our bodies to their youthful vigor with little or no hard, scientific evidence—or a highly selective interpretation of scientific data—to back up their claims. But the quest is the same. It's the final frontier, the only one left for us to conquer."

Mia sighed glumly. "So I guess what we're dealing with here is a madman."

"Sounds like it."

Mia put the phone down, fighting with the notion that the *mad scientist* tag that she'd been keeping at bay when thinking of the man who held her mother, probably wasn't far from the truth.

Chapter 39

⁓⊘⁓

The hakeem sank back in the armchair of his study, feeling blissfully invigorated.

The morning's treatment, a weekly regimen he had religiously followed for years, had given him its customary boost. He relished the crisp autumn air, breathing it in with big, hungry gulps as the cocktail of hormones and steroids coursed through his veins and made his skin feel as if it were electrified. The rush cleared his head and his eyes and heightened his senses, almost slowing down everything around him. It was the best high he could possibly imagine, especially since it didn't involve his losing control, something that would, for him, be inconceivable.

If only people knew what they were missing.

In addition, the news from Beirut was promising. Omar and his men had grabbed the assistant professor. One of them had been killed, another badly wounded—he would have to be taken care of, as a trip to a hospital, even one in a friendly part of town, was out of the question, and he was apparently too badly wounded to be sneaked over the border—but, all in all, the operation had been successful.

It was a shame the American hadn't been killed. The hakeem sensed that the man's interest was becoming a problem. He was too close to the situation, too . . . committed. Omar had informed the hakeem that the American had taken the Bishop woman's laptop, as well as a file, from her apartment. One file. Standard procedure in such an investigation, or was there more to it? Yes, admittedly, an American woman had been abducted, and the Americans took such things more seriously than most, but the man's stubborn determination hinted at something more personal at work.

Did he know what was really at stake?

He'd ordered Omar to take extra precautions from here on. The Iraqi dealer's phone call was imminent. The book would soon be his.

Things were looking good.

Better than good.

Somehow, with the clarity afforded to him by the fresh dose swirling inside him, he knew that this time, finally, he really was close.

He shut his eyes and sucked in a deep breath, relishing the prospect of imminent success. With his mind gliding along unhindered, images of home soon swooped into his mind.

Reminiscences.

Of the first time he'd taken notice of the chapel's unusual offerings.

The first time he became aware of his unique heritage.

ᥠᥐᥐᥝ

He'd been inside the chapel before, of course. He'd grown up there, in Naples, a city where, to this day, his ancestor's name was still whispered in hushed tones. But that visit, at the age of nine, had awoken him to the mysteries of his past.

His grandfather had taken him to the chapel that day.

He enjoyed spending time with the old man. There was something solid and comforting about him. Even at that tender age, the young boy—his name was Ludovico, back then—could sense the respect his grandfather commanded from those around him. He yearned for that inner strength himself, especially in the playground at school, where bigger, stronger boys would taunt him because of his ancestry.

In Naples, the di Sangro cross was a heavy one to bear.

His grandfather had taught him to stand proud and take note of his family's heritage. They were princes, for God's sake, and besides, geniuses and visionaries were often derided and persecuted in their own time. Ludovico's father hadn't been interested in understanding what lay in their past, choosing to remain weakly and embarrassingly apologetic about his lineage. Ludovico had been different, and his grandfather had seen it in the young boy and nurtured it. Their ancestor had many startling achievements, he'd taught him. Yes, he'd been called everything from a sorcerer to a diabolical alchemist. Rumors abounded that he'd performed vile experiments on unwitting subjects. Some believed these were related to perfecting the creation of even better castrati, the illegally castrated singers that entranced audiences and drove Italian opera to prominence in the seventeenth and eighteenth centuries. Some went further, claiming that the prince had ordered the killing of seven cardinals who took displeasure with his interests and had chairs made from their bones and skin.

As far as his grandfather was concerned, such talk was indicative of the limited intellect and imagination, and inevitably the jealousy, of Raimondo di Sangro's detractors. After all, their ancestor had belonged to the prestigious Accademia della Crusca, the highly esteemed club of Italy's literary elite. He'd invented new types of firearms such as a rear-loaded shotgun, as well as revolutionary fireworks. He'd created waterproof fabrics and perfected new techniques for coloring marble and glass. Far more than that, however, he'd created a monument of immortal power: the Cappella San Severo, his personal chapel in the heart of Naples.

The hakeem remembered that fateful visit with his grandfather. Set low in the chapel's outer walls, by the entrance, were the barred cellar windows to what was once the prince's laboratory. Inside, the small baroque church was resplendent with the most unique paintings and works of art. Marble statues, the most famous of which was Sammartino's *Veiled Christ*, were mesmerizing in their detail, the features on their subjects' faces clearly visible under a thin veil of marble. To this day, experts are puzzled as to how such an effect was achieved.

His grandfather had guided him beyond it, to Queirolo's statue *Disillusionment*. Another veiled wonder, it showed the prince's father trying to free himself from the confines of a net, aided by a winged youth. The hakeem's grandfather had explained to the young boy how the statue represented man trying to free himself from the trap of false beliefs, aided by his intellect.

The basement housed more marvels. A narrow spiral staircase led down to the prince's laboratory, where two glass cases held the infamous "anatomical machines," skeletons of a man, on one side, and a heavily pregnant woman on the other, the veins, arteries, and organs of their entire circulatory systems immaculately preserved using an unknown and still-perplexing embalming technique.

Over the years, his grandfather had taught young Ludovico more about his ancestor's mysterious life. The *principe* had, his grandfather told him, been obsessed with attaining human perfection. The castrati were perfect singers. The anatomical machines were part of his quest to create the perfect human body. His tombstone, fittingly, read, "An admirable man, born to dare everything." It presided over an empty tomb: His body had been stolen. But at some point in his life, his obsession had taken a dramatic turn. And when Ludovico reached eighteen, his grandfather finally told him what had inflamed his ancestor's obsession.

He also gave him Raimondo di Sangro's diaries, as well as something else that he'd prized above all else: a talisman, a medallion bearing the mark of a tail-eating snake, one the young man would always wear, even to this day.

The revelation inspired Ludovico beyond his grandfather's greatest dreams—or worst nightmares.

It had started off well enough. Ludovico had excelled in his studies and had gone on to the University of Padua, where he obtained a doctorate—with honors—in geriatric medicine and in cellular biology. By now a brilliant biogeneticist with a solid reputation, he ran a well-funded research lab at the university, exploring stem cells, hormonal pathways, and cellular breakdown. But, with time, he started to feel the constraints of acceptable science. He began to push the envelope and to challenge the accepted boundaries of bioethics. His experiments grew more adventurous. More extreme.

In a bitter twist of fate, his grandfather died at around the same time. His parents had tried to raise Ludovico as a good Catholic, and he'd been taught, at home and in church, that death was God's wish for us, and that He was the only giver of immortality. His grandfather had tried to lessen the effects of their teachings, and in his death, in that single, passing event, his words would come to pass. It made Ludovico realize that it was not in his nature to accept death, nor to be defeated by it. He wouldn't go down without a fight. The grave—his own, and that of his loved ones—could wait.

Love wouldn't conquer death. Science would.

And so, with that mind-set, his experiments became less acceptable. They soon became illegal.

He was hounded out of the university, chased away by the imminent threat of legal action.

No laboratory in the West would touch him.

Baghdad University would, however, offer him a way out. And, eventually, lead him—or so he now hoped—to the elusive discovery that had taunted his ancestor.

∾∾∾

WITH HIS MIND SPURRED by the chemicals whirling inside him, he found himself going over the events of the last few days, turning them upside down and examining them from fresh angles. Despite his almost rapturous exhilaration at the prospect of getting hold of the Iraqi dealer and the book, he couldn't avoid going back to the American archaeologist's long-lost lover. The notion kept ambushing and undermining his serenity, as if a sensor somewhere inside him had been tripped.

And in his heightened state, another piece of the puzzle, a delicious epiphany, burst from the outer reaches of his consciousness.

How could I not have seen it before?

He ran a quick mental calculation. From what Omar had told him about her daughter's age, the fit was certainly feasible.

More than feasible. It was perfect.

That sly bitch, he mused. She had actually kept that little gem to herself.

He sprang to his feet and strode across his study, flying across the tiles as he barked out an order to be escorted down to the cellar.

∾∾∾

EVELYN BOLTED UPRIGHT as soon as she heard the key jangle in the door's lock.

She didn't know how long she'd been in there, or even whether it was day or night. All sense of time and place had receded into irrelevance in the brutal isolation of her cell. The one thing she did know was she hadn't been in there that long, and that, if previous kidnappings in Beirut were anything to go by, she still had a long, long way to go.

The door swung open and her inquisitor stepped in. He wasn't wearing a lab coat this time, which Evelyn found faintly reassuring. He gave the small cell a quick scan, like a stern hotel manager surveying a guest room, then sat down at the edge of her bed.

His eyes were alive with a manic energy that was deeply unsettling. "I think you forgot to mention a small detail during our last little chat," he told her playfully.

She wasn't sure what he was referring to, but whatever it was, he was way too delighted at his discovery for it to be good.

"This roving Casanova of yours," he said, glowering with irritating condescension. "Tom Webster. I'm amazed you still feel so strongly about him, so protectively. Given how he left you."

He leaned in, eyeing her with relish, as if savoring her apprehension at his little mind-game, and as he did, she spotted the medallion through the folds of his buttoned shirt. The brief glimpse was all she needed to recognize the Ouroboros symbol on it, and right then, she knew there was a lot he—and Tom—had been keeping from her about the long-lost occupants of the chamber in Al-Hillah.

"Pregnant," the hakeem rasped. "I'm not mistaken, am I? Mia . . . she's his daughter, isn't she?"

Chapter 40

~~~

A man's voice broke through Mia's dour thoughts.

"You must be Mia Bishop."

She turned. The man standing before her extended his hand. "Bill Kirkwood. I was looking for Jim?"

As she met his hand, she took in his features. He was a pleasant-looking guy, but there was something aloof in his manner, a reserved hesitance, that discomforted her. "I don't know where he is," she said. "He left me here about an hour ago."

"Ah." He seemed to hover for a moment before adding, "I'm sorry about what's happened to your mom."

Mia wasn't sure how to answer that. She went with "It comes with the territory, I guess."

"Not lately, it hasn't. Not in Lebanon. It took us all by surprise. Still, I'm sure she'll be fine."

Mia nodded and let an awkward silence settle between them.

"So I hear you had another Wild West adventure," he ventured.

Mia shrugged. "I seem to have a knack for being in the wrong place at the wrong time."

"You could look at it that way. Then again, the fact that you were there that night and that you reported what happened to your mom could end up saving her life."

Her face brightened. The thought brought her a hint of solace. "I hope so. You knew her?"

Kirkwood nodded. "A little. UNESCO. We've been funding some of her digs out here. She's a great lady, we have nothing but the highest of respect for her, you know. And this whole thing is just so . . . awful. Tell me, Mia—may I call you Mia?"

"Sure."

"How did she seem to you?"

"What do you mean?"

"You were the last one to see her before she was kidnapped," Kirkwood reminded her. "Did she seem nervous about anything? Worried, maybe?"

"Not particularly. She was a bit rattled by Farouk—you know, the Iraqi dealer—his showing up out of the blue took her by surprise. But otherwise . . ." Her voice drifted as she noticed that his eyes had wandered to the desk and settled on the writing pad. It was covered with notes she had scribbled during her calls and littered with doodles of the Ouroboros.

Kirkwood cocked his head to one side, intrigued. "The symbol on one of the books," he half-noted, half-asked. "From Iraq."

Mia felt slightly rattled. "Yes," she answered, somewhat surprised that he knew that.

"Do you know what it is?"

"It's called an Ouroboros." She wasn't sure how much to say and settled for "I don't know much about it." She forced a smile, which she knew didn't reach her eyes. She wondered if he noticed.

"You think that book is what the kidnappers are really after?" he asked.

She felt conflicted.

Kirkwood must have seen it, as he preempted her unease. "It's fine. I'm working with Jim on getting Evelyn back. He told me about your chat. Said you took him to her apartment." He paused. "We're all on the same side here," he added with a hint of a smile as he leaned in and studied her notes.

She relaxed and nodded. "It's the one thing that links Evelyn, the cabal's chambers, the book, and the hakeem. It's got to mean something."

A puzzled look clouded his face. "The hakeem?"

A knot formed in her throat. She knew she'd screwed up the second she'd said it. She fumbled for the right words to get her out of her spot, but they wouldn't announce themselves. "He's . . . you know, in Baghdad," she mumbled. "Maybe you should ask Jim about that."

Just then, mercifully, Corben showed up.

Another man was with him, younger than Corben, someone she hadn't met before. He had short chestnut hair, a thick-set neck, and wore a navy blue suit with no tie. Corben seemed surprised to see Kirkwood here and gave him a small nod. As Kirkwood acknowledged him back, Mia caught a barely perceptible unease in Corben's expression as he glanced down at the desk, where her doodles were in view.

Corben motioned to the man with him. "This is Greg," he said to Mia. "He'll take you to the hotel whenever you're ready and he'll stay with you. We're going to put you up at the Albergo. It's a small hotel in Ashrafieh"—the Christian side of town—"you'll be fine there."

"Okay." Mia nodded to Corben.

"It's where I'm staying," Kirkwood added, before turning to Corben. "Anything on that phone tap?"

"Nothing yet," Corben said matter-of-factly.

"So what are you going to do?" Kirkwood asked.

"I'm driving back into town to be within striking distance." Corben shrugged. "Maybe we'll get a break." He turned to Mia. "I'll give you a call later to make sure you're all sorted out."

"I'll be fine," she said.

Corben looked at her, then nodded to the other agent as if to say, *All yours.*

As Corben turned to leave, Kirkwood said, "Good luck. And keep us posted."

"I'll let you know as soon as I have news."

For some reason, Mia didn't think Corben was too keen on following through with that. More than that, he seemed a bit wary of Kirkwood.

Which meant that she probably ought to be as well.

∞

KIRKWOOD LIFTED the plastic lid and pulled out a cup of coffee from the coffeemaker in the lobby of the annex. He ventured a sip. Surprisingly, it wasn't half-bad.

He replayed his little chat with Mia. It was obvious that she, and therefore Corben, knew far more than they were saying. During his briefings, Corben hadn't said anything about the kidnappers having a specific interest in any of the artifacts, let alone mentioned the book specifically, nor had he brought up Evelyn's discovery of the underground chamber. And yet Mia clearly knew about both.

And Corben certainly hadn't mentioned this hakeem. Even though the man was clearly an intrinsic part of the equation.

Even more interestingly, Mia had said the hakeem was in Baghdad. He knew hakeem meant "doctor," and the sound of that didn't set well in his stomach.

He felt a deep-seated unease. There were agendas he didn't know about. And the Iraqi dealer was still far from being in safe hands. He needed to know what was really going on, and the place to start was with Corben. Which wouldn't be easy. Kirkwood's contacts within the UN were rock solid. His contacts within the intelligence community were less so. The UN, however, did—purposefully at times, unwittingly at others—play a significant role in the Iraq war, particularly during the whole WMD debacle. Kirkwood could use his contacts to mine that vein while looking for other ways to get into the Agency's inner workings.

He also needed to get more information regarding Mia's background, but that would have to come through other methods. He didn't think it would be too difficult.

He took another sip from his cup, fished his phone out of a pocket, and dialed.

Chapter 41

Corben checked his watch. It was quarter to twelve.

Fifteen minutes to liftoff.

He'd been sitting in the Nissan Pathfinder for half an hour, waiting. He didn't mind. He liked the peace. It gave him time to think things through calmly, methodically, and evaluate the various options that could open up. He had to have options. In his business, things rarely went exactly according to plan.

He stretched the stiffness from his bones, took a final sip from the double espresso he'd picked up, and chucked the paper cup into the back footwell. The caffeine rush was now coming onstream, and it felt good. Or maybe it was just the anticipation.

He glanced down at the seat next to him and pulled the Ruger MP9 from its case. It was an ugly little piece, but highly effective. He checked its magazine. It was filled to capacity. Thirty-two rounds. He pressed down on the uppermost cartridge, feeling the give in the springs, and rotated it slightly, making sure it was properly seated, before ramming the magazine back in. He made sure the firing selector was on FULL-AUTO. In that setting, it could spit out its entire load in a little under three seconds. In the hands of a "spray-and-pray" crackhead, most if not all of those rounds would probably miss their mark. Corben, on the other hand, was experienced enough to make them count.

Three extra magazines were in the case, all fully loaded. He also wore a holstered Glock 31 on his belt. It had only seventeen rounds in it, but they were .357s that could punch through car panels as if they were paper.

He needed the firepower.

He'd thought things through and had decided that, despite the increased risks, he needed to do this alone. He was able to sell it to his station chief on the basis that Farouk was easily spookable and had to be approached with lightning speed as well as with utmost care. An army of foreign agents showing up would make him run.

He'd briefly—very briefly—considered bringing Mia along. Farouk—who'd be expecting a carload of Lebanese cops—didn't know Corben. He had no reason to believe him or to trust him. But Mia and Farouk had locked eyes the night of Evelyn's kidnapping. Her presence at the pickup point could definitely have given the Iraqi some comfort, but it wasn't really an option, not given how dangerous it could be and what she'd already been through that morning. Her presence would have been inappropriate and would have severely cramped Corben's style at a time he'd need to think fast and move faster.

Corben wasn't about to involve the Fuhud either, not when he didn't know whom he could trust there. He knew he'd probably be up against a carload of shooters. He just hoped he'd get to Farouk before they did and avoid turning whatever corner of Beirut the Iraqi was holed up in into another firing range.

Which was the key question, really. Where would Farouk be calling from? According to the signal from Ramez's phone, the kidnappers were in the Malaab area, in the southern end of the city. Corben had to position himself somewhere where he'd have a chance at beating them to Farouk. He'd studied a map of the city and crossed off some areas as being unlikely hangouts for an illegal immigrant with a strong Iraqi accent and probably little money. East Beirut was one such area. The glitzy downtown too. The southern part of the city was its own fiefdom and off-limits to outsiders.

Which left West Beirut.

Corben had chosen to wait outside the Concorde multiplex. It was on a main road that bisected West Beirut diagonally and was close to other wide arteries he could use to get across town if he needed to. If the call came in from anywhere near the university, which was where Farouk was last seen, Corben would be closer to him than the goon squad, and he'd stand a decent chance of getting to him before them. Assuming they didn't have a forward guard on hold.

He'd raided the armory for the weapons, signing out a Kevlar vest as well, which, judging from the stiffness in his back, clearly wasn't designed for comfort. He'd also decided to use one of the cars that didn't have embassy plates. If there was going to be trouble, he didn't want his vehicle to be that easily identifiable.

Leila's voice crackled through his cell phone's Bluetooth earpiece: "We're getting something."

Olshansky added, "Looks like they've finally pulled Ramez's phone out from whatever hole they've been keeping it in."

Corben heard some voices speaking in Arabic in the background, the kidnappers coming through the speakers in Olshansky's batcave.

The words became clearer. He pictured the man saying them, possibly the leader of the kidnappers, the one he'd seen outside Evelyn's apartment.

Leila worked fast, speaking intermittently at each pause in the man's voice: "He's telling Ramez it's almost time. . . . He's asking him if he understands exactly what he needs to get Farouk to do. . . . Ramez's saying he understands. Can't really hear him properly, but he sounds terrified. . . . He's reminding him that he promised to let him go if he does it. . . . He's telling him he can keep his mouth shut, no one needs to know, that kind of thing." There was a pause, then the voice came back. "The guy's telling him not to worry, everything's going to be alright. To be careful. Not make a mistake. His life's in his own hands now. It's up to him." The man paused for a beat, then spoke again.

Leila said, "He's now telling his men to get the car ready."

❧❧

FOR THE FOURTH TIME in the last half hour, Farouk asked the man seated next to him for the time.

He was sitting in a small café in Basta, a run-down and crowded part of town, far from the marble-clad skyscrapers and the McDonald's with valet parking. This warren of narrow streets was choked by haphazardly parked cars and rickety old pushcarts teetering with food, cheap clothing, and pirated DVDs. The area was also teeming with antiques dealers, their wares hogging the narrow sidewalks and forcing pedestrians onto the street. Farouk knew the place from years back, having sold some Mesopotamian artifacts to a couple of local dealers he hadn't seen since and didn't want to risk contacting.

It was also a good place to melt into, a good place to lie low.

His clothes felt uncomfortable and stank; he couldn't remember the last time he'd had a bath. He hadn't gone back to the Sanayi' garden square after seeing Ramez. He'd felt paranoid about returning to the same place for a second night. Instead, he'd hung out in Basta, loitering in old cafés and antiques bazaars, subsisting on *ka'ik* and juice from street vendors. He'd spent the night huddled against a crypt in the nearby cemetery, fretting about his own little high noon. Which, according to the slightly irritated man with the honey-flavored *arghilé* water pipe next to him, it now was.

He thanked the man, got out of his chair, and shuffled past a few backgammon players and across to the counter, his heart in his throat. He asked the owner, a round man with a prodigious mustache, if he could use the phone—something he'd previously mentioned to him— again assuring him that it was a local call. The man gave him a wary look before handing him the cordless handset.

Farouk turned away, reached into a pocket, and pulled out the crumpled piece of paper on which Ramez had written down his number. He set it on the bar, sucked in a comforting drag off his cigarette, and dialed.

∿∿∿

RAMEZ FELT THE WORLD around him slow to a surreal crawl as his mind counted off each passing second.

He was still tied to the chair, with the musty sack still on his head. It felt unbearably stifling and only accentuated his throbbing headache. He couldn't stand the torture of having to sit back, wait, and pray that Farouk would make that call as promised.

Adding to his discomfort, he now became aware of a stabbing pain in his groin and realized his bladder desperately needed draining, but now was not the time to bring it up.

He knew they'd have to take the sack off his head if and when—no, just when, no ifs. Couldn't have ifs. Just focus on the when—the call came in. Surely, they couldn't expect him to speak to Farouk with it on. And they might want to mouth him instructions during the call. He thought he'd keep his eyes shut, in case they were worried about his being able to identify them, or at least he'd just look down and avoid eye contact. He'd wanted to ask them about that, but decided against it, worried that he might alert them to something they weren't necessarily bothered about. He tried not to think about what it meant if—as he would have expected—they were bothered about it.

The phone's ring jolted him like a live current. Someone then yanked the sack off his head, doubling his shock.

His eyes weren't properly focusing, still adjusting to the cold neon in the windowless basement. He thought he recognized the man who was looming over him, from when he'd been shoved inside the car. The man was studying Ramez's phone, which now rang again. Ramez imagined his captor was making sure it wasn't a number that was on the phone's memory—Farouk's number wouldn't be recognized.

Ramez met the man's gaze. He couldn't look away. All notions of avoiding eye contact were gone. The man—dark-haired, clean-cut, but with fearsome, dead eyes—gave him a look of such silent ferocity that it almost choked Ramez. He raised a cautioning and threatening finger at Ramez, shot him a look that meant *Careful,* in no uncertain terms, and clicked on the phone before holding it to Ramez's ear.

"*Ustaz* Ramez?"

Ramez breathed out. It was Farouk—he'd kept calling him *ustaz*—professor—during their chat. He nodded hopefully at his captor. The man returned a quietly encouraging nod, motioning for him to speak before leaning down, his head close to Ramez's, and tilting the phone out so he could also hear Farouk.

"Yes, Farouk." Ramez's voice was a little too high-pitched, and he adjusted it down, trying not to sound flustered. "I'm glad you called. Is everything okay?" His mouth felt dry, the words fumbling out like cotton balls. He licked his lips.

"Did you speak to them?" Farouk asked with an evident crackle of desperation in his voice.

"Yes. I spoke to the detectives at the Hobeish station, the ones working the case. I told them what you asked me to say."

"And?"

Ramez glanced sideways at his captor. The man nodded to him reassuringly. "They're willing to do as you asked. They don't care about the pieces and they're not interested in sending you back to Iraq. They're just desperate for your help in getting Evelyn back."

"Are you sure? You spoke to someone of authority?"

"I spoke to the head of detectives," Ramez assured him. "He gave me his personal guarantee. No charges and full protection until this is over. Then you're free to do what you like. If it all works out, they'll even help you get residence papers."

Ramez heard a pause on the line and wondered if he'd overdone it. His heart skipped a beat and he raced ahead. "They're desperate, Farouk. They want to find her, and you're their only hope. They need you."

"Thank you," Farouk finally muttered down the line. "Thank you, *Ustaz* Ramez. How can I ever repay you? You've saved my life."

"Don't worry about it," Ramez simply replied as tidal waves of guilt and relief collided inside him. He bit back his turmoil.

"What do they want me to do?"

Ramez's eyes darted sideways at his captor. The moment of truth.

His captor nodded. Time to bring that puppy in.

"You just stay where you are. Don't go anywhere. They're waiting for my call," Ramez said, trying desperately to control the quiver in his voice. "They'll come and get you. They're just waiting for me to tell them where to go." He paused, a lump of thorns stuck in his throat, before asking, "Where are you, Farouk?"

The four seconds of silence that followed were unquestionably the longest and most petrifying in the assistant professor's eventful life.

And then Farouk spoke.

Chapter 42

Corben already had the engine running as he listened to Farouk's fearful words. Leila's voice boomed over them through Corben's earpiece.

"He's in a coffee shop in Basta. You have to take the Ring and get off before the elevated section."

Corben darted a glance over his shoulder, saw a fifty-yard gap between him and an approaching car, and decided it would have to do. He spun the wheel and floored the pedal. The Pathfinder bolted out of its parking spot and, its tires screeching, pulled a U-turn and rocketed down in the opposite direction.

As he sped towards the old broadcasting house, Corben drew up the city map in his mind's eye and cursed under his breath. He knew where Basta was, and if he was right, he and the goon squad were pretty much equidistant from where Farouk was holed up.

Every second counted.

"Leila, do you have the exact location in Basta pinned down?" Corben knew navigating through the narrow, clogged streets of the market area might be a problem.

"Yes, he's going to be waiting outside a big mosque. Tell me when you take the exit ramp and I'll guide you there."

"What's going on with Ramez?"

"He told Farouk to sit tight and wait, they should be there shortly."
She paused for a second. "They just hung up."

⌒⌒⌒

RAMEZ WATCHED HIS CAPTOR click off the phone and order his men to
move. There were two of them, one older and one younger than their
boss. Both displayed the same hard, emotionless expression, their eyes
utterly barren of even the slightest hint of humanity. They left the room
swiftly, leaving Ramez alone with his captor.

"That was good, wasn't it? I did exactly as you asked, didn't I?" Ramez asked, his breath coming short and fast now.

"*Azeem,*" the man replied tersely—perfect.

Ramez felt tears welling up in his eyes as he watched his captor nod,
then casually flick the phone into his lap. Ramez looked down at it,
then raised his eyes to his captor, smiling nervously, his heart racing,
his nerves bursting, convincing himself that despite all logic, despite the
most basic common sense, he would be freed.

That faint delusion was ruthlessly stamped out as his captor drew
a handgun out of his belt, swung it straight at Ramez's forehead, and
fired.

⌒⌒⌒

AS THE PATHFINDER raced past a lumbering taxi by the Sanayi' garden
square, Corben heard two quick shots rip through his earpiece, followed
by a third one a couple of seconds later.

The controlling shot. To make sure.

His muscles tightened.

Bastards.

He knew it was inevitable. He's already played it out in his mind, and
he didn't have any illusions about how these guys operated. They had
no further use for the assistant professor, not after he'd handed them
Farouk on a silver platter. Not that Corben believed the man had much
choice. Once they'd grabbed him, he was dead either way. His only
choice was about how much pain he was going to have to suffer before
taking that call.

He heard a whimper in his earpiece. He knew it was Leila.

Olshansky's voice cut in, "Jim, did you hear that?"

"I heard," Corben replied flatly.

He knew it was hard on anyone to hear something like that, but there was no time to console Leila. He needed her—and Olshansky—focused.

"Leila. I'm gonna need those directions."

It took a couple of seconds, but then he heard a sniffle and her voice came back, choked up and quivering. "Where are you now?"

"Just getting onto the Ring." The elevated highway that linked East and West Beirut loomed ahead.

"You need to take the first exit ramp just after the tunnel." Her voice was now clearer and, he noted, harder.

He was a couple of minutes away.

∞

OMAR GLARED dead ahead as the car raced down the newly carved avenue that cut through the city.

He needed this to work.

He wanted Farouk. Badly.

The last couple of days had been subpar. He prided himself on his cold efficiency, a stiletto in a world of blunt axes. Tasks such as the ones he'd been assigned since this affair had begun were his bread and butter. But he'd already lost two men—three, really, if you factored in the one with the obliterated shoulder, though they were all as easily replaced as the cars that had been damaged in the encounters—and the little shithead was still out there.

The American had also become a major thorn in his side. He'd embarrassed him, and that was unforgivable. Omar would need to deal with him, at some point, regardless of the implications. He'd find a way. Timing was everything. He'd wait for the opportune moment, for one of the country's recurring political meltdowns. Then the deed would go unnoticed, except by those whose opinion he valued, the truth buried under more pressing concerns.

He saw the turn leading to the antiques market and told the three men accompanying him to check their weapons.

He wasn't heading back without his quarry.

∞

CORBEN SLAMMED on the brakes as he emerged from the tunnel on the Ring. A wall of cars blocked his way.

The four-lane, elevated highway was a main artery linking both sides of the city. Any obstacle on it—a scrape between two drivers, an ancient, conked-out truck, a car crippled by sniper fire—choked the traffic into one lane. Random, unexpected traffic jams were part of the driving experience in Beirut. People were usually creative in dealing with them. Invading the lanes of oncoming cars was one way of making road usage more flexible. The Ring, unfortunately, had a big and insurmountable central barrier. And the exit ramp Corben needed was still a hundred yards away.

Corben couldn't see what was causing the jam. He looked back. A couple of cars were pulling up beside him, but nothing was directly behind him. He slammed the gear into reverse and hit the gas.

The SUV lurched backwards and dove into the tunnel. The tunnel was too short for anyone to bother turning their headlights on, and the shift from harsh sunlight to total blackness made it difficult to tell if any cars were coming at him. It took a beat for his eyes to adjust, and when they did, he spotted a car barreling straight at him.

He cursed under his breath as he lifted his foot off the gas and guided his car as close to the side wall as he could. The oncoming car swerved to its left, causing another car behind it to brake hard to avoid it, and rushed past him, its horn blaring down the tunnel. Corben hit the gas again and guided the car back, narrowly missing another passing car and finally emerging out of the tunnel.

He kept going until he reached an upramp that led to the intersection that straddled the tunnel, then slammed on his brakes, threw the gear into drive, and flew up the ramp.

"I had to back out of the tunnel," he yelled into his phone. "I'm heading up to the main square over it."

Leila's voice came rushing back. "Okay, you're going to need to take the first right and then left after that. Just head down that road and you'll see the fire station on your right."

Corben followed her instructions, but the going was slow. The narrow streets were heavy with traffic, the oddly parked cars and street vendors' carts turning it into an obstacle course. Precious seconds turned into minutes as he navigated the SUV through the mess, shouting, hitting the horn, and waving cars to one side as he plowed through until he finally reached the fire station.

"I can see the station," he exclaimed.

"Turn right and head up that road," Leila shot back. "The cemetery wall's on your left. Take a left where it ends and you'll see a mosque about fifty yards down that street, on your right. That's where he'll be."

He practically leapfrogged over the cars ahead of him and finally spotted the mosque. It squatted between some old antiques bazaars. He slowed right down as he approached it, conjuring up Farouk's photo from Evelyn in his mind's eye as he scanned the street for any sign of Farouk or the hakeem's hit team.

He spotted him.

The Iraqi dealer was standing there, waiting nervously, as directed.

Chapter 43

❧

The Iraqi was unmistakable, even in a setting where he didn't exactly stand out. His posture—guarded, darting furtive glances up and down the street, trying to melt into the background—confirmed it for Corben.

Corben glanced at the oncoming cars and gave his mirror another check, wary of the hit team's imminent arrival as he pulled up outside the mosque. He lowered his window as he stopped.

Farouk looked over. Corben saw that he must have noticed his interest in him, as apprehension immediately took hold of the dealer's face before he threw a glance in the opposite direction, as if looking for salvation, and backed away a few steps.

Corben slipped out of the car, trying to move as fast as he could without alarming Farouk. He raised his hands in a placating gesture.

"Farouk. I'm a friend of Evelyn's. You need to come with me."

Farouk's eyes darted up the street and back at Corben as he continued to back away from him, the apprehension morphing into outright panic.

"Farouk, listen to me. Ramez was kidnapped this morning by the same men who took Evelyn. It's a trap. The cops aren't coming for you, the kidnappers are. They're on their way here right now."

"No," Farouk muttered, before turning and bolting down the street.

Corben frowned and tore off after him, cutting through the swarm of pedestrians blocking his way. Farouk wasn't moving too quickly, and Corben reeled him in fast. Farouk glanced over his shoulder before suddenly darting into an antiques bazaar. Corben followed him in.

The narrow alleyways of this miniature mall were lined with various shops only accessible from inside the bazaar. The passages were cluttered with furniture and trinkets, a few of them old, most of them forgeries manufactured locally to exacting standards. Corben glimpsed Farouk receding into the darkness to his left. He raced after him, dodging Turkish marquetry side tables and Louis XVI chairs, flying past stunned shopkeepers who yelled out after him. He reached an intersection and saw Farouk to his right, heading down a passage towards another entrance, one that gave onto a side street. Corben accelerated, drawing on every reserve of energy inside him, and closed the gap, reaching Farouk just before the exit. He leapt and grabbed him, pushing him to one side against the glass frontage of a carpet seller.

"What are you doing?" he barked at him as he shook him by his collar. "We don't have time for this bullshit. They'll be here any second. I'm trying to save your life."

Farouk stared at him with petrified eyes. His lips trembled as he struggled for words. "But Ramez . . ."

"Ramez is dead," Corben rasped. "You want to be next?"

Farouk's eyes dropped numbly as he stood there and just about managed to shake his head.

"Come on," Corben ordered as he pointed him back towards the main entrance.

Just as they turned into the passage that led up to the street, Corben spotted the pockmarked killer. He was on the sidewalk just outside the bazaar, scanning the street for any sign of his target.

Corben shoved Farouk back behind a large armoire that hogged a big chunk of the pathway and pulled out his handgun. He motioned to Farouk to stay silent and peered out. The man was still there, scowling into the street, severe displeasure radiating from his cavernous eyes.

He was also blocking Corben's route back to his car.

Corben glanced behind him, made sure the passage was clear, and pushed Farouk back into the bazaar. They skirted the edge of the furniture displays and turned into the side alley they had taken before.

"Come on," Corben urged him as he led him back the way they had come, towards the side entrance he had spotted earlier.

Corben poked his head out and made sure the narrow side street was clear before emerging through the cluttered displays. Squinting as his eyes adjusted to the musty daylight, he prowled down the broken sidewalk, making sure Farouk was close behind, holding his gun low and close to his leg to avoid causing alarm.

He reached the street corner and sneaked a look towards the mosque. The Pathfinder was half a block down, tantalizingly close. Around fifteen yards beyond it was the head thug, still prowling outside the bazaar's main entrance. Across the street, closer to him, Corben also spotted a double-parked Mercedes sedan. He saw the pockmarked man dart a glance at the car's driver, who returned the signal with a shake of the head. There had to be at least one more man somewhere around, but he couldn't see him.

He waited a beat, picked his moment, and told Farouk, "Move," as he led him out of their cover. He walked quickly, keeping Farouk close, trying to get as much cover from the passing pedestrians as he could, his grip tightened against his weapon, his eyes scanning left and right at the targets ahead.

He was within reach of his car when a younger man with nervous eyes and a slit of a mouth emerged from a coffee shop to his right. The instant recognition was mutual. The man drew his gun and ducked back behind an old man who was stepping into the coffee shop. Corben's hand hovered for a split second, looking for a clear shot he didn't have. The frightened old man screamed and moved sideways against the wall. Corben's shot was still partially blocked and he stayed his trigger finger. Instead, he did something else. He grabbed Farouk from behind and stuffed his handgun into the dealer's neck.

"You want this, huh? You want me to kill him?" he blurted at the killer.

Corben pushed Farouk forward as he stuck behind him. From the corner of his eye, he saw the pockmarked man beyond the Pathfinder react to the commotion and draw his weapon. His advantage would only last a second or two more. He edged closer to the SUV and saw the killer from the coffee shop go clear of the passersby as he looked on in confusion. Corben turned his gun on him and pumped two rounds through his chest, the .357s lifting him off his feet and slamming him backwards across tables and chairs.

"In the car, *now!*" he yelled to Farouk, pushing him towards the passenger door. All around, people were scurrying and diving for cover. He spotted the head thug, rushing over from the bazaar's entrance, and loosed a couple of rounds in his direction before pulling his door open and jumping in.

Corben spurred the car to life and hit the gas. He pushed Farouk's head down, yelling, "Stay down," at him as the Pathfinder charged into the street, towards the parked Merc. His mind racing, he quickly decided he couldn't just drive off. He was in a maze of narrow streets, and there was no telling how quickly the traffic would slow to a crawl, or even just stop. They'd soon catch up with them. He needed an extra advantage.

As the Pathfinder careened by the Merc, he stood on the brakes, lurching the heavy car to a screaming halt. He pulled out the Glock and swung it around. The surprised driver dived sideways as Corben unleashed three quick rounds at the Merc's front tire, obliterating it and causing the Merc to drop downwards. That would buy them some time. He floored the pedal again and screeched off, but as the car accelerated, he spotted a fourth killer emerging from a side street on Farouk's side, who trained his handgun at the Pathfinder and fired. The shots crunched through the car's right side just as, in the rearview mirror, the hit team's leader was shouting at the shooter as he caught up with him. Corben knew he'd be berating him for endangering Farouk. The hakeem needed him alive, which was why Corben had used him to distract the first shooter.

He glared ahead, trying to remember the fastest way out of the rat hole they were lost in. As he did, he heard a groan from Farouk.

He turned and saw the dealer wincing with pain, a crimson patch blossoming alarmingly from his side.

Chapter 44

❧

Corben forged ahead for about a mile, threading the Pathfinder through the early-afternoon traffic. On the seat next to him, Farouk writhed and groaned. The dealer kept checking his wound in disbelief, his blood-soaked hands pressing on it as Corben had told him to, all the time muttering to himself and lamenting his fate in Arabic.

Corben had one eye glued to his rearview mirror, but there was no sign of the hakeem's men. He knew Farouk was in pain, but he needed him to hang on a little bit longer until Corben was sure they were safe. He finally veered off the main road close to the wide concrete canal of the now dry Beirut River, rumbled down a dusty alleyway, and pulled over by some shuttered old garages.

"Let me see it," he told Farouk before reaching across and, carefully, checking his wound again. It was a clear in-and-out shot to his right flank, entering through his lower back and exiting just above his hip. Farouk wasn't in huge pain, which probably meant his stomach and his liver hadn't been hit, and given that he was still alive, it was a safe bet his aorta hadn't been severed. But Corben knew there would be internal damage, and while Farouk's bleeding wasn't profuse, he was still losing blood.

Choices needed to be made.

Farouk's breathing was coming in ragged, intense bursts. His eyes, wide with fear, looked to Corben for reassurance. "How is it?"

"It looks like it missed the important parts. You're going to be fine." Corben glanced around the car, but couldn't find anything to give Farouk to hold against it. "Keep your hands pressed down on it. It'll help stem the bleeding."

Farouk put both hands on the wound and grimaced with pain. Sweat was trickling down his face, and his lips quivered as he spoke. "Do you know where the nearest hospital is?"

Which was what Corben had been considering.

"I don't want to risk taking you to a hospital," he told Farouk flatly. "These people have contacts everywhere. You won't be safe there. I'm going to take you to the embassy. It's only twenty minutes from here."

Farouk's expression went from perplexed to somewhat relieved. The embassy was a safe choice. They'd probably have the best doctors brought in.

He leaned back and closed his eyes, as if to shut out the world.

Corben slid the car into gear and drove off. "I need to know some things from you. Who's after you?"

"I don't know," Farouk replied, wincing as the car hit a bump on the old, cracked asphalt.

"Well, you must have some idea. How did these people find out about the relics? How did they find you?"

Sinking lower into his seat, Farouk explained about Abu Barzan inviting him to broker his stash; about Hajj Ali Salloum finding a buyer; about Farouk's saying the book with the tail-eater wasn't part of the deal, Ali's client wanting the whole collection, the killers showing up at Ali's, and the power drill.

"Why didn't you want to include the book in the sale?" Corben asked.

Farouk's expression clouded with remorse and regret. "I knew *Sitt* Evelyn would want it, and that she'd help me in return."

Corben nodded. "You were with her in Iraq when she found the underground chamber." It was more a statement than a question.

Farouk first seemed a bit thrown that Corben knew as much, then he relaxed somewhat. "Yes. She spent a lot of time trying to understand what it meant. And when they killed Hajj Ali, I had to run, I knew that was what they were after, but I didn't know why."

Corben processed it quickly. It pretty much fit into his general take on what had happened, but he now had the full picture. But it left a crucial question unanswered.

"So where is it?"

"What?" Farouk seemed confused.

"The book. Where is it?"

Farouk winced, then said, "It's in Iraq," as if he expected Corben had known that all along.

Corben turned to him in surprise. "What?"

"Everything's still with Abu Barzan, where else?" The words were tumbling out fast and desperate. "He wasn't going to just hand anything over to me before I had the money to pay for it. He didn't even bring the pieces to Baghdad, it was too dangerous to travel with them. He kept them in Mosul."

"You told Ramez you had them," Corben shot back.

"I told him I was selling them," Farouk protested. "He must have assumed I had them here with me. They're not mine."

Corben scowled at the road ahead, thinking. He'd factored that in as a possibility, but he'd thought it more likely that Farouk had brought the book to Lebanon with him and kept it somewhere safe while he found Evelyn.

"This Abu Barzan. He's in Iraq?"

"I think so," Farouk answered weakly. "Probably back in Mosul."

Corben fumed quietly, his mind racing. The option tree he'd considered before picking up Farouk had been chainsawed into obsolescence. "You have his phone number?"

"Of course."

Corben pulled out his cell phone. "What is it?"

Farouk looked at him fearfully. "What do you want to tell him?"

"I'm not going to say anything. You're going to talk to him. You're going to tell him you have a buyer. That's what he asked you for, isn't it? Corben waved the information over with his hand. "What's his number?"

ᔆᔆᔆ

As CORBEN DIALED, Farouk suddenly felt uncomfortable with the man who had—or at least, so he claimed—rescued him. The same man who had, moments earlier, shoved a handgun in his face and bluffed with his life.

His head was spinning, his eyelids feeling heavier now, and the burning sensation in his midsection was getting more intense. He cursed his luck, he cursed fate and God himself and wished he could reset the clock, wished he'd never thought of Evelyn and her interest in the tail-eater, wished he'd left things well alone, passed on the goods to Ali's buyers, flicked a kiss from his lips to his forehead in gratitude and taken the money.

Even Baghdad was better than this.

Corben listened for a moment, then handed him the phone. Farouk took it with a trembling hand. The distant, irregular whine rang in his ear.

After a couple of rings, Abu Barzan answered in his gruff, heavy smoker's voice. "Who's this?"

"Farouk." He noticed that Abu Barzan's voice had come across somewhat louder than normal, and he could hear a radio in the background. He thought he might be in a car.

"Farouk," Abu Barzan boomed through, jovial as ever. "Where the hell are you?" He added a burst of jocular obscenities to describe his friend. "I tried calling you but your line's dead."

"I'm with a buyer," Farouk said bluntly. "He wants the pieces."

Corben glanced over at him. Somehow, Farouk managed to coax out a half smile.

Corben drove on.

"You're too late," Abu Barzan informed him with a haughty chortle before throwing in another colorful insult. "I already sold them."

The news hit Farouk like a tempest. "What do you mean, you sold them?" he flared up.

"I'm on my way to deliver them as we speak."

Farouk's heart rose. "So you still have them?"

"They're right here with me."

"Well, I'm telling you I have a buyer." Farouk saw Corben turn at his alarmed tone and felt a surge of concern about Corben's reaction. He tried to regain some composure and gave Corben a reassuring not-a-problem shake of the head.

"Well, sell him something else," Abu Barzan was saying. "You've got a whole basement of priceless junk in that shop of yours, don't you?"

"Listen to me," Farouk hissed into the phone, trying not to appear perturbed and failing. "Some people are after one of the books you're selling. Bad people. They killed Hajj Ali, they've killed others. They've kidnapped a friend of mine, a woman, because of it, and I've just been shot, do you understand me?"

"You've been shot?" More obscenities followed, though not at Farouk's expense this time.

"Yes."

"You okay?"

Farouk coughed. "I'll live."

"Who's been kidnapped then?"

"An American woman. An archaeologist, here in Beirut."

"You're in Beirut?"

"Yes," Farouk replied, exasperated. "Look, these guys are serious. They'll come after you."

Abu Barzan shrugged. "I'm sorry for what you're going through, but it's not my problem. I'm meeting my buyer tomorrow evening, I'll hand them over and get paid, and then it'll be his problem. But thanks for the heads-up. I'll keep my third eye open."

Farouk scrunched his face and sighed heavily. He felt as if he were drowning from the inside. He wasn't really surprised. Not only was Abu Barzan a grubby pig of a man, he was a sleazeball who'd sell his own children if he could find a buyer who wasn't put off by their crappy genes after taking one look at him.

Farouk told Abu Barzan, "Stay on the line," then turned to Corben, his mouth twitching with pain and frustration. "He says he's sold them. He's on his way to deliver them right now."

Corben thought about it as he coaxed the car on, then said, "Does he still have the book?"

Farouk nodded and asked Abu Barzan about the book, describing it specifically. Abu Barzan replied that he thought he had it. The deal was for the entire consignment.

"Ask him how much he's getting for the lot," Corben told Farouk.

Farouk immediately realized it was the right play, nodded, and asked.

Abu Barzan laughed. "Your buyer's got deep pockets?"

"Yes," Farouk, at his wit's end, insisted patiently.

The answer came back: "Three hundred thousand dollars. Cash."

He told Corben and made a surprised, impressed face like *That's a huge offer.*

Corben mulled it over, then said, "I'll give him four."

Farouk's eyes widened. He relayed the offer.

Abu Barzan scoffed. "That was quick. This guy serious?"

"Of course he is."

"He'd better be." Abu Barzan's tone was more serious now. When it came down to hard cash, he didn't mess around. "So tell me. What's so special about this book?"

"I don't know and I don't care," Farouk blurted angrily. "I'm just trying to save the woman's life."

"Spare me the soft sell, will you?" Abu Barzan took a deep, wheezy breath. "Alright. I'm interested. But I need to call my buyer. Least I can do is give him a chance to beat your guy's offer."

Farouk informed Corben. Corben asked him to find out how long it would take.

"He called me today," Abu Barzan said. "I'll call him now. What's your number?"

Corben told Farouk to say they'd call him back in five minutes. Farouk did, then hung up as the Pathfinder turned off the main coastal highway. The foothills that harbored the embassy loomed in the distance.

Farouk curled into his seat and sucked in a deep breath, trying to push away the burning pain in his gut and taking solace in that he was still breathing and in the hope that—contrary to expectations—things might just end up better for him than they had for his friend Ali.

Chapter 45

Kirkwood leaned against a bench in the courtyard behind the annex and waited. He was raked with frustration, unable to ask the questions he needed to ask, feeling precious minutes slipping by while he could only sit back and watch helplessly. He was checking the time yet again when his phone rang.

He saw the incoming caller ID and frowned. He stood up, glancing around to make sure he wouldn't be overheard, and flicked it open.

"I just got a call from an interested buyer," Abu Barzan's voice thundered in his ear. "He's offering me more than you are for the collection, my friend."

"I thought we had a deal," Kirkwood noted irritably.

"We did, and we do. But it's a nice offer, and I'm a businessman, you know?"

A real competing buyer, or just a shakedown? Kirkwood wondered. Either way, he had to play along. "How much is he offering?" he asked with affected patience.

"Four hundred thousand."

Kirkwood mulled it over. Another buyer, out of the blue. Offering far more than the collection was worth. If it was the same group that held Evelyn, then getting hold of the pieces would make her expendable.

To say nothing of the fact that he wasn't about to let anyone have them either. Not that easily.

"I'll give you five, but on one condition. We're not playing this game again. You want to be careful here. You know I'm good for it, you won't have a problem with me. But there are some dangerous people out there."

"So I hear," Abu Barzan agreed soberly. "I'll tell you what. Make it six hundred and the whole collection's yours. Including the book."

Kirkwood's chest tightened. Abu Barzan wasn't supposed to know about the book. Kirkwood didn't want to take the bait, nor did he want to give him the impression that paying up was that easy. He let him stew for a moment, then said, "Okay. Six hundred. But that's a huge price and you know it."

"Oh, believe me, I know it. I'll see you tomorrow night."

"This new buyer," Kirkwood asked quickly. "Anything you can tell me about him?"

Abu Barzan chuckled throatily. "Sorry, my friend. Just another crazy American, like you. Trying to get his hands on that book. Maybe I should hang on to that one, what do you think?"

Kirkwood barely contained his displeasure. "I wouldn't recommend it," he replied tersely.

Abu Barzan laughed again, mockingly. "Relax. From what I hear, it sounds like it's cursed. I'll be glad to get rid of it. Don't forget the extra cash."

And with that, he hung up.

Kirkwood stared at his phone for a moment before putting it away. He thought about the timing, and something didn't feel right. This new bidder was specifically after the book. The only people he knew of who could have been in touch with Abu Barzan were Evelyn's kidnappers and the Iraqi dealer Corben was trying to bring in. Had he failed? Had the kidnappers gotten hold of the man?

He walked into the main villa and climbed up to the ambassador's office. The ambassador's secretary informed him the ambassador would be in a meeting for another hour or so. Kirkwood thanked her. He went back out and crossed over to the annex and made his way to the press office.

Mia was still there, where he'd left her earlier. She was reading something densely worded that she had accessed on the Internet and seemed to be deeply engrossed by it. He couldn't see a heading, and the text was too small for him to make out what it was about.

"Have you heard anything from Corben?" he asked.

"No." Her expression was lined with concern. She checked her watch.

Kirkwood had already checked his. He knew it was past twelve o'clock. His eyes rose and met her gaze, his anxiety mirrored in her eyes.

The noon call would already have been made.

They'd know soon enough.

∾∾∾

THE PATHFINDER EMERGED from the congested coastal strip and began its climb towards Awkar.

The SUV's engine groaned as the wide, flat road narrowed into a series of winding bends that snaked up the foothills of Mount Lebanon. Unregulated and irregular buildings lined the road, thinning out as the climb progressed, the gaps between their stone façades widening to reveal more of the lush forests that loomed beyond.

Corben called Olshansky and gave him the number of Abu Barzan's cell phone. He told him he needed a lock on its position, which was most likely in northern Iraq. He also told him that the phone was probably being used at that very moment, and that Corben was also after whoever was on the other end of that call.

He made sure Olshansky understood to pull out all the stops on this one.

They were now ten minutes away from the embassy, and Corben didn't have much time to evaluate his options. He needed to call Abu Barzan back, though he suspected he already knew the outcome. Regardless, he wasn't ready for the interference that would inevitably descend on him the minute he entered the embassy compound.

He spotted a side road he had used before, slowed down, and took it. It was a narrow lane of cratered asphalt. He followed its path, past some scattered houses and low buildings that soon gave way to the pine forest. The track leveled off before starting to head downhill in a series of tight bends. He was about a mile off the main road when he pulled over into a small clearing and killed the engine.

It was a secluded spot, cool from the dense tree cover that was occasionally pierced by ethereal rays of sunlight. It was also deathly quiet, save for the mating song of countless cicadas that echoed around them.

Farouk scanned the trees, then turned to Corben, confused. "Why are we stopping here?"

"I don't want to make the call from the embassy."

Farouk seemed bewildered. "Why not?"

"I'd rather get this sorted out before we get there," Corben said calmly. "Don't worry about it. We're two minutes away. We'll be there before you know it."

He checked his watch. It was time. He picked up his phone, logged it back to the second-to-last dialed call, and hit the green button. A few seconds and it started to ring.

He handed the phone to Farouk as he heard Abu Barzan pick up on the first ring.

Farouk listened for a moment before turning to Corben, his face contorted with pain and dismay.

"His buyer's offered six hundred."

Corben expected as much.

He knew it would be pointless to counterbid. The relics weren't worth anywhere near as much, which meant the buyer was definitely after the same thing he was and was probably prepared to pay what it took to get them. Still, he thought of bidding up. Whether he'd ever have to come up with the cash was a different matter. But before he could even answer, he noticed that Farouk still seemed to be listening intently to Abu Barzan.

The expression on the Iraqi's face darkened even more. "He's saying there's no need for you to offer more money," Farouk relayed, his breathing labored. "He's saying his client's known he was getting the pieces all along, which means that if anyone's killing people for them, it's obviously not his buyer. And he's more than happy with the price. He thanks us for ramping the price up, but the deal's done."

Corben frowned. It was slipping away. He needed an advantage, and the only card he could play was weak, one that could work as much as it could backfire, depending on Abu Barzan's politics, which he had no time to assess, and his propensity to be intimidated.

He decided to give it a shot. "Does he speak English?"

Farouk nodded.

"Give me the phone."

Farouk mumbled a brief introduction, convinced Abu Barzan to stay on the line, then handed the phone to Corben. It was sticky with blood.

"I can't outbid your client," Corben told him, "but I'd like you to reconsider my offer."

"I'm sorry, my friend," Abu Barzan chortled. "I know my buyer's real, I know I'll have my money tomorrow, and I'll go back to Mosul a very rich man, but I don't know anything about you. Besides, you have an expression in America, no? Something about money talking and bullshit walking?"

"I just need you to think about a few things," Corben told him calmly. "It's not all about cash. I work for the U.S. government, and I can think of worse things than having us owe you a big favor. The way things are shaping up in Iraq, we're not gonna be out of there for a while. And you might find that having a friend in the system could come in handy one of these days, you know what I'm saying?"

Abu Barzan went silent for a beat. When he came back, the relaxed mocking in his tone was gone, replaced by an icy disdain. "You think telling me you work for the American government is going to make me want to help you? You think you can do things for me in Iraq?"

The politics were clear. "Better to have us owe you than be pissed off at you, that's for sure," Corben countered flatly, knowing that wasn't going to work either.

"Now you're threatening me?" Abu Barzan spat back, following it with a torrent of inspired abuse. He was on his second "Fuck you" when Corben hung up.

Farouk was staring at him with round, baffled eyes. "What did he say?"

Corben shook his head slightly. "He's not interested."

Farouk sighed heavily. "Then you have nothing to trade for *Sitt* Evelyn."

Which was true. But he knew who had the book. And he now had his phone number.

Abu Barzan had told Farouk that he was on his way to deliver the goods, and he'd added that he'd have his money "tomorrow evening." That gave Corben a little over twenty-four hours to track him down. If Abu Barzan was traveling and needed to stay in contact with his buyer, he wouldn't probably have time, nor would he risk, changing phones. Corben felt reasonably confident that Olshansky would nail down his position.

Thinking about it now, Corben realized things hadn't gone too badly. Sure, the discovery that another buyer was out there did complicate things. On the other hand, it also drew out someone Corben was just as interested in finding, someone who'd been hiding in the shadows successfully long before Corben had even gotten wind of anything. And that, in itself, was a welcome development.

Which left Farouk.

Sitting there, wheezing and groaning and bleeding all over Corben's borrowed embassy car.

Corben knew wounds like this. He knew that on TV, people who got shot were always told they were lucky it was "just" a flesh wound and would be bouncing around a few days later with nothing more to show for it than a big white bandage. The reality was very different. Most shots needed hospitalization and IVs. Infections set in easily and were commonplace. And a wound such as Farouk's would require, at best, a month of serious hospitalization. It was also highly likely he'd feel its effect, in some way, for the rest of his life.

And that was a problem.

As he had told Farouk, a hospital wouldn't be safe, not from the hakeem, given his contacts in the Lebanese police force. Besides, the last thing he wanted was for the hakeem to know Farouk had been shot. And even if the hakeem didn't grab Farouk outright, he'd find out what Corben now knew, and any leverage Corben had over the hakeem would be lost.

The Fuhud detectives would get involved. The head of station. The press too, probably. Every move, every choice Corben made, or wanted to make, would be pored over with a microscope. The ambassador and the Lebanese government would also get sucked in. If they found out about Abu Barzan's pieces and managed to get hold of them, they might set up an exchange with the hakeem and trade them for Evelyn. The hakeem would have what he was after, he'd recede into the shadows, and Corben would be left with nothing but frustration and tons of paperwork. And if the hakeem couldn't get to Farouk, or if no exchange went through, he'd also disappear.

That ruled out the hospital.

He couldn't keep Farouk at the embassy either. They didn't have the medical facilities there. It would be bad enough if Farouk died while in hospital, but if he died while he was at the embassy . . . The ambassador was a principled, honorable guy who wouldn't keep Farouk's presence a secret, not from the State Department, nor from the local authorities. Farouk's death on U.S. soil would create a shitstorm that would ruin everything.

He wouldn't get what he was after.

Thinking it through dispassionately, he couldn't see that Farouk was of any further value to him. The man had only gotten drawn into this accidentally, and now that Corben knew what Farouk knew about Abu Barzan, the Iraqi had become obsolete.

More than obsolete.

He was a liability.

Whichever way he turned, all Corben saw coming out of bringing him in was questions, obstacles, complications, and grief.

Which didn't really leave him much choice.

He turned to Farouk. The wounded Iraqi looked like a mauled animal, curled up and drenched in blood. His face glistened with sweat and looked even more ashen in the pale, diffused light of the forest. His whole body was shivering, and his trembling hands, caked thick with blood, still pressed down meekly on his wound. He was staring at Corben with scared, half-dead eyes that were barely managing to stay open.

He opened his cracked, dry mouth to say something, but Corben calmly gestured to him to stay quiet. He leaned over to him and said, "I'm sorry."

Farouk looked at him with faint puzzlement.

Corben's arms lashed out towards him. One hand went behind his head, holding it in place. The other slammed onto Farouk's face, squeezing tightly, clamping his mouth and nose shut.

Farouk's eyes rocketed wide and his arms flailed upward, but there was no strength left in them. Corben swung an arm down and darted a punch right next to Farouk's wound, causing him to exhale in a muffled howl of pain as he bent forward. Corben shoved him right back against the seat and kept the lock on his breathing. Farouk started coughing and wheezing with a heavy, gurgling sound, his eyes almost popping out of their sockets as he stared at Corben in primal horror. Corben increased his vise grip on him, feeling the Iraqi's strength drain, feeling the last wisps of life abandon his battered body until the futile resistance stopped altogether.

Chapter 46

Through the window of her room in the press office, Mia noticed the Pathfinder driving past the annex, headed for the rear of the compound. The driver's-side window was down, allowing her to spot Corben as he guided the SUV into a parking slot in a covered bay that was kept away from the main building as an additional safety precaution against booby-trapped cars.

She sprang to her feet and looked out, her pulse racing as she concentrated her gaze on the car. The angle hadn't allowed her to see anyone in the passenger seat. Interminable seconds crawled by before Corben finally appeared from behind the bay's bunkerlike shelter.

Mia's heart sank. He was alone.

Even worse, he was covered in what could only be blood. And as if that weren't enough, the grim scowl that darkened his face said it all.

Mia felt her knees buckle. She slid back into her chair, feeling a great tearing deep inside her.

No Farouk.

No way of getting the book.

Nothing to trade for her mom.

CORBEN SHUT HIS EYES and let the torrent of hot water flush the weariness out of his aching body. The embassy's gym was a windowless, isolated haven tucked deep into the basement of the annex, and right now, its shower cubicle afforded Corben a momentary respite from the blood and the grime of what had become his most intense day since being posted to this unsettled city.

He'd thought carefully about what he would tell his bosses—the station chief and the ambassador—before calling in and giving them a heads-up while driving back to the embassy. Farouk had been shot. Mortally. He'd died before he could get him to a hospital. And at that point, there was only one option open to him: He needed to make sure the kidnappers didn't find out Farouk had been killed. If they did, they might assume that the relics' location was lost with him, and if so, there'd be nothing to trade for Evelyn.

He couldn't bring his body to the embassy, which was technically U.S. soil. He couldn't hand him over to the cops either. Given how pervasively they seemed to be penetrated, the kidnappers would find out Farouk was dead long before his corpse went cold. He had to make him disappear. For a while, anyway. To buy himself some time to come up with another way to get Evelyn out.

So he'd driven deep into the pine forests east of the city and dumped his body there, off a small trail that was hardly used. No one had been around. If and when the body was eventually discovered, Corben and the embassy had total deniability. Yes, Corben had driven off with him, but the man had been wounded in the shoot-out and had bolted out of the car when it got stuck in traffic and run off. An entirely plausible theory would be that the men who were after him, and who had killed the assistant professor, had caught up with him. By then, the whole affair would probably be done and dusted, and no one would be too concerned with the fate of an illegal alien, let alone one from Iraq.

Corben didn't really have a choice. It was a tough decision he had to make, there and then. It was either that or jeopardize the whole endeavor. Which he wasn't about to do. The brass ring he was reaching for was far too momentous for that.

He shook his misgivings away, and his thoughts soon migrated to something more productive. Olshansky had gotten a preliminary hit on

Abu Barzan's cell phone. It wasn't in northern Iraq, as assumed. The phone signal was roaming somewhere in eastern Turkey, close to the Syrian border. Olshansky would need a bit of time to get a tighter lock on it. He'd told Corben that he was confident he'd be able to track down the man for him, but that working backwards to trace whomever he'd been in touch with would be harder, adding some technobabble about incompatible network systems that Corben tuned out.

The location didn't surprise Corben. A foreign buyer wouldn't risk venturing into Iraq to take delivery of the pieces, and Mosul—where Abu Barzan was coming from—wasn't far from the Turkish border. Corben knew the area reasonably well. It was predominantly Kurd, on either side of the border, as was Mosul. He guessed the buyer would have arranged for the transaction to take place in Batman, Mardin, or Diyarbakir. All three had airports that were serviced by regional flights and private charters, and all were within a few hours' drive from the Turkish/Iraqi border.

It was an exchange Corben didn't want to miss.

Farouk's revelation of a buyer paying over the odds for Abu Barzan's little trove threw all of Corben's plans into question. Up until that point, the hakeem had been Corben's main target, the only man on his radar whom he knew to be chasing the dream with ruthless abandon. This mystery buyer was now at least as interesting to Corben as the hakeem. Somehow, he'd managed to hear about the book's availability before the hakeem. He'd trumped him into securing it. Hell, he could well know more about it and its significance than the hakeem. The question was, was what he knew enough to make the hakeem irrelevant to Corben's plans, or was his work incomplete? Did he have the treatment figured out already, or would he need the hakeem's extreme resources and facilities to turn the dream into a reality?

Two targets were now in Corben's crosshairs. One would inevitably contact him: The hakeem would assume Corben had Farouk—and the book—and would want to trade. The other would be making his way to a quiet rendezvous somewhere in eastern Turkey. Corben needed to be there for it, but he had to find a way to do it on his own terms and without involving his colleagues at the embassy. At this point, apart from the mystery buyer and Abu Barzan himself, no one else knew about the imminent transaction. He wanted to keep it that way for now, at least until he could set up his trip to Turkey on his own terms. He needed to choose his words carefully if he was going to pull it off without attracting undue attention.

Either way, the endgame was near.

∽∾∽

KIRKWOOD STUDIED Corben's face as he listened to the agent's briefing with deepening unease.

Things hadn't gone according to plan. Admittedly, Corben had been winging it. There were never any guarantees that they'd be able to intercept the call to Ramez, much less actually beat the kidnappers to Farouk. Corben had done remarkably well to get hold of the Iraqi before them, and he'd almost pulled it off, if it hadn't been for an unlucky round that had found its way into Farouk's side.

He scanned the other faces around the room. The ambassador and Hayflick, the station chief, were also listening intently as Corben presented his thought process with impressive clarity.

"So what are we left with?" the ambassador asked. "Do we know where he stashed the pieces Bishop's kidnappers are after?"

Corben shook his head. "I didn't have time to get that from him. He was in shock, just rambling incoherently in Arabic before his body gave up on him."

The ambassador nodded glumly.

Kirkwood kept his eyes locked on Corben. He wondered if Corben also knew that there was no stash to be found. The call from Abu Barzan had raised some troubling questions in Kirkwood's mind, and since Farouk hadn't been grabbed by the kidnappers, the other bidder wasn't one of them. Which meant it was someone else. And the timing was too coincidental to discount the possibility that the other bidder was linked to Corben, if it wasn't actually him.

Which threw up some disturbing realizations.

One was that Corben was, quite possibly, well aware of the forthcoming Turkish transaction. The other was that, given the ulterior agenda he seemed to be pursuing, getting Evelyn back safely might not exactly be a priority for him.

"You think the kidnappers will get in touch?" Kirkwood probed.

"They've got to," Corben speculated. "Right now, they think we've got Farouk, which means they've got to assume we also have his stash. And that's what they're after. I've got to think they'll make contact and offer to trade Evelyn for it. At least, I'm hoping they do. Right now, it's looking like our only chance of getting her back."

A sobering silence descended on the room.

Not good enough, Kirkwood thought. He wasn't comfortable with the wait-and-pray strategy, nor with the potential danger of a bluff trade if they did call. He needed to instigate things. "We need to send them a signal," he suggested. "A message. Let them know we're ready to trade." He turned to the ambassador. "Maybe you could make a statement to the press. Something along the lines of 'We're waiting for word from the kidnappers so that we can work things out and give them what they need to bring this matter to a mutually beneficial conclusion.' That kind of thing."

The ambassador's expression clouded. "You know our policy on negotiating with terrorists openly. You want me to go on TV and invite them to make a trade?"

"They're not terrorists," Kirkwood reminded him. "They're antiquity smugglers."

"Come on, Bill. It's a nuance no one's going to pick up on. For most people who'll be watching, they're one and the same."

Kirkwood frowned with frustration. "What about the Bishop girl? A daughter making an emotional plea for the return of her mother."

"I don't see a problem with that," the ambassador conceded. "Okay. I'll set something up. But it's going to be tricky to pull off a bluff like that, given that we don't have the pieces."

"If we get that call and they want to trade, we'll get her back, regardless," Hayflick assured him. "We can set it up so it's to our advantage."

Kirkwood turned to Corben. He thought he spotted a hint of discomfort in his hardened expression, but the agent's face wasn't giving much away. He just acknowledged Kirkwood's suggestion with a small, thoughtful nod.

At the back of Kirkwood's mind, something else was vying for attention. More and more, he was feeling it would be inevitable. He and his partners were all in agreement on this. *Do your best to get Evelyn out without exposing the project. But if you have to, then use the book.* Not having seen the book yet, he wasn't sure that giving it up would expose anything, but it could jeopardize their work and put a legacy that was hundreds of years in the making at risk.

It wasn't a decision he had to make just yet. It was irrelevant as long as the kidnappers hadn't made contact.

He felt a silent vibration in his pocket and fished out his phone. He glanced at the caller ID. It was his main contact at the UN. "I'm sorry, I have to take this," he apologized to the others as he got out of his seat and stepped away from the table.

The blunt voice on the other end went straight to the point.

"That thing you asked me about," his contact at the UN said. "This hakeem. I think I've got something for you."

∾∾∾

THE CONTRITE WORDS coming out of Omar's mouth inflamed the hakeem.

"He got away, *mu'allimna*. The American has him."

The hakeem seethed with disbelief. How could Omar have failed him—again? The man had all the necessary advantages. He had the resources, the contacts, the firepower, and still he failed.

Omar rattled off his explanation and his excuses, but the hakeem silenced him with a ferocious rebuke. He didn't need to hear the details. He only cared about results. And he needed people who could provide him with the ones he wanted. When this was over, he'd have to see about having Omar replaced. They'd need to get him someone more reliable. More capable. Someone who would get the job done.

He allowed his breathing to settle and focused on his next move. He knew he still held a trump card. They'd give him what he was after in exchange for the woman, he didn't doubt that. But the trade would carry risk, and given Omar's track record of late, pulling it off without leaving a trail was by no means assured. The hakeem was loath to take unnecessary risks, but Omar's ineptitude had made a big one unavoidable. Hostage exchanges were never foolproof, not for either party.

Something else was coursing through his veins, something far more poisonous than the looming threat of the exchange: The American had humiliated his men yet again, which meant he'd humiliated him. It was a personal affront, a grave insult, one that the hakeem found intolerable and unforgivable. The transgression had to be punished. Order needed to be restored.

"Call your contacts. Do it now. I want to know everything there is to know about this American," he rasped. "Everything."

Chapter 47

Cocooned inside her hotel room, Mia watched herself on TV with subdued detachment. She stared through the screen as her own face loomed bizarrely back at her, reciting the carefully worded plea that Corben had given her before handing her over to the embassy's press attaché. The image on the screen wasn't registering. It felt like an alternate reality, a surreal parallel universe that she was watching through a tear in some *Matrix*-like continuum, except that it wasn't. It was real. Starkly, unquestionably real.

With a heavy heart, she'd called her aunt's house back in Nahant just before the news conference. Her aunt had picked up, her sunny voice indicating that she hadn't yet read anything about the kidnapping. Mia built up some courage with a brief exchange of banter, then, with great care, she told her aunt what had happened. It was a hard conversation to have, but her aunt was a strong woman who, though hugely concerned, took it stoically. Mia alerted her to the press conference while assuring her that every effort was being expended to find Evelyn and get her back safely, adding that, yes, she would be careful too. She'd hung up, feeling a constricting ache in her chest.

She turned the volume down and brooded over Corben's grim update. With Farouk dead and his stash missing, there was nothing to trade for Evelyn. Which was really bad news. She'd thought about going back to Evelyn's apartment, looking through her stuff, seeing if she could find another book, something with the tail-eater symbol on it that they could use, something to entice the kidnappers into a barter, but Corben had shot that idea down pretty quickly. He'd been there, done that. He'd found nothing in her apartment that they could substitute for the book.

Besides, it was all moot right now. The bastards hadn't made contact.

She silently hoped—prayed—they would. They had to. What was the point of taking her, if it wasn't to trade her for something?

The news moved on to some other uplifting event. She clicked the TV off and looked around the room. She hated the utter loneliness of it and thought back to the previous night, to being at Corben's apartment. Even though she barely knew him, his presence was comforting. She realized she'd been through more with him, in the brief hours she'd known him, than she had with most men she'd dated. She wondered whether to call him, to see if there was anything new, but she buried the thought, certain that it would be a bad idea.

She glanced at her bed and knew that sleep, if it was to come, needed to be coerced, bribed, enticed.

She picked up her key card and her cell phone and headed for the door.

ᏇᎧᎧ

IN HIS DARKENED LIVING ROOM, Corben switched off his TV and made his way to his bedroom. It had been a ferocious day—probably his most challenging, ever. He'd been fueled through it by a torrent of adrenaline, but that well was now bone-dry. He felt the weariness of battle in every pore of his body, which was crying out for a respite. He wasn't about to argue with that.

He climbed into bed and killed the lights. The blackout blinds blotted out the outside world, and he let his mind drift. It resisted for a while, stubbornly churning over the tasks ahead.

His thoughts settled on Evelyn Bishop's call to Tom Webster. Corben had asked a data-mining analyst at Langley to feed the name into the system. There were too many hits—the name was surprisingly common. Corben had given the analyst an estimated age and some target backgrounds to narrow the field, but pinning the name to an identity, if it happened at all, would take time.

He moved on to the more pressing matter at hand. The last update from Olshansky showed the Iraqi dealer to have settled in for the night in Diyarbakir, a small town in southeast Turkey, around fifty miles from the Syrian border. Corben had thought the man would go for Mardin, which was a couple of hours closer to the Iraqi border. Both had airports, but Diyarbakir's was larger, the town bigger, and visitors didn't risk drawing as much attention. Using triangulation, Olshansky had the dealer pinned down within a radius of fifty yards, which, in a remote place such as Diyarbakir, was as good as it got.

Corben needed to figure out how to get there without alerting his colleagues to what he might find there. The Agency had people in the general area, but he didn't want to delegate this. He wanted to be there himself and didn't want Hayflick or anyone else, for that matter, to know the real reason. He thought he would use Olshansky's phone tracking to justify the trip. Say it was someone Farouk had called from the café. A person of interest. Diyarbakir was only three hundred miles away. It wouldn't take more than a couple of hours to fly there in a small plane. He'd need to arrange it first thing in the morning if he wanted to get there in time for when his mystery buyer showed up.

The thought of that encounter pleased him and lulled him into a desperately needed sleep.

<hr />

TWO FLOORS UP from Mia's room, Kirkwood glanced up from his laptop and half-watched her statement on his TV. He'd already seen it on one of the other local channels. The embassy's press handlers had done a good job, as had Mia; her mom's kidnappers would definitely get the message.

His attention was mired elsewhere, and his eyes dropped back to the screen of his laptop and to the baleful file that his contact inside the UN had e-mailed him. He'd read it once already, and he was about to read it again.

It was the hakeem's file.

The file shed light on Corben, as the agent assigned to track him down. Corben himself was solid. His assignments had been bread-and-butter

Agency fieldwork in the Middle East, nothing too vicious or too wet. It was the information relating to the hakeem that had shaken Kirkwood.

His contacts in Iraq had mentioned someone asking about the Ouroboros on a few occasions in recent years, but he was never able to find out who was behind the inquiries. People were scared to talk under Saddam.

Even more so, in this case.

He went through the dossier again, his chest constricting with revulsion. The findings in Iraq were beyond heinous. Autopsies that had been carried out on some of the bodies found after the raid on the hakeem's compound confirmed, with appalling detail, what the man had been working on. There was little doubt as to what he was after.

Many of the techniques he was attempting had been tried out on lab animals, mostly mice, and had varying degrees of success in rejuvenating the animals or prolonging their lives. The thing was, the hakeem wasn't using mice. He was performing the same experiments on humans.

One such experiment, famously undertaken by Italian and American neuroscientists in the early nineties, was to transplant tissue taken from the pineal glands of younger mice into older mice, and vice versa. Simply put, the older mice got younger, and the younger mice got older. The former looked healthier, were able to run around their cages and spin their wheels with startling vigor and outlived control animals of the same age; the latter's fur lost its luster, they slowed down to a point where they could no longer perform basic tricks that they could easily manage before the transplants, and they died sooner. Autopsies on the animals also showed that some of the internal organs of the older mice that had received the transplants from the young mice displayed striking signs of rejuvenation. And given that the pineal gland is responsible for the production of the hormone melatonin, the rejuvenation was attributed to an increase in the recipients' melatonin levels, which sparked the melatonin supplement craze.

The full picture, however, wasn't as promising: Scientists who took a closer look at the results discovered that the mice that were used in the experiments had a genetic defect that actually prohibited them from producing melatonin. Attributing their improved physiology to melatonin was therefore patently absurd. But proving that melatonin wasn't responsible for their healthier and longer lives didn't negate that they did, in fact, look younger and live longer. Something was responsible for it. It just wasn't the melatonin.

The autopsies indicated that some of the hakeem's experiments were to find out if pineal-gland grafts and transplants had the same effect in humans. Running such experiments on humans wasn't easy. The pineal gland, which is only the size of a pea in humans, is located at the core of the brain. It's mostly active up to puberty, then gets calcified in adulthood and is thought to become obsolete. Which means that the only pineal glands worth harvesting had to come from children or teens, and the endoscopic surgery to reach the glands was complex, delicate, and carried high risks for the donor.

Which wasn't a problem if you had an endless supply of expendable kids.

The other major problem was that life-extending experiments were mostly performed on species that had short life spans, to be able to actually observe and document the changes within a reasonable time frame. Mayflies were ideal, given their one-day life spans. Nematode worms, which live for two weeks or so, were also commonly used, as were lab mice, although their life spans of around two years made them less than ideal. Humans needed much longer periods of observation for any significant change to be noticeable. This meant that after undergoing the hakeem's extreme treatments, his test subjects had to remain incarcerated for months, or years, before the results of his experiments were apparent.

The autopsies showed that the hakeem wasn't just playing with pineal glands. Other glands such as the pituitary and thymus glands were also part of his repertoire, as were testicular glands in males and ovaries in women. In some victims, he had limited his experimentation to studying the effects of various hormones and enzymes on the test subjects' bodies. His work was remarkably advanced, encompassing both prolongevity staples such as telomerase as well as more recent fixations such as the PARP-1 protein. The equipment at his disposal was state-of-the-art, and he was clearly a skilled surgeon and molecular biologist.

Invariably, his test subjects suffered horrible deaths. Some of the men, women, and children who were wheeled into his operating chamber were farmed for whatever parts were of use to him and simply discarded. Others, the recipients, endured long periods of living with the effects of his demented procedures, and when their bodies finally gave out, he clearly had no qualms about opening them up to have a look at what went wrong before chucking their remains into mass graves.

Kirkwood felt nauseous. A bile of anger burned the back of his throat. He knew of scientists who had decamped to less conscientious countries where they could carry out their grotesque experiments without worrying about activists and ethics committees. But this was different. This went far beyond anything he'd ever considered humanly possible.

This was true evil.

The most shocking part of it was that Corben, according to the file, had been tasked with finding the hakeem.

Not to take him down.

To harness his talents.

It wasn't a first. Governments were always happy to forgive past trespasses, no matter how horrific, and dance with the devil if it meant getting their hands on innovative and valuable research. The U.S. government was one of the early adopters of that model. They did it with Nazi rocket scientists. They did it with Russian experts in nuclear, chemical, and biological warfare. And, it seemed, they were happy to do it with this hakeem.

Corben's assignment was to find the hakeem and bring him into the fold. Evelyn's kidnapping gave him a way to connect with him. But it had to mean that in their eyes, she was expendable. A means to an end. Nothing more.

He flashed back to Abu Barzan's unexpected phone call. The surprise bidder. At the same time as Farouk had mortally been wounded.

While he'd been in Corben's custody.

Before he'd died.

How far were they prepared to go?

He had to adjust his plans.

Kirkwood wondered who else was in the loop. Were they all in on it? Hayflick, the station chief—probably. The ambassador—maybe not. Kirkwood hadn't gotten that vibe from him, but then again, these people did lie for a living.

He'd need to call the others, inform them of his discoveries. He knew they'd agree. He had to short-circuit Corben's assignment, even if it meant jeopardizing the project. Evelyn's life depended on it, as did the lives of countless innocents who could find themselves on the monster's operating table.

Images of the hakeem's victims ambushed his every thought. He knew he wouldn't be falling asleep anytime soon.

∽∂∽

A FLURRY OF MUFFLED THUMPS jolted Corben awake.

He sprang up, his eyes barely registering the ghostly 2:54 A.M. reading on the alarm clock on his side table, his foggy brain still booting up and struggling to process some noise at the very edge of his hearing threshold: rapid footfalls, rushing stealthily across the cold, tiled floor of his apartment, coming straight at him.

He realized what was happening, his hand instinctively diving into the side table's drawer for his handgun, but just as his fingers felt its grip, the door to his bedroom burst open and three men whose features he couldn't make out in the darkness bolted in. The lead man kicked the drawer shut, slamming it hard against Corben's wrist. Corben reeled with pain, turning back in time to glimpse the man's raised arm arcing down at him like a lightning bolt from above.

He thought he spotted a gun in its grasp a split second before the strike connected with his skull and sent him crashing into a sudden and absolute blackout.

Chapter 48

⦶

The roof terrace of the Albergo Hotel was soothingly mellow, a pleasant change from the chaotic bustle of the bar at Mia's previous hotel.

She hadn't been here before. Lost among jasmine and dwarf fig trees, a handful of people were scattered in the dark recesses of this suspended oasis that overlooked the city's rooftops and the sea beyond. She found a quiet corner and was soon in the comforting embrace of a martini. E. B. White had dubbed the drink his "elixir of quietude," and right now that was working just fine for her.

She was too lost in her own thoughts to notice that she was the only solo person here. A lot had happened in the previous forty-eight hours, and her mind had a lot to work through.

She was looking for a waiter to order a refill when Kirkwood appeared and joined her. They shared a round and dabbled in some awkward chitchat, briefly commenting on the hotel's charms and the city's contradictions. Mia could see that his mind was elsewhere. His eyes radiated a deep unease, and something was obviously haunting him.

He was the first to veer them back to the grim tide they were swimming against.

"I saw the broadcast. You did great. It'll do the trick. This hakeem will definitely get the message. They'll call."

"But then what?" Mia asked. "We don't have anything to offer them, and trying to pull off some kind of bluff . . ." She let the words drift.

"The guys at the embassy know their stuff," Kirkwood assured her. "They'll figure it out. They managed to get to Farouk before the hakeem's men, right?"

She could see that he wasn't thrilled by the prospect either, but she appreciated the effort. "Yeah, and look how well that turned out."

Kirkwood found a half-smile. "I've got my contacts in Iraq working on it. I'm pretty confident they'll come up with something."

"What? What could they possibly find that could make a difference?"

He didn't really have an answer he could give her. A waiter glided over and discreetly replenished their carrot sticks and pistachios, then Kirkwood said, in a surprising change of tack, "I never knew Evelyn had a daughter."

"I wasn't around," Mia said. "I lived with my aunt. In Boston. Well, near Boston."

"What about your father?"

"He died before I was born."

A shadow crossed his face. "I'm sorry."

She shrugged. "They were together. In Iraq. In that chamber. One month later, he dies in a car crash." She raised her glance to Kirkwood. All light had abandoned her voice. "This tail-eater. It's one hell of a good-luck charm, isn't it?"

Kirkwood stayed silent, and nodded somberly.

"I mean, what the hell is this nut job thinking?" she blurted out angrily. "Is he looking to revive some biblical plague, or does he really expect to find a magic potion that'll let him live forever? I mean, how can you even begin to reason with someone like that?"

Kirkwood raised an eyebrow. "You think the hakeem's after some kind of fountain of youth? Where'd that come from? I've seen his file. It doesn't mention anything about that."

Mia brushed it off and, almost self-mockingly, mentioned her conversation with Boustany about elixirs.

Kirkwood took a sip from his cocktail, as if weighing his next words. He put the glass down and looked at her. "Well, you're the geneticist. You tell me. Is it really that insane?"

"Please," Mia scoffed.

He wasn't scoffing back. He was serious.

"You're really asking me if it's possible?" she said.

"I'm just saying, face transplants were considered impossible a few years ago. They're doing them now. If you think about the medical advances that have been achieved in the last few years . . . it's staggering. And the hits just keep on coming. We've mapped out the human genome. We've cloned a sheep. Heart tissue has just been successfully created from stem cells. So, I don't know. Maybe this is possible."

"Of course it isn't," Mia replied dismissively.

"I saw this documentary once. About this Russian scientist, back in the fifties—I think his name was Demikhov—he was researching head transplants. To prove it was doable, he grafted the head and upper body of a puppy onto a bigger mastiff and created a two-headed dog. The thing ran around happily and survived for six days." He shrugged. "And that's just one we know about."

Mia leaned forward, her eyes bristling with conviction. "Transplants are about reconnecting nerves and veins and, yes, maybe even spinal cords one day. But this is different. This is about stopping the damage that happens to our cells, to our DNA, to our tissues and organs, with every breath we take. It's about errors in DNA replication, it's about molecules inside our body getting bombarded by free radicals and mutating wrongly and just degrading over time. It's about wear and tear."

"But that's my point. It's not the years, it's the mileage," he said pointedly. "You're talking about cells getting damaged and breaking down, which is very different from saying they're programmed to live a certain length of time, and then die. It's like, if you buy a new pair of trainers. You wear them, you jog in them, the soles wear out and the shoes fall apart. If you don't wear them, they don't just disintegrate after a few years in their box. Wear and tear. It's why we die, right? There's no ticking clock that tells our body its time is up. We're not programmed to die, are we?"

Mia shifted in her seat. "That's one line of thought."

"But it's the one that's carrying the day right now, isn't it?"

Mia knew it was. It was a specialization she had flirted with, but she'd ultimately veered off into another direction, knowing that anti-aging research was the embarrassing relative no one wanted to talk about. Biogerontology—the science of aging—had been having a tough time since, well, the Jurassic era.

In official circles, it wasn't far removed from the quackery of alchemists and the charlatanry of the snake-oil salesmen of yesteryear. Serious scientists, clinging to the traditional belief that growing old is inevitable, were wary of pursuing something that was doomed to failure, and even warier of being ridiculed if they attempted to explore it. Governmental bodies wouldn't fund it: They dismissed it as an unachievable pipe dream and were loath to be seen funding something that their electorate didn't really believe—because of what they'd been told and taught—was achievable. Even when presented with compelling arguments and breakthroughs, the holders of the purse strings still wouldn't go near it because of deeply held religious beliefs: Humans age and die. It's the way of the world. It's what God intended. It's pointless and immoral to try to overcome that. Death is a blessing, whether we realize it or not. The good will become immortal, of course—but only in heaven. And don't even think about arguing it with the President's Council on Bioethics. The prevention of aging is, even more than Al Qaeda, an evil threat to our dignified human future.

Case closed.

And yet, in a broader context, scientists had been spectacularly successful in prolonging human life so far. Average life expectancy—the average number of years humans are expected to live—hovered between twenty and thirty years for most of human history. This average was skewed downwards due to one main cause: infant mortality. Three or four infants died for every person who managed to evade the plague, dodge the blade of a sword, and reach eighty. Hence the low average. Medical and hygienic advances—clean water, antibiotics, and vaccines—allowed babies to survive to adulthood, allowing this average to increase dramatically over the last hundred years in what is referred to as the first longevity revolution. It hit forty in the nineteenth century, fifty in 1900, and it was now around eighty in developed countries. Whereas early man had a one-in-twenty-million chance of living to a hundred, that's now one in fifty. In fact, since 1840, average life expectancy had been growing at a quarter of a year every year. Demographers predicting an upper limit to our expected life spans had consistently been proven wrong.

The crucial difference was that life extension had been achieved by developing vaccines and antibiotics that weren't conceived with the aim of prolonging life, but rather, to help combat illnesses, an unarguably noble goal. The nuance was critical. And only recently had a paradigm shift occurred in the medical-research community's attitude towards aging, from perceiving it as something inevitable and predestined, to considering it something far less draconian:

A disease.

A simple analogy was that, until recently, the term *Alzheimer's* was only used when referring to sufferers of that form of dementia who were under a certain age—around sixty-five or so. Any older than that, and they didn't have a disease—they were just *senile*, and there was no point in doing anything about it. It was part of growing old. This changed in the 1970s, when a demented ninety-year-old was treated no differently from a forty-year-old with Alzheimer's—both were now equally considered to be suffering from a disease that medical researchers were working hard to understand and cure.

Much in the same way, "old age" was now, more and more, being viewed as an illness. A highly complex, multifaceted, perplexing illness. But an illness nevertheless.

And illnesses can be cured.

The key realization that triggered this new approach was a deceptively simple answer to the fundamental question "Why do we age?" The answer was, simply put, that we age because, in nature, nothing else did.

Or, more accurately, almost nothing ever did.

For thousands of years—throughout virtually all of human evolution—in the wild and away from the cosseting care and advances of the civilized world, humans and animals hardly ever reached old age. They were ravaged by predators, disease, starvation, and weather.

They didn't get a chance to grow old.

And nature's preoccupation has always been to make sure its organisms reproduce, to perpetuate the species—nothing more. All it asked of our bodies, all we were designed to do from an evolutionary point of view, was to reach reproductive age, have babies, and nurture them until they were old enough to survive in the wild on their own.

That's it.

That was all nature cared about.

Beyond that, we were redundant—man and beast alike. All of the cells that made us up had no reason to keep us alive beyond that.

And since we didn't stand a chance of surviving much beyond the age of reproduction, then nature's efforts were—rightly—concentrated on stacking the odds for us to reach that age and replicate. Natural selection only cared about our reaching reproductive age, and—rightly, and again unfortunately for those of us who wanted to stick around a little longer—it chose a short life span for us to reproduce in because that was more efficient: It made for shorter time between generations, more mixing of genes, which gave greater adaptability to threatening environments. All of which meant that a process—aging—that never actually manifested itself in nature, in the wild, couldn't have evolved genetically.

Nature, while it was evolving us, didn't know what aging was.

In other words, aging wasn't genetically programmed into us.

This had led to a radical new outlook on aging.

If we weren't programmed to die, if we were killed by wear and tear—so the argument now went—then maybe, just maybe, we could be fixed.

Chapter 49

⌒⌒⌒

Aburning twinge of smelling salts assaulted Corben's senses and shook him back to life.

He was immediately aware of a sharp pain that throbbed at the back of his head, and he felt oddly uncomfortable. He realized that his hands and feet were all tied to each other behind his back, his legs bent all the way backwards in a reverse-fetal position. He was also still in his boxers. His mouth and cheek were pressed against something hard and prickly that felt like sandpaper, and his throat felt parched. Instinctively, he tried to lick his lips, but found dry soil instead. He spat the grit off and coughed.

His eyes darted around, rushing to process his surroundings, and he saw that he was lying on the ground, on his side, out in some kind of field. Somewhere quiet. The headlights of a parked car were beating down on him; beyond them, he could see that it was still night, although the faint glimmer of a morning sun was hinting from behind a mountain range to his right.

A mountain range. To the east. He archived the thought, guessing that he must be somewhere in the Bekáa Valley. And if it was almost dawn, it meant he'd been out for at least a couple of hours. Which tallied with how long it would take to drive there from Beirut, especially at that time of night when the roads were deserted.

As his nerves endings flickered awake, more pains and bruises announced themselves across his body. He tried to shift to a position that was less awkward, but his effort was rewarded with a sharp kick from a booted foot to his ribs that sent a searing pain through his side.

He coiled forward, straining against the nylon cuffs on his limbs, still on his side, his face and side digging into the rough soil. He turned upwards and saw the pockmarked man leering down at him.

"Khalas," he heard a voice snap. Enough.

He sensed movement from the corner of his eye. The man who owned the voice was approaching through the glare of the headlights. From his low vantage point, Corben could only make out the shoes— leather moccasins, expensive-looking—and the dark slacks. The face towered far out of reach.

The man stepped right up to him until his feet were inches from Corben's face. Corben tried to roll slowly, awkwardly, slightly more onto his back, but his bent legs blocked the move. The man just stood there, staring down at him as if he were an insect. Corben couldn't really make out his features, but he could see that the man was slim, clean-shaven, and had longish silvery hair.

The feeling of vulnerability and helplessness was disconcerting. As if to confirm it, the man raised his foot and brought it over Corben's face, then casually pressed down, slowly, resting the sole of his shoe on his nose, not really putting his weight into it at first, then gradually leaning down harder, crushing his nose and cheeks, sending an excruciating pain shooting across his face as his head was mashed into the ground.

Corben tried to wriggle free, but the man's foot had him pinned down. He let out a tortured, half-muffled yell for him to stop.

The man didn't, prolonging Corben's agony a few more seconds before finally pulling his foot away. He glowered down at him, studying him. "You have something I want," he said, his voice laced with a mocking disdain.

Corben spluttered the sand and grit out of his mouth. "And you've got something—someone—we want."

The man raised his foot again, hovering it just above Corben's face, threatening. Corben didn't flinch. The man just held his foot there for a beat, as if he were about to squash a bug, before pulling it back. "I don't think you're in any position to play hardball," he told him calmly. "I want the book. Where is it?"

"I don't have it." Through his daze, Corben registered the man's accent. Southern European, for sure. Italian, possibly. He stored the thought.

The man nodded to someone behind Corben. Before he could see who it was, another sharp kick plowed into his side.

Corben screamed out with pain. "I'm telling you I don't have it, God damn it."

The man seemed surprised. "Of course you do. You have the Iraqi."

"I don't have it yet, alright? I'll have it tomorrow." Corben's voice bristled with rage. He tried to get a clearer look at the man's face, but his vision was still warped from the pressure of the man's shoe, and the car's headlights were blinding the little eyesight he had. "He didn't have it on him," he added angrily.

The man studied him from above. "I don't want any more games. Get me the book, or I'll make your life a living hell. Which, as you can see, is well within my ability."

Corben glared up at him with fierce resolve. "I'll get you the book. I want you to have the book. But I want something else."

A puzzled tone infected the man's voice. "Oh?"

Corben could feel his pulse throbbing in his ears. "I know what you're working on."

The man's lips pursed with doubt. "And what am I working on?"

"I saw your lab. In Saddamiya. The mass graves. The body parts. The blood bank." Corben studied him. His vision was clearing up, and the man's features were coming into focus. He concentrated his gaze on him, then added, "I was there, hakeem," and spotted the flinch, the tell of recognition.

And in that instant, he knew he'd found his man.

Up until that point, he'd suspected it, he'd assumed the doctor from Baghdad was also behind Evelyn's abduction, but he wasn't sure. He'd never seen a picture of the hakeem nor heard his voice, let alone met him in person. And although this wasn't how he'd hoped to have his encounter with the beast—far from it—there he was, standing before—or rather, over—him.

A confusing rush of horror and elation surged through Corben. "We had some forensic experts take a look," he went on. "They checked out the dead bodies, the traces of the surgery, the equipment you left be-hind. The body parts in the jars. Their conclusions were . . . startling."

He paused, gauging the man's reaction. The hakeem just looked down impassively, his mouth and eyes narrowed to thin slits. Corben gave him a moment to let his words sink in, then asked, "Do you have it figured out?"

"You want my research, is that it?" The hakeem mocked dismissively. "You're here to offer me the blessing and patronage of the American government in exchange for sharing my work with you?"

"No." Corben's eyes hardened. "Not the American government's. Just mine."

Chapter 50

"From what I've read," Kirkwood told Mia, "identical twins have the exact same genes, but they don't live as long as each other or die of the same causes—and I'm not talking about the ones that get hit by a bus. Studies have shown that the DNA of each twin develops its own harmful mutations. If aging was genetically coded into us, then they'd age the same way. But they don't. The damage in their cells accumulates randomly, just like the rest of us."

Mia took another sip from her glass, grinding over his questions. "You do realize what 'fixing' us entails? We're talking about cells like brain and heart cells that don't replace themselves when they die, chromosome mutation leading to cancer, protein accumulation inside and outside the cells . . . There are several distinct ways in which our body falls apart with time."

"You mean, with wear and tear." Kirkwood grinned.

"Yeah, well, life's about wear and tear, isn't it?" Mia shrugged. "I'm not about to move to some stress-free monastery in Tibet and spend my days humming show tunes and meditating in order to gain a couple of decades."

"After Beirut—might be a tad boring," he joked.

"Actually, on second thought—I'd happily take boring right now."

Kirkwood nodded empathetically, then his expression went serious.

"All I'm saying is, it's possible. We just don't know how yet. Cancer is believed to be curable, right? We're working on it. We might not find that cure for another hundred years, but the odds are, one day, we will. It's part of our MO. Not so long ago, infections ranging from simple viruses to flu pandemics were the main causes of death. The plague was considered a curse from God. We learned different. Now we've tamed those illnesses, we live long enough to experience heart disease and cancer. A hundred years ago, they were thought to be incurable, unlike infections. They were believed to come from within us. We now know that's not the case. And once they're tamed, who knows what the effects will be for the rest of the body."

Mia studied him curiously. "You seem to know a hell of a lot about this."

Kirkwood smiled. "I kind of have a vested interest."

She looked at him, unsure of how to take that.

He paused, as if encouraging her moment of uncertainty, before adding, "We all do, don't we? I don't think anyone wants to die any sooner than they have to."

"So you're really into this? Do you also starve yourself and pop a couple of hundred pills a day?"

Many leading biogerontologists followed a regular exercise regime—the single universally accepted way to a healthier and longer life. They also self-medicated with vitamins and antioxidants and were careful with what they ate. The latter was occasionally and unwisely taken to extremes, as severe calorie restriction was known to extend life—in animals, not in humans—although most would agree it had serious shortcomings in the quality-versus-quantity department.

"I look after myself, sure," he conceded. "What about you?"

She held up her glass sarcastically. "That, and bullets—kind of not ideal if you're hoping to break that hundred-year barrier," she scoffed. She put her glass down and scanned the man's face. There was something unsaid in his expression, a guardedness that she couldn't really penetrate. "Seriously, though," she insisted. "You're more keyed into this than someone who's just looking after himself."

"We've got this small division in the UN—the World Health Organization?" Kirkwood ribbed her. "I've sat on some committees. We have a whole range of initiatives dealing with aging, but it's mostly to do with improving the lives of the old. But we also host debates and prepare some in-depth studies, which I take the time to read—having a vested interest and all." He looked at her intently. "You know all about the advances in molecular biology that are taking place. Science and technology are experiencing exponential growth. This accelerating growth rate has the potential to shrink distant projections to a tangible near future. What we think might take hundreds of years to achieve could only take a few decades. Replacement organs could be grown from stem cells; stem cells themselves could be injected into the body to repair it. The possibilities are endless. And I'm not even talking about distant dreams like artificial intelligence and nanotechnology. I'm talking about what we know is doable. And if our bodies are fixable, if the cellular wear and tear can be stopped or repaired once, there's no reason why the process can't be repeated. It would be like having your car serviced every ten thousand miles. It could just make us live much longer, or, if you push that notion to its logical conclusion, we could even be—in fact, it seems to me that a lot of scientists now seem convinced that we are—on the threshold of achieving medical immortality. And if that's what this hakeem is after . . . it would explain a hell of a lot, wouldn't it?"

Mia's face pinched together as she considered the possibility. "You really think some primitive alchemists working a thousand years ago could have figured out something that we're only starting to realize might be possible?"

Kirkwood shrugged. "Mold was used as an antibiotic in ancient Greece. Less than one hundred years ago, scientists perfected it and named it penicillin, but it's been around for thousands of years. Same for aspirin. I'm sure you know your Phoenicians used it, as did Assyrians, Native Americans, and countless other peoples. After all, it's not rocket science. It's just a simple oxidation process of a powder taken from the bark of willow trees. We now think everyone should take a small daily dose to keep heart disease at bay. Just yesterday, I was reading about how the people of Chile are rediscovering the remedies of their indigenous Mapuche tribes for all kinds of diseases, and how well they work. There's a lot out there we don't know about. All it takes is one compound, maybe some powerful free-radical scavenger that can repair the oxidative damage to our cells. One compound. It's not that impossible to imagine."

"But still," she countered, "with everything we know, with all our knowledge, we haven't been able to work it out."

"It would be a fair point if a lot of effort was going into preventing aging, but it's not. Very few people are actually working on it. Scientists aren't exactly motivated to go into that field. Government gurus, church leaders, and "deathist" scientists tell them it's not possible, and even if it were, they keep telling us it's not something we should want. The media's quick to jump on anything that sounds promising, which has the effect of turning any serious enterprise into an apologist joke. Any serious scientists considering the field are—rightly—worried about being lumped in with the army of charlatans out there selling youth and getting nominated for the Silver Fleece Awards. They know they won't get funding the minute they mention their work has to do with antiaging—they don't even use the word anymore, it's now cloaked under the term *longevity medicine*. They're worried about working on something that, if you're going to prove it works on humans, takes decades to show results, which can be hugely disheartening when the odds are you're going to fail, and if you're going to be mocked along the way . . . You're a geneticist. Would you go into it?"

Mia shook her head glumly. It was too close for comfort. Her whole field, it seemed, was a minefield these days.

"You see my point," he went on. "You know how the government feels about your line of work. They're not even ready to back stem-cell research. Same goes for the Church. So the funding and the incentives aren't there. But things are changing. The new megarich are getting older. And they're interested. They don't want to die unnecessarily. And to figure out something like this either happens by fluke, or with a lot of hard work and a lot of money. How much did we spend on the Manhattan Project? On putting a man on the moon? On the war in Iraq? Doesn't seeing if we can fix the human body and eradicate the diseases and ravages of old age deserve one-tenth of the same funding? One-hundredth even? We don't even have that. Do you know how many people die of age-related diseases every day? One hundred thousand. One hundred thousand deaths a day." He paused and shrugged. "Maybe it's worth thinking about."

He set his drink down and gave his words a moment to sink in. "Don't get me wrong. If that's what this hakeem's working on, I'm not saying he's justified. His methods are beyond insane. He's a monster who deserves to be drawn and quartered. But maybe—just maybe—what he's after isn't that insane. And if it isn't, imagine what would happen if it were discovered."

Mia finished off her drink and sat back. She was drunk with the possibilities. "I think I'm starting to understand his level of commitment. If he thinks it's even remotely possible . . ." Her face brightened with a realization. "He's got to be desperate to get his hands on that book. Which might give us an advantage in getting Mom back."

"Absolutely." Kirkwood paused. "Have you discussed this with Jim at all?"

She shook her head. "Up until an hour ago, I wasn't really sure there was anything to discuss. Why?"

"I was just wondering what his take on it was. We've only talked about the operational details of what was going on."

"He thinks the guy's working on a bioweapon. Maybe he should know about all this too. I'll call him in the morning."

Kirkwood winced with discomfort. "I'd leave it. It doesn't really affect his plans."

"Yeah, but if this is possible, if that's what the hakeem is after . . . maybe it changes things."

Kirkwood's expression darkened. "Not in a good way, as far as getting Evelyn back is concerned."

Mia felt a ripple of worry at the sudden seriousness of his words. "What do you mean?"

Kirkwood looked away for a moment, weighing his words. The frown hadn't left his face as he leaned in. "Think about it. Jim's a government agent. If there's something like this out there, if they know that's what the hakeem is really working on . . . what do you think they would do? Hand it over to a lunatic? Or keep it under wraps?"

Chapter 51

⟋⟋⟍⟋⟍⟋

Corben's remark took the hakeem by surprise and paused him, if only for a moment. "And your help and patronage is supposed to be even more attractive to me than your government's, is that it?

Corben looked up at him, his voice calm and unwavering. "I was asked to find you. To track you down. But that was four years ago. A lot's changed since then." He adjusted his position slightly, trying to alleviate the discomfort of the harsh soil.

"The WMD mess crippled us," he continued. "*Intelligence report* became a dirty phrase, synonymous with White House fabrication. It turned us into pariahs. The antiwar movement and the press savaged us. People got fired or shuffled around, my boss included. Priorities changed. Everyone was busy backstabbing and pointing fingers and scurrying around trying to save their own asses, and a lot of stuff got lost in the mix. Your file was one of them. The Agency lost interest."

"But you didn't," the hakeem observed drily.

"I wasn't sure. The odds were that you were a waste of time, a wild-goose chase. You were running experiments, you had all the resources and human guinea pigs you needed, but I had no idea if you'd been successful in your work. And you'd pulled a mother of a disappearing act. I would've let go. Moved on. But there was this symbol, carved into the wall of one of your cells. The snake, the tail-eater. Data-mining hadn't turned up anything on it that was relevant, but when I did some old-fashioned digging around through our archives in Langley, I found something. An old file, long forgotten. A report from an Agency man in the Vatican. A memo about an old case from the eighteenth century involving the tail-eater symbol, a false marquis, and a prince who believed the man hadn't aged a day in over fifty years." Corben noticed the hakeem's jaw take on a sharper, more pronounced line. "And it made me wonder if you were just another quack—God knows, there are enough of them out there—or if you were really onto something. So I kept an open mind. You know those detectives who can never let go of an unsolved case that marked them? You were mine. If any of this was real, it was my golden ticket out of the sleaze pit of intel work, a big fuck you to the ungrateful and self-righteous bastards in D.C. who are more than happy to use us and then hang us out to dry, a way to ride off into the sunset sipping Cristal in the back of a Maybach."

Which was, at least until that phone call to Abu Barzan, the truth. Now, though, Corben was no longer sure the hakeem was the most direct route to the fountain of youth, if there was such a thing at all. Not until he knew what the mystery buyer knew. But he didn't want the hakeem to know that. Not yet, anyway. Not if he wanted to get back to Beirut in one piece.

"After Baghdad," Corben concluded, "I got posted out here. Kept my eyes and ears open, in case something popped up. And here we are." His tone hardened. "No one else knows about your involvement. No one's aware of the link. They just think this is about smugglers fighting over the spoils of war. It's what I've made them think. And I can keep it that way."

The hakeem glanced away, nodding to himself almost imperceptibly, seemingly processing his captive's words.

"What do you think you could possibly offer me that I don't already have?" he finally asked.

"Oh, I can think of a number of things. Access to our intel, to our resources. Research. I can also provide you with a safety net. I don't know where you've been holed up since Baghdad imploded, but this part of the world's not the most stable, and if it blows up around you again, you might want to relocate somewhere less . . . distracting. I can organize that. New papers, a new identity. And if you do have something the world wants, something people will be willing to pay big bucks for, then I can be your front man. I can be your beard and legitimize it. And you don't need me to tell you there's a lot of money to be made."

The hakeem remained poker-faced, staring down at Corben as he brooded over his words. After a short moment, and in the same dismissive tone, he simply said, "I don't think so," and motioned to someone behind him.

A ripple of alarm coursed through Corben. He strained to see what was going on, but couldn't. "What do you mean, you don't think so?"

A man appeared from the direction of the car, carrying a small briefcase. He flicked it open and held it up, its lid facing Corben and masking its contents. The hakeem dipped into it. When his hands reappeared, they held a syringe and a small bottle. He gave the man behind Corben an indifferent nod. The pockmarked man reached down and grabbed Corben, pinning him in place while the hakeem plunged the needle into the small bottle and filled the syringe with its contents.

"I mean you're going to tell me where the book is, my men will bring it to me, and then I'll decide about whether or not to let you live."

"There's no need for this, I'm telling you—"

The pockmarked man hit Corben in the gut, punching the air out of him. He felt his arm being twisted into position, a tourniquet quickly applied below his shoulder, as the hakeem leaned in, squirting an air bubble out of the syringe.

"Where's the book?"

Corben's eyes locked onto the needle. "I told you I don't have it."

The hakeem injected Corben. Seconds later, the searing sensation rocketed through his veins, turning his blood into lava. Corben screamed out from the pain, the hakeem hovering over him, watching him with detached curiosity.

"Where's the book?"

"I don't have it," Corben yelled back.

The hakeem pushed the plunger further in. "Where's the book?" he rasped.

Corben's skin felt as if it were frying from the inside. His eyes were blurry, drowning in tears. "In Turkey," he blurted. "The book's in Turkey."

The hakeem pulled the needle out.

The burning receded, as if it were vaporizing itself out of Corben's fingers and toes.

"Go on."

Corben took a deep breath, his body still shivering from the drug's effect. "Farouk, the Iraqi dealer who came to see Evelyn. He didn't have it with him. He was just brokering it. And the dealer who has it is on his way to deliver his whole stash to another buyer."

That last part ignited the hakeem's interest visibly. "Another buyer? Who?"

"I don't know."

The hakeem held up the needle threateningly.

"I don't know," Corben insisted. "He wouldn't tell me. I tried to counterbid, but the other buyer bid even higher."

He hadn't wanted the hakeem to know about the other buyer and cursed inwardly, noticing that the hakeem's mind was clearly thinking the same thing he was, desperate to find out who the other interested party was.

"Where is this exchange taking place?"

"I don't know yet," Corben said grudgingly. "We're tracking him. It looks like he's spending the night in Diyarbakir. The trade's going down tomorrow." He scowled at his captor. "If you want that book, you're going to have to work with me on this. I'm the only one who can get that information from our intel guys, and if I don't show up at my desk in the morning, all bets are off."

A faint smile played on the hakeem's lips. "Oh, I'm sure you can get the information by phone. I can't imagine CIA agents having to punch in every morning. Just as long as you don't forget to make your sign-in call."

The hakeem was well-informed: He knew of the Agency's routine requirement for field agents to call in at specified times every morning to confirm they were okay. Corben watched the hakeem as he thought things through for a moment, before adding, "What excuse were you planning to use to justify your little excursion to Diyarbakir?"

"I was going to be checking out someone Farouk called. Without mentioning the book."

The hakeem nodded. "I want that book," he said firmly. "And even more than the book, I want to know who the other buyer is. I'll get you to Diyarbakir without your people knowing about it. But in the meantime, I'd prefer to keep you close. If you need a way out later, you'll be able to say we grabbed you from your apartment and forced you along." He fixed Corben intently. "Take my men to wherever this exchange is taking place. Bring me back the book and the buyer, and we can talk about our future. Do we have a deal?"

Corben's eyes hardened. He nodded. He didn't have much choice. The man was, if anything, methodical.

There was one more issue to discuss. "What about the woman? Evelyn Bishop? You heard the ambassador's announcement. It would strengthen my hand if I get her back at some point."

The hakeem shrugged. "Like I said. Get me the book and the buyer. Maybe after that, you can stage a miraculous escape and free her too." He looked a question at the pockmarked man and asked him something in Arabic.

Corben strained to look over his shoulder and saw the killer pull out Corben's cell phone from a pocket. He'd taken out its battery, which he held in his hand.

The hakeem nodded, then stowed the syringe in the briefcase and motioned to his men to take it away. He turned and walked off, flicking a terse signal to his men. They approached Corben.

"So is it real?" Corben called out after him.

The man kept walking.

"Does it work?" Corben shouted out, persisting.

The hakeem stopped, turned, the corners of his mouth breaking in a thin, wry smile. "I hope you won't try to be too clever. I can always find room for you in my little clinic. Do we understand each other?"

Corben locked eyes with the hakeem. He realized the man would be impossible to rein in, and Corben knew he'd have to adjust his plans accordingly. If the other buyer knew his stuff, Corben would ditch the hakeem. The thought of bringing the sick bastard in or—even better—pumping a bullet through his forehead seemed hugely satisfying right now.

The hakeem got into a waiting car. He was driven away while his men converged on Corben, gagged him with some packing tape, lifted him off his feet, and carried him off like a roped steer before dumping him into another car's trunk and slamming it shut.

Chapter 52

The dusty morning sunlight conspired with the car horns and street vendors to wake Mia up. In truth, she hadn't slept well at all despite the cushy comfort of her bed. As if the whole notion of the hakeem's insane aspiration being possibly not-so-insane wasn't enough, Kirkwood's closing words had sent her mind into a confused spin. The three martinis probably didn't help on that front either.

Kirkwood was right. They had to keep this quiet, at least until Evelyn was safe.

Which meant keeping it from Corben.

Thinking back, Mia had sensed a wariness in the agent when she'd first seen him around Kirkwood. What was the real reason for that? Did the agent know more than he'd shared with her? She thought back to Corben's telling her about the lab in Baghdad. He'd suggested that it was about bioweapons, but he hadn't given her a satisfactory explanation of why the hakeem was after the codex, repeating—annoyingly, as far as she was concerned—that it was irrelevant to getting Evelyn out. If the hakeem's experiments had to do with longevity, surely the CIA's experts would already have figured that out.

Which meant they'd want to keep it under wraps.

Either she was way off the mark, which she thought was quite likely. Or, on the off chance that what she and Kirkwood had speculated about last night was real, Corben was hiding things from her. Which, she reminded herself, wouldn't be that shocking. He was a CIA man. He had a job to do. Not telling her the whole truth wouldn't exactly be keeping him up at night.

On the other hand, she didn't know much about Kirkwood. She'd felt a certain distance, a hesitancy in his manner, almost a shyness—about something. But he also exuded calmness, a confidence that came with well-honed knowledge. He'd appeared in Beirut wanting to help get Evelyn out, he was with the UN, and that was pretty much all she knew. Mia realized she had to be careful with him too. The same reasons that would have her be wary of Corben had to apply to Kirkwood too.

Her mouth felt dry and her stomach was grumbling in protest. Deciding that the buffet would provide a quicker fix than room service, she quickly slipped on some cargo pants and a shirt and headed out to the hotel's restaurant.

She was lost in her thoughts and waiting for the elevator when its doors pinged open. Kirkwood was standing inside.

A silver attaché case and a backpack were by his feet. He looked as if he was leaving.

Mia stepped inside, her eyes darting from his face to the bags and back. Something caught in her throat. "You're leaving?"

His face tensed up, as if he'd been caught out. "No, I . . ." he stumbled, "I'll be back tonight."

She nodded, sensing his discomfort. She decided to probe a little deeper. "Look, I've been thinking about what we were talking about, and I think I should let Jim know." She studied his face. "Maybe it'll help."

            ◦◦◦◦◦

KIRKWOOD HADN'T SLEPT WELL either. His chat with Mia, at the rooftop bar, deeply unsettled him. He'd nudged at the truth with her, then he'd pulled back. Which left her with a lot of questions. Questions that could get her into trouble.

Corben and his handlers obviously had their own agenda. Evelyn was expendable, Kirkwood knew that. Mia hadn't posed much of a threat to them, but if she started asking too many questions, making a pain of herself, they might feel threatened. And he knew what these people did when they felt that way.

He'd made that mistake before. Keeping quiet about the real significance of the tail-eater had put people in danger. He didn't want it to happen again.

And he certainly didn't want it to happen to Mia.

"Let's talk about this some more before you do that," he said as they stepped out of the elevator. His eyes swept the lobby and noticed the agent guarding Mia sitting by the hotel's entrance, reading a newspaper.

The agent nodded to Mia, who acknowledged him back before turning to Kirkwood.

"I know you're not sure about Jim's motives," she pressed on, "but he's been pretty open with me about what they have, and—"

"Please, Mia," Kirkwood interrupted, "you've got to trust me on this." He checked his watch and winced.

He'd wanted to tell her everything the night before. He'd thought of calling her room earlier that morning, to fill her in on what was going on, but he'd held back.

He took her aside, into the small library bar, out of the agent's eye line. No one else was in there. "We got a hit early this morning, out of Iraq," he lied. "I'd put the word out through our contacts on the ground there. We've been heavily involved in trying to secure the country's historic heritage, especially after the fiasco at the National Museum four years ago. We've offered rewards and amnesties in the past, and the strategy's been very successful. It's also helped us develop a significant network of contacts within the antiquities community. Anyway, we think we know who's got the pieces Farouk was trying to sell. A dealer in Baghdad who knows—well, knew—him told one of our people there that Farouk had mentioned the items to him. He said Farouk was brokering them for another dealer, a man from Mosul." He'd skirted around the difficult part, but he was back on track now. "Farouk didn't have the pieces with him here in Beirut. That's why he only had the Polaroids."

"So the book's still in Mosul?" Her eyes were alight with interest.

"No. It's in Turkey." He paused, taking stock of her reaction, before diving in. "I'm going there now to bring it back. Come with me. I'll fill you in on the plane."

∾∾∾

QUESTIONS AND confused feelings harried Mia's mind.

She wasn't sure about Kirkwood, but then again, she wasn't sure about Corben either. The only person she could really trust to look out for Evelyn's interests was herself. If the book that could free her mom was really out there, she had to do everything she could to make sure it got into their hands—her hands—safely. But a nagging uncertainty was still vying for her attention, warning her.

"I can't just fly off with you like that," she objected.

"Mia, listen to me," Kirkwood insisted. "There are things you don't know."

That made her angry. "Like what?" she asked fiercely.

He heaved a conflicted sigh. "Look, I'm sorry, but . . . last night. I wasn't being perfectly honest with you. After you mentioned this hakeem at the embassy, I managed to get hold of his file." She could hear the deep concern in his voice. "What we talked about last night. It's exactly what he's working on. And Corben and his people know it."

Her mouth dropped an inch. "The experiments . . . ?" She already knew the answer.

Kirkwood nodded somberly. "That's what they're interested in."

She didn't know which way to turn, but one certainty was hacking its way through the thorns in her mind: She couldn't trust Corben. Not anymore. The verdict on Kirkwood, on the other hand, was still open, but she didn't have much choice. She had to risk it.

"What do I tell the agent out there?" she asked flatly, motioning towards the man guarding her.

"Don't tell him anything."

"He's here to guard me. He's not going to let me waltz out of here with you without checking with Jim." The man's name felt like poison on her tongue.

Kirkwood frowned and thought for a moment. "The restaurant next door's part of the hotel, but it's got its own entrance further down the street. They've got to have the same kitchen. I've got a car waiting for me outside. Go back to your room, get your passport and whatever you need to take with you, and take the stairs down to the restaurant and make your way out from there. I'll be parked around the corner."

She was about to leave when Kirkwood put his hand on her arm. "Please, Mia. Trust me on this. Don't confront Jim about this. Not yet. Not until we know we have the book safely. I don't want to give anyone any chance to screw us on using it to get Evelyn back."

She made a quick study of the man. His eyes shone with sincerity. He was either telling her the truth, or he was a spectacularly effective liar.

Either way, she'd soon find out.

She nodded and headed back to the elevator.

⌒⌒⌒

Kirkwood watched her leave with a knot in his stomach. He was now committed. There would be no turning back.

He checked his watch and decided to initiate a precaution he'd been mulling. He pulled out his cell phone and dialed the number of the scout in Iraq who had first brought Abu Barzan's find to their attention.

The man could be trusted. Years of collaboration, a couple of passed trust tests, and a healthy retainer had proven that.

He couldn't risk calling Abu Barzan himself. He knew that if Corben had in fact been the counterbidder for the book, he and his minders knew about Abu Barzan and had his phone number. They could be monitoring it. And Kirkwood preferred not to announce his real interest to them just yet.

The scout picked up quickly. Kirkwood told him what to do. He had to do it quickly and be brief. He also had to make sure he didn't spook Abu Barzan. He asked the scout to call him back from another number and let him know where the new meeting would take place.

He hung up, picked up the attaché case and the backpack, and headed for the door.

Chapter 53

Fifty miles further east, Corben was lying down on a narrow bed, looking around his stark white cell. The small room was windowless, and he had no idea what time of day it was, but he hadn't really slept and he didn't think more than a few hours had passed since they'd shoved him into the trunk of the car and driven him off.

He tried to imagine what the other prisoners of the hakeem's compound were going through. He pictured Evelyn Bishop and wondered how close she was, and whether she'd ever make it back into the sun's embrace again.

A picture was forming in his mind, and all the pieces seemed to fit. He was either in some town in north Lebanon or in Syria. He thought the latter more likely. The accent of the pockmarked thug and the rest of his cronies gave away their nationality pretty clearly. Corben didn't speak much Arabic, but the little he did know allowed him to identify the different accents—Lebanese, Iraqi, Gulf Arab, Palestinian, Syrian. Also, the car ride fit the profile. The second leg, at least, the one he'd been awake for. A winding road up a mountain and back down, a stop and some chatter—probably the border crossing—followed by more winding roads leading to a city that reverberated with a deafening cacophony of prayer calls, far more noticeably than Beirut.

It had to be Damascus.

The thought angered him. The city had actually been his first—and obvious—guess, back in 2003, when his assignment was officially live, when he'd tried to figure out where the hakeem had escaped to. A lot of Saddam's cronies had made their way there to avoid getting shocked and awed. Despite the deep, long-felt animosity between the two countries, timely conveniences and dovetailing objectives meant that bitter enemies occasionally found reasons to help each other out.

In the case of the hakeem, however, Corben knew the arrangement had nothing to do with politics.

It made sense for the hakeem. He would find patrons who could provide him with the same level of support that he'd enjoyed in Baghdad. Whatever he needed would be provided. His little guesthouse would run at full occupancy. And, when complications—or opportunities—such as those of the last few days arose, the expert, ruthless manpower was readily available.

Speaking of which, the lock clicked open. The hakeem stood at the cell's door. The pockmarked killer, Omar, and two other armed men were with him.

"Time for you to sign in," the hakeem announced. He gestured to Omar, who pulled out Corben's cell phone and snapped the battery back into place. "You need to get the precise GPS coordinates of the Iraqi dealer," he added, then raised a cautioning finger at him. "Remember, thirty seconds. No more."

Corben got up, still in his boxers, and did as told. He got through to Olshansky. No one at the embassy seemed to have noticed anything amiss. Not that they had any reason to. As long as he signed in on time, no alarms would go off.

"Your target hasn't moved since last night," Olshansky informed him. "He's still at the same location in Diyarbakir, but something else came up. Someone called him from Iraq."

"Who?" Corben asked.

"I don't know," Olshansky replied. "The call was too brief to lock it in. The caller just told him to hang up, remove the battery from his phone, and call him back from another phone."

Corben didn't allow the unexpected complication to perturb his countenance. He kept his cool and, without a tremor in his voice, asked Olshansky for the Iraqi cell phone's last GPS coordinates.

"You sure you want them?" Olshansky asked. "He's got to know he's being tracked by now, after that call. He's probably long gone."

"Just give me the coordinates," Corben said simply.

Olshansky sounded a bit puzzled, but acquiesced. "One more thing," he then added. "The Geneva cell phone I've been trying to lock onto—it's not in Switzerland anymore. Its signal bounced off a jumble of satellites and servers before disappearing into a digital netherworld, but its trail definitely indicates a change of region. I'm liaising with a contact of mine at the NSA who's prioritized the trace for us. My guy thinks he might be able to get a lock on its position before the end of the day."

"Do it sooner than that. I need it," Corben replied curtly as he vaulted the information.

He had his suspicions about where the caller might be headed.

The hakeem looked at him suspiciously and gestured for him to hang up, which he did after telling Olshansky to keep him posted if the Iraqi signal changed location. Omar was quick to take back the phone and pull out its battery. These guys were well versed in covering their digital tracks, Corben thought. They'd kept Ramez's phone live not to miss Farouk's call, but they wouldn't make that mistake with Corben's phone. He wouldn't be able to work backwards to pinpoint the hakeem's lair beyond the broader confines of the city.

He gave the hakeem the coordinates, which he knew were probably worthless, but he didn't have much choice. He had to wing it from here. As he did, Omar punched them into a handheld device—the killer evidently spoke English, Corben noted—and it zoomed to a map of the Syrian-Turkish border, and to the town of Diyarbakir. Omar nodded with satisfaction.

A thin smile broke across the hakeem's aquiline features. "Time to go," he ordered, gesturing for Omar to bring Corben.

Omar gestured to one of his men, who handed him a folded batch of clothes and some boots. He threw them at Corben's feet. Corben slipped them on over his boxers—baggy khaki pants, dark gray sweatshirt, and military boots. Omar pulled out some plastic cuffs and motioned for Corben to put his hands together. Corben grudgingly acquiesced. Omar snapped them into place, then pulled out a black cloth sack. He grabbed Corben's shoulders and spun him around harshly, preparing to slip it over his head. *"Yalla, imshi,"* he grunted. Move it.

Corben had had enough of being pushed around for one day. "Back off, asshole," he snapped back, pulling his arm free and shoving Omar back. "I'll do it myself."

Omar grabbed him, pushing him against the door, yelling, *"Imshi, wlaa."* Corben resisted, but the hakeem interceded, ordering his man to stand down. Omar glared angrily at Corben, then shoved the hood into his hand and stepped back.

〜〜〜

WITH AN EAR GLUED to the door, Evelyn listened intently to the noise outside her cell. She'd heard the door being unlocked and had feared another victim, like her, being brought in or, worse, being collected for another torture session with her demented host.

Instead, she heard a man speaking in English. An American. She couldn't really make out what he was saying, but he seemed to be in solid health.

And now she heard a tussle and realized they were taking him away. The man had resisted.

Her mind flooded with panic. She wasn't sure what to do. Part of her wanted to cry out, to make her presence known to the other prisoner. If he escaped, if he was freed, he'd let the world know she was still alive. But another part of her was terrified. Terrified of getting the man into trouble, terrified of being punished herself for the insubordination.

She couldn't let the opportunity pass.

Screw the consequences.

"Help me," she shouted at the top of her voice. "My name's Evelyn Bishop. I'm an American citizen. I was kidnapped in Beirut. Please let the embassy know." She banged her hands repeatedly against the solid, unyielding door. "Help me. I need to get out of here. Please. Tell someone, anyone."

She stood still for a moment, her nerves frazzled by the effort, her weary body taut with fear and tortured by desperate hope, and listened for a reaction.

Nothing came back.

She slunk down to the floor, a nervous quake in the corner of her lips, and wrapped her shivering arms around her.

∽⌒∽

CORBEN FROZE at Evelyn's screams. He turned and cast his eyes over the series of doors on either side of the long corridor, wondering which cell she was in. She sounded as if she was close by, but the muffled sounds could have come from any of the adjacent rooms.

Not that it really mattered anyway.

He wasn't in a position to do anything about it.

He glanced at the hakeem. The man was unflustered. He seemed to be studying Corben's reaction.

A thin smile broke across the hakeem's thin lips. "It's up to you," he said sardonically. "Do you want to be a hero? Or do you want to live forever?"

Corben let the words sink in. He hated that this freak, this insanely evil monster, could mess with him like that, goad him, tempt him. He hated the hakeem for it; more than that, he hated himself for succumbing to it. A pact with the devil. It never worked out, did it? If he had the opportunity, there and then, to gain the upper hand on his captors, to blow their brains out and free Evelyn and the rest of them, would he have done it?

He wasn't sure.

But if he had to choose, he had to admit he probably didn't think he would.

Too much was at stake.

The prize was too big.

Corben scowled at the hakeem, and gave him his answer. He slipped the hood over his head. And in the darkness of the shroud, he hoped that the haunting sound of Evelyn's scream wouldn't remain branded into his consciousness for too long.

Forever was far too long for that.

Chapter 54

The Beechcraft King Air skirted the lush Mediterranean coastline, its twin turboprops powering it north towards Turkey.

Mia hadn't had much trouble sneaking out of the hotel unnoticed. Kirkwood's car was parked around the corner. At the airport, there were no formalities to go through; she and Kirkwood were driven straight to the small plane that was waiting for them, its props spinning. Its wheels lifted off virtually as soon as they reached it. Clearly, the UN held sway in Beirut, even more so since several thousand of its troops were currently keeping the peace in the south of the country.

Diyarbakir was northeast of Beirut, and the direct flight path would have cut across Syria diagonally, but Syrian airspace was tightly controlled. Kirkwood had decided on a more discreet, if slightly longer, course. They would fly north, keeping well out of Syrian airspace, until they reached the Turkish coast. There, they'd bank right and head east, inland, to Diyarbakir.

She turned away from the distant coast shimmering along the horizon as Kirkwood came back from conferring with the pilots. He sat down opposite her and opened up the map in his hand.

"Farouk's friend is called Abu Barzan," he informed her. "He crossed the border point here, at Zakho, and drove into Turkey yesterday." Kirkwood pointed at the map, showing her the border crossing that was close to the tip where Turkey, Syria, and Iraq met. "He's in Diyarbakir." He indicated a town that was around fifty miles north of the Syrian border.

"Is that where he's meeting his buyer?" she asked.

Kirkwood nodded. "We've got a couple of private contractors meeting us there. They'll take us to him."

It was happening too fast. She wasn't sure what to make of the sudden development. "How did you manage to track him down?"

Kirkwood hesitated. "He wasn't too hard to trace," he offered as he folded up the map. "Mosul's much smaller than Baghdad, and he'd boasted about making a big score."

"How are you going to get the book from him?"

Kirkwood seemed uncomfortable with her questions. "He'll hand over the book and the rest of the pieces, in exchange for us not shipping him back to Iraq for prosecution."

"What about his buyer?" Mia asked. "He could be part of this, couldn't he?"

Kirkwood shook his head. "He's probably just some antiquities dealer from London or Frankfurt," he speculated dismissively. "Hardly our concern. We just need to get the book to trade for Evelyn."

Mia frowned. She hadn't heard anything on that front since making her televised plea, and she wasn't hugely comfortable with being out of touch with the embassy—or even with Corben. "We don't know if the kidnappers have made contact yet," she noted.

"They will. We can set up another press conference, say we caught some smugglers, make sure the book's front and center." Kirkwood looked at her with fierce determination. "Don't worry. They'll call. I'll make sure of it."

Mia nodded and looked out the window, lost in her thoughts.

After a moment, Kirkwood's voice brought her out of her daze. "What is it?"

Weariness lined her face. "It's hard to imagine. That we're doing this. That something like this could actually exist." She shook her head and scoffed, but it was more out of tiredness than anything else. "It's like Frodo's ring. Tempting man with its power over nature, with its promise of long life. Toying with our easily corrupted hearts."

Kirkwood pursed his lips doubtfully. "I wouldn't call it a corruption at all. Dying is such a huge waste of talent. And wisdom."

As the King Air skimmed the thin wisps of cloud, they discussed the profound changes a potential "magic bullet" of longevity would trigger, the seismic shifts in the way we live. Overpopulation was the obvious problem. From the hominids' first appearance on the planet, it had taken us 80 million years to hit the billion mark in the early 1800s. It took well over a hundred years to hit the second billion in 1930, but ever since, we've been addding a billion more every fifteen years or so. This increase comes almost entirely from less developed countries; the more developed countries, in fact, are barely producing enough babies to maintain their current population levels. Still, having five or ten generations of the same family surviving concurrently would cause all kinds of upheavals. More natural resources, food, and housing would be needed. The welfare and pension systems, among others, would require even more of an overhaul than the one they already need. And human relations would be drastically, dramatically different.

Marriage—would the institution still mean anything when no one would really expect to stay with one other person for a couple of hundred years? Children—how would they age and behave relative to their parents? The changes would also extend to work. Careers. Retirement. Would people have to work throughout their longer lives? Probably. Could they cope with that, mentally? What happened to the notion of the old moving on so the young could find their place in life? Would there be room for anyone to ever get promoted? And what about less obvious implications, such as on prison sentences, for instance? Was the threat of a thirty-year sentence as much of a deterrent to someone who expected to live a couple of hundred years?

The more they talked it through, the more Mia realized that if this was real, every aspect of life as we knew it would need to be radically redefined. She'd never really explored its ramifications beyond scientific conjecture and idealized what-ifs, but thinking about it as potentially real, it was as daunting, even frightening, a prospect as she could imagine.

"We'd be living in a 'posthuman' age," Kirkwood said. "And that terrifies the conservative and the religious establishment. But then, that fear is irrational. It wouldn't happen overnight. It would be a gradual change. The 'fix,' if it were ever discovered, would be announced and people would just, well, not age. Or they would age very, very slowly. And the world would adapt. We were already hugely different from those who lived a hundred years before us. To them, we're already 'posthuman.' And we seem to be handling the improved longevity, the medical advances and the technological innovations pretty well."

But then, Mia knew, common sense and the greater good didn't necessarily always prevail. Fear of change, combined with a patronizing, arrogant, and pontifical worldview, was already aligned to block such a discovery. Beyond its dogmatic, conservative mind-set, the government was daunted by the potential costs—never mind the huge potential savings in health-care costs due to chronic age-related diseases—and organizational changes that significantly longer life spans would incur. Big pharmaceuticals were happy to watch our bodies fall apart and sell us disease-management drugs. The antiaging creams, supplements, and hormones that didn't really work were also highly lucrative—$6 billion a year's worth, in fact.

"The people against it," Kirkwood concluded, "they're usually either deeply religious, or they're philosophers who don't live in the real world anyway. They compare us to blooming flowers or use some other inane analogy to celebrate the importance of death, they quote Greek and Roman thinkers or, inevitably, scripture. For them, life is defined by death. I'd say it's the exact opposite: Life is defined by the ambition, the need, the urge, to avoid death. That's what makes us human. It's why we have doctors and hospitals. We're the only species that's aware of our own mortality, we're the only species that actually has the capability, the intellect, the awareness, to aspire to defeat it. It's been an ambition of man ever since we've walked on the planet. It's part of our evolutionary process."

Mia studied Kirkwood and nodded. She agreed with him, but an uncomfortable thought was clawing at her heart. "And in order to get Mom back, we might be handing it all to a psycho?"

ᴄᴏᴄᴏ

KɪRKWOOD WATCHED the confusion and uncertainty clouding Mia's face. He'd been wondering about that too.

He hated having to lie to her, and delaying the inevitable. He wanted to tell her the whole truth, then and there, but every time he tried, something pulled him back. He knew he'd have to. He knew he would. But he still found it staggeringly hard to face her and tell her what she didn't know.

He had a lot to make up for.

Compounding his turmoil was the hakeem's file. Kirkwood had flown to Beirut with a clear mission: to assist in getting Evelyn back, while trying to keep the secret safe. Reading the hakeem's file had thrown those objectives into disarray. Countless victims had died horrible deaths, and many more were at risk.

He had to be stopped.

Kirkwood and his partners were all agreed on this. It had to supersede all other considerations.

Including Evelyn. Including the secret itself.

The hakeem couldn't be allowed to carry on his murderous quest.

Where that left him, Evelyn, and Mia was another matter altogether.

Chapter 55

Through the cloth shroud covering his head, Corben concentrated on the whir of the chopper's turbine. The sound was throatier, lower-pitched, very different from the Hueys, Blackhawks, and Chinooks he was used to. The seat he'd been shoved into confirmed his suspicion. It was positioned sideways, along the outer wall of the cabin, and its fabric was rough and starchy, its padding thin, its metal frame biting into his thighs uncomfortably.

The chopper was military.

Russian-made. A Mil, no doubt.

He'd know soon enough, as he sensed the machine slowing down and banking heavily, both of which suggested an imminent landing. Sure enough, it lurched and began its descent.

He wasn't sure how long the flight had taken, but the feeling he'd gotten of it tallied with the journey he assumed they were making: two hours of flight time or so. Comfortably within the range and airspeed of the big choppers.

They were soon on the ground. He was hustled out of the cabin and heard some shouted orders before the big turbines strained back to full power and the brunt of the rotor wash plowed into him. As the chopper lifted off, he used the likely moment of distraction among his captors to raise his nylon-cuffed hands and pull the sack off his head. Omar spotted it and barked out angrily at him, but it was too late. Corben glimpsed the Mi-25 as it banked and headed back south. He couldn't make out any markings on its camouflaged flank, but it was a military helicopter, and only one country within a few hours' driving range of Beirut had them.

He gave Omar a small grin, an unspoken middle finger, then looked around. Omar had brought three other men with him. They were toting some impressive gear: Corben spotted two sniper rifles, several subma-chine guns, and a couple of packs of additional gear. All of which con-firmed that whoever the hakeem's sponsor was had some serious muscle. The man seemed to have access to significant support and firepower, as well as a seemingly inexhaustible supply of drones. They'd been able to chopper straight into Turkey at the drop of a hat, no doubt aided by the symbiotic, enemy-of-my-enemy relationship between Turkey and Syria, which were both engaged in an ongoing struggle to subdue the nation-alistic aspirations of the stateless Kurds.

Corben realized that any ideas he'd entertained about possibly col-laborating with the hakeem were seriously misguided. Besides being a hard case himself, the man clearly had some heavyweight sponsors to an-swer to. Whoever they were, they were heavily invested in him. They'd have serious issues with inviting an American intelligence agent to their party.

It didn't necessarily displease Corben. He'd taken a serious dislike to the man and to the leather sole of his hand-sewn moccasin. He looked forward to possibly ramming it down the man's throat if this mystery buyer proved useful.

He noticed Omar pulling out the phone they'd taken from him and snapping its battery into place before pocketing it and checking a handheld GPS device. Corben scanned their surroundings. They're been dropped off in a clearing on a small hill, at the edge of a vast plain of arid land. Small patches of greenery dotted the edge of a river, the Tigris, that cut through it, snaking south, where it would eventually cross all of Iraq. About a mile north of their position, looming down on the parched flatlands from its elevated mound, was the ancient city of Diyarbakir.

Omar walked over and handed Corben his phone. "No messages for you," he said in a heavily accented tongue. "So the position of Abu Barzan is still the same."

"Still the same," Corben confirmed. "But we'd better keep it on from here on, in case they call with any changes." If Olshansky didn't come through for him soon, things might get tight. He just had to find an opening and take it.

"I'll keep it with me," Omar said. "For now."

Corben smiled. It didn't even try to find his eyes. *"Intal rayyis, ya Omar."* You're the boss.

Movement caught his eye as two dusty SUVs drove up to meet them. Omar waved them over and yelled out an order to his men to load up.

Within minutes, they were on their way.

✑✑✑

THE KING AIR WAS MET on the tarmac by one of Kirkwood's security consultants. Typically ex-SAS or Special Forces operatives, their services were in high demand since the chaos had overwhelmed Iraq. Per Kirkwood's request, he and Mia were able to disembark in a remote corner of the small airfield, away from prying eyes. They sat in the back of the car that was there waiting for them, a Toyota Land Cruiser with heavily smoked windows, while the hired gun, an Australian who gave his name as Bryan, took their passports in to be stamped at the small terminal. Moments later, they breezed out of the airport compound and were headed to their meeting with Abu Barzan.

"You've made contact with him?" Kirkwood asked the Australian.

"Yeah," he confirmed. "He was a bit put out by the change of venue, but I told him it was just a safety precaution. One of my guys is there, with him."

Mia listened to the exchange with slight puzzlement. "What change of venue? He knows you're coming?"

"I had him moved this morning," Kirkwood told her. "Just in case Corben and the others were onto him."

Something about it wasn't sitting well with her. "Is he under guard or something? I mean, aren't you worried he'll just bail on you?"

Kirkwood seemed to read her suspicions. "I'll explain everything when we're with him, I promise."

∽∽∽

THE TWO DUSTY SUVs made their way across a narrow concrete bridge and climbed up towards Diyarbakir.

The city had grown to become the Kurdish capital of eastern Turkey. The ancient town, squatting on its elevated mound, was surrounded by a massive Byzantine defensive wall. Only the Great Wall of China was bigger. Built of large blocks of black basalt, it housed five imposing gates that led into the old town and had sixteen keeps dotted around its circumference. Newer buildings crawled down its outer ridge and spilled out into the plain around it.

From the back of the lead vehicle, Corben studied his captors. Omar was seated next to him, studying the GPS coordinates on his handheld screen, with one of his men riding shotgun next to the local driver. The back car had Omar's two remaining henchmen, and another driver.

He was wondering if he'd get lucky before his bluff was called, when his cell phone suddenly warbled. Omar checked its screen, then handed it to Corben as he pulled out his handgun and pressed its nozzle against Corben's neck.

"Be careful what you say."

Corben ignored the comment and just took the phone. He glanced at its screen. It was Olshansky.

"Where the hell are you?" his techie asked. "I got a really weird ring-tone on your phone."

"Don't worry about it," Corben countered. "What have you got for me?"

Olshansky sounded excited. "The NSA's got a lock on your Swiss mystery caller. You're not going to believe this."

Corben eyed Omar coolly. "He's in Turkey," he told Olshansky, his voice flat.

"Not just in Turkey, my friend," Olshansky enthused. "He's in Diyarbakir."

"Where in Diyarbakir?"

"Last lock I have placed him at the airport—no, hang on. He's just crossed cells. He's on his way into the city." Olshansky's tone changed to concern. "Hey, are you alright?"

"I'm great. Just let me know when he stops moving." Corben

brusquely hung up, spinning around to scan the roads out his window. "Is this the airport road?" he asked Omar.

Omar relayed the question to the driver in Arabic. The driver nodded.

Corben turned and checked the road behind them. It was empty. "Get your driver to pull over somewhere discreet. Our buyer's on his way in."

Chapter 56

The sun-drenched landscape between the airport and the elevated city was barren and desolate. Mia and Kirkwood's driver had to stop several times as villagers in tattered clothing meandered across the road with herds of sheep and goats, the languid processions escorted by squadrons of flies and trailing an acrid stench.

The Land Cruiser eventually reached the concrete bridge and headed up to the city. The buildings lining the approach were a haphazard, unruly mix of old and new, cheaply built, many further defaced by half-torn election posters and the garish signage of the shops that occupied the street level. The road was crowded with pickup trucks and overloaded sedans carrying everything from watermelons to refrigerators.

The driver threaded his way through the congested obstacle course. Neither he, nor his passengers, noticed the two dusty SUVs that were parked along their route, shielded by a large tanker truck that was unloading water.

As the Land Cruiser glided past Corben's SUV, something about it snagged his attention. It was reasonably clean, it was in good condition, and though he couldn't make out much behind its smoked windows, he'd caught a glimpse of the man in the front passenger seat as the car had been heading towards them, a fair-skinned man with sandy-colored hair wearing black shades.

That had to be the target. Hardly any cars had driven in from the direction of the airport, and this guy wasn't local.

"There." He pointed it out to Omar. "That's our buyer. Follow him."

Omar ordered the driver to do so. The two SUVs pulled out and slithered forward, keeping two or three cars between them and the Land Cruiser.

Corben's muscles tightened with anticipation. He wasn't sure it was the buyer's vehicle, but he sensed he'd gotten it right. Regardless, he'd soon get a lock from Olshansky on the buyer's final destination.

He glanced over at Omar. The hakeem's man gave him a small nod before his lifeless eyes swiveled back to take in their quarry.

The Land Cruiser tunneled through a vast stone gate and entered the old city. The houses here were much older, lower, and were built of distinctive alternating bands of white stone and reddish black basalt. Mosques abounded, their minarets spearing the dense townscape. The uneven, cracked sidewalks were crowded with men, most of them in the traditional baggy black trousers, and women in white headscarves. Narrow, dark streets radiated away from the main road, sheltering children who played in the shade.

The two SUVs shadowed the Land Cruiser from a safe distance. They stopped around the corner of a big market as their target pulled up outside a house adjacent to it.

Two men waited outside. One was an Arab, the other a Westerner. Both looked as if they were packing. Omar asked the driver where they were. The driver explained that this was the Hassan Pasha Ham, an old caravanserai that now housed souvenir shops and carpet merchants.

Corben wasn't listening. His eyes were locked on the Land Cruiser as its doors swung open.

The fair-haired man emerged first, scanning the surroundings with practiced eyes. The shades and the holster bulge under his khaki desert jacket told Corben the man was a hired gun. He exchanged a couple of words with the Westerner waiting outside the house as the Land Cruiser's rear doors opened.

Corben spotted Mia step out first. And if that wasn't enough, the sight of Kirkwood following her tripped the remaining circuits in his brain into overdrive.

He'd been expecting to see Webster. His mind rushed to process the development. Clearly, Webster and Kirkwood were working together. Which explained a lot about Kirkwood's appearance in Beirut, and his interest.

He glanced at Omar, who'd also seen her, but didn't know Kirkwood. Corben just nodded and kept his satisfaction cloaked.

Perfect.

Chapter 57

Mia climbed out of the Land Cruiser and watched the Australian hand Kirkwood the silver attaché case. Kirkwood turned to her. "Give me a minute, will you? Let me make sure he's not going to give us any trouble."

Mia nodded. Kirkwood went into the house with the Australian, leaving her outside with the other hired gun, a South African named Hector, and Abu Barzan's man. Both men acknowledged her with curt nods—the Arab checking her out a touch more obviously than the South African—before they remembered their day jobs and concentrated on the surrounding streets and buildings instead.

The town seemed to have settled into a typically Middle Eastern mid-day torpor. The street was quiet, and few people were going in and out of the bazaar. Down a narrow, cobbled side street, a few kids who hadn't succumbed to the general lethargy played soccer barefoot under some crowded clotheslines. Mia watched as one of the boys bounced the ball repeatedly off his feet, knees, and thighs, to the cheers and taunts of his friends.

Kirkwood's voice cut through Mia's momentary distraction and invited her to join him inside the house. The front door led straight into a large living room that was simple and sparsely furnished and reeked of stale nicotine. Their Australian escort was in there, as were three Arab men, all of whom, she noticed, were smoking.

"This is Abu Barzan," Kirkwood informed her, pointing out a heavy-set, triple-chinned man with dyed jet-black hair, a thick matching mustache, and a prominent mole on his left cheek.

"Very nice to meet you." Abu Barzan smiled, balancing his cigarette off his lower lip while taking her hand into his large, sweaty paws enthusiastically. "This is *Kaak* Mohsen," he said, using the Kurdish term for "brother" and gesturing to an older, more reserved man who quietly gave her a welcoming half-bow, "my dear friend who kindly invited us to use his house, at very short notice," he added pointedly, glancing at Kirkwood, who acknowledged the remark with a nod of gratitude. "And my nephew, Bashar," the Iraqi concluded, indicating a younger, paunchy, and prematurely balding man.

Mohsen offered her the ubiquitous cup of heavily sugared tea. As she sipped from it, she cast her eyes behind the men and picked out the panoply of guns in the room. Two rifles were on a sideboard by a door that led to the back of the house, and Abu Barzan's nephew was holding an AK-47 machine gun and packing a handgun under his belt.

She also noticed Kirkwood's silver attaché case, on the dining table in the corner of the room. Bryan, the Australian hired gun, seemed to be guarding it. On the floor beside it were several wooden crates filled with items wrapped in soft cloth sacks.

Her gaze found Kirkwood. "Does he have the book?" she asked.

"Ah, this famous book," Abu Barzan chuckled throatily, his girth rippling in tandem with his labored breathing. "Yes, of course I have it for you. Here," he said, padding heavily over to the table, picking up a small pouch, and holding it up to them knowingly. "This is the one you want, yes?" He unwrapped the protective oilskin cover to reveal the codex and held it up proudly.

Even from across the room, Mia could make out the snake-eater. The entire room seemed to resonate with promise and expectation.

Abu Barzan set the codex squarely on the table. "Please." He gestured, inviting them over. Kirkwood glanced over at Mia, then approached the table almost reverently. Mia joined him. He reached over to pick up the codex, but Abu Barzan calmly settled his sausagelike fingers over it and flashed Kirkwood a questioning smile. Kirkwood acknowledged it and gave Bryan a signaling nod. Mia watched with a flutter of unease as the man picked up the attaché case and handed it over to a gleeful Abu Barzan, who retreated deferentially.

She wanted to ask what was going on, but her attention was gripped by Kirkwood, who was picking up the codex. He held it up so she could examine it with him.

The cover was in remarkably good condition. The Ouroboros was meticulously tooled into the leather, its scales individually carved out. Kirkwood looked up at Mia, his face radiating nervous anticipation, then, carefully, opened it.

It read from right to left, as with all Arabic writing. Its inside front cover had a blank pastedown, which was common for the period. The first inside page had some Naskhi writing in its center.

As soon as his eyes drank in the words, his face contorted with disappointment.

"What?" Mia asked.

"This is a different book," he said with a dismayed shake of his head. "It's called the *Kitab al Kayafa*," he read aloud. "The book of principles."

For a fleeting second, a look of puzzlement crossed her face at the discovery that he could read Arabic. She watched with rapt interest as he turned the pages and gave each one a quick scan.

Whatever he was looking for, it clearly wasn't there.

She stood in silence as he went back to the first page, and her eyes were quickly lured back by the lines of cursive Latin script that had been added, much later it seemed, in its top corner.

"What does that inscription say? Is that French?" she asked as she struggled to make sense of the highly stylized writing.

"Yes," he confirmed. He read them to himself, in silence. She scrutinized his face. It was locked in deep contemplation, as if the rest of the world had ceased to exist for him. Whatever was written on that ancient sheet of paper seemed to reach deep into his very core.

She waited patiently, not wanting to intrude, then couldn't subdue her excitement any more. "What does it say?"

"It's a message," he told her solemnly. "From a dying man to his long-lost wife." He paused, clearly still processing the words that he'd just read.

After a brief moment, he spoke. "It says, 'To my love Thérésia, how I yearn to see you, to tell you how much I miss you, to bask in your warm embrace once more, and to show you what I now know is real, for it is all true, my darling. Everything I hoped for is true. I have seen it with my own eyes, but even the discovery of a lifetime pales when I think of what it has cost me, that is, being with you and with our dear son, Miguel. Farewell,' and it's signed, 'Sebastian.'"

A look of puzzlement played on his face. He cocked his head, as if toying with a notion, then turned the page and started reading. He noticed something, then flipped to the next page, immersed in its contents, and then to the next, and the one after that. His eyes lit up as they scoured the text, devouring the Arabic script, then a broad smile erupted across his face.

"What?" Mia asked, her eyes riveted on him. "What is it?"

"This is . . . it's marvelous," he said, beaming. "It's real, Mia. It's real."

Chapter 58

⌒⌒⌒

"You see, look, here for instance," Kirkwood enthused, "it refers to how 'the memories of the men and the women of the new society will be challenged as never before' and sets out ways in which to overcome that. And here"—he turned to the previous page—"it talks about how the men and women of the new society should deal with their numerous descendants in their new world. Not just the men. The men and the women."

"I don't understand," Mia confessed.

Kirkwood was still collecting his thoughts. "This book is a code book, a guide on ethics and relationships. It sets out the rules, the principles of living for a society of people whose lives have been radically altered."

"By living longer?"

"Yes. It's about adapting to the new longevity. And it talks about men and women, do you see? Men *and* women." He shook his head. "After all those years, he found it. He actually found it."

Kirkwood wasn't making any sense. "What are you talking about?"

"Sebastian Guerreiro. He devoted his life to finding the right formulation, and it cost him everything—his wife, his son—but he made it, in the end. He made it. He must have found another book, or maybe a stash of books, another hidden chamber like the one your mom found—

only this one had the full formula in it. It's real." He beamed. "It exists."

A swarm of questions clouded Mia's thoughts. "How do you know that? I mean, this book could be theoretical. How do you know it isn't just a philosophical treatise exploring how a society would work, how it would function if such a substance existed?"

"Because Sebastian already had part of the formula," Kirkwood told her. "He found—well, he was entrusted with—a book, similar to this one. Same cover, same style . . . It described a series of experiments using a substance that seemed to arrest the aging process. The experiments had led to a formulation, a way to prepare an elixir, but the book wasn't complete. The last part of it was missing. Sebastian didn't know what was in the rest of the book. He didn't know if they had been successful, if there even was a full formula, one that really worked, or if the book just described the failed experiments to try and get it to work properly. But he still thought it important enough to devote his whole life to finding that out."

"But this book doesn't have the formula in it?"

"No, but it confirms that it's out there. The calligraphy in this book—it's the same as in the one Sebastian had."

"You've seen it?"

"Yes," Kirkwood confessed, slightly hesitant. "It's the same cabal, the same group, I'm sure of it."

Mia felt her head spinning. "How do you know all this? Who was this Sebastian?"

"He was a Portuguese inquisitor." Kirkwood looked at her, a hue of deep pride suffusing his face. "He was also my ancestor."

ON THE ROOF of a two-story house slightly down and across the street from Mohsen's home, Corben listened to Kirkwood's words through the headphones linked to the directional microphone Omar was aiming.

Omar glanced at him. The Arab was listening in too and seemed to understand what was being said as he nodded.

"Your ancestor?" Mia was angrily asking. "What the hell's going on? Who the hell are you?"

"Mia, please, just . . . please." Kirkwood paused, then they heard him say urgently, "Where did you find this book?" clearly asking Abu Barzan.

"I don't know, I'm . . . I'm not sure," an Iraqi voice, obviously Abu Barzan's, replied in a not entirely convincing stammer.

"Don't do this, alright? Not after everything we've done to get here. You've been paid a small fortune already. Where did you get this?" Kirkwood insisted fiercely.

After a brief pause and what sounded like a deep tug on a cigarette, the Iraqi finally said, "I came across it in a Yazidi village. A small place, in the mountains north of Al Amadiyya, near the border. It's called Nerva Zhori," he admitted somewhat ruefully.

"Were there other books there with this symbol on it?" Kirkwood asked intently. "Did you see anything else there like this?"

"I don't know. The village's *mokhtar*"—the term referred to its equivalent of a mayor—"asked me to go through a storeroom of old rubbish they had there, to see if there was anything I could buy," Abu Barzan said. "I took a few things, some old books, a few amulets. They didn't care what I took, they just needed some cash. Since the war, people are desperate, they need to sell whatever they can to try and make some money."

Kirkwood paused, then said, presumably to Mia, "Once your mother's out safely, we need to go there. We have to talk to this mokhtar and find out how this book ended up there."

"Why?" Mia asked.

"Because Sebastian disappeared somewhere in the Middle East while looking for the formula," Kirkwood explained, the passion in his voice cutting through the static hiss of the directional microphone. "And this is the first time we've found a clue as to what happened to him and where he ended up."

Omar reached up and pressed his finger to his earpiece, and a breath later, he turned to Corben and nodded as if to say, *That's all we need.*

Corben gave him a terse shake of the head, like *Not yet,* but Omar wasn't interested. He'd already reached for his handheld radio and, in a low murmur, issued the kill order.

Chapter 59

❧

"Wait a second," Mia insisted, "you still haven't answered my question. What do you mean he's your ancestor? Who are you? What are you really doing here?"

"It's a long story." Kirkwood looked around, clearly uncomfortable with having an audience. "Let's get everything back to the plane. I'll tell you the rest there."

Two muffled thumps disturbed the stillness outside the house. Barely noticeable, except to Bryan, who was positioned closest to the front window.

"No," Mia flared up. "You're telling me now. I've had enough of you and Corben drip-feeding me what you think is—"

"Quiet," Bryan interrupted tersely. He'd edged over to the side of the front window. Mia and Kirkwood went brusquely silent and watched as Bryan, careful to use the wall for cover, peered out from behind the netted curtain.

His colleague, and Abu Barzan's man, were sprawled on the ground. The South African had blood pooling under his head. The Arab was leaking from the chest area.

"Get down," Bryan ordered, pulling out his handgun and darting away from the glass. "We've got company."

He peered over again carefully and scanned the rooftops opposite.

He caught a glimpse of a sniper looking for a shot and ducked behind the wall just as a couple of more silenced, high-velocity rounds punched through the window and crunched into the tiled floor, showering the front of the room with shards of broken glass.

Bryan swung back out and loosed a few rounds towards the rooftop while, behind him, everyone in the room scrambled for cover. Kirkwood clutched the book as he hustled Mia behind the dining table, his eyes scanning the room for options. Abu Barzan grabbed the attaché case with one hand and pawed a handgun with the other. His nephew and their host had also reached for their weapons, and all three were backing up towards a door at the back of the room.

"Is there another way out?" Kirkwood shouted to Abu Barzan.

The big Iraqi was half-crouched, scouring the windows nervously as he retreated deeper into the house. "Yes, at the back," he said nervously. "Through here."

By the window, Bryan fired a few more rounds, emptying his magazine before rushing back to join Kirkwood and Mia.

"How many could you see?" Kirkwood asked.

"I just saw the sniper." Bryan nimbly slapped a full magazine into his handgun. "Who are these guys?"

"I don't know," Kirkwood said as several shots obliterated the lock on the front door before a military boot kicked it in.

"Take cover," Bryan yelled as he upended the dining table and flung it on its side, diving behind it before leaning out, looking for a target.

A tirade of eerily silenced gunfire from outside raked the room before one of the attackers burst in, firing as he ducked away from the door. Bryan tracked him and squeezed off a few rounds, hitting him in the thigh. The man yelled in pain as he tumbled behind a sofa. As Bryan leaned out, looking to finish him off, another shooter slung his arm in and pumped two silenced shots, one of which caught the Australian in the shoulder.

He winced with pain as he darted back behind the table, checking his bloodied wound with his good hand.

"Get out the back way," he muttered to Kirkwood and Mia through clenched teeth, beads of sweat dripping down his forehead.

Kirkwood protested, "We can't leave you like—"

"Just go, mate," Bryan ordered. "Get the hell out of here before it's too late."

And with that, he swung out and fired at anything that moved by the door, cutting down the first man he had injured and pushing back the other shooter who was moving in.

Kirkwood turned to Mia, yelling out, "Come on," before bolting out from behind the table, the codex still under one arm. Mia followed, hot on his heels, as they rushed through the doorway towards the rear of the house.

They slipped past the stairs that led to the upper levels of the house before reaching the kitchen. They'd barely stepped into the cluttered room when they heard more gunfire and thuds, then Abu Barzan came rushing back through the kitchen door alone. He wasn't fully in yet when his eyes met Mia's just as something struck him from behind and sent him crashing to the floor and writhing in pain as a crimson patch blossomed in his left thigh.

Kirkwood herded Mia back into the house, shouting, "Back the other way, quick."

She tore her eyes off the fallen Iraqi and hurried back towards the living room.

∽∽∽

CORBEN STOOD next to Omar, muscles clenched, his hands still nylon-cuffed in front of him, and watched as the first gunman charged into the house.

He'd seen the two guards outside cut down by the sniper, who had just made his way back to them. Omar had already sent three men around to the back of the house, and Corben knew they'd cut off any retreat from there. Right now, he couldn't do anything. He just stayed close to the wall, biding his time, looking for an opportunity, and watched helplessly as Omar's men went about their business.

He knew their orders were not to harm the American buyer—he'd heard Omar repeat the orders several times—and felt a flush of anger as he thought of Mia being trapped in the shooting gallery.

Omar hadn't said anything about her.

He heard gunshots coming from behind the house, then a barrage of rounds hammered the doorway around them. Omar scowled at the house, listened intently, and ordered the sniper in.

The gunman nodded, peered in, swung an arm in, and fired several rounds. A low growl of pain from inside told Corben the second of Kirkwood's escorts had been hit. He looked at Omar. The hakeem's man had heard it too. A psychotic gleam flitted across his murderous eyes as he ordered his men to finish him off.

ᴄᴏᴄᴏ

IN THE LIVING ROOM, Bryan slammed in his last magazine and peered out at the front of the house one last time. Both shooters were taking cover. He couldn't stay behind that overturned table much longer—they'd rush him sooner or later. His shoulder was hurting more now, the wound quickly getting colder, the blood loss starting to hit his head.

He had to make a move.

He leaned out, saw some movement, and squeezed off several careful rounds before scuttling, fast and low, towards the doorway the others had disappeared through. He spotted the shooter from outside glancing in and slammed a couple of shots his way as he reached the doorway.

He dived into it and rushed towards the back of the house. He reached the stairs just as Kirkwood and Mia did, coming back from the kitchen. Not a good sign—he was planning to follow them out the back of the house.

He saw Mia glance upwards, then yell, "This way."

Urgent orders in Arabic erupted in the front of the house, and the shooter he hadn't wounded came after him. Bryan took cover on the stairs, counted down a few seconds to himself, and bolted out, blasting the man with a chest hit that dropped him like a piece of blubber.

That was when the first of the three bullets struck him in the back.

ᴄᴏᴄᴏ

MIA HAD BARELY TAKEN the first few risers, Kirkwood charging up close behind her, when a small volley of bullets crunched into the walls of the narrow hallway below all around Bryan. She looked down to see the Australian take cover and return fire, only to be struck in the back seconds later by a shooter who had followed them in through the kitchen.

She felt a spasm of horror deep within her at the sight of the man's body collapsing to the floor as the bullets plowed into him, but steeled herself and willed her legs to keep going. She bounded up the narrow steps feverishly, Kirkwood following, and quickly reached the first floor. The stairs continued to another level.

"Keep going," Kirkwood yelled, but she was already on her way up, completely at the mercy of her overworked instincts.

Another flight of stairs and she'd reached a wooden, horizontal trap-door with an old latch that, mercifully, wasn't locked. She pushed against it, flung the door open and rocketed up, and found herself on the flat roof of the house. Kirkwood clambered up after her before slamming the trapdoor back shut, but there was no lock on it from the outside, and nothing heavy to block it with.

Kirkwood scanned the roof, found a piece of rusted metal rebar, and jammed it through the latches on the door. It would hold, but not for long.

Mia spun around, her eyes scrutinizing the small, whitewashed space, hoping for a miracle. A big pigeon coop occupied the center, by the trapdoor. She strode around it, her nerves overwhelmed, her mind racing to process her options, which turned out to be nonexistent: The house was freestanding, surrounded by streets and passages on all sides.

There was nowhere for them to go.

Chapter 60

❧

Corben watched as Omar, gun drawn, surveyed the front living room before yanking him in like a dog on a leash and rushing through the house with him.

He spotted the wounded shooter by the doorway and crossed over to him in a few quick strides. He was slunk down, huddled against the wall, and looked as if he wasn't doing too well. The body of the second shooter to go in lay by his feet. Omar took cover beside the open door and yelled down the hallway, asking for updates. A voice yelled back that someone called Rudwaan was dead—one of the two shooters Omar had dispatched to the back of the house, either the third member of his hit team or one of the drivers who'd met them—but that the other hired gun had been killed and that the American and the girl had gone upstairs.

Omar glared angrily, then dragged Corben out by his neck and slipped deeper into the house. They met up with the surviving shooter who'd come in through the back. The body of Kirkwood's other hired gun was all bent up at the foot of the stairs, messy with blood.

Omar looked up, thought for a nanosecond, and turned to Corben. He brought his handgun up and shoved its nozzle under Corben's chin. His eyes burned into him, the fury seething out of every pockmark in his scarred face.

Corben didn't flinch. He either died here, now, or he'd have a chance.

The hakeem's man barked to the shooter to stay with Corben and watch him, then rushed up the stairs after Kirkwood and Mia.

∽∽∽

KIRKWOOD AND MIA moved around the roof in a daze, trying to divine some kind of escape, flicking anxious glances from the low parapet surrounding them to the trapdoor and back.

They'd gone all the way around the edge of the house and were back where they started.

The shooters would soon be there.

They had to do something.

Kirkwood headed for the side with the narrowest gap separating it from the next house and called out for Mia to follow him. They reached it and stood by its edge. It was a six-foot gap to the next flat roof, that of the bazaar, which was long and had many protrusions they could use for cover.

But it was a six-foot leap over a three-story chasm that led down to the narrow cobbled passage below.

"Can you jump it?" he asked Mia, his voice frantic, his eyes darting back at the trapdoor, expecting it to fling open any second.

"Are you nuts?" she shot back.

"You can do it," he insisted.

"I'm not jumping this."

Loud thrashes against the trapdoor rattled them.

Kirkwood's eyes lasered into Mia's. "You can do this," he yelled fiercely. "You have to do it."

Another jarring burst against the trapdoor. It creaked open, its hinges juddering. It wouldn't last much longer.

Mia looked at the bazaar's roof, then back at Kirkwood.

"Jump over, and I'll throw you the book. Don't wait for me. Just go. Make your way to one of our embassies, insist on speaking with an ambassador, only with an ambassador, do you understand?"

She seemed to be looking into him, her mind swamped by a flurry of questions and emotions.

The trapdoor thudded again.

"Why are you doing this?" she asked. "Who are you? Why should I trust you?"

The questions were like spears through his heart. He felt a wild grief and a raging fury take possession of him at the same time. "Because I was with your mother in that chamber in Al-Hillah," he told her.

A look of utter mystification washed over her face.

"Because I'm pretty sure I'm your father," he added desperately, feeling as if his soul had been sucked out of his body there and then.

Another loud thump and this time, the trapdoor gave.

Kirkwood and Mia both turned in tandem as the pockmarked killer burst out of the opening and clambered onto the roof.

"Go now!" Kirkwood ordered her.

Mia looked down to the dark passage below, raised her glance to the man who had just told her he was her father, and nodded. She was too numb to speak, her mind submerged under a deluge of questions. She simply took a few steps back, charged forward, and flung herself into the air.

The ordeal lasted less than a breath as her legs flailed in the air in big, rotating sweeps before she tumbled heavily onto the roof of the bazaar, rolling on its dust-swept surface. She righted herself and sprang back to her feet, her teeth rattling and her head spinning from the harsh landing, and rushed back to the parapet.

Kirkwood stood there, his face breaking into a radiant smile of relief as he saw her straighten up unscathed.

A shadow was rushing up behind him. The same pockmarked man she'd seen in Beirut each time the madness started. He had a gun in his hand.

"Behind you," she shouted.

Kirkwood glanced back, turned to her, dropped his eyes and slid one last glance at the book he gripped in his hands, and in one fluid motion, he flung it to her.

It twirled in the air, spinning around itself, a priceless ancient Frisbee, before landing in her arms just as the killer reached the parapet. She saw him raise his handgun at her, she saw death about to reach out from its nozzle and rip the life right out of her, only the man she knew as Bill Kirkwood lunged at him from the side and tackled him, pushing his arm away and sending the bullet careening into dead air.

"Run," Kirkwood yelled as he struggled against the armed killer.

And despite every yearning, every emotion, and every instinct gluing her feet to the ground, she did.

∽⌒∽

IN THE DARKNESS at the bottom of the stairs, Corben watched the nervous shooter guarding him as they both listened to the repeated blows echoing down from above. It sounded as if Mia and Kirkwood had locked themselves into a room. Omar would break through soon, of that Corben had no doubt.

It would soon be over. If he was going to try something, he had to do it now.

Only one man watching him.

A nervous wreck, at that.

Time to party.

Kirkwood's dead gunslinger was blocking the stairs. Further down the hall, one of Omar's dead shooters was sprawled on the ground. Something of interest was lying by his arm.

Corben's eyes snared his guard's nervous look, then glanced sideways, down at the body of Omar's man, and turned to his guard in mock surprise.

"The book. It's there, look." Corben pointed down at the bloodied floor. And he took a step towards the dead shooter, keeping an eye on his guard, testing his reaction.

The shooter yelled at him, warning Corben off, but Corben stared him down and kept moving, his voice even louder. "It's the book, asshole, you understand? *Al kitab.*"

And he took another step, raising his cuffed hands in a gesture of helplessness, then pointed downward. *"Al kitab,"* he repeated. "It's what your *mu'allim* wants, numb nuts."

The shooter kept shouting and raised his gun, his eyes darting nervously up the stairs after Omar, unsure what to do. Corben was committed now, he was in a zone and wasn't going to back out. He kept reaching down, yelling, "The book, okay? *Al kitab,* you understand?" And with that, positioning his back to the gunman, his fingers grabbed the fallen man's silenced gun and he spun to face the wide-eyed Arab and pulled the trigger, hoping to a God he didn't believe in that its magazine wasn't empty and undergoing a small conversion in matters of faith as several rounds drilled into the man's chest and punched him backwards before dropping him to the floor in a bloody mess.

⁓⁓⁓

ON THE ROOF, Omar shoved Kirkwood off him with a vicious head butt and pushed himself to his feet. He held him at bay with his handgun as he scanned the roof of the adjacent bazaar.

There was no trace of Mia or of the book.

He grabbed Kirkwood by the neck and pulled him to his feet. He took one last look across the roof, then gave up and yelled at Kirkwood to move. He pushed him through the trapdoor and herded him down the stairs, prodding him in the back with his handgun.

He was livid.

He'd lost the book, when it was right there, within reach. But he had what the hakeem wanted even more: the buyer. Unscathed. Ready for questioning. But it wasn't a success, not by any means. Apart from the book, he'd lost several men.

He had to get out of there fast. The Turkish police would, no doubt, be rushing over, alerted by the gunfire.

He followed Kirkwood down and saw Corben's back as they reached the bottom of the stairs. He barked out angrily to the man he'd left guarding the American.

Corben turned to face him slowly, unthreateningly, his expression a blank sheet.

And in the darkness of that dusty hallway, Omar didn't see the gun in Corben's hand, not even when it spat a 9mm round that spun out of its nozzle and cleaved a path straight through his forehead.

Chapter 61

⌒⌒

Kirkwood watched Omar fall to the ground beside him and tumble down the last few steps, headfirst, until he lay still in a mangled, splattered heap by Corben's feet.

Corben looked up the stairs. "Where's Mia?" he asked urgently.

Kirkwood studied Corben's eyes. He was still processing the eruption of the last few minutes. The killers were Arab and had to be the hakeem's men—only Corben was with them. Which didn't compute. "What are you doing here?"

Corben seemed to be busy processing things himself. "They grabbed me last night."

"How did they know about this rendezvous?" Kirkwood pressed. "Through you? You've been keeping tabs on Abu Barzan?" His tone had an overtly accusing tone to it.

Which didn't faze Corben. "We don't have time for this," he countered bluntly. "Where's the book?"

"Mia's got it. And trust me, she's long gone by now." Kirkwood watched Corben for a reaction. "Can't blame her, really, what with all the bullshit she's been hearing about how getting her mom back's your top priority."

Corben glanced up the stairs after Mia, then confronted Kirkwood's gaze. "Clearly, it's yours too," he shot back, his voice laced with cynicism. "I mean, that's the only reason you're here, right? Nothing to do with tracking down the formula your ancestor was after."

The mention tripped Kirkwood's mind. Corben couldn't have known about that—not unless he'd been listening in. Which had to mean that he wasn't here as a prisoner. He was already working with the hakeem—only something about his plans had evidently changed, given that he'd just killed the man who seemed to be the leader of the hakeem's hit team.

Corben glanced towards the front door, then bent down to Omar's body, pulled a knife from one of his pockets, and cut his hands free. He rubbed the blood back into his wrists, then retrieved his cell phone from the fallen Arab and quickly checked its battery. It was fully charged. He took its battery out and put it away, then turned to Bryan's body, picked up his submachine gun, which he slung over his shoulder, and rifled through his pockets. He found some extra magazines, which he took, as well as the Land Cruiser's keys, which was what he was really after.

Kirkwood saw him cast his eyes to the back of the house, as if wondering about something.

"Come on," he ordered Kirkwood as he stepped over Omar's body and stole deeper into the house.

"Where are we going?" Kirkwood asked.

Corben didn't answer.

Kirkwood followed him into the kitchen. Corben gave the alleyway that ran behind the house a quick check, then stepped back inside. Abu Barzan was lying in the corner of the room, facedown, a dark pool of blood under him. By his feet was the attaché case.

Corben picked it up. He turned. Kirkwood stood there, facing him. He looked at the agent quizzically, then held out his hand for the case.

Corben shook his head slightly. "I think I'll hang on to this. Make sure it gets back to the UN safely. Wouldn't want them to miss it now, would we?" A thin, mocking smile broke through his stern expression.

Kirkwood held his gaze for a moment, then nodded with silent frustration. The gloves were off, clearly. There was no point in dissembling. He looked down, and his eyes fell on one of the Iraqis' weapons, a handgun, on the floor beside him. It was tantalizingly within reach.

Corben had seen it too.

Kirkwood's muscles went rigid. He locked eyes with Corben. It was as if they could read the thoughts etched across each other's face.

"Not a good idea," Corben cautioned.

"There might be more of them out there," Kirkwood bluffed. "You could use another shooter."

Corben shook his head dismissively. "They're all accounted for." He waved the gun towards the back of the house, motioning for Kirkwood to head out. "Let's go," he ordered.

∽∽∽

MIA'S FINGERS CLUTCHED the codex tightly as she huddled behind the parapet on the roof of the bazaar.

She kept darting nervous glances back at the house she'd escaped from, but no one seemed to be coming through the trapdoor after her. Not that it made her feel any calmer. Her heart was still pounding feverishly as she tried to make sense of what had happened and, even more pressingly, of what Kirkwood—or whatever his real name was—had told her.

Because I'm pretty sure I'm your father, he'd said.

Which didn't make sense.

He couldn't have been with Evelyn at Al-Hillah. That was thirty years ago, and he didn't look as if he was even over forty.

The only possible explanation was one she wasn't yet ready to entertain.

Besides, he'd also said that his ancestor was looking for the complete formula for the elixir. That it was incomplete. And if it was incomplete, then it didn't work, and he couldn't be using it.

She shook the whole notion out of her mind. It simply wasn't possible. It couldn't be. He was lying to her, he had to be. Which was the safe and comforting conclusion to cling to, except that she couldn't do that. She'd looked into his eyes as he'd said those words, as he'd explained about his ancestor Sebastian, about the codex, about who he was. Everything about him screamed of sincerity. She'd had that same feeling when they'd spoken on the plane, and earlier, at the rooftop bar of the hotel. He wasn't lying. For some reason she couldn't quite fathom, she was sure of it.

Which meant that everything she considered impossible had to be revisited, questioned, and—if her instincts were right—reclassified without the *im* prefix. And that included the impossibility of his being her father.

She heard movement below and peered over the lip of the parapet. She froze as she spotted Kirkwood, heading down the narrow alley at the side of the house. Another man was following him. She craned over the edge to get a better look, and her heart turned over when she realized it was Corben.

What's he doing here?

She wasn't sure it mattered, and her spirits rose at the sight. He'd managed to save Kirkwood from the hakeem's men, and they were both safe.

She was about to spring up and make her presence known when she noticed something as they moved into the street, past the dead bodies of Abu Barzan's man and Kirkwood's other bodyguard. Corben was walking behind Kirkwood. He had a submachine gun slung over his shoulder and was carrying the attaché case. He also held something in his other hand. A handgun.

The whole body language was wrong. There was tension between them, in the way Kirkwood was walking warily in front of Corben.

It was almost as if he were a prisoner.

⌒⌒

CORBEN WALKED BEHIND Kirkwood as he directed him to the Land Cruiser, gripping the attaché case in one hand, the silenced handgun in the other.

As they walked up to the SUV, his eyes calmly scanned the surrounding houses. He caught a glimpse of a young boy, peeking out at them from an open window before being pulled back by his fearful mother. He sensed movement in other windows. They had to be quick. The Turkish police were probably already on their way—they were always on alert throughout the region, due to the constant threat from Kurdish PPK separatist militants, whose home turf this was—and Corben had no interest in explaining himself to them, or to anyone for that matter, just yet.

They reached the Land Cruiser. Its windows were down, and Corben could see that its doors weren't locked. "Get in the car," he ordered Kirkwood in a low rasp, "and don't do anything stupid."

Kirkwood climbed into the passenger seat as Corben chucked the attaché case and the submachine gun into the back of the SUV. He looked up and scrutinized the roofs above them. He couldn't see her anywhere, but he knew she had to be watching.

"Mia," he bellowed upwards. "Come on out. It's safe. We've got to get out of here now."

᙮᙮᙮

MIA STAYED LOW as Corben's voice echoed up from the street.

The last thing she wanted was to be abandoned here, alone, in this godforsaken corner of the world, surrounded by dead bodies. The *Midnight Express* analogy was coming to life alarmingly in her mind's eye. She wanted to believe that Corben was on their side, that he was here to save them, that he was trying to get her mom back. He'd obviously killed the hakeem's men. Which had to be a good thing. So what if he knew about the hakeem's experiments? So he'd lied to her about what this was all about. Big deal. She didn't "need to know." And it didn't mean he wasn't also trying to get Evelyn back.

"Mia," Corben yelled again. "We've got to go. Come on."

She shut her eyes and imagined Corben and Kirkwood driving off without her, and the thought suddenly horrified her. She couldn't face being left behind.

She subdued her warring emotions and, with the fear of making a huge mistake throttling her stomach, rose to her feet.

᙮᙮᙮

SITTING IN THE LAND CRUISER, Kirkwood felt a surge of anxiety wash over him as he listened to Corben's calls.

He had to do something. He was sure Corben wouldn't want Mia around once he got his hands on the book. She knew too much.

He had to warn her.

He reached out and flung the door open and bolted from the car.

"Mia, don't come out," he yelled, scanning the roofs around him. "Stay away."

Corben dashed after him and tackled him a few yards from the Land Cruiser. He grabbed him by the collar and stuffed the gun in his face.

Kirkwood scowled at him defiantly. "What are you gonna do, shoot me?"

Corben held him there for a breath, seething with anger and frustration. "Get up," he ordered, pulling him to his feet and shoving him towards the Land Cruiser. He stopped at the car, cast one last glance up at the roofs, then pushed Kirkwood into the car and climbed in behind him.

ᓇᓇᓇ

MIA'S BREATH CAUGHT as she spotted Kirkwood dart out of the car and run down the street. Her whole body stiffened as Corben caught up with him, floored him, and manhandled him back to the car.

She sank back to her cover and watched as Corben climbed into the car, and her heart sank as she heard its engine churn to life before it screeched off and disappeared around a corner.

She pushed herself to her feet, the blood draining from her face, feeling dizzy. She looked down at the quiet street. The Land Cruiser was well and truly gone, leaving a plume of dust and the two dead bodies in its wake. Stunned and curious people were cautiously emerging from the adjacent houses and from the bazaar.

She glanced at the old book in her hands and noticed that her nails had clawed deep into its leather cover. She felt like ripping the damn thing to pieces and screaming her lungs out in rage, but instead, she looked around, saw what looked like the overhang of a stairwell, and made her way towards it.

Chapter 62

M ia ducked out of a side entrance to the bazaar and into the cobbled alleyway from which Corben and Kirkwood had emerged. She could see increased activity in the main street outside the house as people realized the threat was gone, and she snuck the other way, heading back into the alley.

As she turned the corner, she saw a hulking figure stumbling out of the house. It was Abu Barzan. The big man was slowly inching his way out, all hunched over, one hand pressed against his thigh, his trousers drenched with blood. The alley was strewn with several dead bodies. He stopped at one of them and crouched down, running his hand over the dead man's face. Mia realized he'd found his nephew's body.

She edged up to him. He turned to her, sucking in deep, laborious breaths. He had pained, half-shut eyes, and his jowly face glistened with sweat.

"I'm sorry," she muttered, avoiding looking too closely at the fallen man by his feet.

Abu Barzan just nodded stoically, his expression bristling with anger and defiance.

"Let me see it," she said, pointing to his wound.

He didn't react. She reached out hesitantly and ripped his pants open around the wound to uncover it. She could see an entry puncture as well as an exit one in the thick flesh of his thigh. Noting that the bleeding wasn't intense, coupled with that he was standing and breathing, she thought that his femoral artery probably hadn't been severed by the bullet or by bone fragments. This negated the risk of his bleeding to death, but the wound needed to be dressed quickly to lessen the blood loss and avoid infection.

"I don't think it's shattered any bone," she observed, "but it needs cleaning."

A high-pitched siren wailed faintly in the distance. Abu Barzan looked at her with anxious eyes. "I have to go," he grumbled, and started to limp away.

"Wait." She followed, stepping over the fallen gunmen. "You need to go to a hospital."

He waved her off. "A hospital? Are you crazy? I'm half-Kurd," he spat back. "How do you think I'm going to explain this?"

Mia nodded somberly. "I'm not sure I know how I'm going to explain this myself."

Abu Barzan studied her for a beat, then said, "Come."

She put an arm under his shoulder and helped him keep the weight off his injured leg as they slipped away into the dark back alleys of the old town.

∽∽∽

CORBEN KEPT A CLOSE EYE on his rearview mirror as he guided the Land Cruiser out of the city and headed south, towards Mardin.

He had a big decision to make, but the more he thought about it, the more he believed he could pull it off. He had Kirkwood, who could unlock the mystery if properly motivated, and Corben was, if anything, an expert on inspiring. He had a window of opportunity during which he could misbehave: He'd been abducted in his sleep, the front door of his apartment would testify to that. He would say he was a prisoner of the hakeem. Everything he did was with a gun to his head. Enough said.

The problem was Kirkwood.

He couldn't be allowed to walk away from this. Not with what he knew. Mia—that could be finessed. Kirkwood was more complicated.

"You really with the UN?" Corben asked him. His handgun nestled in his lap.

"Last time I checked," Kirkwood answered flatly, staring ahead blankly.

Corben nodded, impressed. "Six hundred grand. Not exactly chump change." He waited for a reaction, but none came. "How many of you are there?"

He detected a flicker of confusion in Kirkwood.

"What are you talking about?"

"How many of you are there looking for this thing? I mean, there's you, and there's Tom Webster, right?" Corben fished. "You're able to fly in at the drop of the hat with a case full of cash. I'm thinking you guys have some decent resources to draw on."

Kirkwood ignored the comment. "Where are we going?"

"We're both after the same thing. I say let's see it through all the way." Corben paused, glancing over at Kirkwood. "Besides, I miss the mountains. Clean air up there. Good for the lungs," he deadpanned.

The Iraqi border was a couple of hours' drive away. He debated whether to call in, inform his station chief that he'd been kidnapped, say he'd managed to get away and was now shadowing the Iraqi smuggler behind the kidnapping, and get them to call ahead and make sure he was allowed through the border crossings unhampered. He decided against it, preferring to keep his cohorts in the dark a little while longer. And although he didn't have a passport or any ID on him, he had a far more effective travel document in the back: a case full of dollar bills. In that desperate land, he knew a few of those greenbacks would open most doors. From there, it wasn't far to Al Amadiyya. If everything went smoothly, they'd make the village Abu Barzan had spoken of by nightfall.

"What are your plans for it, if it's out there?" Kirkwood asked bluntly. "Can't imagine our government's anywhere near ready to deal with something like this. Preserving the status quo and all." He turned to face Corben. "'Cause that's the plan, isn't it? Bury it—along with anyone who knows about it?"

Corben smirked and let out a small chortle. "Probably. But it's not mine."

Kirkwood raised an eyebrow. "Oh?"

Corben glanced at him, a wry smile crinkling the edge of his mouth. "Let's say I have a more entrepreneurial approach to life." He paused. "Question is, what are you guys planning for it?"

"A better world for everyone," Kirkwood replied, seemingly thrown by Corben's cavalier attitude. "And I mean *everyone*."

Corben shrugged. "So I guess we're on the same page."

"Except for one pesky little detail. I'm not prepared to kill for it."

"Maybe you just haven't yet had to face that choice."

Kirkwood let it simmer. "What if I have?"

The insinuation intrigued Corben, but he masked the feeling. "Then I'd say I care more about making the world a better place than you do," he replied nonchalantly.

"And where does Evelyn Bishop fall in all this? Collateral damage?"

"Not necessarily." Corben glanced over at him. A motivational tool had just presented itself. "Help me figure this out, and nothing will give me more pleasure than taking the hakeem down and getting her back."

Corben cocked an eyebrow, waiting for Kirkwood's reaction, and smiled inwardly. He had him thinking, which was good. It meant he'd be spending less time trying to wrangle his freedom.

Corben decided to nudge him a little further in that direction. "By the way, when were you and Webster planning on telling Mia that her dad was still alive?"

ᴄᴏᴄᴏ

KIRKWOOD STIFFENED at Corben's jocular tone. At least Corben didn't know the whole truth, he reminded himself.

At least he didn't know that he was Tom Webster.

He thought back to what Corben must have overheard back in Diyarbakir and replayed the conversation in his mind. Corben assumed the formula didn't work, not for anyone. Which was why he hadn't made the leap.

Let's keep it that way, he thought.

The name he'd used with Evelyn drifted his thoughts back to her. Guilt consumed him. If he'd told her the truth back then, in Al-Hillah, maybe she would've been more careful. She would have known dangerous people would be after this. They always were. They came out of the woodwork the minute they got a sniff of it. It was the way of the world. Had been for hundreds of years.

Evelyn wouldn't have been kidnapped.

And he would have known he had a daughter. A daughter who would have grown up with a father. He'd have made sure of that. He'd have found a way.

He remembered the look in Mia's eyes when he'd told her the truth, and it gutted him again, just ripped his insides out and left nothing there but a gaping black hole.

At least, he thought with a trace of solace—at least she was safe now.

～～～

MIA SAT ON A RICKETY CHAIR in the smoke-filled room. She sipped from a glass of water as the wiry old man with bloodstained arms finished dressing Abu Barzan's wound.

The antiques dealer had guided her through the back streets of the ancient town to the house of another of his contacts. Despite their occasional fratricidal tussles, the Kurds all shared a hated common enemy and helped each other out when it came to keeping out of the clutches of the MIT, the Turkish intelligence service—the local variant of the *mukhabarat*.

Three other men were in the room, all locals, all smoking. They were arguing vociferously among themselves and with Abu Barzan, in Kurdish. Mia couldn't understand what they were saying, but they were clearly angry about what had happened. One of their own had been killed, after all, as well as Abu Barzan's nephew, and the debate was clearly on as to what the repercussions—and potential reprisals—could be.

The doctor finished his work and left the room, taking the others with him and leaving Mia alone with Abu Barzan. A leaden silence hung between them as the wisps of smoke thinned out and vanished, then Abu Barzan turned to her.

"You still have the book," he observed. It sat squarely on the table, in front of her.

She nodded, lost in her thoughts.

"What are you going to do?"

"I don't know." She'd pondered that question while the doctor had been working on Abu Barzan's wound and hadn't reached a conclusion. "I can't go to my embassy. I don't know who to trust anymore." She told him about what had happened in Beirut and about Evelyn's kidnapping. He flushed angrily when she filled him in on what she knew about the hakeem. Saddam had already used nerve gas on the Kurds. They weren't exactly his chosen people. It was quite possible—likely, even—that he'd gleefully culled the hakeem's guinea pigs from their ranks.

She told him about Corben, but avoided mentioning what Kirkwood had told her on the roof, merely painting him as a UN official who was trying to help.

She was still grinding that one over herself.

A skeptical expression crossed his sagging face. "This UN man. The one who was buying this"—pointing a thick finger at the codex—"you trust him?"

The comment surprised Mia, then she remembered seeing Kirkwood handing him the silver attaché case. It all fell into place. "He was your buyer all along, wasn't he?"

Abu Barzan nodded. "Six hundred thousand dollars. Gone." He heaved a desolate sigh.

Mia's brow furrowed as her thoughts drifted back to Corben. At the back of her mind, something was clamoring for attention, and she couldn't quite put a finger on it. She remembered seeing Corben carrying the attaché case, but something didn't fit. He'd been alone. No backup, no SEAL team, no Turkish forces assisting him—and they were our allies, after all.

He was operating on his own. A rogue agent.

A tremor of concern rattled through her. Kirkwood. Corben had him. And if there was any chance of getting her mom back, it was with him.

She tried to imagine what Corben's next move would be. Evelyn didn't matter to him, that much was obvious. He'd killed the hakeem's men, which wasn't exactly the best "let's get together" signal if the intention had been to make contact with him.

Corben was following his own, personal agenda.

Which meant that he'd be going after it. And that meant he'd be headed for one specific place.

"Do you want to get your money back?" she asked Abu Barzan, her voice alight with hope.

Abu Barzan raised his eyes to her, a dour and confused expression on his face.

"Can you get us across the border?" she added, breathless.

Chapter 63

⌒⌒

The sun had arced into a hazy, midafternoon sky as the Land Cruiser crossed into Iraq.

Corben had pulled over at a makeshift fruit stand on the road out of Idil, close to the border, and picked up a couple of bottles of water and some bananas for him and his prisoner. He'd untied Kirkwood—having secured his right wrist to the handle in the passenger door to make sure he didn't try to bail—and they'd both relieved themselves by the side of the road. He'd then driven past the long line of empty fuel trucks and buses waiting to cross into Iraq and pulled up at the Turkish border post. The loutish and overzealous soldier manning it was quickly subjugated by a more accommodating officer, who, his eyes flickering at the sight of several months' salary being dangled before him, had generously kicked in a map of the region before allowing them to leave his country.

Corben and Kirkwood had then driven across the barbed-wired no-man's-land that separated the two frontiers. The bleak strip was even more desolate than the flatlands it separated. A couple of hundred yards later, they'd reached the Iraqi border post, where a guard in flimsy camouflage fatigues had also gleefully pocketed a small roll of bills and hastily waved them through.

Corben stopped at a gas station just outside Zakho, once he was sure that his border bribe hadn't backfired on him and that no one was following them. He filled the car and checked the map for Nerva Zhori. His eyes had trouble locating it, but after a twinge of concern, he finally spotted the small village, marked by the tiniest of letters, tucked away in the mountains, almost straddling the Turkish border.

They'd have to drive south to Dahuk, then turn left and head northeast, past Al Amadiyya and into the highlands. He checked the car's clock and looked up at the sun's level and ran a quick mental calculation. Barring any major holdups, he thought they might just be able to make it before sundown.

He folded up the map, slid a glance at Kirkwood, and hit the gas pedal.

∽∾∽

FROM THE LUMPY BACKSEAT of the old Peugeot, Mia watched the flat, rocky, mind-numbingly barren landscape unfurl outside her open window. Not a tree was in sight; instead, a row of anorexic electricity poles lined the narrow road, the wires linking them sagging lethargically. They reminded her of the telegraph lines of the Wild West, which was fitting, she thought, given the day—days, in fact—she'd had so far.

Abu Barzan was seated next to her, wheezing heavily between deep drags off a Marlboro. Two other men that she'd met at the doctor's house were in the front of the car. She'd lost count of how many cigarettes Abu Barzan and his buddies had lit up during the journey. A dark patch stained his trouser leg, blood having seeped through the bandage, but it wasn't getting any bigger. The doctor in Diyarbakir seemed to have done a good job, but then, given the unrest in the region, he probably had some practice.

Despite Abu Barzan's wound, they'd decided to leave Diyarbakir and drive off immediately. Their route would be longer than the one Mia and Abu Barzan assumed Corben would be taking. They couldn't risk crossing the official border at Zakho, not with Abu Barzan's bullet wound. Mia didn't have her passport either; she'd left her bag in the Land Cruiser. They also didn't know if Corben had gotten the contacts he surely had within the Turkish intelligence service to tighten the border crossing behind him, just in case. Instead, they would drive fifty miles farther east, along the main road that skirted the border, until they reached the base of the Chiyā-ē Linik mountains. They'd be smuggled into Iraq from there.

They crossed a couple of small, breeze-block border towns before the steppes gave way to undulating foothills. An imposing mountain range rose in the distance, and before long, the road got windy and ascended rapidly, the tired car listing and straining under the effort.

The sun had disappeared behind the peaks towering over them by the time they turned off the main road to head south through a narrow valley. A small river coursed through it, and the Peugeot bounced down a gravelly path alongside it for a couple of miles before the road petered out in a small clearing where four dour-faced men were waiting for them.

They'd brought mules—loaded with gear, and, Mia noticed with a tinge of gratitude, saddled—and were armed with Kalashnikov submachine guns and rifles.

The driver cut the engine. Mia climbed out and watched as the men helped Abu Barzan out of the car. They exchanged hearty kisses to each others' cheeks, coupled with big, backslapping bear hugs, and impassionedly bemoaned Abu Barzan's gunshot. Once the intense ritual was over, Abu Barzan turned to Mia.

"We go now," he stated simply, inviting her to the fly-infested mule that waited lazily by his side.

She glanced up at the daunting mountains bearing down on them and nodded.

ᨆᨆ

CORBEN VEERED OFF the main road ten miles past Al Amadiyya and onto a winding dirt trail that headed north. The four-wheeled drivetrain of the Land Cruiser was getting a real workout, groaning in protest as the SUV struggled up the mountain along what wasn't much more than a mule path.

"Abu Barzan said it was a 'Yazidi' village," Corben recalled as he wrestled with the wheel, trying to avoid the larger rocks in their way. "You know much about them?"

"Only that they're devil worshippers," Kirkwood mentioned casually, with a wry smile.

"Good to know." Corben shrugged.

It was a common misconception, but one that, right now, watching the annoyance across Corben's face, gave Kirkwood a modicum of pleasure.

More accurately, the Yazidis, also known as the Cult of Angels, were a small, peaceful sect who had resisted Islam for centuries. Their religion, which included Zoroastrian, Manichean, Jewish, Christian, and Islamic elements, was claimed to be the oldest on earth. They rejected the concepts of sin, the devil, and hell and believed in purification and redemption through metempsychosis—the transmigration of souls—and, yes, they did worship Satan, only as a fallen angel who had repented, been pardoned by God, and had been reinstated in heaven as the chief of all angels. Saddam had a particular loathing for the Yazidis. He'd nurtured the *devil worshipper* tag, using it to carve a fault line between them and the Kurds. After the first Gulf war, during his revenge attacks on the Kurds, Yazidi villages were brutally raided and sacked. Men were executed, their own families made to pay for the bullets used in the killings.

The landscape grew progressively more lush, more closely resembling the densely forested mountains farther north. As the Land Cruiser labored up the steep trail, the temperature also dropped markedly. Sunset was less than an hour away by the time they spotted thin spires of smoke rising into the early-evening sky. Soon after, the bare village came into focus.

Corben parked the SUV on a small shoulder just off the rocky trail. He pocketed a small wad of hundred-dollar bills, tucked his handgun behind him under his belt, and glanced over to Kirkwood.

"Help me do this," he reminded Kirkwood, "and I'll help you get Evelyn out, you have my word on that."

Kirkwood didn't seem mollified. "It's not like I have much of a choice, is it?"

"You want this too," Corben reiterated. "Let's find it. We can figure out the rest later."

Kirkwood shrugged and nodded. Corben knew Kirkwood was right in that he didn't have much of a choice. He also knew the lure of what they might find in that village was pretty hard to resist.

He freed Kirkwood's wrist, and they headed into the village.

Nerva Zhori was a small, forgotten settlement, nestling safely in a

cleft in the steep mountainside. Low stone walls, interrupted by the occasional rusty metal gate, lined both sides of the central, dusty alley; behind small courtyards littered with wheelbarrows and building material,
low mudbrick houses squatted among scattered poplar trees, one side of
them backing up against the rising mountain, the other looking down
at the drop of the hill and the forest below. Mud was the material of
choice in these mountains; even the reed roofs were covered by a thick
blanket of dried earth. A few pickup trucks, old and weathered, dotted
the lane. A row of ducks waddled across the lane while cows and horses
grazed in wild fields behind the houses, picking at patches of tall grass
in the otherwise barren soil. The harvests were long gone, and the harsh
mountain winter was approaching.

As the two men advanced into the village, a few local faces stared at
them. A couple of children and an old woman stopped what they were
doing to watch them pass. They didn't get many visitors up here, but
the Yazidis were known for their mild, accepting manners and their hos-
pitality. The two men acknowledged their hosts with small, friendly nods
that were cautiously returned. Corben studied the faces of the villagers
who eyed them somewhat nervously, then picked out a young boy.

"Do you speak English?" he asked.

The youth shook his head.

"Aawiz itkallam maa il mokhtar"—I need to talk to the chief—
Corben told him, hoping the boy understood some Arabic. The Yazidis
were Kurds and spoke the northern, Kurmanji dialect of Kurdish. He
assisted the translation by reaching out to the boy's hand and stuffing a
hundred-dollar bill in it, reiterating, *"Mokhtar."*

The youth hesitated, then nodded apprehensively. He stuffed the bill
in the back pocket of his pants, then gestured for them to follow him.

Corben gave Kirkwood a triumphant nod and followed their local
guide.

❧❧❧

A BURNING SENSATION blazed across Mia's back and legs as the silent convoy snaked its way up the winding trail. They'd mounted the mules
hours earlier, and despite trudging on without a respite, she didn't feel
they were getting any closer.

They'd come across rifle-bearing shepherds, guarding their flocks of sheep and goats from roaming packs of wolves and hyenas—the thought of which only added to her discomfort—and armed smugglers who led cigarette-laden donkeys up the mountain, acknowledging each other's presence with grunts and vigilant, silent stares.

The mountains were riddled with trails, and it was impossible for the authorities on either side to cover all of them, so they had simply given up. The border was porous, but getting across required a level of commitment and fitness that Mia was only just beginning to understand.

The landscape around them was markedly different from the flat wastelands they'd left behind. Deep valleys filled with rushing water cleaved through the dramatic ranges that towered above them. Pistachio forests and clusters of tall poplars dotted the otherwise inhospitable terrain, all of it crisscrossed by a maze of hidden paths.

"How much further?" Mia asked.

Abu Barzan conveyed her question to one of his men, then replied, "One hour. Maybe more."

Mia breathed out despondently, then steeled herself and straightened up. She soldiered on, driven by the anger at being deceived, the need to find out the truth about her father, and the desperate need to rescue her mother.

～～～

THE BOY LED CORBEN and Kirkwood past a battered Toyota pickup and into a dusty front yard. The low house that nestled against the hill was no different from any of the others. Not exactly Gracie Mansion, Corben mused, as he followed the boy up to the front door.

The boy pushed it open and announced their presence. A gruff voice bellowed out from deeper in the house. The boy took off his shoes and placed them alongside other, tattered shoes. Corben followed suit, as did Kirkwood.

Corben cast a glance across the house as they made their way past a small kitchen and through a doorway into a low-ceiling corridor. His eyes dropped to the floor as he reached the door to another room, and as he stepped in, something that didn't fit registered at the threshold of his consciousness. Faint traces of bootprints were on the tiled floor just inside the room. He tensed up subconsciously, but it was too late. A shaft of hard steel was prodding him in the back.

Before he could turn, he spotted the slim, familiar figure, sitting cross-legged in the faint light, his silvery hair slicked back, watching him with ice-cold, detached eyes. He was seated on the floor—there was no furniture in the room, nothing but cushions scattered around its perimeter—and had his small medical bag by his side. He still had the needle in his hand. Beside him was a heavily armed bruiser whose thick arms were clasped on the shoulders of a terrified-looking local. Corben guessed it had to be the mokhtar. The man was sweating profusely and rubbing his forearm.

The rest of the room quickly fell into focus. A TV flickered silently in a corner. A small fire crackled in the tin fireplace. Next to it, three heavily armed men held a woman and four children—a boy in his late teens, and three girls—at gunpoint.

"Glad you could join us," the hakeem announced drily. "We've just been having the most illuminating chat."

Chapter 64

Corben spun around quickly, his arms lashing out to grab the gun digging into his back, but he wasn't quick enough. His opponent swung his arms up with lightning speed, hammering Corben with the butt of his Kalashnikov and catching him squarely in the jaw. Corben thudded to the ground, his skull seared with agony.

His eyes struggling to regain focus, he turned to see the hakeem push himself to his feet and take a couple of steps towards him. Curiously, the man didn't seem interested in Corben. He bypassed him to home in on Kirkwood.

"So this is our mysterious buyer," he intoned, his eyes moving over Kirkwood's face with undisguised fascination. "And you are . . . ?" He left the question hanging.

Kirkwood just stood there and watched him, without replying.

The hakeem gave a brief chortle, then, without taking his eyes off him, raised the needle he was holding and said to Corben, "Would you be so kind as to educate our guest as to my persuasive powers?"

Corben groaned as he lifted himself off the ground. "Tell him what he wants to know," he complied grudgingly. "Believe me, it'll save you some pain."

The hakeem's eyes remained locked on Kirkwood, his expression now tinged with smugness.

Kirkwood looked at the man the hakeem had been working on. The mokhtar, who was dressed in traditional, local garb, seemed to be drowning in pain and, Kirkwood somehow thought, in shame. "Kirkwood. Bill Kirkwood," he flatly informed the man circling him.

"Any other names you'd care to add to that?" the hakeem teased. "No?" He paused, studying his prey. "Very well. We'll leave that for now." A puzzled look played across his face. "I don't see the book anywhere. Where is it?"

"I don't have it," Kirkwood replied crisply.

The hakeem arched a skeptical eyebrow.

"He doesn't have it," Corben interjected. "He gave it to Evelyn Bishop's daughter. She's probably being escorted to our embassy by now."

The hakeem brooded over the information, then shrugged. "I suppose it doesn't matter. It didn't contain the formula anyway, did it? I mean, you said so yourself. And there was no reason for you to lie." He scrutinized Kirkwood, then added, "Not to Miss Bishop. You wouldn't lie to her, now, would you?

Kirkwood felt his blood turn to ice. He realized the hakeem must have been listening in. His mind raced to remember exactly what he had said in that room.

"And yet, you still rushed here," the hakeem continued. "To speak with this man." He aimed an elegant finger at his seated victim. "What were you hoping to find out from him?"

Kirkwood stayed quiet.

"Perhaps you were hoping to find out what happened to your ancestor? And, with a bit of luck, find out what he discovered?" The hakeem moved to the window and stared out. "Fascinating man, your ancestor. A man of many talents. And many names," he mocked. "Sebastian Guerreiro. The Marquis of Montferrat. The Comte de St. Germain. Sebastian Botelho. And those are just the ones we know about. But then, I suppose, he lived a very full life, didn't he?"

Each of the names dropped into Kirkwood's stomach like a pallet of bricks. There was no point in dissembling. The man was clearly well-informed. "How do you know all this?"

"Well, if you know anything about your ancestor," the hakeem replied haughtily, "you're bound to have come across a mention of one of mine. Perhaps the name rings a bell. Raimondo di Sangro?"

The bricks had just turned to acid.

Kirkwood knew the name well.

The hakeem edged right up to Kirkwood, his eyes brimming with grim interest. "Brings a whole new meaning to the term *full circle*, don't you think?"

His expression grew more serious. "I'll save us all some time. As I said, our gracious host and I"—the hakeem nodded dismissively at the mokhtar—"were having a lovely little chat just now. And if anything, it confirmed to me that generational memories run deep in remote places like this." He pointed to the walls of the room.

Kirkwood looked around the room and saw what he meant. Faded portraits of the mokhtar's ancestors loomed down from behind weathered glass. They held a place of honor on the main wall of the room.

"People don't have video games and cable television to keep them entertained," the hakeem went on. "Instead, they gather around fireplaces and tell each other stories, passing on their life experiences. And the Yazidis, in particular, have a phenomenally strong oral tradition, one that was perhaps founded by necessity, given that their most sacred writings are gone." The Yazidis' holy book, the *Mashaf Rash*—the Black Book—was long lost. The common belief among them was that it was taken by the British, and that it was currently sequestered in a museum somewhere in England. In its stead, they had a tradition of talkers, who could recite the entire lost book from memory. "And it seems that this dear man's grandfather once told him about a man who came down from the mountain, a sheikh no less. The man was delirious with a horrible fever—typhoid or cholera would be my guess—and in his final hours, he spoke in many different languages, languages they'd never heard. He created something of a stir, which is understandable."

"He died here?" Kirkwood asked.

"So it would seem," the hakeem confirmed sardonically. "We were about to go out and have a look at his grave. You want to see it?"

Chapter 65

⤳〜⤳

Sebastian rode away from the docks with a feeling of profound contentment. On clear, golden evenings like this, Lisbon was truly a magnificent city, and he was glad to be back.

It had been far too long.

He'd fretted about moving back to the country, let alone the city, of his birth, but the choice had proven fortuitous. Like the city, he was experiencing a rebirth, a reinvention that was—for both—a marked improvement over their previous incarnations.

The city had been devastated by a massive earthquake on the morning of November 1, 1755, All Saints' Day. The churches were crowded with worshippers honoring the dead when the first shock struck. A second jolt followed forty minutes later. The waters of the Tagus River rose and thundered through the city, wiping out most of it. Fires took care of the rest. By the end of that day, the city was a smoldering wasteland. Over thirty thousand of its citizens were dead, most of the rest homeless.

The Marques de Pombal, the effective ruler of Portugal, handled the disaster with exemplary care and efficiency. Shelters and hospitals were hastily improvised, and troops were summoned to deliver supplies to the needy. He also drafted visionary architects, who quickly refashioned the old, medieval city into a stunning European capital.

The city's rebirth wasn't just physical. Pombal's enhanced prestige, due to his handling of the disaster, allowed him to rid the country of influences he had long fought against. Of particular relevance to Sebastian was that Pombal had dissolved the Jesuit order, expelled its members, and turned its headquarters into a hospital. The Palace of the Inquisition, flattened by the earthquake, was never rebuilt.

Sebastian and Thérésia had arrived in Lisbon in the midst of the reconstruction. The lack of records and the infectious optimism he found there both suited him well. Anyone who knew him from his days as an inquisitor was long since dead. And with the expulsion of the Jesuits, any lingering ghosts from his darkest days were finally swept away.

And so the Comte de St. Germain had retaken the first name his parents had bestowed on him, Sebastian. As a precaution, he'd given up his original surname, electing to use his mother's surname instead, Botelho. He'd invested in a small sugar refinery in the Alfama district, converting the raw cane from the colonies in Brazil into the kitchen staple that he exported across Europe. Sebastian's business was flourishing, as was his home. He'd married Thérésia in a small ceremony that was held in a church in Tomar, and their son, Miguel, was born two years later.

He'd also banished another lingering ghost from his past the day he and Thérésia had left Paris together.

Her radiant face drifted into his mind as he rode past the arcaded buildings of Commerce Square and headed home. The day's business had been successful, the contract satisfactorily concluded. He nudged his horse into a full gallop, relishing the brisk, salty air as he skirted the burnished waters of the Mar de Palha—the inland "sea of straw"—before heading north into the low, rolling hills that hugged the city.

An intangible sense of dread ambushed him the minute he was told that Miguel was still out riding with Thérésia. He'd recently bought him his first pony, and Thérésia enjoyed putting their son astride its small saddle and walking him around the estate's lake. Sebastian knew they never stayed out this late, not at this time of year, not when the sun was already melting into the surrounding hills and surrendering to the rapidly encroaching chill of night.

He didn't bother with his horse and headed down the sloping meadow, his strides gathering pace until he was tearing through the olive and lemon groves. His heart froze as he burst out from the trees and spotted the pony, grazing innocuously and very much alone. He hurried over to it, scanning the edge of the lake with panicked eyes, and spotted Thérésia, lying prone on the ground, a hundred yards farther down the shore. Miguel was nearby on a rocky outcropping, sitting next to a man whose brooding deportment Sebastian recognized even from that distance.

The man pushed himself to his feet, his fingers firmly clasped around the boy's little hand, as Sebastian rushed to Thérésia's aid. Mercifully, she was still breathing. He couldn't see any blood, any cuts or wounds. She was just dazed. Sebastian guessed di Sangro must have struck her and knocked her down before wresting control of their son.

"Miguel," she muttered worriedly as she stirred at Sebastian's touch.

He nodded to her as he flung off his overcoat and tucked it under her head before standing up to face his tormentor.

Di Sangro's face and posture bore witness to the decade of grief and frustration that he'd lived through since their last encounter in Paris. His shoulders were drooped, his hair now a shock of gray, his skin shriveled and pallid. The tall, lithe, ravenous *principe* of Naples was gone. In his place stood his decaying shell, frittered away by time and by his own obsession. Only the seething hunger in his eyes hadn't dimmed.

"Let go of the boy," Sebastian raged.

Di Sangro held firm. "You owe me, *marquese. Occhio per occhio, dente per dente.*" An eye for an eye, a tooth for a tooth. He pulled out a dagger from under his belt and held it close to the boy's cheek.

Sebastian understood. Di Sangro's son hadn't survived the wound he'd inflicted on him that night on the Île de la Cité.

"You came after me," Sebastian said fiercely as he stabbed a finger at the prince, trying to keep his anger in check and failing. "You put him in danger."

"Just as you put your own son in danger by refusing me," di Sangro shot back.

Sebastian took a step forward, but di Sangro quickly tightened his grip on the boy and nudged the blade against his neck.

"*Tranquillo, marquese,*" he warned him. "That's far enough."

Sebastian stopped and raised his open hands in a calming gesture.

"I'm sorry about your son," he said with genuine regret, keeping his eyes fixed on di Sangro. "Let him go. It's me you want."

"I have no use for you," di Sangro rasped angrily. "I only want what you know. Tell me the truth now and perhaps I just might consider it *soldi di sangue*." Blood money. "Perhaps that way," he added ruefully, "my son won't have died in vain."

"You still believe I have what you seek," Sebastian said calmingly, keeping his hands out in front of him, taking careful, measured steps towards the prince.

"I know you do—" di Sangro started, then his voice suddenly wavered. Sebastian was now five yards or so from him, and with each step, something changed in the prince's expression. Confusion flickered across his weary eyes as he scrutinized Sebastian's face.

His mouth dropped slightly. "You've . . . you've aged?" he asked, loosening his grip on the boy slightly, his gaze still fixated on Sebastian.

Di Sangro's eyes weren't deceiving him.

The day Sebastian and Thérésia had slipped away from Paris together, he'd stopped using the elixir. There would be no looking back.

The reborn Sebastian Botelho of Lisbon would wither away and die like an ordinary man.

He'd never truly regretted that momentous decision, and in his rare moments of uncertainty and remorse, he only had to look into the mischievous grin of his six-year-old son to know that he hadn't made a mistake. There would be no more secrets, no need to escape into new identities, and, best of all, no solitude. He would share the rest of his numbered days with a woman he loved, grateful for every sunrise by her side.

Until that fateful evening.

Di Sangro stared at his nemesis. He had markedly changed since Naples and Paris. His face was lined. His hair, now streaked with gray, was receding around his temples.

Sebastian just stood there, allowing the bewilderment to seep through di Sangro's resolve. He noticed the prince's hold on his son loosen even more as, almost in a trance, he edged closer to get a better look at him.

"But . . . I thought . . . ?"

Sebastian leapt at him, one hand keeping the dagger at bay while the other struck di Sangro flat in the chest, knocking him off-balance and sending him to the ground.

"Go to your mother," Sebastian yelled to Miguel, who hurried to Thérésia's side as Sebastian pinned his enemy. He picked up the fallen dagger and brought it to di Sangro's neck.

"Why can't you leave me alone?" he hissed.

Di Sangro dropped his eyes, their fiery light snuffed out. "What would you have done, in my place?"

Sebastian pulled his blade back. "I too have wasted my life searching for something that doesn't exist. I tried to tell you, but you wouldn't listen."

The prince nodded ruefully. "So you really don't have it?"

Sebastian shook his head. "No."

A look of heartfelt dismay flooded the *principe*'s face as the finality of the reply sank in. He reached inside his shirt and pulled out the chain he wore around his neck. He fingered the medallion with shivering fingers. "So this?" he said, holding it up to Sebastian.

"Nothing but a trick, a mirage," Sebastian said in a hollow voice. "A siren that lures men and wrecks their lives against the rocks of its false promise."

He looked at di Sangro and released his hold. He pushed himself up to his feet and extended a hand to di Sangro. The prince took it, got up, and looked away at the glassy water of the lake, the dejection seeping into every corner of his tired body.

"Such a shame. A tragedy. For us all." He turned to Sebastian. "Imagine if it were true. Imagine how it would change the world. What a gift it would be. To have more time to spend with those we cherish. To have more time to learn, to travel, to discover . . . to truly live."

Sebastian nodded glumly. "Go home. Go back to your family. Enjoy the time you have left. And leave me in peace to enjoy mine."

Di Sangro took one last look at him and nodded.

ᔓᔕᔕᔓ

THE BOISTEROUS VOICES and laughter roared all around him, but di Sangro couldn't hear any of it. He just sat at his corner table in the small tavern, a broken man, nursing yet another jug of ale, staring at the dancing flame of the candle before him, lost in the abyss of his mind.

All this, for nothing, he lamented. Years wasted. Time, money. His son's life. And for what? To end up like this, old and withered, drowning in bitter ale, hundreds of miles from home.

Despite the glaze obscuring his thoughts, he scoured his memory for every piece of background he'd gathered, every word he'd heard, every nuance he'd picked up on during his dogged pursuit of the man who now called himself Sebastian Botelho. Every now and then, the disparate thoughts would emerge from the crevasses of his mind and threaten to coalesce into an affirmation he was yearning for, but each time, the doubt would set in and send them scattering into the shadows. Images and voices competed for attention inside him—the Contessa di Czergy and her recollections of Venice, Madame de Fontenay in Paris, among others—but each time, the shuttered face of Sebastian Botelho would appear, godlike, and overwhelm them into submission.

For hour upon hour, he replayed his encounters with the man, the words they'd exchanged, the revelations he'd seen—or thought he'd seen—in his eyes. And in that jungle of confusion, a few words kept clawing at him. *You don't want to know,* principe. *Trust me. It is not a gift, not for any man. It is a curse, pure and simple. A curse from which there is no respite.*

Respite.

He concentrated on that word and on the haunted look in the eyes of Botelho—the Marquis de Montferrat, at the time—when he'd uttered them all those years ago.

What if respite was what Botelho had finally found? What if he'd had the elixir, but had—for some demented reason di Sangro couldn't begin to fathom—decided to stop using it.

He threw the mug to the floor and rubbed his eyes harshly, trying to wipe away the fog that was clouding his thoughts. His heart thundered in his ears as the angry realization materialized before him.

He'd been tricked.

The *marquese* had done it again. He'd played him like a fool. Yes, Botelho was older. But that didn't mean he never had it. It meant he was no longer using it. And, like the old fool that he now believed he'd become, di Sangro had allowed the *marquese* to hoodwink him into believing him and abandoning his quest.

"Bastardo," he bellowed as he hurled himself to his feet and staggered out of the crowded inn, fueled by the raging fire in his veins.

∽≈∽

SEBASTIAN WATCHED the faint shadows from the moonlight inch their way across the walls of the bedchamber.

He couldn't sleep. The idea of losing Thérésia or Miguel to di Sangro still seethed inside him. He wondered whether he ought to have killed him, there and then, but it was too late for that now. Besides, he didn't know whom the *principe* had brought with him, whom he'd told about what he suspected. Killing him was no guarantee of peace.

His sanctuary had been compromised. The intruder, more than the man himself, was the words he'd spoken, which still rang in Sebastian's ears.

Imagine if it were true. Imagine how it would change the world. What a gift it would be. To have more time to spend with those we cherish. To have more time to learn, to travel, to discover . . . to truly live.

He'd imagined it many a time, as had Isaac Montalto, as had Sebastian's own father before him. A gift they all dreamt of giving mankind. A burden that had rested on his shoulders alone. A promise on which he'd reneged.

Di Sangro was right. It was a tragedy.

He couldn't ignore it any longer.

Thérésia stirred beside him, her smooth skin silhouetted against the pale sheets. From the concern in her eyes, he knew that, as on so many previous occasions, she could read the thoughts written across his troubled face.

"We have to leave, don't we?" she asked.

Sebastian simply nodded and embraced her.

∽≈∽

DI SANGRO BURST into the stately mansion at first light like a demon, brandishing a sword in one hand and a pistol in the other, screaming for Sebastian to appear before him, but his shouts went unanswered. He pushed and kicked at the servants who appeared and tried to reason with him and bounded up the central staircase to the upper floor, where the bedchambers lay. He kicked in the carved double doors to Sebastian and Thérésia's bedchamber, only to find it empty.

They were long gone, and in his heart of hearts, he knew he'd never see either of them again.

He dropped to his knees, the weapons tumbling noisily onto the tiled floor beneath him, and wept.

∽∾∽

SEBASTIAN WATCHED as the porters carried Thérésia's chest and dressing case onto the ship. The harbor was teeming with vessels of all sizes, from the small, Phoenician, crescent-shaped *fragatas* that performed lighterage duties around the port to the three-masted tall ships that plied the Atlantic and linked the old port city to the New World.

His heart contracted at the thought of the crossing his wife and son would soon be undertaking. The decision had haunted his every waking moment since they'd all abandoned their house on that night, barely days ago.

They would never find peace. Not from di Sangro, not from others who would inevitably hear about it. Not as long as they were together.

And he had work to do.

A promise to keep.

A destiny to fulfill.

"Why won't you change your mind and let us come with you?" Thérésia asked him. Miguel stood beside her, holding her hand, watching in wonderment as the last crates were loaded onto the towering vessel.

"It's not safe," Sebastian answered, the words barely escaping through his lips.

He knew what he was talking about. He'd been there before—and he was about to journey there again. He'd return to Constantinople. Assume the persona of a sheikh, just as he'd done half a century earlier. And travel into the Levant, to the bustling cities of Beirut, Jerusalem, Damascus, and Baghdad, and across the mountains and deserts in between, in the hope that this time his search would be more fruitful.

The ship's first mate called for the gangway to be withdrawn and the lines released.

Thérésia's hand gripped Sebastian's tightly. "Come back to me," she whispered in his ear.

He took her in his arms and kissed her, then knelt down and kissed his son.

"I'll do my best" was all he could promise.

And with a tremulous heart, he watched as the ship's sails unfurled and took away the only true happiness he'd ever known.

Chapter 66

⌒⌒⌒

They were marched out of the house at gunpoint—Kirkwood, Corben, along with the mokhtar and his family—under a patchwork sky of purples and grays. Frothy clouds scudded along the horizon, backlit by the setting sun.

The cemetery was at the far end of the village. Simple gravestones clustered around the *mazar*, a small, conical local funerary monument. The mokhtar led them through the rough, barren ground until they reached a small headstone. He stopped there and, with a morose expression etched across his face, pointed it out.

Kirkwood knelt down and examined the old marker. The austere piece of limestone barely jutted out of the ground. It was bare, except for a small, circular carving in its center. Kirkwood reached out and brushed the moss and dust away from its edges. The head of the snake appeared more clearly, its simple detail eaten away by the passage of time.

He noticed something else below it. He passed his fingers over the etching, clearing the detritus of time off it.

It was a date, in Arabic numerals.

"Eighteen oh two," Kirkwood read out in a hollow voice.

His mouth felt dry as a feeling of infinite loss came over him.

So this was where his journey had ended.

The hakeem's voice broke through Kirkwood's swirling memories, scattering them. "Eighteen oh two," he repeated, thinking aloud. "My ancestor died in 1771. Not a huge difference, you might say. Except for one minor detail. Our ancestors met in the middle of the eighteenth century, around 1750 or so. At the time, your ancestor, according to di Sangro's diary, seemed to be a contemporary of his, that is, approaching the age of forty. Which means that, at his death, he would have been, oh, close to a hundred years old. But here's the thing. My ancestor died an old man. Your ancestor, well . . . according to the story that was passed down, the man who came down from the mountain and died here wasn't an old man. He had walked down the mountain, alone. And it was a fever that killed him, not old age. The mokhtar was very clear about that. Which either means that your ancestor found something up in those mountains that kept him young, or—and this is the explanation I favor—that, as the *principe* suspected, he'd been using the formula for years. Only you said he didn't have the complete formula. Which I find confusing. He abandoned his wife and his child to travel to this dangerous and distant corner of the globe, to search for something he already had?"

Kirkwood stiffened. "He didn't have it."

The hakeem took a menacing step forward, and his brow darkened gravely. "You know something? I think you're lying. I believe he had it," he said acidly. "I believe my illustrious ancestor was right all along. I believe Sebastian Guerreiro used the formula to live an extraordinarily long life. And," he added fiercely, "I believe you're doing the same."

Kirkwood tried to rein in his anger and his fear. "You don't know what you're talking about." His voice didn't waver.

He felt Corben's eyes on him, but didn't dare turn to him. The hakeem was watching him too closely.

"Really?" the hakeem coldly observed. "Let's see."

He barked an order to his men. Two of them trudged off and disappeared behind one of the houses. The remaining guards raised their machine guns cautiously, watching over Corben and Kirkwood like hawks.

Moments later, the two men returned, bringing back a prisoner who was dressed in camouflage fatigues and whose hands were cuffed. The prisoner's head was concealed under a black cloth sack, like the one they had used on Corben. They stood the prisoner next to the hakeem and backed off.

Even before the hakeem made his introduction, Kirkwood saw through the baggy outfit and the mask. The realization paralyzed him. He glanced sideways at Corben, but he couldn't read the agent's shuttered expression.

"You were saying . . . ?" the hakeem asked gruffly, before yanking the sack off his prisoner.

Evelyn's eyes squinted a few times, adjusting to the light. Then she saw Kirkwood standing before her, and her jaw dropped.

"My God . . . Tom?"

Chapter 67

The sight of Evelyn's bewildered eyes sent an ice pick through Kirkwood's heart.

"Evelyn, thank God you're . . ." He shook his head with anguish. "I'm so sorry."

The hakeem was scrutinizing Evelyn's reaction with resounding satisfaction. He turned to Kirkwood, his face beaming with the most irritating complacency, and stepped closer to him until he was only inches away.

"I know plastic surgery does miracles these days, but this . . ." he said to Evelyn, waving his hand down Kirkwood's body, "this is far more than cosmetic, wouldn't you say?"

"You're . . ." The words were catching in her throat. "How is it possible?"

The hakeem nodded to one of his men, who grabbed Evelyn and pulled her back. The hakeem turned to Kirkwood, his face contorted with renewed menace. "You have the formula," he seethed. "What are you really after?"

Kirkwood summoned any reserves of will he had left and held firm. "The same thing you want."

"But you have already have it," the hakeem rasped.

Kirkwood didn't respond.

The hakeem grabbed a gun from one of his men and shoved it against Evelyn's head. "You already have it, yes?"

Every nerve in Kirkwood's body bristled with fury, but he held firm and didn't react.

The hakeem's finger tightened against the trigger. "You already have it, yes?" he raged.

Kirkwood just scowled at him mutely.

"Have it your way then," the hakeem hissed, his sharp voice slicing the air, and he blinked his eyes over to Evelyn, his wrist bending slightly as he prepared to put a round in her head—

"Wait," Kirkwood yelled.

The hakeem turned, the gun still held there.

Kirkwood looked at Evelyn, then dropped his eyes to the ground. "I have the formula," he muttered.

Without looking up, he felt everyone's stare on him.

"I don't get it," Corben blurted out. "What the hell are we doing here then? Why are you here? What are you so desperate to find?"

Kirkwood heaved out a ponderous, frustrated sigh. "The experiments in the book we have . . . they weren't complete. The formula doesn't work on . . . everyone."

"What do you mean, 'not everyone'?" the hakeem asked, bringing down the gun.

Kirkwood glanced at Evelyn, then raised his eyes angrily at the hakeem. "It only works on men."

The hakeem processed his words, his face lighting up with a manic euphoria. "So you've been using it?"

Kirkwood nodded. "The book Sebastian found wasn't complete. It was partially burnt, and the last few pages—who knows how many, really—were missing. The experiments it detailed hadn't been satisfactorily completed, at least not in the pages we had. There was still this critical flaw. For many years it was pointless to try and figure out the reason for the deficiency and try to fix it. Science wasn't yet advanced enough, and besides, there were more important problems for our best minds to work on, more urgent diseases to overcome. It's only in the last fifty years, really, that we've felt the time was finally right to devote some serious scientific resources to try and solve this riddle."

" 'We'?" the hakeem asked, waving the handgun questioningly.

"We're a small group. There are four of us. Carefully selected and approached by the descendant of Sebastian who's been bequeathed with the . . . the burden. It's something my father started."

"And he, in turn, passed it on to you," the hakeem surmised.

"Yes." Kirkwood turned to Evelyn. "That's why I couldn't stay with you. I had taken an oath, and it wasn't a life I could share with anyone. Not when I was taking the elixir. We had to work on fixing it, on figuring out how to make it work for everyone, and our cells, our blood, was part of the experiments. But it all had to be kept secret. We couldn't risk letting the world know of its existence. If it ever came out, if it were available—and it's not complicated to prepare, not in its current form anyway—it would turn society on its head. Men living a couple of hundred years, while women only lived a third as long and died off . . . it would redefine our world, it would rewrite all the rules of our civilization."

"Oh, I don't know," the hakeem mused cynically, keeping a bemused but interested eye on the mokhtar. "Muslims and Mormons take on several wives, and it seems to work for them. This would be the same, only sequentially."

Evelyn still looked dumbstruck. "Is that how long it gives you? Two hundred years?" she asked.

Kirkwood nodded. "It seems to more or less triple our current life expectancy, if you start taking it once your body's fully grown. It doesn't make us immortal. We just age very, very slowly. It slows down the decay in the cells and allows a radically decelerated senescence. Then, eventually, the cells go into free fall."

The scientist in the hakeem couldn't resist asking, "How does it work?"

Kirkwood shrugged. "We're still not sure. It seems to act like a supercharged free-radical scavenger. We've found that it changes the way DNA normally wraps itself around some chromosome proteins. As a result, some genes are enhanced while others are repressed. One of the genes that are enhanced is an antioxidative stress gene. But for some reason, something about the chromosomal difference between men and women, at a core mitochondrial level, inhibits its effectiveness in women."

"It's like 4-phenylbutyrate," the hakeem enthused. The drug, recent experiments had shown, had a startling effect on fruit flies, extending their lives dramatically. "Only for humans."

Kirkwood nodded reluctantly. "Exactly."

Evelyn's eyes were riveted on him, telegraphing a cocktail of anger, disappointment, wonder, and horror. "How old are you?" she asked, fear gnawing on the words as they slipped out of her throat.

Kirkwood had already said more than he'd intended, but he couldn't lie to her. "I was born in 1913," he reported in a low voice. "Sebastian was my grandfather."

He tore his eyes away from Evelyn's shocked expression and glanced at the others. Corben was staring at him coldly, as poker-faced as ever. The mokhtar had been listening intently too, though, as he rubbed his forearms nervously, he was more visibly rattled.

"And so that's what you've been doing, all these centuries," the hakeem accused Kirkwood indignantly. "Using it secretly in your little coven, depriving the world of life, instead of announcing it, sharing it, inviting the greatest minds in the world to help you fix it?"

"We've got some great minds working on it," Kirkwood protested fiercely. It was a sore point, the source of much guilt. "Some of the most gifted scientists around."

"Well, maybe you should have had more people working on it," the hakeem shot back, stabbing the air viciously with his gun to punctuate his words, his finger still worryingly close to the trigger. "Maybe they would have found the solution by now. Instead, you choose to hide it, to selfishly keep it to yourselves."

"You think this is fun?" Kirkwood lashed out angrily. "Never being able to get close to anyone?" As he spoke, he glanced at Evelyn, and his voice softened. "Watching everyone you love, everyone you care about, wither away and die? Besides," he added, turning back to the hakeem, "what if there wasn't a fix? What if they'd never managed to make it work for everyone?"

"Well, clearly, your grandfather seems to think they did," the hakeem observed, his voice laced with contempt. He nodded to himself, grinding Kirkwood's words over, thinking things through. When he raised his eyes, a Zen-like resoluteness had spread through them.

"I want the formula," he said calmly. "And you'll give it to me, we both know that. But don't worry. It'll only be a temporary measure.

Something to keep me amused while my men explore these mountains." He turned to the mokhtar. "What do you say? You think you can point me in the right direction?"

The mokhtar lurched back a step, the blood draining visibly from his face as he butted into one of the hakeem's men. His eyes wide as saucers, he shook his head repeatedly as beads of sweat materialized at the rim of his headdress.

The hakeem's features grew dark and threatening as he stepped in closer to him. "An incomprehensible, intriguing man comes down off the mountain, spouting words in all kinds of languages, carrying a mysterious book in which he writes a final message in a foreign hand. He dies here, in this village. You want me to believe your ancestors weren't curious about where he came from? You seriously expect me to believe they didn't go out looking for where he came from?"

The mokhtar was shaking his head repeatedly, darting glances left and right, anywhere but at the tall, hell-bent foreigner who was breathing down on him.

"Well?" the hakeem asked. *"Jaawib, ya kalb,"* he ordered him viciously. Answer, you dog.

The mokhtar mumbled something. He didn't know anything.

The hakeem's eyes narrowed, then he turned to the gunman who was standing guard over the mokhtar's family and nodded disdainfully at the children. The guard herded them over roughly.

Kirkwood felt his pulse quicken and he instinctively inched forward, but the gunman standing next to him stopped him with a firm hand.

The hakeem raised his gun towards the children. "Which one goes first?" he asked the mokhtar. He aimed at the teenage boy. "The boy? Or maybe"—he swung the gun around recklessly at one of the little girls—"her? Choose one," he ordered.

A tear streaked down the mokhtar's cheek, and he muttered, "Please," as he dropped to his knees.

"Which one?" the hakeem shouted fiercely, his eyes blazing with manic determination.

"Tell him," Kirkwood yelled out angrily.

The mokhtar shook his head.

"Tell him," Kirkwood repeated fiercely. "It's not worth their lives," he added, glancing at the man's terror-stricken children.

The mokhtar mopped his face with his hands, then, without looking up, nodded his acquiescence and mumbled, "I'll take you. I'll take you where you want to go."

Just then, something struck one of the hakeem's men squarely in the chest, yanking him backwards, a red cloud erupting. The man dropped heavily to the ground as the rifle shot's report echoed in the hills around them.

Chapter 68

~~~

Several other rounds crackled around the cemetery, scattering the gunmen and their hostages in a panicked frenzy.

Kirkwood darted for Evelyn, but the hakeem was closer to her and snared her just as three rounds struck a nearby gravestone. Kirkwood ducked for cover and could only watch as, with a handgun pressed against Evelyn's head, the hakeem dragged her to the low wall of the graveyard. The bullets seemed to be coming from behind a house at the edge of the village. One of the hakeem's men was with him and was intermittently rising from his cover and peppering the source of the gunfire with carefully placed rounds.

Kirkwood tried to go after Evelyn, but another of the hakeem's men was firing back from behind the *mazar*, and the fire directed at him was also pinning Kirkwood to his cover. He glanced to the far end of the cemetery and spotted Corben, hustling the mokhtar and his family to safety and helping his children over a kink in the wall. The hakeem spotted him too and barked at the man crouched with him to stop them. Corben also heard the shout and turned. The gunman raised his weapon, looking for the shot. Corben pushed the mokhtar over the sag in the wall and leapt over it himself just as a couple of bullets bit into the bricks behind him.

More rounds crunched into the markers around Kirkwood, looking for the shooter sheltering behind the small monument. To his left, the hakeem was still huddled against the low wall, his arm clasped around Evelyn's throat, but he was inching his way to the opposite, downhill side of the cemetery, pulling Evelyn along with him. Beyond the wall lay a forest of tall poplars. Kirkwood swallowed hard. They were at the far end of the village, and whoever was firing at them was coming from the opposite direction. They weren't surrounded. And that meant the hakeem could potentially escape.

Kirkwood couldn't allow him to take Evelyn again. But right now, he was helpless to do anything about it. He watched with roiling frustration as the third surviving member of the hakeem's squad, who was huddling behind the wall by the entrance to the graveyard, sat up and sprayed a cartridge-load of bullets at his attackers, ducked and reloaded, then rose again and spat out some more rounds before lurching backwards violently, the back of his head blown open. The shooter who'd gotten him then made the mistake of leaning out of his cover recklessly to check out his success. The gunman escorting the hakeem rose up and dropped him with a single bullet to the chest.

The hakeem and Evelyn reached the edge of the cemetery. Kirkwood saw Evelyn try to make a run for it, but the hakeem lashed out and pinned her down ruthlessly. Kirkwood's blood was boiling. He couldn't sit back anymore. He saw the gunman close to the hakeem get hit while returning fire, saw the hakeem's attention snagged by the squirming man beside him and darting terror-stricken glances over the wall, and decided he would make his move.

He bolted across the cemetery, head low, fists clenched, eyes locked on the hakeem and Evelyn. No bullets came his way, and he kept rushing. He was ten feet from them when the hakeem noticed him.

The hakeem spun around just as Kirkwood tackled him, his left arm lunging out at the handgun in the madman's right hand. A round went off just as he hit him, jarring his senses and sending a flash of pain erupting across his left shoulder. He heard Evelyn scream as he rode the adrenaline wave and butted a knee into the hakeem's chest. The hakeem wheezed out heavily. Both of Kirkwood's hands were now clasped around the hakeem's handgun, fighting desperately to keep it clear. Another shot rang out, but the gun was aimed downward and the bullet harmlessly kicked up some dirt as it burrowed into the ground.

"Move away," Kirkwood shouted to Evelyn, unable to take his eyes off the hakeem to judge her proximity.

The hakeem elbowed Kirkwood's jaw, bone crunching against bone heavily, sending a bolt of pain searing across Kirkwood's head. His grasp on the hakeem's hand weakened, and the madman used the moment to wrestle the gun free. He swung it around at Kirkwood, but Kirkwood didn't blink and just lunged at him with total commitment, slamming him against the wall with all of his weight and sending the handgun spinning out of his fingers and biting into the ground.

Their eyes locked in a split second of unmitigated and absolute loathing. Their eyes darted within nanoseconds of each other at the fallen weapon. Then Kirkwood sensed movement to his side. He turned to see the surviving gunman, the one positioned behind the *mazar*, spinning his weapon toward him. His heart missed a beat before a couple of rifle rounds punched the stonework of the monument, forcing the gunman back into cover. Kirkwood dived at Evelyn, pulling her to the ground before turning to face the hakeem, who gave him one final leer before clambering over the low wall and disappearing behind it.

"Come on," Kirkwood yelled to Evelyn as the last surviving gunman returned fire feverishly. He crawled forward, shielding Evelyn, trying to put more gravestones between him and the shooter. The pain in his shoulder flashed angrily with every move. He'd managed a few feet when the gunman turned his attention to them again and leaned out to take another shot at them, but before he could make the kill, several rifle rounds plowed into him, knocking him backwards savagely, a burst of wild bullets from his submachine gun cutting up the still air over the cemetery before dying out with him.

An eerie stillness descended on the cemetery. Kirkwood eyed Evelyn, his shoulder burning, his mind racing, wondering if they were finally safe.

"Hello?" he shouted out to no one in particular, hoping that whoever had intervened was friendly.

The voice he heard back blew through him like a gale of joy. "Kirkwood? Mom?" Mia was yelling. "You okay?"

He looked at Evelyn, his face bathed with relief. "We're fine," he hollered back. His eyes scanning the hakeem's fallen men and watching out for any unseen threats, he got up carefully, wincing from the pain in his shoulder.

Evelyn stood with him. Mia and a few armed men were racing down from the village.

Evelyn reached out to check his shoulder. He pulled back as she touched it, the wound throbbing with a deep, burning pain. "It's alright," he assured her before glancing towards the forested hill that dropped down from the cemetery.

The hakeem was still out there.

Evelyn saw it in his eyes. "Tom," she cautioned him.

He was already striding towards the hakeem's fallen man.

"Tom, don't," she urged as he leaned down and picked up the dead shooter's submachine gun. He checked its magazine, found a couple of fresh ones on the dead man's belt, pocketed one and rammed the other into place, and chambered a round just as Mia and Abu Barzan's men reached them.

"Stay with your mom," Kirkwood told Mia before rushing to the wall. He climbed over it awkwardly, trying to protect his injured arm, then darted a quick look at Evelyn and Mia before he disappeared down the hill.

"What are you waiting for?" Evelyn shouted at the men with Mia. "Go with him. *Sa'idoo*," she insisted in Arabic. Help him.

They nodded and bolted after him.

Chapter 69

Kirkwood ran through the silent, darkening forest, the ragged bursts of his breathing pumping deafeningly in his ears, the pain in his shoulder blazing with every heavy step, his eyes scouring the trees for any sign of the hakeem. The urgent, determined footfalls of Abu Barzan's men chased after him.

His head was feeling cloudier, his eyes heavier, as the blood loss was starting to undermine the basic functions of his body. He clenched his jaw and drew deeper, plundering his last reserves of energy, allowing his anger and his revulsion to push him on.

At the very edge of his consciousness, he heard a slow whine, an engine coming to life. It grew louder and more frenzied with each step he took, the blades of a rotor cleaving the air with increased ferocity.

The realization summoned a desperate jolt of adrenaline that carried him farther down the slope. He pictured the chopper before he saw it, imagined the hakeem waving, leering down at him as it took off and ferried him to safety, and the thought propelled him even faster.

He couldn't let him escape.

He couldn't even let him live.

Through the confusing interplay of light and shadow of the poplars, he caught a glimpse of the hakeem climbing into the monstrous machine. He burst out of the cover of the trees, and the full ferocity of the rotor wash and the turbine's ear-piercing scream hit him head-on as the chopper lifted off.

The chopper, a Mi-25, was facing him. It looked like a horrific mutant wasp, its fuselage disfigured by a rash of glass cockpit bubbles and gun turrets, two small wings sticking out of its sides and laden with rocket launchers and other pods. Two pilots, sitting in tandem, were at their controls, facing him through the glass, urging the chopper into a quick ascent.

Kirkwood raised his gun and started firing.

Full auto.

One full magazine, then another.

Everything he had.

Each round found a searing echo in his shoulder, but he kept a firm grip on the machine gun, emptying its load mercilessly, showering the lumbering vulture rising before him with a torrent of bullets. He watched as they sparked off the chopper's metal skin like darts bouncing off a tank, but he kept adjusting his aim, and a few of them managed to find the forward pilot's bubble, the first of them drilling into it and splintering it, the next few evidently cutting into flesh and bone as a red puff gruesomely splattered the inside of the cracked windshield.

The huge chopper lurched to one side, its engine groaning into a sudden frenzy just as Abu Barzan's men reached him and joined in. It tilted at a severe angle as it sideslipped through the air, and its rotor clipped the edge of the grove of poplars. The massive blades hacked into the tips of the tall trees, and for a moment, the forest seemed like a giant web that had snared a prize catch. Kirkwood watched, grim-faced, his feet edging instinctively backwards, his mind fast-forwarding to the explosion that would consume the hillside and obliterate him, and he thought of Evelyn and of Mia as the Mil teetered precariously. It looked as if it were about to tilt sideways and plow into the trees, but just when it seemed terminal, the copilot seemed to regain control. The machine pitched back violently and rolled the other way, extricating its blades from the trap of the trees before rising into clear air.

It rotated as it rose, snubbing its attackers with its tail as it banked around before heading away from the mountain. Kirkwood watched it recede with a reeling horror, the rage and utter frustration flooding through him, then he heard something from behind, coming from higher up, from the village. It sounded like a loud snap, something he hadn't heard before, and was quickly followed by a whooshing sound that sliced through the air above him. He looked up to see the thin contrail of a narrow, white tube that was streaking across the patchy sky, arcing its way towards the chopper, rushing forward and catching up to it. The contact triggered a small explosion that was almost immediately followed by a massive fireball, the blades of the big rotor detaching themselves and spinning off wildly in all directions, the hulking fuselage somersaulting over itself before plummeting to the ground and erupting in a gargantuan cloud of fire.

ᴄᴏᴄᴏ

EVELYN AND MIA raced down the hill and found Kirkwood resting against a tree. His face was beaded with sweat, his skin pale and sallow, his eyes barely able to stay open, but he perked up somewhat at the sight of them. Two other men were with them, one of them still clutching his SA-14 shoulder-held missile launcher. The men—Abu Barzan's Kurdish friends, as Mia explained—whooped with delight and exchanged hearty backslapping hugs with their two buddies. In the distance, the black smoke still billowed upwards into the dying light.

Evelyn watched over Kirkwood as Mia quickly went to work on stemming the blood loss from his wound.

He didn't know where to start.

"Evelyn," he told her faintly, the last vestiges of strength abandoning him, "I never . . ." He broke off, the sheer weight of his regret catching in his breath.

She met his gaze straight on. "Later," she told him.

He nodded gratefully, but there was one thing he couldn't wait for. He glanced at Mia, who read through his look. He turned to Evelyn.

"Is she . . . ?" he asked, knowing, hoping for the answer, but his breath caught nevertheless.

"Yes." Evelyn nodded. "She's yours."

"So what do we call you?" Mia asked. "Bill? Tom? Something else maybe?"

"It's Tom," he confessed with a contrite half-smile, turning to Evelyn. "Tom Webster."

A confused rush of conflicting emotions swamped him, a heady cock-tail of guilt and euphoria. He couldn't help beaming at the sight of his daughter, up here, with him, with her mother, having somehow man-aged to get there and save them, and now patching him up. He suddenly felt very old, but for the first time in his life, he took pleasure in it.

His pensiveness was interrupted by the sight of a figure rushing down the incline from the village. It was the mokhtar's teenage son. His face was gripped by dread.

The words tumbled incoherently out of his mouth, but Kirkwood quickly made sense of what he was saying.

Corben was gone.

And he'd taken the mokhtar with him.

Chapter 70

⤮

The two horses charged up the ridge, their hooves kicking up the loose stones and echoing through the trees. The light was weakening with every second, and total darkness wasn't far off.

Corben had no choice. They had to leave the village, there and then. He had to make his escape while the others were still preoccupied. Before they turned their attention on him.

The mokhtar led the way up the mountain, careful not to venture too far ahead of his captor, who had him on a literal tight leash. Once they were outside the village, Corben had tied a rope around the man's waist and strapped the other end to the pommel of his saddle. Corben had also relieved one of the hakeem's fallen men of his AK-47. He'd wanted to get more gear from the Land Cruiser—the attaché case with the cash, for one—but they'd parked it on the approach to the village, and he thought it more than likely that Abu Barzan and his men would already have rifled through it on their arrival.

Their sudden interruption—with Mia, to boot, whom he'd also spotted alongside one of the shooters—was as irritating to him as it had been impressive. He was curious as to how they'd managed to make it there, but he had his suspicions. He chided himself for not having bothered to check the dealer's body in that kitchen back in Diyarbakir, but then again, maybe that wasn't a bad thing. The burly man and his crew may well have saved his life.

All things considered, he wasn't too worried about his current situation. Officially, he was brought here at gunpoint, and the hakeem was now, in all likelihood, dead. He and the mokhtar had seen the helicopter getting blown out of the sky. Evelyn was safe, as was Mia.

Mission accomplished.

He didn't think the two women or Kirkwood—rather, the man claiming to be Kirkwood—would be a problem. They wouldn't want to create a stink about what really happened. That would risk exposing Kirkwood for what he really was, and he knew none of them would want that. They'd probably go along with any story he chose to tell.

The main thing, he reminded himself, was that the prize was now within reach. And once it was his, he'd be in a great position. It was the key to the kingdom. If things got sticky, in any way, he'd be able to negotiate from a position of supreme strength.

Either way, he expected to become a pornographically wealthy man reasonably soon. And, as an added bonus, he would enjoy those trappings for a very, very long time.

❧

MIA CURSED INWARDLY as she struggled through the dusty trail of the horsemen ahead of her. This wasn't exactly what she was looking forward to after her backbreaking, leg-numbing, four-hour mule trek earlier that afternoon.

Three others were accompanying her this time. The mokhtar's eldest, his son, led the pack. He had—with anxious hesitation—admitted knowing where his father was taking Corben. The mokhtar had shared the secret with him at the onset of the Iraq war, in case anything should happen to him. Two other men from the village followed close behind him, with Mia bringing up the rear. The men were all armed. The villagers had also appropriated Kalashnikovs off the hakeem's dead men, while the mokhtar's son, whose name Mia learned was Salem—the boy was only sixteen—carried an old hunting rifle.

The decision to go after them now, and not wait for morning, was a tough call. The mountains would soon be forbiddingly dark. It would be hard for them to see where they were going, and the trails were steep and treacherous. The night also brought out other dangers. Wolves, hyenas, and jackals roamed the deserted, bleak ranges in search of scarce food.

The mokhtar's son had been adamant about leaving immediately, and his feeling had been echoed and supported by his mother. Corben and his captive didn't have that much of a head start, and if they kept moving at night, they'd be hard to catch up with come morning. Mia's joining them was another issue. She'd insisted on going with them. She'd lived through this with Corben and felt she had to see it through. She thought that if it came to that, she might be useful, to mediate, to get through to him, given the time she'd spent with him. Beyond that, she somehow felt it was her responsibility now. The connection to it ran through her blood.

She had to protect it.

The hastily arranged posse had grabbed as much gear as they could: flashlights, torches, blankets—the temperature, in these high altitudes, dropped significantly after the sun set—and water. And as she caught one last glimpse of the village before it disappeared behind a ridge, the clipped words of her father rang through her head. Her father—the thought was still hard to countenance and would be, she suspected, for quite a while. He'd confirmed to her that, yes, the elixir was real. That one would also take a while to sink in. He'd then added the caveat that it only worked on men, but that the full formula was somewhere up in those hills, and that Corben was after it not to help the government suppress it, but to use it for his own material gain.

Which they couldn't allow.

Kirkwood—no, Tom, she corrected herself—and his colleagues also wanted the full formula revealed to all, but it had to be handled with extreme care and with meticulous planning. It would be a daunting task to release this to an unsuspecting world; it would lead to a seismic change for all of humanity—perhaps the most momentous change ever. Every aspect of life would be affected.

Not exactly the kind of thing you'd want to entrust to a murderer with contemptible motives.

They pushed the horses as hard as they could, up a hidden trail that snaked up through clefts in the mountain and across passes through the craggy peaks. Mia turned to cast a nervous eye at the horizon as the sun slid behind the peaks behind her. The trail became harsher, steeper; the footing looser, more slippery. Ancient gnarled pines, beaten down by harsh weather over countless decades, loomed down on them, clinging to vertical rock faces that threatened to engulf them at every turn. Still, they pressed ahead, horses faltering on narrow passages, pebbles and loose earth skittering downhill under their heels, the last of the day's light now surrendering to the onslaught of nightfall.

The air cooled down as vertiginously as they climbed, its chill seeping through Mia's thin layer of clothing with ruthless ease. She tried to ignore it for a while, but it was soon clawing at her bones. She unfurled the blanket that had been hastily tied to her saddle and wrapped it around her. With the horses grunting against the incline, they eased their way up a winding, interminable pass that nature had cleaved through the mountain's crown.

By the time they finally emerged on the other side, the darkness was firmly entrenched. A three-quarter moon hung low ahead of them, casting a pale, silvery glow across a long, deep valley that lay below. It looked like a big, black inkblot, its lower reaches lost in the shadows, protected by a bastion of soaring peaks beyond which lay an endless succession of undulating valleys and mountains. Mia strained her eyes, trying to see where the mokhtar's son was leading them, but she was rebuffed by the faint light. He seemed to be having trouble too and soon pulled out a lighter and ignited the tip of one of the torches they'd brought along.

The small convoy slowed down, moving more carefully now, down the softly sloping trail and into a thicket of trees. The shadows of the bare branches scuttled and danced around them. Beyond the flickering glow of the torch, the stillness was oppressive. There was no wind, no cawing of birds, no goat bells. Nothing but the horses' labored breathing, the drowsy clatter of their hooves, and the gunshot that rang out and tore one of the villagers off his mount.

The horses started as another shot bit into a stone outcropping by the second villager. He leapt off his horse without managing to subdue it and took cover behind the rocks, while his mare charged down the trail, neighing furiously and disappearing from view. Mia slid off her saddle, pulling her horse to the relative safety of the tree line. The mokhtar's son did the same, ditching the torch, which burned on regardless.

Mia scanned the darkness ahead. She couldn't tell where Corben was positioned. Two more shots rang out, crunching into trunks, dangerously close to them. Corben was a good shot; she already knew that.

Corben's voice bellowed through the choking silence.

"Turn around and head back. I don't want to have to hurt any more of you."

She heard the mokhtar start to shout something out before a thud muffled him and ended his outburst.

"Jim," Mia called out after him, "let him go. They're not going to abandon him."

"I won't hurt him," he yelled back. "Once I've got what I came for, I'll let him go."

Whispers to her left snared her attention, and she spotted the mokhtar's son and the villager conferring. They mumbled a few hushed words, then slipped out stealthily from behind their cover, fanning out in wide arcs. As he passed by her, the mokhtar's son flashed her a parting gaze, the fear in his eyes unmistakable, even in the dying glow of the torch.

Mia's heart sank at the thought of harm coming to the boy, of more blood being spilled.

"Jim," she urged, shouting out into the darkness. "Please. Don't do this."

He didn't reply.

He knew better.

∽∾∾

CORBEN WATCHED the trees with hawklike concentration, alert to the slightest movement in the forest of shadows around him.

Mia's presence troubled him. What the hell was she doing here? Hadn't she risked enough already?

He gritted his teeth and pushed the thought of her from his mind. He needed to stay focused. The mokhtar had given away their position by shouting out his warning, and although Corben had sideslipped away by a few trees, he was still vulnerable.

They'd stopped for the night—the trail had become too dark for them to trudge on—when he'd heard his pursuers' approach. He hadn't expected the others to come after them that evening. He'd taken one out. He was pretty sure there were four of them altogether, including Mia. Which meant he had two more gunmen to worry about.

The odds didn't particularly bother him. Besides, it was always better to be the one holding the high ground. They would have to flush him out, and that meant they'd have to show themselves. He just had to be ready.

My kingdom for a set of night-vision goggles, he mused. And some thermals. He shivered against the cold and tried to tune it out. Then he sensed movement to his left.

Careful steps, inching their way towards him.

A hunter's movements.

He shut his eyes for a few seconds to sensitize his retinas, then opened them again and scanned the trees. Which was when he heard a step crunching against the gravelly soil, only this one was coming from his right side.

Chapter 71

‿∽ ∾

Mia's heartbeat thundered in her ears as she strained to see into the brutal darkness. She hated the feeling. She knew someone would soon be dead—again—and she couldn't do anything about it.

The night suddenly lit up with flashes of muzzle fire, and gunshots echoed through the trees. She counted at least a dozen, irregularly spaced, different, and heard horses whinnying frenziedly and bolting, their hoofbeats clattering into the distance—then silence.

Not quite silence.

Groans.

Pained, injured moans. Followed by shouts, in Kurdish.

Angered, furious, pained wails.

She bolted out into the open and rushed towards the source of the noise, dodging tree trunks and loose stones, trying to stay on her feet.

The first man she reached was the other villager. He was down, injured but still alive. He'd been hit in his side. He was in a lot of pain and was visibly scared. He beseeched her for some help, his eyes struggling to stay open. As she got down to have a look at his wound, she heard the mokhtar scream out wildly and turned her attention to the source of the shouts. She saw a shadow moving through the trees up ahead and heard more gunshots, then the distinct clicking sound of an empty magazine.

She gestured to the villager, indicating that she'd be right back, and heard the boy cry out to his father. The boy coughed violently, more of retch than a cough, clearly badly injured. She crept forward, closer to the skirmish, and found Salem, the mokhtar's son, lying on the ground. He was bleeding from just below his shoulder, and the wound seemed dangerously close to his upper lungs. He coughed up some blood, confirming the probable puncture there, and its severity. The mokhtar was there, by his side, his face contorted in worry and anger, his trembling fingers clasped around a rifle. He held it aimed at a couple of thick trees that rose up around ten yards away.

"There," he muttered, pointing the rifle at them, as if indicating a cornered prey. "Come."

He advanced cautiously, the gun held level in front of him. Mia followed in his footsteps. They edged through the trees, one step at a time, until they rounded the two hulking trunks.

Corben lay there on the ground, his back propped up against the larger of the trees. He was also hit, somewhere in his midsection. His shirt was drenched with blood, and an empty Kalashnikov was still in his hands.

He looked up at the mokhtar with drained eyes. The mokhtar started cursing him fiercely, nudging the rifle threateningly at him, then he went berserk, shrieking louder, getting ready to pump a bullet into Corben's brain.

Mia stepped in front of him, blocking him, yelling, "No!"

The man was livid, rattling on in Kurdish, pointing back at his injured son, screaming abuse at the fallen agent. Mia kept shouting "No" back at him, repeatedly, again and again, waving her arms angrily, until she finally grabbed the muzzle of the rifle and pushed it away.

"Enough," she hollered. "Enough already. He's down. Your son's hurt. So's another of your men. They need help."

The mokhtar grudgingly tilted the rifle downwards, took one last scowl at Corben, and nodded.

She watched him turn away and head back into the shadows. She knelt down beside Corben and lifted the AK-47 off him, saying, "You won't be needing this anymore, right?"

He nodded, keeping his dazed eyes on her.

She checked the wound. It was to his abdomen. It was hard to tell what the bullet had damaged on its way into him. A lot of organs were crammed in there, and most of them were crucial.

"How painful is it?" she asked.

"It's . . . not great," he said, wincing.

Whatever it had hit—stomach, liver, kidneys, intestines—the damage needed to be fixed quickly. Gunshot wounds to the abdomen were almost invariably devastating. From the level of bleeding, Mia thought there was a decent chance that his aorta hadn't been ruptured, but if that was the case, all it gave him, if he didn't get treated soon, was a slight extension to the minutes of life he would have if it were.

"We need to get you back to the village."

He nodded faintly, but the somber acceptance in his eyes told her that he knew he'd never see it.

The mokhtar hurried back to her. He was gripping the lead of a horse, one of the ones he and Corben had ridden up. "There's no sign of your horses," he stammered. "This is the only one we have left."

Mia scanned the obscurity around them. She couldn't see any sign of the other horses either.

She heaved a dejected sigh. "Your son needs medical attention quickly. And the other man, from your village . . ."

"Shāker, my cousin. He's dead," the mokhtar informed her, his voice as tenebrous as the forest around them.

Mia nodded. She knew what had to be done. "Take the horse, with your son. You can ride down with him. I'll stay here with Corben."

"I can't leave you here like this," the mokhtar argued. "We can put him on the horse and walk him down together."

"There's no time for that. He needs help fast."

The mokhtar shook his head with frustration. "You came after me, to save me."

"Then hurry down and send for help," she insisted. "Go on."

The mokhtar studied her for a beat, as if committing her face to memory, then nodded. "I'll help you make a fire."

"No, just go. I can do it."

He looked at her with eyes that were dark with remorse. He gave in reluctantly, threw one last angry glare in Corben's direction, then led the horse away from her, towards his fallen son.

They split up the lighters and the torches—the mokhtar would need to see his way down—and the blankets they managed to recover. Moments later, the mokhtar helped his son onto the saddle before climbing on behind him, and with a final, heavy-hearted wave of the torch in his hand, he rode off. Holding up a flaming torch of her own, Mia watched him ride off, her eyes clinging desperately to his receding figure until the darkness swallowed him up entirely.

Chapter 72

She checked on Corben again. There wasn't much she could do for him, apart from keeping him warm. With a different kind of chill seeping into her bones, she sought out the bodies of both villagers. She found them, one, then the other, lying on the cold ground, bereft of life. She checked each of them for pulses, just in case, and felt a bile of anger at Corben's reckless actions rising in her throat. Remorsefully, and with a tremble in her hands, she pulled the jacket off one of them and brought it back to cover Corben.

She then got to work on building a fire. The winter rains hadn't yet arrived, and the twigs and branches she collected were dry and brittle. She managed to get a good fire going opposite the tree Corben was against and gathered a small pile of additional wood to keep it fed.

She wondered how long it would be before help arrived. Given that they'd ridden for close to two hours to get to this spot, she reckoned it would take at least twice as long before anyone appeared, probably even longer given that they'd be making the entire journey at night—and that was assuming they would actually attempt it at night and not wait until morning. A warm feeling spread through her as she thought of Evelyn and Tom wistfully. She knew they wouldn't wait till morning, and yet, at the same time, she didn't want to put them in any more danger.

The exhaustion—both physical and mental—was overwhelming the last traces of adrenaline that had kept her going. She surrendered to it and slid down to the ground beside Corben. They just lay there in silence for a while, staring at the bonfire, listening as it crackled and popped, watching as the flames licked and curled around the twigs before pulling them down and consuming them.

"Last thing I remember is going out to meet my mom for a drink," Mia eventually said. "How did we end up here?"

Corben chewed on it for a brief moment. "Because of assholes like the hakeem. And me." His hollow voice was laced with regret.

Mia turned to him. "You wanted it that badly?"

He shrugged. "It kind of beats everything, doesn't it?" He winced. "Everything except a bullet in the gut."

"Did you kill Farouk?"

Corben nodded faintly. "He was badly hit, but . . . yes."

"Why?"

"Greed. Self-preservation." He mulled his words. "Greed, mostly." He leaned around so that he was facing her. "I'm not a good person, Mia. I wasn't trained to be good. I was trained to be effective. To get things done. And I've done some questionable things, some awful things that were applauded by my superiors." He shook his head with remorse. "I guess somewhere on that road, I decided I could also do it for myself."

"So my mom, me . . . we were just, what? Useful?"

He shook his head faintly. "There was no master plan. It just kind of took me—took us all by surprise and sucked us all in. Something happens, an opportunity pops up, and you go after it. But the last thing I wanted in all this was for you to be put in harm's way, to get hurt. That's the truth. And regardless of my motives, I always thought I'd get your mom out, as soon as it was possible. The thing is, in my business, the first lesson you learn is that things rarely work out the way you plan them." He coughed up a bit of blood and wiped it off his mouth. He looked up at her. "For what it's worth, I . . ." He shook his head, as if deciding against saying it. "I'm sorry. About everything."

Just then, a spine-tingling cry shattered the stillness of the night. It was the unmistakable howl of a wolf. Another quickly responded, its cry echoing around them.

Not a wolf.

Wolves.

They never hunted alone.

A sudden feeling of dread wrung Mia's gut. Her eyes swung over to Corben. He'd heard them too.

"It's the blood," Corben reported gloomily, straightening up. "They've smelled it."

Another howl pierced the night, this one much closer.

How quickly did they travel?

Mia sat up, her eyes and ears on high alert.

"The guns," he mumbled. "Get the guns."

Mia hurled herself to her feet and pulled a flaming stick out of the fire. She scurried away on rubbery legs towards where she remembered the mokhtar's son had fallen. She thought she remembered seeing the mokhtar put the boy's rifle down there. She'd seen submachine guns by the two fallen villagers, but they were further afield, and she wasn't sure she dared venture that far.

She advanced cautiously, sweeping the lighted brand left and right, scanning the murky obscurity for any sign of the predators. Her eyes picked out the old hunting rifle, propped up like a talisman against the tree where the mokhtar's son had lain. She stepped towards it, and just as she reached out to grab it, she saw the gray forms lurking in the shadows. Her heart skipped a whole bar as she watched them skulk there, eyeing her. She stabbed the brand at them, causing them to flinch and retreat a step, but they weren't easily cowed. They inched forward again, baring their teeth menacingly, their sleek bodies taut with anticipation.

She steeled herself and sliced the air with the brand, shouting at them as she took a careful step to the rifle. She snatched it with her free hand, its weight taking her by surprise, then pulled away, keeping her back to the bonfire, retreating while swinging the stick manically around her. Farther away, she heard yelps and angry snarls, and the three wolves that had been stalking her rushed off into the darkness. She heard them working feverishly on something and realized they had found the villagers' dead bodies.

She hustled back to Corben before they came back for more. He'd managed to get himself up and was half-crouched, his back to the fire, a flaming brand in his hand. Mia handed him the gun.

"What about the automatics?"

"I couldn't get to them," she said fearfully.

Corben checked the rifle and frowned. It was a Russian SKS carbine, ex-Iraqi-army-issue. Its magazine had a capacity of ten rounds. Corben thought he'd heard two of them go wild, and the third had ripped through him, which meant he had seven shots left, if it had been fully loaded. He felt under its barrel. Its bayonet, normally swiveled, tucked in under it and nondetachable on the military-issue weapon, had been taken off, much to his dismay.

Mia was watching him from the corner of her eye. "What have we got?"

"Seven rounds, tops," he informed her glumly.

The ghostly shapes soon materialized in the darkness around them, the golden glint of the flames flickering in their eyes. They swirled around Mia and Corben like a legion from hell, crisscrossing each other's paths calmly, almost as if they were conferring with each other and planning their onslaught. They snapped their jaws and bared their teeth, taunting their prey, darting forward and lurching back just as fast, playing with them, testing their defenses.

Their fetid smell clawed at Mia's nose as she lunged at them, her eyes stinging from the heat of her torch, her back inches from the raging bonfire that licked hungrily at it.

"We're not going to be able to hold them off forever," she hissed to Corben, "and there's more than seven of them."

Corben had been thinking the same thing.

His eyes had been scouring their perimeter, trying to gauge how many they were up against. From what he could see, there seemed to be ten of them, maybe a dozen. At least, those were the ones he could see on the front line.

He faltered, his strength long gone, his legs living on borrowed time. A couple of the predators decided to push a little harder and darted at him, their long muzzles wide-open, their wet tongues slobbering ravenously, their sharp fangs gleaming in the firelight. He stabbed back with his brand, struggling to remain on his feet, the throbbing of an overtaxed heart deafening in his ears. The wolves dodged the flames with ease, pulling back with lightning agility. As if sensing his faltering life force, one of them decided to go for the kill and leapt at him, paws and jaws flung wide and aimed at his neck. Corben squeezed off a round that caught it in midflight, and it yelped and dropped like a sandbag, at his feet. Another grabbed the opportunity and pounced at Corben, who stopped it with another shot. The others seemed momentarily spooked by the gunshots and the sudden deaths of their brethren and retreated, receding into the darkness.

"You alright?" Mia asked, her eyes still locked on the shadows stalking them.

Corben could barely stand or keep his eyes open. He felt as if he were sinking into a smothering abyss.

"We're going to need those automatics," he rasped through clenched teeth. A burning sensation, more fierce than the heat from the bonfire, was scorching him from the inside. "Where's the nearest one?"

"Down that way." Mia pointed in the direction of the fallen villagers. "But they were too far to reach, I told you."

"We don't have much choice. I'm not going to get the rest of them with the handful of bullets this piece of junk has left in it. And without them, we're dead anyway. The fire's going to give out sometime. They'll just wear us out, it's what they do. And I don't know about you, but I'm not too keen on ending up as wolf feed."

"What do you want to do?" Mia asked, her mouth dry with fear.

"Grab two big fire sticks. The biggest you can carry. We'll head out there, back to back. Take it one step at a time, keep them at bay. If I need to, I'll use the bullets I have left. If we can get to one of the guns, I think I can take them out. What do you say?"

"Can you make it there?"

Corben wiped the beads of sweat streaming down his face. "Never felt better." He grinned. "Shall we?"

Mia met his gaze. No matter what he'd done or what his intentions had been, he'd still saved her life more than once, and maybe, just maybe, he was going to do it again. Which had to count for something.

"Come on," he blurted, coughing up some blood. "While we're young," he added, a sardonic glint in his eyes.

Mia bent to the foot of the bonfire and pulled out two large, flaming logs.

She nodded at Corben.

"Lead the way, but stay close," he told her.

With her back against him, they crab-walked, sideways, inching away from the fire, heading into dark waters, swinging the torches back and forth, surrounding themselves with a ring of protective fire. Step by step, they edged closer and closer to the spot where one of the villagers had fallen, the image of the man's dead body getting torn apart by the wolves clawing at their debilitated minds. All around them, the creatures snapped and snarled, lunging and pulling back, running around, their glowing eyes locked on their prey.

In the dim firelight, Corben spotted the shredded carcass of the villager, and, not far from it, the glint of the AK-47's barrel.

"That way," he grunted to Mia, adjusting their trajectory, angling towards the weapon of their salvation.

He felt his legs about to give out, but willed them to stay with him a bit longer, and with a Herculean effort, he managed to edge them over to the fallen machine gun.

"Keep them off me while I check it," he managed, as he reached down and picked up the gun. It felt as if it weighed a ton in his hands. He grunted and winced as he lifted it up, then steadied himself and clicked out its magazine, pushing against the top cartridge with his fingers, checking its load.

"Well?" Mia asked, desperation ringing in her voice.

"We're good to go," he shot back, barely able to stand now. He set the selector to semiauto and half-turned to be able to see her face. She was looking at him, her eyes ratcheted wide with nervous anticipation.

"Take this," he told her, handing her the rifle. "I'll take down as many as I can, but if they get me, you'll have to finish them off with this. The safety's off. Just aim and squeeze, okay?"

She managed a smile. She opened her mouth as if she wanted to say something, but he knew now was not the time. She knew it too.

The creatures were now in a frenzy, sensing the final confrontation and the imminent kill. One of them bunched up its hind legs and pounced at Corben. He squeezed the trigger, and the wolf jerked in midair and fell dead just as the others swarmed in for the kill.

Corben loosed off more rounds, swinging the gun left and right, spitting death at them. His body was running on pure momentum now, each shot resonating across him, pushing him backwards against Mia, his fingers stuck in a death clutch on the gun's handle and magazine. One after another, the wolves fell, stopped in midair as if hit by an invisible sledgehammer or slamming against a nonexistent glass barrier, toppling on top of each other, littering the ground with fur and bone and blood.

With two remaining wolves snapping at his feet, the firing pin slammed against the empty chamber in a loud clunk. One of the wolves leapt up at him. He spun the wooden stock of the Kalashnikov upwards and batted it off him. It righted itself almost immediately, as if he had swatted it with nothing more than a rolled-up newspaper. Before it could come around for another frontal attack, he'd flicked the machine gun in his hands, gripping it now from its barrel, like an ax, and brought it down heavily on the creature, pounding it once, twice, desperate yelps slicing the still air.

"Jim," he heard Mia yell, but before he could turn, he was hit from behind by the last surviving wolf. He felt its teeth digging into his neck, its claws carving into his back, and the first wolf recovered, spun on itself, and joined in. The weapon fell from his hands and he saw the earth rise up to meet him as he plummeted to the ground. The pain was surreal, his body getting ripped to pieces from all quarters, but he was already numb to it all, his neurons long exhausted and no longer able to transmit any sensations to his depleted brain. He wasn't sure, but he thought he heard a gunshot, then another, and another still, and the movement on him stopped, the mauling ceased, and the teeth and claws that had buried themselves in his body froze in place.

He rolled onto his back and felt the light leaving his body. He saw Mia's vague form grunting as she yanked at the beasts that had been tearing at him, pulling them off him, and then he saw her face looming down at him, studying him with a combination of horror and sadness, tears from her eyes dripping down onto his lips, their salty taste resuscitating the dead cells they were landing on, her soft fingers moving across his face and clearing something off his forehead, her lips moving and saying something he couldn't quite fathom, a mesmerizing halo of distant stars shimmering around her heavenly face, and he decided it would be a good way to die, better than any he had ever imagined for himself or thought he deserved. He might have managed a smile, but he wasn't sure of it, as he drank in a final warming sip of the glorious elixir before him before it faded to black and all feeling deserted his pillaged body.

Chapter 73

M ia just sat by Corben's body for a long while, not moving. Her skin resonated with a shivering that wouldn't stop, and her eyes stared out into the darkness, avoiding the mounds of dead bodies, man and beast, that littered the ground around her.

Eventually, noticing that the brand she was still clutching was dying out, she rose to her feet and trudged over to the bonfire. She didn't even bother looking around for more wolves, too weary and bone-tired and drained to care.

Nothing came at her.

With numb hands, she fed the fire again, then shrank down, her back to the tree Corben had been leaning against, and cupped her face with her hands.

Dawn was far off. She'd lost all notion of time, but she knew she had a long night ahead of her. It didn't matter. She wasn't going anywhere. She was going to stay there, riveted to that spot, until someone—or something—came and plucked her off it.

A lone, distant howl broke the stillness.

It wasn't answered.

The creature sounded mournful, as if lamenting the great loss of life, the monsoon of death that had drenched the parched soil of the mountain.

And then she saw them.

Distant lights, flickering in and out from behind trees, a slow convoy snaking its way towards her.

She strained to get a clearer picture of who, or what, they were, but they were far off. They would disappear behind a ridge, then reappear a few minutes later, slightly closer. Gradually, they made their way to her, traveling in silence, a muted procession. When they finally came into view, she saw that there were several of them, on horseback, half a dozen or more perhaps, holding up flaming torches and oil lanterns.

She didn't recognize any of them. She didn't think they were from Nerva Zhori—she'd met a lot of the villagers in the commotion after the helicopter had exploded—then she saw the familiar face of the mokhtar as he climbed off his horse and approached her with a weary smile and a blanket.

He draped it over and led her to a waiting horse, the others watching her every move in respectful, if intrigued, silence.

Chapter 74

∾ ∾

Philadelphia—December 1783

The fireplace crackled in the small but comfortable room as Thérésia stared out the window. A light dusting of snow was falling on the trees outside, the flakes twinkling in the suffused moonlight as they glided to a gentle rest.

She knew he wouldn't be coming back.

She'd known it at the quayside in Lisbon, almost two decades earlier.

Had it been that long ago?

Her face relaxed into a bittersweet smile at the memories floating through her mind.

Thérésia hadn't wanted Sebastian to leave, but she knew he had to. Those years in Lisbon had been the happiest, the most fulfilling of her long life—living with him, traveling in his company, learning with him, and, of course, raising their young son together. She had never wanted it to end, she desperately wanted him to stay or take her and Miguel with him, but she realized it wasn't possible. He had to follow his destiny, and she had to keep their son safe.

His leaving her, and her move across the ocean, had—as he'd promised—brought her peace. No one had bothered her or Miguel—Michael now—since they'd settled in Philadelphia. The City of Brotherly

Love had lived up to its name. The last few years had been turbulent—
revolutions usually are—but, mercifully, she and Michael had survived
the turmoil and with the Treaty of Paris now signed, it looked as if the
worst was well behind them.

How long she would live to enjoy the peace, though, was a question
now haranguing her. The small, hard lumps that had appeared under
her arms and in her left breast were troubling her. She had prided herself
on her independence and her fitness throughout the troubled times of
the conflict and was certainly as fit as a sixty-year-old widow—that small
lie had readily been accepted upon her arrival in the new city—could be.
But since discovering the lumps, she felt a tiredness in her bones when
she woke up every morning, a shortness of breath, a heaviness in her
head that accosted her in worrying waves. She knew that the blood that
had, in the last week, appeared when she coughed was a bad augur.

She didn't have much time left.

She wondered how Sebastian was keeping. She imagined he was
drinking the distillation again and smiled inwardly at the thought that
he would be little changed from how she remembered him. She caught
a glimpse of her own, wrinkled face reflected back at her in the thin glass
of the window and willed him to success. What a wonderful gift it would
be. A most worthy of quests . . . even if it did cost her the love of her life
and cost Michael his father.

She saw her son appear at the gate and make his way into the house.
He had grown into a fine young man and had performed admirably
during the troubles, working alongside his mother at liaising with the
French envoys who were assisting the revolutionary effort against the
British. His diplomatic and organizational talents were evident, and
throughout the conflict she had imagined great things in his future, in
his adopted homeland. But with each passing day, he also reminded her
more and more of Sebastian. She could see it in his eyes, in his stance,
even in small things such as the way he held a quill. And as the boy grew
into the man, she knew she couldn't ignore his unique provenance.

She also couldn't ignore his father's legacy.

She had promised Sebastian she would never tell the boy what had
led his father to leave them. Sebastian had made her promise it to him,
and, at the time, she saw the sense in it. He wanted his son to have a

normal life. He didn't want him to have his life ambushed by an oath he had himself made. It was his burden to bear, not his son's.

It was a promise she could no longer keep.

She owed it to Sebastian. To his memory and to his legacy. If he was going to die away from her, alone, in a foreign land, she had to try to ensure that his death wouldn't be in vain.

Deep down, she knew he would have wanted her to.

"Mother?"

She heard Michael take off his boots and make his way to join her in the sitting room. She turned to him, the pain in her limbs receding at the sight of his radiant face. She saw the quizzical expression on his face at the sight of her and saw his eyes drop lower to the ancient, leather-bound book with the strange circular symbol tooled into its cover that she held to her chest.

"I have something to tell you," she told him as she invited him to join her.

Chapter 75

M ia stirred in the narrow bed. Beams of dusty sunlight bathed the room around her. Still weary and foggy-brained, she pushed herself up to her elbows and looked around. Plain, hand-finished walls, simple oak furniture, and lace curtains greeted her in hushed silence.

She scoured her mind for clarity, and a cloud of confused images slowly drifted into focus. She remembered being part of a slow convoy, riding into the night, leaving behind the mangled corpses. She remembered the furtive glances of the men and women accompanying her, as well as the mokhtar, riding directly ahead of her, keeping a supportive eye on her as they snaked their way down the mountainside until they'd reached a village she didn't recognize. She remembered being led into one of its houses, sitting at a rickety kitchen table by a blazing fireplace, being offered a hot, herbal infusion of a flavor she wasn't familiar with, and being watched with warm curiosity by the mokhtar and an elderly couple as she drank it gratefully.

She felt as if she had a mild hangover and guessed they must have given her some kind of sedative, which she thought was undoubtedly the right call. The heavy-headedness soon started to lift. A cotton undergarment and a beige, long-sleeved dress, delicately embroidered around its sleeves and collar, had been left for her on a chair by the small window. Some sheepskin moccasins were on the floor next to it. She slipped them all on, opened the window and swung the wooden shutter away, and felt the soothing warmth of the sun on her tired skin.

She looked out. The cluster of low-built houses squatted at the bottom of a valley. They were part mudbrick, part stone, and had the same thatched roofs as those in the Yazidi village. Beyond the small settlement, she could see fields and tended meadows of early-winter earth spreading out to the foothills of the jagged peaks that ringed the valley.

She left her room and wandered through the house but didn't see anyone. She went through the kitchen and out the door. The air was surprisingly warm, markedly different from the chill of night at the top of the mountain, and she could hear nothing apart from a faint breeze that rustled the branches of the pistachio trees, and the burbles and trills of small birds. The utter tranquillity was a shocking contrast to the mayhem of the day—and night—before.

She wrapped her arms around her and wandered down a narrow path, past a couple of small houses and a barn. The place had a Waldenesque, calming feel to it that, right now, was most welcome. It reminded her of a small Amish community in its tidy, unapologetic simplicity and its splendid isolation. She encountered a family—parents and two boys in their early teens—unloading some wood from a horse-drawn cart. They smiled politely at her and kept working. Farther along the dirt pathway, she came across two women who led a mule that was loaded with a basket of bread. They acknowledged her with warm eyes and a half-nod, without stopping.

She kept going, drinking in the serenity and the fresh mountain air, feeling herself coming back to life. She heard faint voices to her right and glimpsed some figures standing at the bottom of a small ridge, deep in conversation. She saw the mokhtar, along with an elderly couple whom she recognized vaguely as the ones who had given her the drink the night before, and—to her wild relief—standing next to them were Evelyn and Webster.

"Mom?" she called out. "Webster?" She couldn't quite bring herself to think of him as *Dad* yet, but she knew it would come.

They turned and saw her and waved her over, beaming. She rushed down the meadow and joined them. They were standing by a small pond. She embraced her mom and, hesitantly, gave Webster a soft hug, wary of his wound.

"When did you get here?" she asked, overjoyed.

"We rode up this morning," Evelyn informed her. "*Kaak* Sulayman"—she pointed out the mokhtar—"very kindly sent someone back to his village to bring us over."

Mia remembered his riding away with his injured son. "How's your son?" she asked him softly, hoping for the best.

"He will live," the mokhtar said, a gleam of relief breaking through his dark eyes. "He will live," he repeated, as if his mantra would help seal the deal.

Mia nodded. The harsh memories of the night before strafed her heart. As if sensing it, her father turned her attention to the elderly couple with them.

"These are Muneer and Arîya," he said. "Your hosts." His movements were slow and tentative, and he winced as he brought down his arm. Evelyn took his hand and held it in hers, supportively.

The elderly couple smiled affably at Mia.

"Thanks for coming to get me last night," Mia told them. They shrugged humbly. She noticed something slightly strained and uncomfortable in their demeanor and saw it reflected fleetingly in Webster and in her mom. She suddenly remembered what had brought them here in the first place and, feeling a surge of excitement, turned to Webster.

"Well?" she asked him. "Do they have it? Have you asked them?"

The whole valley seemed to resonate with promise as Webster glanced conspiringly at the couple, then looked knowingly at her before swinging his eyes over to the pond.

She followed his lead and a puzzled look crossed her face before it clicked. "Is that it?" she asked, pointing at the pond.

Webster smiled and nodded. "That's it."

The pond was unremarkable, a shallow freshwater pool of murky water. Low-lying clusters of thin, small-leafed plants grew all over it.

She bent down to get a closer look. "What is it?"

"It's called *Bacopa*," Webster said. "*Bacopa monniera*. It's also known as the herb of grace, which kind of makes you wonder . . ." He left it at that.

"We call it *jalneem*," Muneer added in surprisingly well-spoken English as he reached down, plucked a stem of it and gave it to Mia.

Mia fingered its thick, glistening leaves and studied its small, white flower. Her heart contracted as a wild exhilaration galloped through her. "What about . . ." She hesitated, looking at them, the key question catching in her throat. She turned to Webster. "Was Sebastian right? Does it work on . . . everyone?"

Webster met her gaze, and with a sparkle of infinite gratification in his eyes, he calmly nodded.

∞

THEY SAT AROUND the small kitchen table and dug heartily into a meal of cornmeal porridge, cheese, bread, and olives that Ariya quickly prepared. Mia worked hard to rip her concentration away from the swirling questions in her mind and will herself to eat, knowing her body needed it.

It wasn't easy.

She was sitting at the threshold of a new world.

The mokhtar had told Muneer what Webster had said to the hakeem, at Sebastian's grave. He'd related the way Webster and his partners had protected the secret. He'd told him that Webster was Sebastian's grandson. Which put Muneer at ease, at least enough to explore Webster's story himself.

"The cabal that had the underground meeting rooms in Al-Hillah," Evelyn asked, "what do you know of them?"

"They were our ancestors," Muneer replied. "That's where it all started, in southern Iraq, towards the middle of the eleventh century.

"A little-known scientist-philosopher by the name of Abu Fares Al-Masboudi, who had studied under Ibn Sina—Avicenna—before moving to Kufa, was the one who first made the discovery. The marshes of southern Iraq were rich in *Bacopa*, and travelers from India had spoken of how the people there had been using it for centuries, but not in that preparation. Which inspired his curiosity."

Webster saw the question in Mia's eyes. "It's like the aspirin we talked about," he told her. "If you chew on a piece of willow bark, it's not going to have the same effect. It's an elaborate chemical process, but it all starts with that plant."

Muneer nodded. "Al-Masboudi started taking it himself and, thinking that it was merely a health tonic, gave it to his wife as well as to two colleagues of his and their wives. After years of taking the elixir, they all started noticing its effects. They realized its ramifications and formed the secret cabal you refer to in order to discuss what to do with it, whether or not to announce it. You have to remember, the world was a very different place back then. Everyone claimed to be after wondrous discoveries, but there was a thin line between experimenting on something and being labeled a sorcerer and hounded out, or worse."

"We studied their writings," Evelyn said, glancing at Webster. "Were they connected to the Brethren of Purity?"

"One of Al-Masboudi's colleagues was with the brotherhood," Muneer confirmed with an impressed nod. "They debated whether or not to let the Brethren in on their discovery, but ultimately decided to keep it to themselves, until they felt certain that it wouldn't be abused by the rulers. Iraq, at the time, under the Caliph Al-Qa'im, was in almost as much turmoil as it is today. The Seljuks were posing a great challenge to the ruling Abbasid dynasties. My ancestors were worried that, if they gave the caliph the secret, they would be killed off, leaving him to bestow a long life on whomever he chose and turning him into a living god. And so they kept it quiet and waited, meeting in secret, modeling themselves on the Brethren, discussing and debating how a new world—one with longer-lived humans—could be made to work.

"As the years passed, people inevitably started talking. And my ancestors found they had to move on to new pastures and start new lives. They migrated north. Eventually, they settled in Yazidi territory"—acknowledging the mokhtar with a slight bob of his head—"and, ultimately, here, in this remote valley."

"And the longer they waited, the more difficult it became to find a way to announce it," Webster noted, more than asked.

Muneer nodded. "Up until recently, it was considered next to impossible to tell others about it. Our thinking has always been that either everyone should have access to it, or it should remain hidden. But for centuries, the whole planet was ruled by self-serving aristocracies and ruthless dictators. There was no fraternity among men, no true democracy. There was slavery. There were wars waged for vanity or greed. It was the few controlling the many. Not that the many were any better. It seemed as if man thrived on causing pain to others, on doing everything possible to rise above others at their expense and regardless of the pain and suffering he left behind. And we knew that something like this would only skew that equation and empower man's darkest instincts.

And so the question became, does man deserve to live longer, or would that only allow him to inflict more pain on his fellow man?"

"I don't think you can paint everybody with the same brush," Webster countered. "There are plenty of good people out there."

"Possibly," Muneer conceded. "You know it far better than we do. But you can understand our reticence. Greed and selfishness do seem to be the central motivators of mankind."

"How did you know all this about the outside world," Mia asked, "from this isolated valley?"

"This isn't a utopia. We've always lived in hiding. And there weren't many of us. We knew that if we were to survive, we had to mix with the people on the outside. So we—the small circle of custodians, if you like—would take turns to leave the valley and travel. We always have. We never took the elixir with us. It stayed here. We roamed the lands, watched how the world evolved. We brought back books and treatises to teach the others. And we waited. Occasionally, we would encounter someone exceptional, someone we believed would be a strong ally, who could perhaps help us figure out how to overcome the obstacles facing us in wanting to share this with the rest of the planet. There was a knight, during the Crusades, who impressed my ancestors in that way." Muneer turned to Webster. "Your grandfather was another."

Webster seemed to be studying Muneer, running a mental calculation.

"No"—Muneer smiled, as if reading his thoughts—"I didn't know him. I wasn't born then. But my father knew him. He's fondly remembered up here."

"How did he find you?" Webster asked.

"We found him," Muneer said, his eyes smiling. "He was in Damascus. He'd been asking about the Ouroboros, looking for books bearing the symbol. My father heard of him and sought him out. He brought him here. He was going to help us spread the word—he was full of optimism and energy, he wasn't afraid of the forces that would oppose this—but that winter, he fell ill with typhoid. He didn't want to die here, he insisted on trying to get back to his wife . . . even though she was continents away."

Mia looked at him in amazement. "And in all these years, you've managed to keep it secret? No one ever left and gave it away?"

"This is a small place," Muneer noted. "People—young people, in particular—need to go out and explore the world. So we don't tell everyone about it. Some leave here and never return. Others come back and bring loved ones with them. So we wait. And we watch. A life of moderation doesn't necessarily suit everyone, but when we feel that person has reached a stage of their life where they're contented with what this valley has to offer, where they're satisfied by working the land and enjoying our simple ways, where they won't feel frustrated by the constraints of this isolated life, then—and only then—we invite them into the circle of custodians, to share in the secret, to enjoy its benefits, and to protect it."

Mia sat back, her mind swirling with the possibilities. She glanced at Webster, and at Evelyn. They were both reading the thoughts written on her face. Her father gave her a small nod. She turned to Evelyn, who was also telegraphing her agreement.

She raised her glance to their host, and with her heart in her mouth she asked, "Can we help you bring this to the world?"

Muneer turned to his wife, and to the mokhtar. He studied her for a beat, then smiled graciously. "Do you think the world out there is ready for it?"

"I'm not sure it ever will be," Mia replied. "But if it's done properly . . . I don't see how we can't try."

Muneer mulled her words, then nodded. "Why don't we do this. Go back to your world. Put your affairs in order. Make sure you won't be missed for a while. Then come back and stay with us. We can take our time, talk things through. And then, if we're all agreed, perhaps we can make it happen together."

Mia looked at her parents. "What do you say?"

Evelyn's face grew serious. "We have to make sure the hakeem's clinic is shut down and that anyone still held there is released." She turned to Webster.

He nodded. "Absolutely. But after that," he told her, then turned to Mia, his eyes brimming with anticipation and with pride, "I think we all have a lot of catching up to do."

Mia smiled, suspecting that they'd have plenty of time to do just that.

Author's Note

〜〜〜

*"To realize our true destiny, we must be guided not by a
myth from our past, but by a vision of our future."*
—MARK B. ADAMS, discussing the visionary
biology of J. B. S. Haldane

At the time of writing this book, there's nothing out there that's been
proven to slow down or arrest the aging process in humans. That's the
hard truth. But scientists are demonstrably making significant progress
in figuring out why we age—and why we die. This progress is mostly
due to the change—the "paradigm shift"—in approach that's described
in this book. Rather than just studying the *symptoms* of old age and figuring out how to deal with them, how to alleviate them, how to patch
up our bodies as they fall apart in what the "deathists" consider its in-
escapable, preordained, and even noble descent into decrepitude, these
"prolongevists" are now trying to figure out *why* aging happens in the
first place and how to interrupt the aging process altogether, daring to
believe that aging, like cancer and cardiovascular disease, can eventually
be overcome, and that living longer, healthier lives wouldn't be a bad
thing.

The scientists working in this arena are facing a Herculean task: Not
only do they need to contend with the most perplexing scientific issue
to ever face mankind, they also need to deal with the prejudice that's

associated with the field of longevity medicine, as well as the fierce ethical debate that engulfs them at every turn. Those at the forefront of this most difficult, contentious, and worthy of fields—Aubrey de Grey, Tom Kirkwood, Michael Rose, Cynthia Kenyon, Leonard Guarente, Bruce Ames, and Barbara Hansen, to name but a few—are to be applauded and encouraged. One of them could—and, quite conceivably, *will*—make a discovery at some point in the future that will do nothing less than redefine humanity. This book is also dedicated to them.

For those of you interested in finding out more about this subject, I'd recommend starting with Bryan Appleyard's eminently readable and very thorough new book *How to Live Forever or Die Trying*. I'd also highly recommend *The Fountain of Youth*, a collection of hugely insightful essays edited by Stephen Post and Robert Binstock. *The Quest for Immortality*, by Jay Olshansky and Bruce Carnes, is also pretty much required reading on the subject.

I'd also recommend checking out Sherwin Nuland's take on Aubrey de Grey's theories in his article "Do you want to live forever?" on the Web site of MIT's *Technology Review*, which can be accessed at www.technologyreview.com. Also, www.futurepundit.com has a great archive on aging that's regularly updated.

Mia's journey to Beirut to work on the Phoenician project owes a debt of gratitude to Rick Gore and his compelling coverage of Spencer Wells and Pierre Zalloua's work on tracing the origins of the Phoenicians. For those interested, visit https://www3.nationalgeographic.com/genographic to check out *National Geographic*'s Genographic Project. You can even participate and have your origins traced.

As for the historic parts of this book, a lot has been written—and dreamed up—about the Comte de St. Germain. The eighteenth century was rich in such ciphers, and hundreds of years later, his name retains its mystique. There's no doubt that he existed, as countless letters and diaries from the period, written by diplomats and aristocrats, will attest. They mention, for instance, that he "thoroughly understood herbs and plants, and had invented the medicines of which he constantly made use, and which prolonged his life and health." A great deal of his legend, however, was underpinned by what is believed to be one of the great literary hoaxes, the *Souvenirs de Marie Antoinette*, purportedly written by the Countess d'Adhemar in the nineteenth century, and a bestseller in its time. Was St. Germain a mystic, a possessor of great secrets, an enlightened being—in the words of one of his contemporaries, "the most enigmatical of all incomprehensibles"? Or was he just a brilliant charlatan, a cunning swindler who was able to charm and hoodwink the gullible aristocrats around him?

Much more is known, however, about Raimondo di Sangro. For the sake of this story, I've taken a few liberties with his life, but if you're ever in Naples, I heartily recommend a visit to the magnificent chapel he left behind, the *Capello San Severo*, with its mysterious veiled statues, its bizarre iconography, and the creepy "anatomic machines" that stand guard outside his basement laboratory.

From Gilgamesh to St. Germain and on to Aubrey de Grey and the tireless pioneers working to solve this most cruel of riddles, the yearning to stick around and experience more of life is—no pun intended—as old as man. Not only do we live our lives with an awareness of our inevitable and impending deaths, but we are the only species to have—and bear the burden of—that awareness. Being aware of it, it's only natural to want to resist it. And no matter how many obstacles and hindrances the "deathist" camp puts up, that determination will ultimately prevail. At some point in the future, frailty and senility will be postponed significantly, perhaps indefinitely.

And I don't know about you, but I think it would be very cool to meet my daughters' grandchildren and be fit enough to teach them to ride a bicycle one day. . .

Acknowledgments

I need to begin by thanking my wife Suellen for generously sharing me with Mia, Evelyn, Corben, and the rest of the motley crew of houseguests who invaded our lives over the past year. The good news I can offer her is that with the publication of this book, they're now gone. The bad news is, the new bunch just called from the airport, and they're on their way over.

A number of friends generously shared their insights and their time with me while I was writing this novel, and for their contributions that have shaped it in ways big and small, I'd like to thank (in no particular order) Mahfouz Zacharia, Nic Ransome, Raya and Carlos Heneine, Joe and Amanda McManus, Richard Burston, Bruce Crowther, Bashar Chalabi, Tamara Chalabi, Alain Schibl, Dr. Amin Milki, and Lauren Klee, as well as my family—my parents, my brother Richard, my sister Doris, and my Aunt Lillian.

I'd also like to thank my sagacious and patient editors, Ben Sevier and Jon Wood—without forgetting Mitch Hoffman, who shepherded the book in its early days. Without them or the rest of the great teams I've been fortunate to work with (for the second time now) at Dutton and at Orion, none of this would be possible, and I'm deeply grateful for the consummate skill and continued support of everyone who worked on getting this book onto the shelves and into the hands of our readers.

Last, but hardly least, I've got to mention my überteam at the William Morris Agency. Eugenie Furniss, Jay Mandel, Tracy Fisher, Raffaella De Angelis, and Charlotte Wasserstein: Take a bow. My thanks to you all.